I, MEDEA
A tale of conflict, deceit and vengeance

Jeffrey Peter Clarke

I, MEDEA
A tale of conflict, deceit and vengeance

DOUBLE DRAGON

ACKNOWLEDGMENTS

I thank Lynda Buxton for her helpful observation
plus her care and attention in
checking through to find my numerous
typographical and grammatical errors.

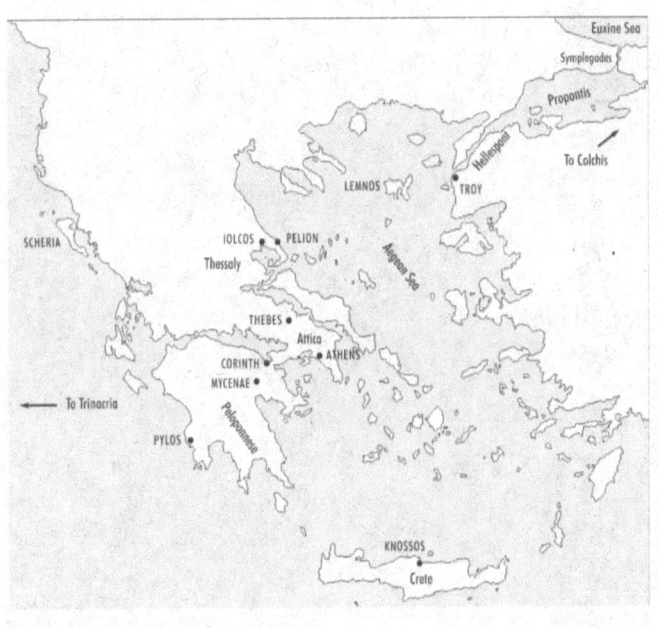

Euxine Sea

Symplegades

Propontis

To Colchis

Hellespont

LEMNOS

TROY

SCHERIA

IOLCOS

PELION

Thessaly

Aegean Sea

THEBES

Attica

CORINTH

ATHENS

MYCENAE

To Trinacria

Peloponnesus

PYLOS

KNOSSOS

Crete

7

Prologue

I, Medea was for long a priestess of that often feared yet never seen goddess Hecate. Hecate, who those knowing of her believe to be an aspect of the moon, of the earth and of the underworld. She is companion to souls of the dead and a mistress of spirits, of magic and witchcraft, all realms of darkness, yet she may at times confer good fortune. Guided by her I used my skills with potions and herbs to assist those in need, the sick and the suffering, but since those golden days of innocence much wickedness has been laid at my feet. Accusations of poisoning, of sorcery and witchcraft, of conspiracy and murder, oh, and responsibility for the death of another man's bride. As for *that* other man, as for Jason and the affair of the Golden Fleece, we will come to both soon enough. But I'll say here and now, though I am condemned by many by my deeds, no one is perfect. Not even the gods themselves are perfect but as they're immortal they do very much as they please, unless almighty Zeus determines otherwise.

I, of course, was not created immortal. I am daughter of a mortal man. That mortal man is, or was, the brutal King Aietes who ruled over the land of Colchis to the east of the Euxine Sea; the Black Sea as it is known to some. Into the east of this Euxine Sea flows the River Phasis and some way up this river stands Aietes' grim city they call Aia. It is there I was priestess at Hecate's temple because my mother, revered throughout Colchis as a minor goddess, had been priestess before my accession and it was with her blessing the goddess bestowed upon me those powers I came to possess.

Yes, there are many who believe my very name to be synonymous with guilt but I know better than most how easy it is to elicit the misunderstanding of others, especially when they have a grudge to bear, and I assure you a good number of them did – at least when they were alive.

And when I claim no one is perfect, I maintain this applies equally to some, if not all, of the characters we are soon to encounter. Perhaps I do them an injustice by referring to them merely as characters for a number were of royal blood – blood, and lots of it being in some cases a result of their presence in this world. Others were adventurers on the lookout for gain, or refugees from adversity, a few were and still are regarded as demigods though that is a matter of opinion, mainly I suppose, *my* opinion. Yes, *mine*, though I will admit to a degree of bias when reflecting upon these people as unlike others, who so readily pass judgement, I knew several rather well and actually married two of them.

I recall in my years of innocence, in those days when I was a naive young girl, how I sat alone in the depths of night, in the silence of a sparsely furnished chamber, my back to a window that framed a crescent moon pale against the night sky as a newly stripped rib-bone. Before me on a stand of twisted copper rested a small white cup of smouldering incense from which spectral fingers of smoke unfurled before spreading upward into darkness. I gazed into the vapours and I saw beyond the temple and beyond the city wall. Yes, I knew those men were approaching and I knew there would be bloodshed. I knew they were coming though at first they were far away. For many days, I stared through shimmering mists but could see only shadows and nameless forms on the water. Only in time, only as their vessel drew closer, would those images begin to resolve.

When I set out to relate this tale I was unsure where to begin as at the start I was not at all involved. So you see I must have another describe much of what follows until such time as I myself am drawn fully into the coming events. Until then I'll excuse myself in advance for those first intrusions.

Chapter 1 - The Pledge

Pelion, a harbour town of Thessaly, lay on the Aegean Sea close beneath the wooded mountain after which it was named. This town, never pivotal in great events, was nevertheless renowned throughout the land for the rearing of fine horses in its extensive stables. Within the almost deserted megaron, the russet-columned main hall of the modest royal palace, there was not to be found the opulent grandeur witnessed in other towns and cities in the Mycenaean world such as gold rich Mycenae, grim walled Tiryns, wealthy Pylos, gauntly fortified Sparta or strongly founded Athens. The frescoed walls of Pelion depicted vivid scenes of hunting and of the natural world rather than those of conflict seen elsewhere. No marching warriors armed for battle strode across these walls though at intervals were hung bronze-tipped spears and figure-of-eight shields, each of these latter almost large enough to conceal the man carrying it. The frescoes and the weapons glowed from the light of burning brands mounted on the wall opposite. At the centre of the hall, flanked by four columns, a broad circular hearth, bounded by finely carved stone blocks, contained at its centre glowing embers where flames had through the previous evening danced. And though the hall was often home to chattering courtiers, the gaudy, bare-breasted, butterfly ladies encountered in those more extravagant, more cosmopolitan cities of the Greek world were not to be seen here. Palace staff and slaves, however, would be on hand when summoned. Two figures already waited at the shadowed far end of the megaron to do the king's bidding.

Before the great hearth that morning sat fair in feature, neatly-bearded Chiron, King of Pelion. He waited patiently, listening for the approach of footsteps. The alabaster throne of Pelion's virtuous ruler was plain but adequately cushioned and his robes, though rich in colour and flowing patterns, did not glisten like those of other rulers with gold, silver or gemstones. In no way a poor man, Chiron thought it improper to appear a gilded icon aloof from his own people. Propped against the throne was a large, tortoiseshell lyre, its gilded wooden frame inlaid with lapis lazuli and silver ornamentation. Chiron may have abjured ostentation, but the lyre, given him by a defeated enemy in the time of his youth, was a most valuable and prized possession, and when the mood took him he played it well.

Chiron's fame rested not only upon his devotion to horses but even more so for the wise advice requested and acted upon by many notable men from across Greece when visiting his stables over the years. Wise advice, yes, but not through wisdom gained by great age, for Chiron was a man of middle years, but rather through listening, reasoning and acute observation.

Now came the footsteps he awaited. At last entered the young Jason, fair-haired, strong and confident as he strode by the hearth. Chiron's blue-eyed, clean-shaven adopted son of some twenty years was dressed in plain, leather-belted linen tunic

14

with sword at his side. The ever present sword, upon which his hand rested, boasted finely crafted, ornate hilt and pommel set with a gemstone and was one of his few concessions to extravagance. The keen bronze blade, however, had served him in full measure the way any experienced warrior demanded it should though conflict was, for the time being, absent from the lands of Thessaly.

Chiron eyed him with anticipation as Jason approached to stand before his father. 'Well here you are my boy. You asked to see me before others began to gather in our hall. There's nothing amiss I hope.'

'There's nothing amiss,' Jason smiled, 'at least nothing I can think of right now, but we need to talk. I know we've touched upon this before but I've felt of late a decision had to be made and now I have.'

'Sit yourself down and we'll discuss matters. You are restless, my boy. Yes, I know you are and have been for some time. You have proved your worth often against our enemies but now you're more restless than ever. It's further challenge you need and I appreciate there is a wide world out there beyond our modest kingdom you ought to experience for yourself.'

'That there is,' said Jason, 'and there's a part of it you are well aware of waiting for me not so far away. You've made it clear from my earliest years how I came to be under your protection and how my true inheritance lay not only here in Pelion but also in our neighbouring kingdom of Iolcos.'

'That is so and I appreciate your feelings, but have I not also made it clear that this first and foremost is your home and always will be – and, of course, your inheritance.'

'Yes, father, you have, and what better home could any man ask for except I must return to Iolcos and, if I interpret your words correctly, take back that which ought to have been mine all along. I *have* to do this. I can no longer continue as I am unless the situation is resolved. It - it follows me of late as a dark shadow. You have your reputation for wisdom and the finest horses in all the lands whereas I have acquired mine in armed conflict. Therefore I must be seen to uphold it. As you so rightly say, I need a challenge; there is another world out there I know too little about. I hoped you would understand, which is why I needed to speak with you today in particular.'

'Of course,' said Chiron, 'and I expected in time you would endeavour to do as you now suggest. Even so, I always hoped you would regard the affair of Iolcos as something of lesser account. There were times, when you were a child, that I determined you should know nothing of what was said to have happened there all those years ago, but then to keep you in ignorance would have been an act of deceit. I'd not wish to face you each day knowing of that deceit - especially when you have risked your life, as I also have, in leading our men and to keep at bay those bandits and those predators who would have pillaged our town, seized our possessions and carried off our women.'

16

'I've had my uses on occasion,' grinned Jason, 'apart from managing our horses much of the time.'

Chiron's eyes brightened, his voice rose with enthusiasm as he continued, 'By the gods you have on both accounts. I recall that last assault upon us only a year ago. We were warned in good time by that shepherd boy who saw their two vessels approach before sunrise. You raised enough of our best men and were ready for them as their first boat arrived. You were down to the harbour before half of their vile crew were able to clamber onto the quayside. I watched that bold red plume on your bronze helmet sway as you cast your spear to bring down their boastful leader, one who bellowed like a bull to instil fear and take from us what is ours. Aye, they must have imagined there would be little opposition from a town famed largely for raising horses. Oh, you struck his head from his still quivering body and as spears and arrows flew I watched you, shield in hand, sword raised as you fell upon them like an avenging eagle, yes as you and your companions, weapons eager for blood, sprang forward to strike down any man foolish enough to remain on the quay. What with all the shouting and cries of those stricken, our harbour waters were soon red with their blood as those of 'em able to do so heaved clear with their oars in panic.' Chiron laughed, threw up his arms then added, 'You raised high their leader's severed head and flung it after 'em – yes, it hit the sail then fell straight into his damned boat! At that moment, I tell you, my pride in you as my son knew no bounds!'

17

'Just a lucky shot,' shrugged Jason, 'but if we'd had any vessels fit for it and enough crew ready to man them I'd have been after those devils and finished the job.'

Chiron relaxed then went on, 'I know that and I recall the look of frustration on your face as you watched them reach open water. Our fighting men, all our people respect you mightily and yet – and yet, yes, I have always believed that one day you would wish to leave Pelion and pursue what you, what I also believe to be your rightful inheritance elsewhere. As you know, it is claimed that King Pelias, the man who still rules Iolcos, had your true father, Aeson, his half-brother, and two of your own brothers murdered so he could get his hands on that throne. True or not, and I cannot say for sure, if you intend to visit Iolcos it must be with a well-armed party, otherwise -.'

'I – yes, I've thought of that but the men of his own town would surely outnumber us if Pelias called on them and that in turn could bring our kingdoms into direct conflict. If I go alone then Pelias won't have reason to feel threatened. It's well known he's outlived his only male offspring so there won't be any problems there, either. What I'm saying is – is that I won't be offering a challenge to any son of his unless he's decided it's to be the child of one of his court women or even a slave.'

'Look here,' said Chiron, 'let's have a drop of wine - I'll call for it now.' He tugged three times on a cord hanging close to one side of the throne. This caused a small bronze gong suspended between the shadowed beams of the ceiling to ring three times and echo about the megaron. The pair of plainly gowned young slaves approached from the far end of the hall, one a dark-eyed, slim girl bearing two richly pattered ceramic goblets, the other, an older, sallow male clutching an ornate flagon charged with honeyed red wine. Silence pervaded for the time it took the male to fill the goblets. During those moments the girl glanced knowingly aside at Jason, a brief grin crossing her face. Jason smiled back discretely as the goblets were handed over then watched as both offered Chiron and himself a bow of respect before retiring out of earshot to their former station.

Chiron raised his goblet to drink then said, 'We have a choice of excellent horses as you well know, so before you ride to Iolcos you must take one of our finest and dress as becomes a man of your status. You'll have to take gifts for Pelias, of course. Take some small but valuable items of adornment – that should keep the man happy.'

'Very well, and I'll make use of the fancy leopard skin tunic I occasionally use on feasting and ceremonial occasions, and over it a decent cloak so at least I won't be looked upon as a peasant. Other than that I'll take nothing but my sword, a flask of water, a small amount of food, the gifts and enough silver to see me through should I need to stay the night at Iolcos. Oh, and I intend to walk so if I leave here at sunrise I'll be at Iolcos early in the afternoon. I've stout enough leather sandals and the pathways will be well defined.'

'Walk!' exclaimed Chiron, his goblet poised in mid-air. 'No, that's – that is too undignified for anyone of my household, let alone my chosen son and heir. And don't forget, my boy, there's a river to cross. I say you must ride all the way.'

'The Anauros will be shallow enough in places at this time of the year and I want to appear before Pelias as though my journey is of no great importance – at least not at first. I know what he's said to have done and what his reputation is so I've no wish to antagonise him.'

'You may not wish to antagonise him,' Chiron responded, 'but I know the man rather well whereas you have yet to encounter him. So let me assure you; antagonising Pelias will not be difficult. He is a calculating and vindictive man – arrogant enough to insist his father was Poseidon himself and scornful of anyone he thinks doesn't believe him no matter how ridiculous his claim sounds. Hmm, I'm not sure anyone does know who his father was. But the more we talk of this, the less inclined I am to see you going through with it. Still, I know they will at this time be celebrating the festival in honour of Poseidon so the laws of hospitality must prevail – even at the court of Iolcos. And,' he continued, pulling a heavy bronze ring from the second finger of his left hand, 'you must wear this, the seal of our house. Pelias will doubtless recognise it.'

Jason accepted the ring, tested the fit, pushed it onto his finger then said, 'Thank you. I'm sorry you disapprove but I owe it to myself and in a way I owe it to you for all the confidence you've had in me.' He grinned widely, drank from his goblet then added, 'And I know about the festival, of course I do - and that's exactly why tomorrow is the day I plan to go.'

***

Cool morning air elated his mood and livened his step as Jason, leather satchel swinging from his shoulder and sword part hidden by his cloak, strode from beneath the stone gateway of Pelion town. Passing him on their way up to the town were the early traders and craftsmen, keen on setting up their stands to display their goods in a market square more restricted than those boasted by larger cities but providing better trade than many. Those knowing Jason offered polite greeting or passing bow. Directly ahead of him, on the rough but well defined wooded pathway leading up from the valley below struggled asses, oxen and provision loaded carts. Amid the lush woodlands lay thriving orchards, olive groves and fine vineyards. Numerous streams wound their way from the slopes of Mount Pelion and beyond into broader, sunlit lands where they meandered on to join the Anauros. And in those more open spaces Chiron's prized horses enjoyed their freedom. The route Jason took would find him before the river well ahead of midday and the broader crossing there he considered would offer less of a challenge at a time of the year when the Anauros flowed steadily.

He arrived at the Anauros to find many people in evidence. There were men and women casting their nets into the river, children dashed busily about, splashing in and out of the water followed by yapping dogs and there were groups of men further along tending their precious cattle. Jason hesitated

21

to peer at the river, seeing it flow more turbulently than he recalled on previous visits when out hunting or fishing. He noted where, a short way up river, water flowed over part-submerged rocks and considered it a suitable crossing place. Close by this on the bank was a small, loosely spread gathering of people. As he approached there were raised voices and laughter though one among them, an elderly, stooping woman in tattered black gown with head cowl, appeared to express herself in a hand-fluttering, agitated manner. Close to the water's edge Jason again stopped. Her voice was raised and her words clear: she was appealing for one of the men to carry her across to the opposite bank but her pleas elicited not sympathy but derision. One man suggested loudly, 'Someone take 'er 'alf way out then tip 'er into the river.'

Jason stepped over as another man remarked, 'Not me - I wouldn't wanna touch 'er.'

'Me neither,' agreed a third, 'though I reckon she could do with a damned good wash!'

They eyed Jason with suspicion but saw from his bearing and expression he was not a man they ought to offend. As all but one of the men began to amble away Jason said to the woman, 'If your need is pressing then I'll gladly help you over the river since I myself intend to cross here.' The woman scrutinized him from beneath her cowl, her piercing, pale blue eyes set within a walnut textured face, her few existing teeth much discoloured and set at various angles in a thin-lipped mouth.

The remaining man turned to leave, saying with a grin, 'Fancy 'er do y'sir?'

The look Jason gave him deterred further comment and as the man strolled away the old woman asked in croaking tone, 'What's the likes of you wantin' to 'elp the likes of me for, eh? You looks a proper gentleman you does.'

Jason grinned, shrugged and replied, 'Well I - I really can't say but offering my help will cost me precious little and if you'd care to accept then I promise I won't dump you when we're half way over as one of those oafs suggested.'

'Well I'll thank you, young master,' she croaked, tugging her gown more closely about herself then folding her arms tightly across her middle as she gazed up hard into his face. 'I'm ready when you are good sir.'

Jason stooped, placed his arms about her frail body and lifted her gently from the ground. She felt light as a small sack of corn and he could feel her bones through the material of the gown. Odd he thought, placing a foot cautiously into chill water, that she did not express the odour of age and bodily contamination he might have expected.

'An' where would you be goin'?' she asked as Jason stepped further in with water surging about his ankles.

'Not very far,' he replied, holding her bare feet clear of the water, 'to the palace at Iolcos as it happens. And you?'

'Oh me, good sir, just to the other side, no further, whereas in Iolcos I say you'll be facin' Pelias, 'er king, unless I'm much mistaken.'

Now well out into the river, treading rocks, with the water almost up to his knees and more turbulent than he had anticipated, Jason said, 'As it happens, yes I will. You obviously know of him. Are you then from Iolcos?'

'From Iolcus – me,' she cackled with a gappy smile as they passed the half-way point. 'Oh no, good sir, I'm not from Iolcus, that I'm not.'

Jason was about to question her further when his left foot slipped from the rock and drove deep into the mud at its side. Teetering, fighting to regain his balance, cursing under his breath, he managed to remain upright but found his sandal embedded firmly and out of sight beneath mud-clouded water. He tried hard, probing about with his foot, but encumbered by the woman, was unable to stoop or to reach down and recover the sandal. The woman said nothing, only clutching hard on his shoulder as he splashed onwards to the nearly deserted opposite embankment where he eased her to her feet, saying, 'There you are, madam. We made it across except I regret to say I'm now minus one of my sandals.' Peering down at his feet, he added, 'I might as well keep the one I still have then maybe I'll acquire a new pair in Iolcos; I hear they have a good market.'

'That they do, Lord Jason,' came her voice, 'but I doubt you'll benefit from it today.'

'What!' he exclaimed, stepping back from her diminutive figure. 'So you know who I am. How is this? You said you'd never been to Iolcus so you must have spent time in Pelion.'

'Oh, I know of you, sir,' she replied, her sharp eyes fixed steadily upon his from beneath the cowl. 'I've lived long, yes, I've been around more years than ever I bothered to count. I've 'eard much in my

24

time. I know of the man who's now your father, Lord Chiron, aye, and what others of little understandin' think of 'im.'

'And what d'you mean by that?' Jason asked. 'My father is the most respected man I know of and he well deserves it.'

She gave out a brief, rattling laugh and replied, 'That as may be, but there are those who've seen 'im only from afar among 'is many 'orses an' make out 'e's 'part 'orse, part man 'imself and call 'im a centaur, if you'll pardon me sayin' so.'

'Half horse and -!' laughed Jason. 'Well maybe that's how he'll be remembered. Now tell me, seriously, how can such as you, and I intend no offence, how can you possibly know anything about me, my father or anything of royal courts? And what else d'you claim to know?' As he gazed at her face, into her fathomless eyes the world all about appeared to fade, time seemed no longer to matter, no longer to exist as words drifted through his mind. 'This shrunken old crone – was she once young enough to experience the pleasures of love and lust? Was she once beautiful like Clymene, the slave girl whose affections I often enjoy in the privacy of my chamber?' The woman's face appeared to waver, her features to soften into those of the younger woman, but when he blinked the illusion was gone and once more he stood by a river in a broad land beneath a wide sky with a breeze on his cheek.

'What do I know, good sir,' she answered, 'aye, what *do* I know. Well I know of the man you're soon to meet. That man murdered 'is 'alf brother who was then king, the man who was your true

25

father. Your two brothers 'e also 'ad murdered an' would 'ave murdered you as well 'ad your mother not fled from Iolcus to Pelios an' left you with Lord Chiron. She told 'im what 'appened but departed soon after so 'e 'ardly knew who the lady was.'

Jason stared hard at her and demanded, 'By the gods where *did* you learn all this? It's accepted my mother had to leave the court of Iolcos when my true father died but as to exactly what happened, well -.'

'So now, good sir,' she interrupted, 'you 'ave to be on your way an' so must I. But you've shown me great kindness an' that I'll not forget – no, Lord Jason, be assured I will not forget.'

'Now look,' he insisted, 'we go nowhere until you explain to me how you could possibly -.' But when the woman lowered her head, turned her back to him and stepped away, it struck him as certain she was no longer willing to talk. Jason continued to stare at her but she remained statue-still. The sound of children calling to one another as they splashed about in the water nearby caught his attention and he knew he had to continue on his journey. The morning was well advanced, the sun hot when he turned to leave her, plodding up to level ground with one foot bare. He hesitated, deep in thought, then looked around, wishing he had pressed her further over her account, but the frail, dark figure he had carried across the Anauros was no longer to be seen.

'Where's she -?' he muttered, gazing in confusion both ways along the riverbank. 'How could an ancient peasant woman like her know

26

anything about -? Ah, that's it!' he exclaimed, holding up his left hand. 'She will have recognised the ring on my finger – of course, that must be it, but what does it matter. I guess a lot of people have been doing a lot of talking over the years and she's had plenty of time to listen.' Glancing down at his bare foot he mused, 'But this, damn it. I suppose I'd better take care not to tread on any sharp stones.' Yet as he walked on, he twice more glanced over his shoulder. When pausing further on to take a drink from his flask, he somehow knew she was telling the truth about Pelias.

***

Well I'm back sooner than I intended to make matters clearer, perhaps a lot clearer. In case you hadn't guessed, the decrepit old hag our dear Jason carried over the Anauros wasn't who or what he thought she was - no, far from it. Not even after she vanished into thin air as soon as his back was turned could he possibly have known. She was, as matters transpired, a manifestation of Hera, Queen of heaven, one of the twelve Olympians - no less the wife of almighty Zeus himself and goddess of women and childbirth if you don't mind. Kindly you might think, but she really wasn't someone to get on the wrong side of and Zeus himself knew that.

But why would she be wandering about looking more like a sack of offal and trying to get someone to help her over a river she never needed to cross? First of all, you see, Hera had no time for Pelias - no, none whatsoever. He'd never shown due respect for her and had a while back murdered, at her very altar, a supplicant who he claimed had offended him. Because Pelias had defiled her shrine with blood she regarded Jason as a means of getting back at him. You might think this was a time-consuming way of going about it when she could have ended his existence in no time at all by other means; an accidental or not so accidental poisoning - an assassination, perhaps, by some bastard son wanting his throne. But being immortal, time is one thing the gods have plenty of and they really do crave entertainment to fill out those endless days, months and years. Yes, eternity can seem quite a long time unless you find things with which to occupy yourself. Anyway, she intended to look after Jason so he could get on with it, as well as for a favour rendered to someone of apparently no importance he thought needed his help in crossing a river. How very touching from a man so skilled in the taking of human life.

***

The sun was past its highest when Jason approached the gaunt city wall of Iolcus. This wall arose above the sea shore on the gulf of Pagasae and presented more the aspect of a fortress than did that of Pelion. Armed, bronze-glinting guards were visible by her main gate amidst the many people passing in and out of the city. It surprised him to see most people were not carrying goods nor were there oxen and carts in evidence. Where, he asked himself, were the anticipated traders? He paused for a time to watch what was happening then continued on. Walking beneath the massive stone lintel of the gate he noted, crouching in shadow against the walls and largely ignored by the chattering throng, were the lame, blind and dispossessed, their hands held out claw-like in pitiful hope of alms. At Pelion such a sight would not be in evidence because Chiron would have taken measures to alleviate their misery. In Jason's satchel were the gifts for Pelias and his own pieces of silver. But what good was silver to these abandoned souls – it would soon be taken from them with little or nothing given in return.

Emerging from the gateway, Jason found himself before a large open space he recognized as the market square although there appeared to be no stalls set up and he could see no goods being traded. Set along parts of the city wall and some larger buildings within were the stylized bull's horns rendered in stone, familiar from his home town but seen also in many towns throughout Greece where mighty Knossos on Crete was emulated to more modest effect. On the far side of the square arose a stone building with pennants flying above and guards standing at the entrance. This had to be the king's palace and close by it where the crowds thronged most densely stood the temple of Poseidon. Jason turned to a passing woman and asked, 'Where might I buy myself a pair of sandals?'

'Buy a pair of -!' the woman exclaimed, looking Jason up and down. 'This is Poseidon's day. We don't do no tradin' 'ere in Iolcos on Poseidon's day. Where you from, then?'

'Oh, it doesn't matter,' he shrugged as the woman, eyeing him dubiously, turned to walk away.

29

Jason approached the temple, pushing through the crowd, noticed by some for his stature and bearing as they stepped out of his way. Now he was close enough to witness a group of robed priests, accompanied by horns and drums as they officiated over a sacrifice. The victim, a black bull held down by a number of robust men, was about to be dispatched by the smooth-headed chief priest in whose upraised hand glinted a long-bladed knife. Jason had in his mind the full description of King Pelias given him by Chiron but as the one in question did not appear to be present on this occasion he turned to the man standing next to him and asked, 'Does your lord and master not attend here today?'

'The king was 'ere some time back,' replied the man, chewing on a fig. 'Comes an' goes as it pleases 'im.'

'Does he now,' muttered Jason, turning to ease his way back through the pressing crowd.

The royal palace of Iolcos was larger and more imposing than that of Pelion. Of three floors in height rather than two, it boasted at ground level and in places above, the familiar downward tapering columns in russet or ochre but in greater number than at Jason's home. Three broad steps led up to the main entrance, its heavy, bronze-banded doors wide open but guarded by two stern-faced men, each wearing a bronze-scaled cuirass, horsehair plumed helmet and holding upright his spear. As Jason approached, the two promptly crossed their spears to prevent his going further and one announced, 'no one is to enter the palace!'

'I came here to speak with King Pelias,' Jason declared.

'No one's to enter the palace,' repeated the guard, shaking his spear toward the newcomer, 'that's what the king's told us 'an that means you.'

One hand resting on his sword hilt, Jason said, calmly, 'Then go and tell your lord the king that a man who claims to be the true son of Aeson is here to see him. I'd prefer we do this the easy way.'

Each guard looked at the other and the second man, levelling his spear at Jason in a threatening manner, said, 'On your way – the king's a busy man with no time for the likes of you.'

The speed at which Jason moved took both men by surprise. In the blink of an eye his sword hissed from its scabbard and flashed through the air to cleave the bronze spearhead from its shaft. Both men recoiled to stare at Jason in alarm as the spearhead clattered down the steps. The first man was not about to repeat the action of the second but stared for some moments before turning about to call through the doorway. His words were unclear to Jason but moments later a slave appeared. 'Show this man inside,' the guard ordered, 'then inform your lord there's someone wants to see 'im.' He gazed angrily at Jason then added, 'I'm sure 'e'll tell 'em who you say you are an' we'll be close by.'

The slave, a wiry youth who Jason judged to be of Libyan origin, gestured for him to follow then to halt in what appeared to be an ante-room. There he asked, 'What message, master, shall I offer to the king?'

31

Jason repeated the message he had given to the guards who, silhouetted in the entrance, stood watching him intently, hands resting firmly on sword hilts. The slave hurried through an inner door, turned right and vanished down a corridor. Glancing back at the guards, Jason well knew that leaving the palace might be less easy than had been getting in. From where he waited Jason could hear voices, laughter and the sound of pipes and drums. He noted also a smell of roasting meat. The slave reappeared with close behind him a gaudily robed and bearded man of later years who Jason, with the king's description still in mind, was certain could not be Pelias.

'You may address yourself to me,' the man said as he studied Jason from head to foot. 'I am Lycon, a companion of the king. I will give him your message but he will see no one today.'

'My message is as this man must have already relayed to you but I'll say more. Tell Pelias I am the son of Aeson who was one-time king here and I claim my right to the throne of Iolcos as your present king has no son to take his place.' Jason raised his left hand before the man's eyes, adding, 'This ring I wear bears the seal of my father's house which I'm sure he will recognize. And as this day is the feast of Poseidon I claim also the hospitality demanded by custom throughout the land. Go now and I will wait here for him to call me.' Peering closely at the ring, the man eyed him once more then retraced his steps while the slave retreated into shadows close to one wall.

Lycon left the corridor to enter the megaron of King Pelias from where originated the odours of cooking. A fire blazed in the central hearth and burning torches set about the walls supplemented incoming daylight from small windows above. Members of his court and his guests chattered, strolled or sat about the great wooden table, at the head of which presided their king. Pelias was a large man, bear-like and pot-bellied - his stature not so much an inherited feature of his ancestry or strength acquired through exertion, but attributable more to a surfeit of food and drink, as his table evidenced. A jewelled leather band about his broad head kept in place mid-length, raven-black hair. His equally dark beard, neatly trimmed to a point half way down his richly robed chest, was laced generously with fine silver wire as if intended to hold every hair in place. It was nevertheless sullied by food. In one hand he gripped a profusely embossed gold cup while his other hand swayed back and forth in rhythm with the music. Two attendants stood close behind the high-backed, ornately carved and gilded chair that served as his throne while the women of his court sang, cavorted, teased and chattered. Their delicately crinkled hair, held in place by coloured linen bands, fell about the tops of patterned, short-sleeved bodices, open at the front in Cretan fashion to display their naked and rouged breasts. Variously-coloured, layered and flounced dresses hung down almost to their soft-sandaled feet. As Lycon approached him the king looked up to ask, 'Well, who is it makin' a damned nuisance of 'imself out there? Can't the guards see 'im off?'

'He confirms his message and more, sire. He brings gifts and wears what he claims to be the seal of Chiron's house. He expresses a claim to your throne and -.'

Lycon never finished the sentence for Pelias began to laugh, rolling from side to side in the royal chair then drinking deeply from the royal goblet. 'A claim to - !' he spluttered. 'So what else 'ave you to tell me before I call for more men to 'ave the bugger dragged away an' flogged?'

'Well, sire, he is fair, of good stature, wears a leopard skin tunic beneath a clean white cloak, has a sword at his side that most certainly could belong to no common man and, er - and he only wears one sandal.'

Pelias ceased laughing. He stared wide-eyed at the man, his goblet poised in mid-air. 'What d'you mean!' he rumbled. 'What's this about one sandal?'

'I mean, Sire, that – that one of the man's feet is bare.'

'One sandal is it,' growled Pelias, his expression darkening. 'Are you sure of this – I mean *quite* sure?'

'Quite sure, My Lord, he most certainly wears only one sandal.'

'Summon Elymos the priest at once!' exclaimed Pelias. Tell that man outside to wait an' I'll see 'im in due course. Meanwhile I want everyone out of 'ere - now!' Pelias struggled up, scraped back his weighty chair and thumped his wine-spattering goblet several times against the

34

table. 'Out!' he bellowed, his voice ringing about the hall. The music faltered and died. 'I want everyone out of 'ere now!' Courtiers and others stared about in confusion. Lycon gestured with fluttering hands for people to leave. 'Out – out - out!' the king demanded, arms flailing from side to side above his head. 'Everyone out of 'ere! Everyone!' He pointed at a male slave cowering between two columns and added, 'Except for you! Stay where you are!'

A tense, gown-swishing ensued, seats clattered as people arose from the royal table to join others making their way from the hall to passages and corridors. For a time, Pelias stood alone, hands pressed flat against the table, his head switching impatiently from side to side until at last Lycon reentered the hall followed by Elymos in his priestly gown, this spattered liberally by the blood of sacrifice.

Facing the priest, Pelias demanded, 'What's this oracle you were on about sometime back regardin' a man with one sandal comin' 'ere - well?'

'Yes, Sire,' replied Elymos, 'it was foretold such a man would arrive one day to avenge his family for deeds committed by – er -.'

'By me,' growled Pelias, 'that's what y're sayin' isn't it?'

'I mean no offence, Sire,' the priest muttered.

'No,' declared Pelias, dragging a sleeve across his mouth, 'I well recall it - hah, all of it, an' I know what you mean. This is – this 'as to be a co-incidence an' no more than that. Anyway, both of

you leave now. Tell the guards to stand by ready to
rid me of this – this whoever 'e claims to be but
send 'im in 'ere first so I can see for m'self who's
responsible for this damned intrusion. Go!'

'My Lord,' said Elymos, shuffling back, 'Our
laws, our traditions and those throughout the land
say we must not harm a guest such as this or any
other during holy celebrations. The gods themselves
would be angered.'

'I thank you for remindin' me,' mumbled Pelias
as Lycon and the priest retreated from his royal
presence.

Lowering back into his chair Pelias waited,
staring across the hall, fingers drumming on the
table. Footsteps approached. Both guards halted at
the entrance with, standing before them, the young
man attired as described and wearing only one
sandal. Jason stepped forward to stand in full view
of Pelias.

'What've you come 'ere for?' demanded Pelias,
squirming about to face the newcomer then peering
down at his feet.

'I have come from Chiron's kingdom to -.'

'You address the king as, My Lord!' shouted
one of the guards, stepping into the hall.

'I address no man in that manner!' responded
Jason, turning to face him with a hand poised above
his sword.

Pelias laughed aloud, waved a dismissive hand
at the guard, who backed away to stand by his
companion, then eyeing the ring on Jason's finger
he said in a calmer voice, 'Sit down – you might as
well 'ave some wine while you're 'ere. He turned to

the waiting slave and called, 'Bring fresh wine an' a clean goblet!'

Each man eyed the other but neither spoke until the slave reappeared with flagon and goblet which he placed in reverential silence upon the table. Pelias slid the goblet to Jason and seeing him eye the flagon with suspicion, poured a generous measure into his own cup and drank deeply before filling the one offered to Jason. 'Well now,' he declared, picking up his knife to stab at a piece of pork, 'I'm listenin' so let's 'ear all y'ave t'say.'

'First of all' Jason began, 'I have here gifts from the house of Chiron.' He reached to lift from his satchel a small but weighty linen bag which he placed upon the table before Pelias. Pelias murmured his thanks, stared for some moments at the bag but did not open it. 'My father, Aeson,' continued his less than welcome visitor, 'was king of Iolcos before you and I hear it claimed that you had him – shall we say, removed, together with my two brothers. Do you confirm or deny this?'

'I – no, I don't deny any of it.' replied Pelias, chomping his food. 'The throne of Iolcos was rightfully mine to start with and the man you claim to 'ave been y'father refused to acknowledge it as did those who followed 'im.'

'And my brothers, who were mere children – how do you account for their deaths?'

'Er, yes, there was some trouble – things got out of 'and; some of my men were drunk an' what took place all those years ago was, well, unfortunate.'

'Unfortunate was it,' Jason responded, 'But my mother managed to smuggle me out of Iolcos before these men of yours got their hands on me also. Now then, d'you know who she was - her name, that is?'

'Y'mother? I can't recall 'er name, no. She was one of Aeson's court women; that's all I can say, though I was told 'e did marry 'er before -.'

'Well,' cut in Jason, 'that confirms he *was* my father, does it not; which means that since you have no male heirs I have a sound claim to the throne of Iolcos.' Jason rose slowly from his seat, all the time staring at Pelias. He slipped a hand over his sword hilt and declared, 'And if it were not for the ceremonies in honour of Poseidon, things might get out of hand again right here and now, and I promise you'd be a dead man before those two guards of yours could make it across the hall. So tell me, what d'you have to lose by agreeing?'

'Damn you,' breathed Pelias, knife-blading more food into his mouth in an attempt not to appear unduly concerned, though twice his eyes darted from Jason to the guards, to his knife and back again to Jason. 'What do I 'ave to lose, you ask. Well I've still a few years 'ead of me as ruler of Iolcus, that's what I 'ave to lose. But —.' Pelias, still eating, stared up at Jason then continued, 'but maybe we can reach an agreement 'ere an' now if you're prepared to listen.'

'I'm waiting and I'm listening,' said Jason, keeping a keen eye on Pelias' knife.

'Very well but think on this,' Pelias continued, 'If you decide to kill me you'll die also. Feast of Poseidon or no, my men will see to it an' no mistake. That would result in our towns goin' to war and that would weaken Pelion as well as Iolcos

38

to the advantage of our outside enemies. Aye, it could bring ruin on both our 'ouses.'

'By Zeus I'll have your answer!' exclaimed Jason. Both guards took a step forwards.

Pelias ceased eating, belched loudly then slid his knife aside, though his hand remained on the handle. 'All right, I will bequeath all I 'ave to you without animosity if you'll render me a service.'

'A service? A service doing what?'

'Sail to Colchis and bring the Golden Fleece back 'ere. I'll swear on the altars of Poseidon an' Zeus, before you an' our priests that I'll then do as I said - provided you swear also.'

Jason stared hard at the man before responding. 'I've heard of this - this Golden Fleece but why should I do that when you can sail off with armed men and get the thing for yourself?'

'Why should you – well it'll allow me time to get my affairs in order. An' why don't I go? Well I can't go. I've no one I want to trust in takin' over 'ere while I'm away since you ask, an' there's a younger 'alf brother of mine wantin' this throne that doesn't 'ave my sensibilities.'

'A lack of trust within your own house,' Jason commented. 'Now why don't I find that surprising. But Colchis is a long way from these lands from what little I know of it.'

'Aye, maybe it's a bit of a journey but if the reputation the Fleece seems to 'ave is true, an' most men believe it so, then it'll bring good fortune to me an' a kingdom an' honour to you as well as anythin' else you get your 'ands on while you're about it. You're young an' spirited, I see that well enough an' you 'ave the time to do this while there aren't any enemies at either our gate or yours.'

'Be that as it may,' said Jason, backing away from the table, 'but you, my friend, are playing for time. Still, I'll accept your oath and I will give mine at both shrines today. I'll return afterwards to Pelion and there I'll think further on how best to fulfil our agreement. But know this, if you have deliberately set me upon a false enterprise then whatever I swear at the temple will mean nothing at all.'

Jason strode away, obliging the guards to move aside as he left the megaron. The two guards stepped forward to their lord and master in anticipation of instructions for dealing with his newly departed guest, but Pelias waved an arm, saying, 'Let 'im alone 'an get back about y'business.' As the guards left to resume their former positions, Pelias relaxed once more into his cushions and laughed to himself. He called to the one remaining slave, 'More wine!' reached for the linen bag left there by Jason, swung it in his hand as if testing its weight then began to laugh loudly.

***

The sun was low, the air cooler and most people had departed the market square when Jason left the temple of Poseidon. He would not attempt to return home or to cross the Anauros in coming darkness. He had adequate silver and decided that if there was good food and a clean bed to be found at any inn, he would spend the night in Iolcos.

The light of a half-moon bathed his room. Jason lay beneath a woollen blanket with sword close at his side and thinking of the events that had passed that day. There were the words of Chiron, the one whose role as his father could never have been bettered. There was the frail old woman he had carried over the river and the words she uttered that had so baffled him, and still did. There was his interview with Pelias and the man's proposals, an interview that now, in the deep realms of night, he considered had passed too easily by far. Still, he and the King of Iolcos had sworn their agreements before priestly witnesses at the city's two most important shrines and so avoided hostilities. Could anything more have been accomplished since his arrival at Iolcos? He turned over in the comfort of the bed and as sleep descended he murmured, 'In the morning I'll have myself a new pair of sandals then I'll be on my way back home.'

***

Our dear, Jason, formidable in combat but otherwise naïve and near clueless about what he'd just let himself in for, was quite pleased with the way things had gone at the time. He and Pelias had sworn their oaths before high priests at the most sacred shrines in Iolcus – shrines, in fact, sacred throughout most of Greece. Pelias' scribes had recorded the whole event on clay tablets and before these were taken away to be baked hard and placed into storage, Jason and Pelias, before three witnesses drawn from the court, had each removed the ring from his finger and impressed his seal of authority into the clay. Jason had, so he thought, secured his succession to the throne of Iolcos and intended to boast about it as soon as he returned home. Pelias, too, was highly pleased at the outcome. Highly pleased, yes, but for a very different reason.

You may have wondered why Jason had not given more thought to Pelias' proposal over the Golden Fleece. As he said, he'd heard about it, and so had many other people for whom, in the main, it occupied vague realms of hand-me-down hearsay. Those in power knew more of it, or thought they did, but we must excuse Jason's prior lack of interest as his involvement with horses, with hunting, womanizing and in the defence of Pelion had determined his priorities. Womanizing – yes. You may recall his passing glance at the slave girl, and hers at him. She'd been a welcome visitor to his bedchamber on numerous occasions, though even as his favourite she wasn't the only one. Her name was Clymene, named after a nymph, if you please.

Had he been warned in advance to learn more about the Golden Fleece before wandering off to Iolcos and had the hand of the goddess not been instrumental in his laxity once there, his meeting with Pelias might have proceeded in a very different manner. Others, you see, had in the past been drawn by the prospect of fame and fortune to recover the fabled Golden Fleece. None had returned alive, as Pelias well knew.

Chapter 2 - The Summons

Jason's arrival at the palace of his father late that following morning caused minimal comment because few people other than Chiron knew he had been absent since sunrise the previous day. Servants and slaves went about their business in the great hall and a girl was singing, accompanied by a lyre played by one of the elderly male courtiers. Chiron was in conversation with two members of the priesthood when Jason entered, his face lit by a boyish grin. Chiron dismissed the priests, rose from his throne and stepped briskly forward. 'A-ha!' he exclaimed, 'you're back with us and looking mightily pleased with yourself. Come and sit by me, I'll call for wine and you can tell me how it all went.' He gestured across the hall to where stood waiting the male slave and the girl, Clymene.

With filled goblet in hand, with flagon placed by Chiron's throne, Jason related his journey to Iolcus, his crossing the Anauros and his assisting of the aged woman.

'And so you showed a little kindness when others had none to offer,' said Chiron. 'That is much to your credit.'

'I, er – yes, I felt I had to help her though I'm not sure why as she looked none too appealing. And I tell you, she seemed to know a great deal about me – about us, and about the affairs in Iolcus. That was very strange. And then – and then she was gone. Oh, and so was one of my sandals; I lost it in the river as I carried her over.'

'A small loss considering your encounter with Pelias was a success as I assume from your manner it must have been. So - tell me about that.'

Jason hesitated, drank from his cup then replied, 'It was easier than I expected but I wonder if Pelias might have ordered me murdered that day had it not been for the festival. After we'd discussed matters his response greatly surprised me. He said he would quit Iolcos if I rendered him a favour and this we agreed formally at the shrines of Zeus and Poseidon. Now, though, I suspect I ought to have held back and looked further into what he was asking.'

'Oh, and what was he asking, and more to the point exactly what did you agree with the man?'

'I agreed I'd sail to Colchis and bring him back the Golden Fleece.'

Chiron lowered his goblet slowly and stared with apprehension at Jason before saying quietly, 'You should never have agreed to that. Was any of this witnessed?'

Jason had rarely seen him appear so displeased as he answered, 'Er, well yes, it was, and each of us applied our seal to it. From the way you look at me and the tone of your voice it seems this was not a good idea. To what have I so rashly committed myself and just what's so special about this Golden Fleece, this - this gilded sheepskin?'

'No, it was *not* a good idea,' responded Chiron. 'It most certainly was not. You know almost nothing about what is claimed for this fleece when one in your position as prince of a royal court should have known something more – at least as much as I think I know. I'll tell you what I've heard about of it here and now, then later we'll have to decide what is to be done. The fleece is said to have belonged to a winged ram created by Hermes. The purpose of this unlikely creature was to rescue two young people, Phrixos and his sister, Helle, who were condemned to death because of a succession dispute somewhere or other.'

'A succession dispute,' commented Jason. 'That sounds familiar enough.'

'Quite so,' agreed Chiron. 'It is said the ram flew to Colchis but on the way the unfortunate girl fell to her death in the Hellespont, the sea that has since borne her name. Phrixos landed safely and was given sanctuary by their newly enthroned king, Aietes, and there he sacrificed the ram as Hermes had ordered him to do. Its fleece, of pure gold and possessing the gift of power, or so it's claimed, was hung up in Colchis, dedicated to Zeus and is believed now to be guarded by a dragon or something of the sort.'

'Oh, really, a dragon,' commented Jason, raising his cup. 'Sounds a quite fanciful tale to me.'

'And well it may be,' said Chiron, 'except that over these last few years, a few have taken it seriously and set off to find what they thought would bring them great wealth and status as it's thought to have done for this man Aietes. Of him I know virtually nothing.'

'Yes, Pelias seemed to believe that owning the fleece would be much to his advantage and now he expects me to go and get the thing for him. Maybe if he'd had a son of his own still living then he'd have been given the job.'

'I think not,' said Chiron, his expression remaining solemn, 'and I'll tell you why: of all those who it's claimed set sail to acquire the fleece, no one has returned. No one at all. I expect he didn't mention that.'

'Well, no he didn't,' mused Jason, 'and I realise now it's why that rogue Pelias had me agree to go and look for it – yes, he must think I won't be coming back so he'll be quite safe on his throne, or at least safe from me. I did warn him; if this was trickery I'd forget about the oaths and make him pay for it and that's what I intend to do.'

'But regrettably,' said Chiron, 'it would be a grave dishonour to ourselves and an affront to the gods if you were to break the oath you made at their shrines. I – we, need time to consider our options though at present, unless we go to war with Iolcus, I see no alternative other than your going through with this damned agreement even if the whole idea of the Golden Fleece turns out to be baseless nonsense. The less people know about something the more they'll make of it as I well know.'

Jason thought for a while then said, 'Either way it's my responsibility is it not.' Again he fell into pensive silence, then lifted his goblet to Chiron, saying, 'Father, since I've seen little enough of the world beyond Thessaly it's about time I spread my wings, and this sounds an interesting enough challenge. Tell me what you know of Colchis and how far away it is.'

'We and those we deal with have hardly any trading links with that part of the world. To the east it is regarded as undesirable, as hostile even, so there is little I can relate other than that it is many days sailing and rumours of the dangers that lie there are also many.'

'Then I will need men, fit and well-armed men, but not so many as will leave our town vulnerable to those who wish us ill; and by that I mean Pelias.'

'I see no alternative,' sighed Chiron, 'none other than a war which could be ruinous to both sides.'

'Then it's decided. But for now I need to bathe and have myself something to eat.' He noted the two figures awaiting summons at the far side of the megaron - one of them, Clymene, and added, 'I'll relax for a time this afternoon and return here before sunset.'

***

'I have thought hard, very hard indeed over this,' declared Chiron as he and Jason sat with well-filled goblets in the warm air of the colonnaded courtyard. Fed by the streams of Mount Pelion a lively fountain sparkled late afternoon sunlight in the bobbing apex of its waters as he continued, 'Many of those people who over the years have visited me for counsel or to acquire a fine horse have been skilled or brave men, most with admirable deeds to prove it, others with deeds of maybe lesser repute but nevertheless acts much to their credit. All of them owe me something and most pledged their support if ever I needed it, many swearing it most willingly upon the sacred altars of our temples. I will send for these men wherever they are and I will include the great Heracles. A boastful man he was, and more than likely still is, and temperamentally unstable at times, but most useful to have around when things are difficult.'

'What d'you mean by temperamentally unstable?' queried Jason. 'Like most people, I always thought of him as a great hero and no less than that.'

'Well since you ask, he murdered his wife, Megara, a daughter of Creon, King of Thebes, though in the end this was blamed upon a bout of insanity brought on by Hera, who the priests of her shrines claim hated him even though he'd taken her name as a part of his own. Rumour has it that through her manipulations he is, or was, obliged to undertake twelve onerous tasks some refer to as his twelve labours, but you know what rumours are – they're just that and often no more.'

'Then I look forward to meeting the great man if he as well as others answer your call.'

'There are many reports of turmoil far to our east but as our own lands are presently untroubled, apart from the family feuds at Mycenae and problems on the island of Lemnos that lies on the route you have to take, I hope these men will welcome the challenge. Should they do so then you all must have a way of getting there and back, and by that I mean a well-founded vessel to carry the men, their arms and the supplies you're likely to need. Going to Colchis may mean you'll be entering dangerous waters.'

48

'It seems you've been thinking hard over this,' said Jason. 'I see no reason to fear the outcome if we're to be so prepared, except for our method of travel. Do we possess the kind of vessel you imagine we'll need? I'm not aware of any.'

'We do not, nor do I know of anyone that does except perhaps for King Minos, but we have only tenuous relations with Knossos. To the mighty Cretan kingdom we and the likes of Iolcus are minor players in the greater scheme of things. But then we do have the finest ship builder anywhere on the Aegean coast.'

'Oh, you mean old Argos,' said Jason. 'Yes, I have seen him at work. I know his skills are most admirable but surely he builds nothing other than fishing boats.'

'Ah, so he does, but they are the very *finest* fishing boats. He has, I know, sailed in Cretan ships and boasts of being familiar with their construction. Anyway, if I make sure he's on board to keep an eye on things then our good friend Argos will have every incentive to ensure this new vessel I speak of is also the very finest. He'll need time to build the thing but it will give me time also to send messengers out on our fastest horses. They'll search throughout mainland Greece and the Peloponnese, even as far as Sparta, for the many men and their companions who I hope will go with you. Their enthusiasm will doubtless be heightened if there are prizes of value to be gained. Yes, some at least will I'm sure be drawn by thoughts of the plunder denied them by Minos' navy as his power in the Aegean Sea does not extend to the farthest north and east.'

***

A month had passed during which men had started to arrive and now a small but growing cluster of tents bloomed outside the city wall of Pelion. This in turn had attracted stallholders, wine sellers, entertainers and scampering children. Cooking fires gave forth rising smoke and the visitors gathered in conversation with people of the town. And present each evening were those women eager to engage with the men for a payment of silver.

One morning when stepping out alone, Jason observed more tents had been erected, including one close by the city gate. Outside this a small group was gathered and music could be heard. He approached to see at the centre of the group a clean-shaven man, some few years older than himself, seated on a three-legged stool and playing a lyre. It was no ordinary lyre but an instrument of exotic and valuable appearance. His shoulder-length fair hair was held in place by a gilded, leaf-patterned band, the edges of his Egyptian cotton tunic colourfully embroidered. On seeing Jason draw near, he stopped playing, placed the lyre aside and, smiling broadly, raised up from his seat.

'I welcome you,' declared Jason, 'and your most pleasing music. Tell me your name, although I think I may already know it.'

'I am Orpheus, sir,' he replied as the other men stood aside. 'I aim to gladden the souls of men and to steer their thoughts away from the bloodshed and violence that for so much of the time has defined our world.'

'Yes, my friend, I recall now your visit to my father, to our king, when I was playing games with a wooden sword. And talking of swords, I see you yourself wear a fine one.'

'I do, sir, ever since bandits fell on me and attempted to steal that which I regard as most precious.' He patted his lyre then added, 'It was your father and his men who saved me and now I'm here at his call to repay that debt.'

'As it seems we all are,' commented one of the men standing close by. 'This 'as to be worth it.'

Jason was distracted by other sounds from a tent further from the city wall where some ten and more men had gathered. One voice carried loudly as if a declaration of some importance was in progress. Jason excused himself and strolled across to witness what was happening. He eased through the small crowd and there before him, as centre of attention, was a large and muscular man, one with a physique fit to deal with any challenge in labour or in combat. His hair, longer than Jason's, was matched by a bushy black beard that covered the sides and lower part of his weathered though alert, blue-eyed face. His powerful body was part concealed by the pelt of a lion, the head of which hung down at his broad back. In his hands he grasped a large wooden club, shaking this high then thumping it hard on the ground as he thundered, '...and then the King of Crete and ruler of Knossos, aye, the great Minos 'imself, 'ad me go out and catch the creature single 'anded – biggest bull you ever saw, damn great white creature with 'orns like scythes! But I mastered it, oh yes, then I got it on board a Cretan vessel and back over to the mainland where we landed at night. I tethered it to a tree and in the mornin' I let it go, aye, it scared the shit out of people when they saw it. They asked me 'ow I'd got it there because the Cretan ship 'ad earlier left so I told 'em I'd 'ad it swim over with me on its back. They still believe that and -.' Seeing the grinning Jason stand there with arms folded, he hesitated then growled. 'And who's this that finds my account so amusin'?'

Heads turned as the new arrival replied, 'I am Jason, son of Chiron, and do I take it you are -?'

He was interrupted by a burst of laughter from some of the men. The figure in the lion skin lowered his club to the ground next to his powerful bow and quiver of arrows, pulled the animals head up and over his own until his face glared through the open, white-toothed jaws. 'I'm 'Eracles,' he bellowed, beating his chest with a clenched fist, 'that's exactly who I am! And what's more I've volunteered of my own free will and brought over one of my lads an' 'elp you out – yes you since I'm told it's you, the son of Chiron, leadin' us all to find this Golden Fleece thing and whatever else we pick up while we're about it!'

As the man eased back the lion's head, Jason said, 'Yes, I realized you must be the famous Heracles but I had to ask. My father and others have told me about you but I understand you are committed to undertake a number of tasks by King Eurystheus of Mycenae and -.'

'Yes, all right, so I am' he growled 'There's twelve of 'em, aye, twelve so-called labours an'

I've reached the eighth. When I 'eard about your scheme I decided I was overdue for a break an' so I left off 'em.'

'I'm sure you are most welcome, my friend,' assured Jason, 'and when my father knows you're here with us he will make his way over to greet you.'

'Aye, good,' responded Heracles, who promptly turned to his tent and bawled, 'Hylas, a drop more wine out 'ere!' Turning to his audience he added, 'He's my squire if y'please.'

From the tent emerged a clean-shaven, short-haired, slim youth with brimming silver goblet that he handed carefully to Heracles. Heracles took it promptly from him, spilling some of the wine in his haste before downing the rest in two ample gulps. He swung the goblet back to the waiting Hylas, reached down to seize and raise high his club then continued loudly with the colourful account of his exploits.

Jason strolled away still smiling. He proceeded tent by tent to count the men, offering greetings where appropriate before making his way in sunlit optimism to Pagasai harbour where awaited the almost completed boat. Few days passed when Jason had not been present to watch the vessel's steady progress from her keel upwards. The work had continued in bright sunlight and days not so bright, to the clamour of linen or leather-kilted, scrambling, sweating men, young and old, hard at work about her hull of cedar and oak with hammer, saw, adze and rope. Smoke drifted across the scene and pervading the air was the odour of pitch applied to the ship almost up to the gunwale and stanchions, the latter to support the upper bank of those rowing who would number altogether twenty-five each side. Above the black pitch her timbers were painted bright red and above her cutwater bow arose a railed platform with curving high over this, a slim and delicate device in the shape of a horn. A similar device graced her stern, also curving back toward the mast which, stepped through the narrow, central deck, now arose proudly to the sky. Her yardarm was this day being hoisted for the first time with the broad, white sail bearing an image in black of Poseidon's trident.

So occupied was Jason by the sight of the vessel that he did not see the stout, balding but bushy-bearded figure in leather kilt approach with swaying gate until the voice shattered his thoughts. 'Does she please you, young sir? She'll soon be ready to launch and ready for yourself to determine 'er course.'

'She pleases me very well indeed,' responded Jason, turning to face him.

'And 'ave you thought of a name for 'er?' he asked.

'As it happens, my friend, yes I have. In consideration of the work you have done here and the magnificent vessel I see before me, I say she ought to be named after you. I'd like her to be called, *Argo* if that pleases you and I ask if you will consider joining us as captain together with sufficient of your own crew and their arms to make up our numbers.'

54

Exposing gappy, discoloured teeth, Argos beamed broadly and clasping hands at his chest replied, 'Young sir, I'd be mightily pleased an' proud to 'ave her named after myself, aye, that I would, but as for serving as her captain – I'd 'oped all along but 'ardly believed you'd consider asking me since I'm not as young as I was.'

'I wouldn't consider asking anyone else unless you refused outright,' said Jason, placing a hand on the man's broad shoulder. 'She may look a splendid enough ship to me but no one could know her better than you and your excellent men, and I'm well informed of your experience at sea before you began your work here at Pagasai. There are also those unpredictable northerly winds I hear sailing men speak of; I think there your experience will be of immense value while I suspect most of those waiting to join us will have little or no knowledge of the route we're to take. But I have to tell you, my friend, there may be more risks involved with our journey than just the wind and sea.'

'Risks, young sir – I've taken more risks at sea than any man I know of, I've sailed some of the most distant waters and I've faced a good few challenges ashore. And it seems to me those men of yours waitin' outside the city wall are fit to face most anythin' the gods might throw at 'em.'

'Let's hope the gods don't throw too much at our men but whatever waits for us out there I look forward to seeing our vessel take to the wide waters.'

'Talkin' of the immortals who guides our ways,' said Argos, 'I've made more than my usual share of sacrifice and prayer at Athena's shrine an' I truly believe she already watches over us, aye indeed I do.'

'I hope your faith in Athena is well founded,' said Jason.

'I reckon it is, young sir,' he beamed. 'After dark yesterday I was down 'ere alone an' I saw – I saw a white owl perched on the bow of our vessel. As I watched, it took to the air, circled a while then vanished into the night. If that is not a sign the Lady Athena 'as blessed our boat then I don't know what is. An' as for takin' to the waters, that will be very soon. We'll 'ave her afloat early tomorrow with my own lads on board to check things over – mainly those men who'll be sailin' with us. The next day she'll be provisioned an' ready to depart if you so wish.'

'Then,' said Jason, 'I'll return to our village of tents and request the men to gather here in the morning. They can witness her afloat and familiarize themselves with the vessel they're to occupy for unknown days ahead.'

'Aye, sir, and they'll need to practice 'ard their rowin' as I suspect it's a task some of those lads 'ave yet to face.'

***

In the brightly frescoed walls of his room they relaxed with the blinds newly raised to welcome morning sunlight. Clymene, running her fingers over his naked chest, said, 'Lord Jason, dear, something has changed. You are here with me now but your thoughts are elsewhere. I sensed this in the night. I sensed it even when we were – when we -.'

'You surely know I'm leaving on a journey to lands far away from here and I may be gone for some time. How far away and for how long I cannot say.'

'Oh, I am a slave of this house and must do as others bid, but no other man can take your place. I will dread the touch of anyone else when you're gone. I will miss you, yes, how I will miss you.'

Jason looked into her dark eyes and saw tears. 'Clymene,' he whispered, 'you need not fear other men. I intend to have my father grant you your freedom. I'm to speak with him soon. I'll ensure you are placed under his protection and serve as a member of our court. You will learn much. You will learn to read the tablets and to set down your own words and you will have others to serve you.'

The girl smiled. She whispered, 'Thank you,' but still there were tears.

**

'Now the vessel is ready,' said Chiron, 'I expect you and your men suffer growing impatience.'

'We do indeed,' responded Jason as members of the court went about their business and a small group entertained with their pipes and songs at one side of the megaron. 'Those who responded to your summons are keen to sail. Their numbers have grown they've been with Argos and his men over the passing days to familiarize themselves with the vessel and learn her ways and her handling once aboard and at the rowing benches. We leave before sunrise tomorrow and head first toward Lemnos where our gallant captain confirms we should arrive early on the third day.'

Each raised his newly filled goblet and Chiron said, 'Aye, Lemnos. I mentioned a while back did I not that there was said to be trouble on the island, tales of people fleeing reported by captains who felt obliged to avoid their port. Yet again these are rumours but you should take great care and first ascertain if you can what's been happening ashore.'

'I think,' said Jason, savouring his wine, 'that there will be few problems our men cannot deal with; they're all fit and well-armed. But of course, we'll keep our eyes open.'

'Then I'll here drink to you and to your Argonauts, aye Argonauts, for that's what they'll be. Oh, and the girl you wanted to have freed – that I will deal with today and she will soon be instructed in her duties as a full member of our court. And as you also wish, she will have a tutor to give her those skills befitting one belonging to a royal house.'

Jason glanced across to where Clymene and the male slave waited. 'Good, it's what I promised her and I believe she'll serve well.'

'Then in the morning,' smiled Chiron, placing a hand on Jason's shoulder, 'I'll see you on board your ship and ensure you have gifts from our house to offer any you consider worthwhile.'

***

'So of now, dear Clymene, you are free and my father and officials of the court will instruct you over your new role. Now you have a new life and much to look forward to.'

They lay once more in the frescoed room and on this last occasion the blind was aside and the night sky with its array of stars was visible.

'But you'll not be here, Lord Jason, so I'll be none the happier.'

Jason leaned aside to kiss her, saying, 'look through our window and you'll see the star of Aphrodite watching over us. Let's not disappoint her.'

Chapter 3 - The Women of Lemnos

Sunlight finger-tipped the higher reaches of Mount Pelion as voices arose from the harbour below. Oars pushed hard against the stone quay and the good ship *Argo* was eased clear with her complement of some seventy men, their arms and armour stowed on sacking with some of their supplies beneath the narrow deck. Seated by the tiller was sun-bronzed Tiphys, their well experienced steersman, who having spent far more time at sea than on land, liked to present himself as a son of Poseidon though his sentiments were here intended as purely allegorical. Those twenty or more of her crew not manning the oars, which now were able to sweep freely back and forth, clambered about her deck and rigging to raise the yard arm and deploy the sail. People had come down from the town to gather about the quay where they cheered and waved. Drums and pipes played, children dashed to and fro climbing on wall and parapet to gain better sight of a vessel larger and more colourfully arrayed with pennants than any they had seen. Even before reaching open water, Jason poured a cup of red wine over the side of their vessel as a customary offering to Poseidon.

Chiron had left the harbour alone and, with a stick to aid him on the steep walk, had reached a vantage point high on Mount Pelion. From there he watched sunlight glint on busy oars as *Argo* reached the open sea. Another, with white gown and cowl pulled about her, watched with sad eyes from a high room in the palace of Iolcos and whispered, 'Athena, watch over and protect him.'

***

Well there we have it, Jason and his worthy crew were on their way and that girl who doted on him thought it was Athena who was going to look after her oh, so loving prince. Well we know it wasn't Athena, don't we – no, she might have been keeping an eye on old Argos and his boat but it was one above even her that was keen on looking after Jason if only to satisfy her own ends. Hera of course, though I dare say after all the sacrifices Argos made to Athena, you really would expect that one to busy herself in helping to keep his precious ship afloat. As for our sweet little Clymene, she had a lot to learn about men – especially the likes of Jason.

***

On lively, sun-glittering waters their vessel proceeded northward for much of the morning under the power of oars and sail. They turned toward the east, rising and falling with the swell, all the time remaining within sight of land. The oarsmen's strokes were accompanied by the playing and singing of Orpheus and though his voice was strong, the notes of his lyre offered meagre contest to the sound of the waves and the rhythmic beat of Argo's drum, which presently determined the oarsmen's stroke. By midday the wind had strengthened, the oars were drawn in, the sail billowed, the rigging smacked and clattered and *Argo* rolled in heavier seas. Jason, seated with his captain close to the stern of the vessel where Tiphys attended the steering oar, asked, 'Does this

61

heightened wind occur often? I've heard talk of it from our fishermen who call it the etesian wind.'

'Aye, Sir as you say, the etesian wind. It blows through much of the year. It tends to rise in the afternoon and abate in the evenin' when we must later 'eave to.'

'I hear it's often possible to navigate at night by the stars,' said Jason.

'That I 'ave done, sir, on a clear night, but there'd be little or no comfort to be 'ad for all our men tryin' to sleep in the confines of the ship. I would not recommend it, no I would not.'

'I'll go along with that,' grinned Jason. 'You're the captain.'

***

On the morning of the third day more land appeared but this time directly ahead, and Argos, having risen from the drum to order his oarsmen to ease back, announced loudly, 'Ahead lies Lemnos, once spoken of as a land of wine and 'oney an' a place where the 'ot springs offer good bathin' - 'owever - !'

They waited in silence for him to continue.

'There's tales of conflict I myself cannot confirm as I've not been ashore there for some years and 'ave met no one of late that 'as. But we need to replenish our food an' fresh water so if Lord Jason agrees, I suggest we enter the main 'arbour to the south of the island and find out what's 'appened there.'

Jason, not as steady as he would have wished on the gently rolling vessel, grasped the side rail and declared, 'Yes, we'll go ashore at Lemnos but those men not needed at the benches are to be armed and ready to face whatever confronts us!'

Argo approached closer to the island and soon they were entering a wide, calm bay sheltered from the wind. The sail was lowered and the oarsmen took their vessel on toward a town overlooking the water.

'I remember this place from years back,' said Argos as he and Jason stood at the bow with hands shading their eyes against a bright sun. 'It was busy then with lots of boats in the 'arbour and plenty more comin' and goin'.'

'I don't see boats going anywhere,' remarked Jason. 'The quay looks deserted though I can make out smoke rising in three, four or more places over the town. There must be people there but for some reason they're keeping out of sight.'

'P'raps they'll show 'emselves or send someone down as we go ashore,' offered the captain. 'They surely must 'ave seen us by now. I don't like it; it's a good thing our men are well prepared for combat, I say.'

In an orchard below the town wall, three girls in plain cotton dresses, each with a basket at her arm, were busy gathering fruit. One peered out beyond the harbour to exclaim, 'Oh, heavens! Look, there's a ship out there in the bay!'

'So there is,' declared a second girl, 'and it will be full of men.' The three lowered their baskets, shaded their eyes and stood watching the sweep of oars as the vessel drew closer.

'Of course it will be full of men,' said the third girl, gazing harder then adding, 'Only men row ships and they'll all be young and strong. We'd better go and report this,' she declared as the three gathered up their baskets.

'No – wait!' exclaimed the first, staring harder still. 'Let me try and count them so we can tell – oh, I think at least some of them are armed because I can – I can see sunlight glinting on bronze!'

'Oooh - big, strong warriors,' breathed the second, 'or maybe they're pirates.'

From the roof of a modest palace another girl peered out to the bay. She turned to leave, pulled her white gown tightly about herself, hesitated for a second glance then hurried to the stairs. In the corridor at the base of the stairs she encountered two women, bare-breasted and crinkle-haired, going about their business in the colourful flounced dresses of a royal court. Both of these she addressed in urgent tones, 'There's a ship in the bay and it's coming to our harbour – we must inform the queen!'

'A ship!' exclaimed one. 'A ship coming here? Are you sure? Are there men in it?'

'Of course it's coming here and of course there are men in it - that's why I'm here right now telling you! It's a large ship and it obviously has to have a crew, so we need to inform the queen!'

The courtiers stared uneasily at one another and one muttered, 'This may not be a suitable time.'

'If there's a ship approaching then it *has* to be a suitable time,' insisted the second courtier. 'We must go to her chamber now!'

With the girl from the rooftop following at a discrete distance, the two pitter-pattered along to where the darkened corridor turned abruptly left. Around the corner they were faced by a bronze-banded oak door and here they stopped, each to look once more in apprehension at the other as one raised her hand to tap lightly. They waited, each holding her breath. There were no sounds from inside and there was no reply. She tapped again, this time harder. Tense moments passed, muffled noises seeped from within then a voice. 'What is it? What d'you want?'

'It's urgent, Madam - very!' responded the second courtier. Still they waited, then the rattle of a bolt and the door opened part way.

A woman in her mid-twenties stood there, her wide green eyes and sharp features framed by long, honey-coloured, somewhat disheveled hair. She wrenched tighter the belt of her patterned robe of fine Egyptian cotton and demanded with barely suppressed anger, 'Just what is it that *cannot* wait until later?'

'My Lady, it's reported there's a ship coming to our harbour.'

'Oh, really, a ship you say. What kind of ship – a fishing boat? Surely that isn't what you've come here to tell me?'

Inside the dimly-lit room they glimpsed an equally disheveled younger girl lolling naked on the queen's bed. The two courtiers turned to let the girl from the rooftop waiting close by give the answer to her question directly but before she could speak other agitated voices approached along the corridor.

'By the gods now what?' breathed the woman as the three girls from the orchard loomed behind those already pressed about her door.

'Your Ladyship,' blurted one of them, waving her hand high 'there's a big vessel coming to our harbour! It's full of men, all armed to the teeth!'

The older woman stepped from her chamber, pulled the door shut and said, 'So you had a closer look at them did you. How many are there? Do they appear to be pirates?'

'Absolutely no - not pirates, Your Ladyship, not such a boat and – and not with a sail like that; I know what pirates look like because as a child I -.'

'Just tell me how many you think there are!' snapped the woman.

'I - I counted twice more of them than all my fingers and toes, and many more still.'

'Maybe they're going to take over our island; that's what it looks like to us,' put in the second girl.

The woman turned to the nearest of her courtiers. 'You - get along to the harbour with a couple of others. If those men land, stay calm, ask them what they want and try to keep them talking until I'm ready.' To the second courtier she said, 'You can tidy and put up my hair and get me out a decent dress. I will go out there to meet them as soon as I'm ready.' At the others she wagged her hands, saying, 'And the rest of you just, go – go – go!' She backed into the room, muttering as she closed the door, 'Men, by the gods – and they tell me there's a whole boatload of them.'

As their captain had his crew shipped oars and prepared to birth at the quayside, one of the crew said to Jason, 'Damned strange this is, sir – there must be people somewhere unless they all 'ave -.'

'Wait!' Jason exclaimed. 'There are three of them – three women coming down the steps from those buildings higher up. Looking at them I'm sure that must be the palace.' Other members of the crew noticed also as Jason added, 'And by their dress I assume they have been sent to meet us by whoever rules here.'

'By Zeus there's a sight for sore eyes!' exclaimed a crewman, leaning aside to obtain a better view of the bare-breasted females.

Argo was being secured to the quay as Jason, assisted by one of his men, donned his bronze cuirass. Other men were arming likewise but the women had advanced no further than the base of the steps. Jason was first to climb onto the quayside from where he called for six of those already armed to join him.

'Should we expect an ambush?' asked one man as they assembled. 'Those three could be a bait an' don't they just look it. There might be archers waitin' up there on them buildin's to catch us all in the open – then what?'

'Pity we 'ad no room on board for decent sized shields,' added another.

Jason, eased on his ornate helmet of gleaming bronze with swaying plume of red horsehair then patting his sheathed sword, replied, 'It's a chance we have to take. Keep a few steps behind me so those women don't feel threatened and I'll speak to them first.'

The men eyed each other and discreetly winked. They strode along warily, turned the corner of the quay and a few steps on Jason halted a respectful distance from the women.

'Why have you come to our island?' called one. 'We have hardly anything of value left since -.'

Jason lifted off his helmet, cradled it under his arm and replied, 'It is not our intention to offer violence or to take anything without payment. I wish only to obtain food and rest for my crew and to replenish supplies for our vessel. We will offer gifts and will pay your Lord in silver for whatever we take. Where might I speak with him and where are your men?'

'Our Lord!' laughed the woman, 'Our men! There are no other men than you on Lemnos unless they're hiding in the hills, and she who rules over this island will soon be here to speak with you. Tell me your name.'

'I am Jason, son of Chiron who rules over the town of Pelion in Thessaly. We call ourselves the Argonauts because *Argo* is the name of our vessel and we are on our way to -.'

His words were cut short by the appearance of three more figures who stepped into sunlight and proceeded gracefully down the stairs. Of the three, one was attired in regal, richly patterned flowing gown that all but concealed her slim form from neck to ankle and about her fair hair was fitted a narrow, glistening band of gold studded with glinting gemstones. Her bare-breasted attendants, one

68

holding a reed parasol above her head, appeared also as women of her court. They joined their companions and the three who had first spoken to Jason now repeated his message as well as her own reply to the regal newcomer. She listened carefully then stepped closer to address Jason. 'I am Queen Hypsipyle,' she announced in a voice of calm confidence. Her attendants stepped respectfully back. 'This is my - *our* island, and as you have been informed, there are no men here. I take it as you are a prince of your realm that you are in charge of that vessel and her crew and are a man of honour.' Her cheeks were lightly rouged, her full lips reddened and sensual. Her green eyed gaze was all the while set upon him.

Jason confirmed his status and that he was indeed their leader as he endeavoured to resolve her name in his mind - 'Hyp-sip-y-le.'

'I understand,' she continued, seeing the remaining men on *Argo* had extracted their arms from beneath the deck, 'that what you and your men require from us is food and somewhere to rest. Both we can provide because our island is fertile and about our town there are many unoccupied homes they may use for their comfort. If you wish to speak with me in private I ask that you first nominate someone to represent your crew and my attendants will show them where they may retire for the evening.'

'I'll do as you ask,' Jason responded, assessing her as a most desirable woman. 'I'll take three of your er – your attendants, to my captain and he will ensure the proper organisation of our men.'

Jason rejoined his crew, most of who were now assembled on the quayside where they gazed in elbow-nudging awe at the women who accompanied their commander back to the ship and those waiting further behind. Words passed between Jason and Argos, including a warning from Jason to, 'Stay alert at all times in case of treachery. There may well be danger here.'

'Danger?' queried Argos. 'What sort of danger? I sense none.'

'I can't figure this place at all,' he replied. 'Hopefully it'll be no more than temptation but have all our men keep to their arms. If there are men of the town hereabouts they might fall upon us during the night. We'll also need to place three or four lookouts close to our vessel.' With a reassuring nod from Argos he retraced his steps to where Hypsipyle and her two attendants waited.

One of the three women close by the vessel whispered to another, 'They look handsome and healthy enough, don't they – particularly the one in charge of them.'

'Yes,' came the reply, 'and I wager her ladyship has him in her bed before long. And it's not before time we've a few to choose from here. A man is what most of us need isn't it. I'd gladly entertain any two of them tonight.'

'Make that any three,' murmured her companion.

Captivated by the sway of her slim figure yet reassured by the keen blade at his side, Jason followed Hypsipyle up the short flight of steps to where they entered and crossed a frescoed hallway.

This opened onto a modest courtyard arrayed all about with perfumed flowers set in large earthenware jars whose surfaces were worked and brightly painted to express swirling sea creatures. It was now, as she paused to smile at him in the flower-fragranced air of the courtyard, that her alluring perfume touched his senses. Jason was pleased to see no evidence of dogs, though here and there he glimpsed a slinking cat. From the courtyard they entered an anteroom then passed through to the megaron of Hypsipyle's palace. The chatter of female courtiers quietened as their attention fell upon Jason. Some of the women stood ready to answer Hypsipyle's call though none appeared to be slaves. All about were the familiar, downward-tapering columns in assorted pastel colours, before him also the circular stone hearth where flames danced, and to the far side a plain but softly cushioned alabaster throne. Much like Chiron's hall at Pelion, there were rich scenes of the natural world displayed about its walls. Unlike his father's megaron, however, there were no weapons of combat hanging there and it was a young woman rather than an elderly male who sat close to the throne strumming her lyre. To Jason her modest experience and ability with the instrument was apparent though still she rendered pleasant notes.

Hypsipyle stepped around to her throne, gestured for her lyre player to cease and for Jason to sit close by on a cushioned alabaster bench where he also placed aside his warrior's helmet. He was aware now of hungry female eyes glancing furtively toward him. Hypsipyle raised her hand to a woman hovering close by, called for wine then turned to Jason, saying, 'You must tell me first about your journey as we drink, Prince of Pelion, and why you require the company of so many armed men if you're not brigands. After that I will satisfy your curiosity about ourselves.'

Her green eyes were again upon him, as if searching into his soul, and he remained silent for a while not caring to match her steady gaze in case it confirmed his other than superficial interest in her. Peace and good order appeared to dominate here thought Jason in those intense moments of silence, yet there was an underlying tension and pressing within his thoughts was their all but unbelievable claim that no men occupied the island.

The girl reappeared and brimming silver goblets were handed to both. Jason, raising goblet to his lips but eyeing it cautiously, drank a small amount, tasted good, honeyed wine then began to relate as briefly as he could the events that had led him thus far, the bizarre episode at the Anauros River, his encounter with the devious King Pelias at Iolcus and the agreement, as he thought best to describe it, that he had concluded. He told her also about the gathering of his crew and the building of *Argo*. Low level chatter, hardly more than murmuring, continued among Hypsipyle's courtiers but their frequent glances assured Jason that he was well established as subject of their thoughts and probably their whispered conversations. As he gave his account, as he drank, Jason appraised Hypsipyle as he would any beautiful woman. A few years older than himself she might have been and though not in the first incandescence of youth she was nevertheless a gloriously ripening fruit.

Sipping her wine, the Queen of Lemnos listened without interruption and when Jason had finished the essence of his account she said, 'Ah, yes, there are many tales of this Golden Fleece but none I thought very convincing. But now, Jason, there is the one question eagerly waiting to take wing from your thoughts: Why are there no men here?'

'Yes, of course, this is – this is most strange. There were – there are, still are tales of conflict on this island but that's all I and some of those with me know.'

'Then I'll explain,' she said in a voice soft and enticing. 'The women here on Lemnos were said to be the most beautiful throughout all the islands of the Aegean but they, men and women alike, never gave thanks, never made adequate sacrifice at Aphrodite's shrine for that honour, and when her priestesses berated them for this lack of veneration they received only scorn. It was to Hephaestus, god of fire, forger and worker of metals that all their blessings and their sacrifices were offered. Aphrodite, in her anger, laid a curse upon the men of the island, young and old alike. She seized upon and turned their minds. She made them see their freeborn young women and their wives as ugly and contemptible. At first we didn't realise what was happening though I above all should have guessed. They began to treat our slave girls as their wives and we, their wives, as no more than chattels undeserving of all respect. Many women were driven from their homes and I had to find refuge for them in our temples and here in the palace. This was barely tolerated by my husband, then our glorious king, who had rejected me utterly. Well, that simply wouldn't do so we in turn decided to treat them as we felt they deserved. Some of our women took it upon themselves to learn the use of – of those plants from which potions are made that were most dangerous when taken. The source of that knowledge remains with us now and was imparted in secret to many of our young women.'

Jason peered at his unfinished goblet of wine and placed it aside as she continued. 'As the men started to fall ill, when a small number began to die through what appeared mysterious causes, they were encouraged to consult Aphrodite's shrine which was attended of course by the very women they despised, yes, and with myself as chief priestess. We convinced them the gods were angered by their behaviour toward us and were not about to render forgiveness unless they quitted Lemnos altogether.'

Hypsipyle leant closer, her gaze ever more beguiling as she went on, 'Feeling vulnerable, as indeed they were, and no longer caring to remain upon this island with us, the men gathered in council outside the town where all agreed it was safer to depart. Despite our protests they took from the palace and from our temples and town everything of worth they could lay their hands on though many smaller valuables we managed to hide. Then they went down to their boats with their elderly parents and their children. Only a few of those older women who were unattached chose to remain. Because those men were all armed we could do nothing to prevent them taking our young ones also. Some of our younger slave girls declined to follow because they were not deceived; in their eyes we were as we really are and always had been. To these girls we gave their freedom. The men took most of the island's boats and departed for other lands but later, some, perhaps thinking over what had happened here, went about telling everyone that we'd set out to murder them all. Others maintained a plague was spreading over Lemnos and that, more than anything has deterred anyone from the other islands coming here.'

'I can see there's no plague,' Jason responded. 'But murder – isn't that what you *were* doing?'

'A few died, yes,' she admitted calmly, 'but that meant the rest of them would take the hint. Our lives had become quite unbearable, we were abandoned, dismissed from their thoughts, and for all those men cared we might have starved to death. Can you then blame us for what we did? And Jason, dear,' she added, leaning back a little, 'let me assure you, that wine I gave you is *not* poisoned.'

'Er – oh, well,' he breathed, picking up his goblet, 'that's most reassuring, and I'm pleased also Aphrodite hasn't blighted our vision. At least not yet she hasn't.'

'No, Jason, due sacrifice has been offered at her altar ever since the men left and she now favours us.' Relaxing on her throne to appraise Jason more fully she added with a smile, 'Perhaps on this day the goddess has favoured us even more.'

'And maybe us as well,' breathed Jason as Hypsipyle leaned across to place burning fingers on his cheek. He was surprised at this act of familiarity yet at once aroused by her touch. The subdued chatter of her courtiers ceased altogether and their attention froze upon Hypsipyle and her male companion. But Jason, feeling this was not the time nor place to succumb to her enchantment, finished his wine, stood up and said, 'Lady Hypsipyle, I regret I must leave you now and be seen among my men. It will be expected of me as their leader.'

'Yes, of course you must,' she said, rising from her throne. 'Meanwhile your men will be provided with food and they will find it easy enough to light fires and prepare meals in those dwellings open to them. There are many hot springs on the island and water from the closest of these is brought by clay pipes into the town and parts of this palace. I will arrange for food and wine to be served here after sunset just for ourselves - should you wish to return, that is.'

'I will certainly return,' Jason assured her as he collected up his helmet. 'And I'll have those gifts for you that we'd otherwise present to a king.'

'We cannot accept material gifts,' said Hypsipyle with a returning smile. 'We have not enough of value left to offer as I have already explained. Perhaps our gifts will for a time be service to one another.'

Jason gave an understanding nod, stepped back, turned and left the hall. Hypsipyle was approached now by an elderly, stick-tapping woman, in long black gown, who had emerged from shadows amidst the columns. This was Polyxo, her one-time nurse who was mother to no one and so had not been abducted from the island. 'Forgive me for overhearing what has just passed,' she said. 'Those men from the ship; you are letting them stay and you have offered them food and shelter.'

'That is so,' agreed Hypsipyle, 'but then I doubt there was much choice to be had. If I'd turned them away, their response might have been less than agreeable.'

'Are we to offer them all food?' she asked, 'I mean good and wholesome food or -.'

'Dear Polyxo, these men are not brigands. Having spoken to their leader, a prince in his own realm, I doubt they wish us any harm and as custom demands, we must consider their need for food and shelter for it's all – well almost all we have to give. You surely don't think we should deal with them in the manner you seem to suggest – do you?'

'Of course not, My Lady - no, of course I don't, but might you nevertheless have accepted the gifts that man offered as would have our one time King of Lemnos - should that not be so?'

'Oh, I'm sure they will have much to offer us,' smiled Hypsipyle.

With a toothless but knowing smile the old woman turned to leave, hobbling across the megaron as others stepped politely out of her way. Hypsipyle watched her go and murmured to herself, 'And I trust those gifts will bring satisfaction to us all.'

Much of the day Jason spent with his crew, ensuring that all was as promised. Never had he witnessed men so elated in their expectations. Only when the sun was low in the sky did he return to the palace, passing on his way several groups of bright-eyed women proceeding in the opposite direction.

***

You must have seen what was coming. Here we had Jason with all his big ideas about winning fame for the greatest exploit he ever imagined and with it the throne of Iolcus. Now he's persuaded into keeping the sex starved Queen of Lemnos satisfied, and not *just* her. As for his men – never had they been so happy at the prospect, never so much in demand and never so spoiled for choice. With guard duties lapsed, most of them felt they'd been transported to a paradise of wild and unbridled lust. Or at least they did for a time. Argos was one of the few who wondered if things ought to have been going the way they were but even he entertained two women most nights in his appointed residence. Daytime, however, would find him down by the quay and checking over every part of his precious vessel to make sure all was as it should be. Argos had years before lost a wife who could never compete with his wanderings and this boat was for all time his only love.

Well, Hera and Athena didn't envisage all those men ending up on Lemnos and neither did Jason, though as you saw, he wasn't sure at first what to do about it. When I think over what happened to resolve the situation I'm convinced it was the work of Hera herself. She must have reached into the mind of the one man among his crew she loathed, yet the one who impressed almost everybody with his grand exploits and his overbearing manner. Clever, really, because it avoided their leader, Jason, being seen as a selfish killjoy intent on spoiling their fun to serve his own ends.

***

Sunlight flickered about the edges of the leather blind as it shivered in a light morning breeze. Hypsipyle was still asleep, honey-hair spread about the soft cushions when Jason sat upright to peer about her gloriously frescoed and richly appointed room. It had been lit only by small oil lamps on those previous evenings when, after they and others had been entertained with music, wine and food, he and the Queen of Lemnos had taken to the pleasures of her bed.

'Fifteen days,' muttered Jason, peering down at her as she stirred and opened her eyes.

'Oh, I was still half asleep,' she sighed. 'What did you say?'

'Fifteen days,' he repeated. 'Fifteen days and my men have altogether forgotten our main purpose in setting sail and given themselves to the pleasures of your island home.'

'As you also have, Jason, dear,' she smiled. 'The younger women here, and there are many more of them, need it as much as do your men. And now I hear some of them claim the gods have sent you for that very reason and Aphrodite is altogether with us.'

He arose from the bed and turned to her, saying, 'But I must complete what I set out to do – to find the Golden Fleece. My own future depends upon it and yet – and yet if I attempt to rally my

79

men and insist they return to our ship I'll probably have a mutiny on my hands.'

'Well, Jason,' she said, reaching out a hand to touch his thigh, 'there's nothing I can do about that is there so I suggest we -.'

Voices were heard from beyond the room, followed by a persistent tapping on the door.

'Who dares to disturb us?' called Hypsipyle, throwing aside the woollen blanket and slipping naked from the bed. More tapping; this time urgent and loud. Jason drew on his linen tunic and sword belt, Hypsipyle grabbed her patterned gown, pulling this on as she stepped across to unbolt and open the door. Jason was close behind with sword part drawn as she asked angrily, 'What is the reason for this?'

'Madam,' came the reply of a portly woman in blemished grey smock, 'there's a man out 'ere seekin' Lord Jason; a big man dressed like a lion and armed with a club! Almost scared the life outa me 'e did! He came bargin' into the kitchens while we was seein' to the food an' -.'

'Wait!' Jason exclaimed, 'I'll deal with this!' He pushed by both women into the passage to find standing there the one he expected and asked, 'Heracles, my friend, what's this all about?'

Heracles, resting on his club, the lion's head swinging grotesquely at his back, replied in a resonant voice, 'Sorry to break in on you, sir, I'm sure, but we 'ave problems brewin' that need your attention.'

'What problems?' queried Jason.

'Some of our men say the demands made on 'em by these women are too great, if you see what I mean, and -.'

'Oh, really,' grinned Jason. 'Not too many of them I imagine - and what else?'

'No, sir, maybe not *too* many but our captain worries also about the neglect of 'is boat, as should we all since it seems there are no other vessels on the island – at least none that's seaworthy. Then there's no guards to keep an eye on things.'

'Let's discuss this outside before I go and bathe,' said Jason, glancing back at an apprehensive Hypsipyle who clutched at her gown. They made their way down a flight of steps then into the still shadowed courtyard where a fountain danced high. There they stood face to face and Jason said, 'I hear what you say; much as we find it so compelling to remain on this island we have soon to leave and what you have told me may offer an answer. Those of our men still obsessed by what's on offer here must be persuaded by you, Argo and myself to sail on but we must not stir their anger to the point where they confront us with refusal. I hope all of them will see good sense and depart Lemnos with us.'

'Well, sir, they'll be takin' their mornin' food now,' he declared, thumping his club on hard flagstones then causing Jason to step back abruptly as he swung it over his shoulder, 'so I'll go an' put it to 'em in a more direct manner than maybe you'd care to do, with yourself an' our captain followin' up to talk more sense. I've faced far greater tasks, that I 'ave!'

Jason thought for some moments than said, 'Yes, as you say, we have to act but we'll allow them one more night to prepare themselves for what to many will be an agonizing decision.'

'Agonisin', your Lordship – when we're at sea I'll show 'em a bit of agonisin' - I'll show 'em what 'ard work at the oar really is so we win back a bit'f lost time!'

Heracles was as good as his word. When the cooking fires burned and smoke swirled all about the clustered houses and alleyways where the Argonauts resided, he strolled among them with his lion's head in place. A pair of crewmen walked ahead with rams' horns blaring, hesitating from time to time for Heracles to thunder out his message. 'Gather before the palace at midday, lads!' he roared. 'Before the palace at midday if y'please an' even if y'don't please!'

They heard his message to a man but listening to his voice, seeing the expression on his face as he glowered through the open, white-toothed jaws of the lion's head, and the manner in which he held high his club, none considered it advisable to interrupt him in order to ask why.

When the sun was at its highest they began to gather in uneasy silence about the open space between palace and quay to find Heracles standing beside Jason and Argos on the steps where they would easily be seen and heard. A short way behind Heracles awaited his squire, Hylas.

'On the orders of Lord Jason, our leader' declared Heracles in a voice that rang across to the quayside, 'we leave to continue our voyage at first light tomorrow! That's the orders I and all of you 'ave to follow as 'ell now confirm!'

Ripples of muttering and disquiet spread among the men as Jason announced, 'I understand your reluctance but we must leave this island for all your sakes and not just mine. We have a great journey ahead so ask yourselves how long most of you can afford to be away from your homes and what troubles could next arise there in your absence. You all gave your word to my father! Dishonour will fall forever upon any who break that promise and the gods above know it!'

'We catch fish an' 'unt for food durin' the day!' called one man. 'Some of us could live out the rest of our days 'ere!'

'No, my friend!' Jason responded as the men shuffled about, looking from one to the other, 'the novelty would eventually wear off and when it did you'd find there was no way of leaving without the skills you would need to repair or build a vessel!'

'That is so,' declared Argos, 'ours is the only seaworthy vessel on Lemnos an' she demands a worthy crew!'

'Continue with me as you have sworn you would,' said Jason, 'and if you so wish, on our journey back with our task completed, you may return to the pleasures of this island!'

There was further muttering and shuffling among his crew but when this subsided there was no voice of dissent.

'I'll muster our men before sunrise tomorrow, sir!' confirmed Heracles, ensuring as he spoke that his remark was heard by all. The women of the palace watched and listened from above and Heracles, looking up at them, shouldered his club and growled, 'Huh, women –all right in their place they are but this is a man's world an' it suits me that way.'

***

In the twilight of dawn the women of Lemnos town, some young, some not so young, lined the quay to watch the Argonauts depart with sail filled and pennants flying. Most were silent though a few wept while others clung to a friend or to a sister for consolation. One stood aside from the rest, part way up the steps to her palace; Hypsipyle, in plain white gown, her hair fallen loose about her shoulders as she raised a hand in sad farewell. Jason acknowledged her with a wave of his arm but was unable to see her tears. She had given him a finely decorated cloak, left carelessly behind by a noble of Lemnos when he and the rest of the men had fled. This Jason now wore.

The majority of men, straining at their oars, could only call back their raucous goodbyes while those not at the benches waved from mast and rigging. Tiphys, seated once more at his steering oar, twisted about to wave an arm at the woman he so cherished and who he had promised to find again on the Argonaut's return.

As their vessel proceeded into the open bay her captain, joined by Jason who stood by his side in the bow, said, 'there were only four of 'em I couldn't account for. They must 'ave 'idden away or been 'eld there by the women. Aye, some of those women – well -.'

'That still leaves us with over sixty fit and able men,' remarked Jason. 'Quite enough for the task ahead I'd say.'

'Quite enough, young sir,' agreed Argos. 'But those missin' four will sooner or later see the error of their ways. What's more, though, I expect our time there will result in an increase to the island's population before too long and give those women somethin' more to get on with.'

'Oh, I'm sure it will,' muttered Jason. Then he added, 'And once we're clear of the island I'll make our offer of wine to Poseidon.'

Chapter 4 - Their Perils begin

This day began with calmer seas than on their journey from Pelion and once beyond Lemnos' southern bay and passing around the island, other vessels appeared with greater frequency. Sometimes propelled by oars but usually under sail in a steady breeze, the Argonauts proceeded eastward. When rowing to the beat of Argos' drum the men sang loudly to sea and sky with the voice of Heracles loudest of all.

When the winds favoured their progress and the oars were drawn in they talked, laughed and cast out fishing lines. A few had gaming boards to occupy their time and wagers were made but all were entertained by the voice and the lyre of Orpheus. They boasted among themselves over their encounters with the women of Lemnos, each man maintaining his so-called conquest had been greater than that of others. A small number mentioned in passing how they had enjoyed those other fruits of Lemnos, those they had found growing in the orchards.

One of the crew, Telamon, had with him a pebble shaped piece of rock crystal he called his 'Firestone,' and, watched intently by those close by, he held this steadily to concentrate the sun's rays and ignite tinder of the small braziers over which they cooked their catches. When ashore he was also to prove a man of considerable skill with the bronze razor for those, including Jason, who had no desire to grow a beard.

It was midafternoon when the channel ahead appeared to be narrowing and Argos stood to address his crew, 'Over there if you've not sailed this way before,' he announced, gesturing to his right, 'is the mighty city of Troy. An' as it's the 'Eellespont we're soon to enter, we'll get by the city quick as we can in case they think we're traders with goods to exchange for grain an' try to charge us for the privilege.'

'I've heard many people speak of Troy,' said Jason. 'Those who sail to cities beyond the Hellespont are said to resent her control of passing trade and the taxes she imposes. My father tells me there's been talk of war over past years with the great cities of the mainland combining against her but it seems nothing has happened so far.'

His captain turned to Jason, saying, 'Yes, I've 'eard that also. Maybe sooner or later somethin' will 'appen to light the spark of conflict. For now we'll row an' use what wind there is to get clear. Hah, what wind there is, I said, but now it seems there's 'ardly any at all and soon may be even less. The lads will 'ave to pull 'ard as they can.'

As if hearing his words, Heracles, kilt clad and minus his lion skin, part rose and called out from his bench located at the higher row of oarsmen, 'Let's see you match my stroke, you idle buggers! Come on - match it now!'

'Aye they'll 'ave to,' grinned the captain, sitting to take charge of the drum. 'They won't want to break it if 'e's determined the speed will they. I'll 'ave to match 'is beat, that I will, and not 'e mine I reckon.'

The oarsmen were pulling vigorously, all straining hard to match their beat with Heracles who appeared to find the task not at all difficult as they entered the channel with Troy passing slowly to their stern. No Trojan vessel could be seen approaching but Heracles was not about to ease up and instead cried out, 'C'mon! Keep it up! Let's show 'em over there what we can do!'

'We'll have to slow soon,' said Jason as the channel narrowed further. 'I can see most of our men are not up to this. Better get our Heracles to quell his enthusiasm.'

'That I will, young sir,' Argos replied, setting aside his drumsticks. 'I'll do it now before some of our lads gives in to fatigue.' But as he stood to call out to Heracles a loud crack, the sound of splitting wood, caused the men at the benches to ease back and raise their oars as the blade end of a shattered oar bobbed by. With a resounding curse, Heracles rose from his seat, swung up the remaining length of his oar for all to witness then hurled it spinning into the sea. 'Look at that!' he called out to Jason and Argos, 'There's no damned strength in the thing!'

'Congratulations!' responded the captain, 'Now you've busted it we're an oar short an' we don't carry no spares!'

'So what d'you have to say?' demanded Jason, stepping down to the strip of deck. 'You've had a great deal to say about many things, my friend, so how about this?'

The crewmen turned their heads, the boat swayed gently as Heracles glared at him, hands planted defiantly on his hips. 'Very well, your 'ighness,' he declared, 'when we put ashore I'll take an axe an' I'll seek out good timber wherever there's any to be 'ad an' I'll carve out a new oar. Aye, an' a better an' a stronger one than that you gave me!'

Jason was joined by Argos, who addressed the crew. 'All right, lads, keep us on course 'till we're clear of other vessels. After sunset we'll put ashore an' see what the mornin' 'as to bring.'

'I take it you're familiar with this whole area,' said Jason as the men resumed rowing at an easier pace and Heracles sat staring into space with arms folded as though the whole affair of the broken oar had nothing whatsoever to do with him.

'That I am with much of it, young sir,' his captain replied. 'The channel narrows further an' twists around a bit before openin' out again as we enter the Propontis an' that leads us to the Euxine Sea where lies Colchis. The mainland to our right is Mysia an' between 'ere an' the town of Abydos is woodland so our boastful friend over there can maybe find 'imself a useful length of timber on the other side. There are freshwater springs as well should we care to take on more water.'

Daylight was beginning to fade when they manoeuvred the good ship *Argo* into a sheltered cove and there, with the vessel secured, her crew disembarked, taking with them their arms. Some of the men set about gathering brushwood for cooking; their fires ignited from one of the small braziers that had been maintained on board the vessel. Orpheus played his lyre, the men chatted, ate, drank and laughed while reminiscing further over their stay on Lemnos with increasingly colourful accounts. Prominent in voice among them was the once more lion skin attired Heracles who stood with club raised to emphasize the tales of his many alleged encounters though only those closer to him felt obliged to show interest.

But when the fires had died and stars dusted the sky above, the men were unable to find sufficient space about the cove for all to sleep in comfort. Some returned to the vessel, preferring to find rest at their benches or on the deck. Jason and his captain were sat deep in conversation on an embankment when Heracles approached with the ever present club resting on his shoulder.

'I'll be off at first light,' he informed them gruffly. 'I'll carve an oar same size as the others though it'll not be quite so fancy – still, I'll be the one usin' it.'

'Very good,' commented Argos.

'And I look forward to seeing what a splendid job you make of it,' grinned Jason.

Heracles stepped away grumbling incoherently. Jason and Argo would sleep close to where they were on soft grass.

The night passed without incident. In the cool of morning, to the cry of sea birds but with the sun yet to rise, Jason, Argos and their crew were awake, a few strolling about with others already returned to the boat. 'We didn't keep any fire for the morning,' remarked one. 'We've nothing to light the brushwood with.'

We'll 'ave to wait until we're aboard with the sun well up,' responded a companion, 'then Telamon can use 'is magic pebble to light another.'

'Hylas!' boomed out the voice of Heracles. 'Hylas, you buggr, where are you 'idin'?' Heracles peered around the men by the water then over at the boat. 'Hylas!' he called again. This time there was a reply from the boat itself so Heracles shouted once more, 'Hylas, bring over an empty water jug an' get one of the others to fetch me an axe!'

The linen-kilted youth, with copper, two-handled jug swinging from one hand, eased himself awkwardly over the side of the vessel and called back, 'All right, I'm coming!' and, waist-deep in the water, headed for dry land.

With club presently at rest, Heracles waited until Hylas had waded ashore then called, 'Is one of 'em bringin' me that axe?'

'I don't know if anyone heard me,' came the reply. 'They're all very busy so maybe they didn't.'

'Well leave the damned jug 'ere and go back for the axe. I should' 'ave been 'ard at it by now!'

With a look of resigned exasperation Hylas returned to the ship and after some delay returned, bronze axe in hand, to his impatient master. 'Will that be all?' he muttered, handing over the axe.

'No it won't! Bring that jug an' follow me. While I'm lookin' for a decent length of wood you can get us some fresh spring water to refill our flasks, if y'don't mind.'

***

I witnessed this choice little episode later through those on high - via Hecate in fact. Not as it happened, of course, since I had no knowledge of what was to occur at the time. No, it lived on through the memories of others and of the gods themselves who found it rather entertaining, as did I.

Young Hylas wandered off into the woods with his jug, disgruntled over the brusque and unsympathetic treatment handed down by his renowned master. He paused a while to gaze about, heard only birds chirping and felt pleasantly at ease. He trudged deeper into the forest until he observed, some way ahead and sheltered amidst a grove of trees, a likely looking pool. He approached this but on hearing other sounds he stopped to listen. There were pipes playing soft, sensuous music, though from where the sound came he was unable at first to determine. There were voices. Female voices. Sweet voices singing. They were nearby so he crept around the pool to take a closer look while endeavoring not to be seen. Yes, illuminated by shafts of sunlight falling through the trees, there were seven young women, all of them minus their clothes and bathing in another, larger pool a short way beyond the one our Hylas had first come upon. Clutching his precious jug, he moved closer then hesitated, part hidden by a bush, not knowing quite what to do yet stirred deep within by the sight of them. The girls were laughing but as he watched, one of them turned to look directly his way and called, "Hello – won't you come and join us."

Hylas stood bemused, then they all looked at him, with two others rising higher in the water and gesturing for him to approach. Fascinating, I thought, and so did our young Hylas because he moved out from behind the tree and stepped cautiously over to the pool where they waited smiling, some pushing corn blond hair from their eyes, all now standing upright in sun-glinting water to offer him full sight of their alluring nakedness. The pipes still played as he stared mesmerised, as he felt himself stirred deeply within and elsewhere. Here were seven young women, all of them slim and beautiful – naturally, and all bright-eyed with pouting full lips.

"W-who are you?" he asked, ogling each in turn and lowering the copper jug to hang by his side. 'I mean, why are you, er -?"

They eyed him up and down, laughed like gently tinkling bells as one replied, "We're nymphs, dear one, and we bathe here often."

"Yes, bathing - it's what nymphs often do," chimed another. "It's ever so good for you."

"Ever, ever, *ever* so good for you," added one of her equally seductive companions

"Would you care to join us for a while?" asked the first.

"We do hope you will," cooed another as they continued to eye him invitingly. "In fact you really must."

Well it was after all a sacred grove even if that hadn't occurred to Hylas who, being in the flush of youth, now had other things on his mind. Yes there were seven of these brazen tarts, if you'll excuse my words, and it seemed they'd all taken a fancy to him. This was a better prospect even than Lemnos had been because here and now his master was nowhere in sight. Hylas experienced a momentous change of mind over his association with, and obligations to, the bullying Heracles, and the grand expedition of the Argonauts for a Golden Fleece, which meant absolutely nothing to him anyway. Yes, he decided they were of no importance at all, even before three of our lovely ladies glad-eying him, had climbed from the pool to step close and run fingers about his shoulders and chest. They insisted Hylas *must* join them so with wide-eyed enthusiasm he laid his jug aside, tested the water with his toe then slid into the pool with a lecherous grin brightening his face.

When Hylas didn't return - well he wasn't going to, was he, Heracles put aside his axe and the almost completed oar that had kept him so busy hacking away that morning, and set off to find his so-called squire. Bawling his name, cursing aloud, waving that stupid club uselessly in the air, he searched here and there until he came upon the larger pool and spotted the empty jug. He stood gazing about for a long time, for once deeply worried because, in spite of everything, he was very fond of Hylas. *Very* fond, if you see what I mean. After a while he concluded Hylas must have run off somewhere for good, fed up of his role in life or fallen into the pool and drowned, though without a body floating there in calm water, that seemed most unlikely. Heracles collected up the abandoned jug, wandered back with ever searching glances, hurriedly finished the oar, called out several times again while looking hard about, then set off reluctantly to join the others at the ship thinking that's where Hylas must have gone. If so, he intended to make the young man account for the gross neglect of his duties.

To his dismay he arrived to find the cove deserted and peering seaward, spotted *Argo,* well out into the channel, her sail filled, her oars glinting early sunlight with each stroke. Yes, they'd gone and left our mighty Heracles behind because, great hero and self-proclaimed son of Zeus or no, most were fed up of hearing him bluster on and on and on through his lion's head jaws about his exploits and his labours and waving his club around to make sure everyone was listening. Son of Zeus my arse!

"Damn the lot of you!" he yelled at the receding vessel, then he flung the roughly finished oar to the ground and smashed it into pieces with his club. After that I lost interest in Heracles though I heard later he'd muscled his way onto another vessel then made his way back to Mycenae and to King Eurystheus where his next so-called labour was to be determined.

Ah, yes, you must be wondering about the true fate of not so poor Hylas. Well he may not have been visible to Heracles but he certainly was to those girls, all of him. But of course it couldn't last; being eternally young, as nymphs are, they'd have worn him out long before his time. One of the girls, Dryope, gave up being a nymph and took him all for herself. I'll say no more about that.

***

'It's what the men voted for,' said Argos as they stood together at the bow of the vessel, 'or at least most of 'em did, though I thought we were goin' to 'ave a deal of trouble from those who wanted 'im to stay with us. Still, it was a pity.'

'A pity, yes,' agreed Jason, 'but then the great Heracles was becoming a liability when he should have been an asset. It seems he had more on his mind than we realized.'

'You mean those tasks imposed on 'im by Eurystheus?'

'Yes,' replied Jason, 'maybe that's why he was so cantankerous. Now, when and where d'you suggest we next go ashore?'

'Tomorrow afternoon, young sir, will see us close to the domains of Amycus who rules over the land of Bebrycia. It's a pretty lawless place as I recall an' most of 'em were said to be pirates, includin' the so-called king 'imself, aye, a man of reputed violence to 'is own people. It's a persistent rumour among sailin' men. Still, there ought to be food on offer there as long as we stay on our guard. But for now we've no shortage of provisions so for tonight I suggest we anchor close in an' I dare say most of our crew will want to go ashore as usual.'

'Very well my friend, then tomorrow I look forward to meeting this unruly Amycus.'

Early light saw *Argo* again plying open water. The weather that day was fair, the current with them and the wind from the north was light. They were rowing at an easy pace with the sun in early descent when, passing a number of fishing boats, they approached their next destination, the town of Bebryces from where Amycus ruled. The land there arose steeply so that the buildings were terraced back away from the unpretentious and roughly fortified palace. As *Argo* sailed closer, people began to gather on the quayside though some appeared to be armed men with bronze-glinting spears.

'Their harbour looks quite small,' observed Jason from *Argo's* bow.

'It's much as I remember it from years ago,' said his captain, 'but there'll be enough room for us to tie up. What sort of welcome we'll get, if any, I'd not care to guess at - rules of 'ospitality or no.'

'I see no reason why there should be trouble as long as we pay for anything they let us have.'

'We can but 'ope,' muttered his captain. 'Aye, we can but 'ope.'

With the sail down, most oars drawn aboard and with Tiphys the tiller man standing to better judge their distance, *Argo* was gradually manoeuvred into position close to some small fishing boats, the only other vessels in the harbour.

'They'll not 'ave set eyes on a boat like this before,' commented Argos, seeing how the crowds had grown and how many stared in awe. 'Do we offer gifts for the man? I imagine that's what 'e'll expect.'

'We have stowed away items of value as you know but I'd rather pay him in silver; I don't intend to treat any brigand as a king.' Their vessel was secured to the quay and the onlookers, mainly elderly and children were being dispersed by those increasingly numerous men carrying arms. Jason said, 'He must by now have been informed of our presence but may have chosen not to come out and meet us here. As this man we're to confront may not be so welcoming, I'll send Echion as our herald. My father recommended him for such work should it prove necessary and surely Amycus will not disrespect established convention. But I suggest most of our men remain on board until he returns with their arms close by and ready to use.'

'I think so, young sir, yes, I do. It looks as if they're already prepared for confrontation.'

Jason had called for Echion and the man now joined him dressed in the white and gold tunic of a herald and holding his oak staff with gilded tip. He was the first man to step ashore and found two of the guards ready to escort him to the palace. The remaining armed men continued to look on and Jason waited as his crew, overseen by Argos, chattered among themselves. Argos next rejoined Jason and both men stepped onto the quayside to wait a short distance from the guards, who stared idly at them but said nothing. Jason noted how the guards, though armed with sword and spear, were dressed in leather or linen kilt and padded leather corselet as well as light helmets of varying design, so were suited better for mobility than for the field of hard combat.

It was some time before Echion reappeared, now in the company of a man whose richly appointed robe would have been appropriate for the court even though its grizzled wearer appeared otherwise. A member of the court would have been even-mannered and respectful but his surly approach was all too obvious as he addressed Jason and his captain. 'Lord Amycus says 'e wants to know who you are, what y'doin' in 'is 'arbour and where's this fancy ship of yours off to.'

They appraised the man's stubbled face and unkempt brown hair, his ill-fitting, less than pristine gown Jason considered must once have been the property of someone else, then replied, 'Tell your lord I am Jason of Pelion in Thessaly and this man is captain of my vessel. We are sailing to Colchis and are prepared to offer you silver for modest provisions. If this is not convenient then we'll continue on our way.'

'Silver!' laughed the man. 'Our ruler 'as more silver than 'e knows what to do with! But 'e's looked out of 'is window an' says the one in charge 'ere is to come up an' see 'im an' there'll be a goblet of good wine waitin' - right?'

Ignoring the dubious expression on Argos' face Jason replied, 'Then kindly go ahead and I'll follow you.'

As they walked away Argos turned to Echion and said, 'I don't like this, no I don't; the young master shouldn't 'ave gone off alone with that bugger – no 'e shouldn't.'

'From what I saw there may be no immediate danger,' responded Echion, 'but I doubt it'll be in our interest to stay for long. It would appear they have few visitors and I saw no sign of any market other than a few country traders.'

Jason followed the man up a short flight of steps to an unguarded entrance topped by a massive, roughly finished stone lintel, its heavy oak doors reinforced by bronze bands. More windowless steps where firebrands burned led to the King of Bebrycia's megaron though the term, suggestive of a large hall, was hardly appropriate. Beneath the soot-blackened ceiling an odour of cooking permeated the air and smoke from a number of burning braziers, supported by bronze tripods, drifted up to unobstructed windows. The plain stone walls bore no frescoes but were adorned with a random assortment of arms and armour, some, evidently intended to impress by their fine workmanship and ornamentation. About the hall stood a number of rough wooden benches on which were displayed goods of considerable value; gold and silver goblets and larger vessels, some with inlays and some glinting with precious stones. About these were strewn valuable items of personal adornment, bracelets, pectorals and other personal decorations, many strung or set with gemstones. Jason murmured to himself, 'I wonder who the rightful owners were.'

Amycus was seated upon a tall, elaborately carved and gilded wooden throne. A large and powerfully built man of some forty years with gold-banded shoulder-length dark hair, his short beard was laced liberally with gold and silver wire. His richly embroidered robe, seemingly out of place with the less than refined surroundings, covered a plain, heavy linen tunic, at the side of which could be seen a tooled leather sheath from which protruded a dagger with sapphire-topped hilt.

'This man,' announced Jason's escort, 'says 'e's from Pelion in Thessaly, 'e's called Jason and says 'e's on 'is way to Colchis.'

Amycus stared at Jason, whose attention had been caught by contents of the hall and the shadowy people lounging thereabout. There were a number of sullen looking male slaves waiting to one side of the hall but close to Amycus were arrayed five female attendants, all of less than half the man's age, all bedecked at ear, neck, arm and finger with precious adornment. Their long dresses consisted of white Egyptian cotton so fine that they revealed almost as much as much as they concealed.

'Aye, the 'erald said that much,' rumbled Amycus, staring at Jason, 'on yer way to Colchis an' all.' His gap-toothed smile was almost a sneer as Jason, arms folded, responded with a broader smile, 'Yes, that's about it if you don't mind our brief visit.'

'D'you want wine?' asked Amycus, about to raise his hand.

'I'll miss the wine for now,' Jason replied, 'it's the wrong time of day.'

'Oh, wrong time of day, is it,' slurred Amycus. 'Do pardon me, your 'ighness.'

The girls, their wide-eyed attention on Jason, giggled, then at a dark glance from Amycus, fell suddenly quiet as he continued, 'An' you want victuals from us – that it? An' yer 'willin' t'pay.'

'Fruit from your orchards is all we ask for, nothing more,' replied Jason, thinking it not a good move to place himself and his crew under more than minimal obligation to this boorish man.

'Aye,' growled Amycus, rising from his seat to impress with his stature, 'you'll 'ave fruit an' pay for it up front but not with silver. I've enough of that as it is. I'm fond of good sport an' good wi'these, you see.' He lifted his hands, splayed his fingers, fingers too thick or misshapen to hold any but the largest ring, clenched his fists and shook them before Jason, saying, 'See these do yuh?'

'Just about,' muttered Jason, a hand drifting discreetly down to his sword hilt.

'I use 'em whenever I can,' informed Amycus. 'Aye, whenever! I enjoy nothin' more than a good set to so get yer best man, if you 'ave one, to come an' meet me down by the 'arbour an' see 'ow long 'e can last. After it's done you'll maybe 'ave yer fruit an' maybe I'll let yer ship leave.'

'As you wish,' agreed Jason. Amycus' last phrase puzzled him as he saw no reason why he and his crew could not depart as soon as they wanted, even if it came to a clash of arms. No reason whatsoever, until that is, he returned to the harbour.

'They've moored one of their boats across the entrance an' tied 'er up so we can't get out,' said Argos as he and Jason clambered onto the deck of their own vessel. Both noted how visibly restless their men appeared to be, with all eager to respond to the situation and all waiting for a decision.

Jason eyed the vessel in question, one built for speed rather than capacity, a pirate's boat, and considered how she and her crew might best be dealt with. 'Yes, I see there are twenty or more armed men on board but that's as many as she'll hold. Right now this rogue wants one of our men to meet him for a fist fight before he'll move that boat out of our way. The man's built like an ox though I'd say he's seen better days and probably lumbers like one. We have two choices – we go along with him or we take up arms, board that vessel of his and do what needs to be done.'

'If we leave matters too long, young sir,' informed Argos, 'we'll maybe find ourselves in open water after dark an' before knowin' where to gain land. That I'll make the best of but we do 'ave on board one I say is fit to take on the man you describe.'

'Ah, yes, I know him, of course I do, and we met once at my father's court – it is Polydeuces.'

'That's the man, sir, that it is, an' though 'e's no boaster an' never looks for trouble, when put to the test 'e'd stand up to the likes of 'Erecles an' that's sayin' a lot.'

'It certainly is, but I suspect whatever happens we'll still find ourselves adrift after dark so as you say, we'll have to make the best of it. If he's willing, take Polydeuces forward while I talk to the rest of our crew.'

Watched by Amycus' men from the boat positioned close by across the harbour entrance, Jason strolled casually along the deck, assuring his crew that matters were in hand and what he expected they might have to do. He returned to the bow of the ship where waited Argos and Polydeuces, the latter a fair-haired, lightly stubbled, athletic but well-muscled man of impressive aspect.

The soft-spoken Polydeuces listened intently as Jason explained the situation, adding, 'This Amycus is a boastful brute of a man but I'd say age and agility are on your side. But watch for those rings on his left hand.'

Polydeuces nodded and said with a calm smile, 'I'll take the fellow on, sir, and I'll make as good a job of it as I'm able.'

103

'Very well,' said Jason, 'I'll have our herald inform him then all we can do is wait.'

They watched Echion, staff in hand, set off once more from the quay and vanish into the palace. Jason and his captain strolled up and down the deck, chatting to their men while Polydeuces remained in the bow tensing and flexing his muscles, ignoring the jeers and insults that drifted across from Amycus' men in the blocking vessel. Close to the stern Jason stooped to address the crewman who possessed the lens-shaped crystal stone. 'Telamon, do we have enough kindle and wood for you to get five or six of our braziers burning?'

'We do, sir, just about,' the man replied, 'but we've no fresh fish aboard yet, just dried pork, lamb maybe and some vegetables.'

'That doesn't matter, my friend. What does matter is that we have good fires burning when the spectacle we're about to witness gets started. Make it look as though we really are preparing to cook our food.'

'Aye, sir, I'll see it's done right away because the sun is weakening.'

When Echion returned, people were once again gathered about the quay where the guards, each with spear in hand, maintained a clear space between it and the palace. Observing this, Jason said to Argos, 'It looks, my friend, as if the word's got out; I don't expect Amycus will keep us waiting too much longer.'

Smoke was rising lazily from *Argo*'s braziers when two guards emerged from the palace entrance, followed by a pair of white-robed priests carrying rams' horns. The onlookers ceased their chatter. The guards took up position either side of the door with the priests standing together at one side. The priests stepped forward and raised their horns. A raucous blaring shivered the air, causing a flock of birds to rise in panic from the palace roof. The noise ceased and from the main door emerged Amycus in wide-belted, finely tooled leather kilt and sandals. He sauntered down the steps and moved out into the open, grinning, clasping and shaking his hands back and forth above his head while glancing from side to side at the onlookers. He came to a halt, lowered his arms and peered across at the trapped vessel. Still there was silence.

Polydeuces stepped casually onto the quay, rubbed his hands slowly together and gazed up at the sky as if preparing for no more than an evening stroll. The silence was broken. Cries of encouragement for Polydeuces arose from the men aboard *Argo* while from those gathered ashore came shouts of encouragement for their lord and master. Amycus' grin broadened, he punched the air with clenched fists then stooping, gestured with a curling finger for Polydeuces to approach, though Polydeuces was already strolling with easy gait toward him.

'Well who's the pretty boy we 'ave 'ere!' growled Amycus. 'Yer about t'meet Amycus so tell me y'name while yer still able t'speak!'

'My name is Polydeuces,' he answered, calmly, as the pair closed, 'but that's no concern of yours. Are you ready?'

'Oh-oh-oh, am I fuckin' ready!' cried Amycus, glancing from side to side once more at his onlookers. 'Well yer name'll be no concern of yours soon!' With that he lunged forward, right fist raised to swing a vicious punch at his opponent, a punch that might have brought down an ox but one that met only air, for Polydeuces, having smartly dodged the blow, delivered a fist-flashing left to the side of Amycus' head that caused him to stagger aside. His expression granite-grim, Amycus recovered quickly and spun about to face Polydeuces once more with a cry of, 'So the pretty boy likes a good dance does 'e!' Amycus glared hate, spat hard in contempt, crouched, lurched from side to side then sprang forward once more with fist drawn back. Polydeuces deflected the oncoming blow, sprung aside and struck again, his right fist impacting the other man's jaw with a resounding crack, another hard blow following with his left. A gasp arose from the crowd as Amycus reeled but Polydeuces would not allow him to recover a second time, striking again and again to face and body with both fists until Amycus, mouth ajar, eyes staring wildly from a bloodied face, swayed back and forth, tottered then toppled heavily to the ground, arms akimbo. Polydeuces stepped back, flexing his fingers, as three of the several guards positioned to keep away the awed onlookers, dashed across to assist the ruler of their land with spears levelled at his assailant. Polydeuces retreated cautiously toward his vessel as one of the guards laid down his spear and bent low to examine Amycus. The man remained motionless for a time then raised up to exclaim, 'Lord Amycus is dead!' Pointing at Polydeuces who had now almost reached the ship he shouted to the other guards and to the crowd, 'Our leader is slain by the 'and of that man!'

One of the guard's companions dashed forward with spear raised high to cast at Polydeuces. He was about to hurl the shaft on its deadly course but the weapon never made its intended flight. A death proclaiming hiss and Jason's arrow, shot from the quayside, struck the man to pierce deep through the leather corselet at his chest. A garble of voices arose from the crowd as with a cry he fell to the ground, his spear clattering aside.

'To your arms, lads - to your arms!' cried Jason, clambering onto *Argo's* deck.

Polydeuces, too, was back on board and her crew, though with their swords and spears well within reach, had risen with their bows and arrows ready to shoot at close range. From that side of the vessel facing the obstructed harbour entrance sped a flock of vengeful shafts, many piercing flesh as the men on board the enemy ship, realizing what had taken place ashore, scrambled to engage in combat. On the side next to the quay Argos and three of his crewmen, seeing more armed men head toward them with sword and spear at the ready, leapt to slash through the ropes that held their boat. *Argo* was freed and, with oars thrusting hard against the harbour walls she was drifting away from the quay, but those men close enough were hurling their spears. One struck a crewman through the neck, its bloodied blade protruding through as the dying man tumbled into the water. Another was hit in the thigh as he raised his own spear and fell screaming overboard beyond hope of rescue. But the arrows of *Argo's* men did better service at such close range and very soon, with four of the guards down and others hit, the remainder, their spears gone or of no use, retreated to safety. Others of Jason's crew swung the burning braziers by their chains and tipped their brightly glowing contents into those smaller boats moored close by. *Argo* had drifted near enough to the blockading ship for her crew to engage at close quarters. Jason, his deadly blade serpent-hissing from its sheath, was first to leap down onto the enemy boat, cleaving helmet and skull of the man who confronted him as others from his vessel followed close with grim-faced intent. In the turmoil of clashing bronze, amid shouts and cries, the men on the blockading boat were outnumbered and quickly overwhelmed, several dead or wounded, the rest leaping overboard into bloodied water for safety where some, through the weight of their armour, soon vanished below the surface. The enemy boat was already cut away with over half of *Argo's* crew taking to their oars so as to heave their own vessel clear while the remainder braced themselves on the deck, ready to loose their arrows at any of Amycus' men who dared approach the quayside. With considerable satisfaction did Jason, his captain and *Argo's* crew observe the smaller boats moored by the quay smouldering heavily or fully ablaze under thick, drifting smoke that already was obscuring the dead Amycus' palace.

'I'd call seeing the end of Amycus a fair day's work,' remarked Jason as flames bellowed and the pall of smoke grew larger. 'I regret, though, our own losses.'

'I regret them also,' informed Argos as their ship gained open water. 'I see we've lost three good men, two at the quayside and one in their damned boat. We've two wounded; one is Telamon though it's hardly more 'e's got than a scratch and 'is fire makin' pebble is safe. The other man took a glancin' spear on 'is shoulder but 'ell more than likely survive if we let 'im rest.'

'Yes,' said Jason, 'I've seen both and I think also they'll recover well enough. Telamon says he'll try to preserve our remaining fire as the sun isn't strong enough now for him to light another. As for Amycus, he'll have spawned any number of sons so I expect they'll soon be fighting over who gets his palace and his loot.'

'Aye, young sir, I expect they will an' pity it is we couldn't get our 'ands on some of it. But for now we must find ourselves a safe moorin' before dark or I'll need to 'ave us anchored in mid-water, which the men won't be too 'appy about.'

Twilight was descending when *Argo* was guided into a deserted cove and hauled part way onto shallow ground. Telamon had been successful in preserving his single fire and with newly gathered brushwood, a number of his brazier's offspring were soon brightening the darkness. Food was handed about together with enough fish hauled from the water to ensure every man had a good meal. Enlivened by wine and encouraged by

Orpheus whose lyre had lain protected within the bow of their vessel, some of the men sang in raucous voice while others recounted their experiences of earlier that day.

Chapter 5 - Curse of The Harpies

Early morning light saw *Argo* return to deep water where she would face the next phase of her journey sail raised, pennants flying and with a welcome breeze behind. Standing in the bow with Jason later that uneventful day, Argos said, 'As you see before us, young sir, the channel is narrowing; this they call the Thracian Bosporus.'

'Very much narrowing from what I make of it,' said Jason. 'How well d'you know this passage?'

'A half day beyond is the furthest I ever sailed so I know it's navigable an' it leads directly into the Euxine Sea that some call the Black Sea. We now pass the west coast of Bithynia on our right and when we reach open water we turn eastwards along the north coast and continue toward Colchis. Before then, apart from what I've picked up from others, I'll be as much a stranger as yourself an' our crew but I understand from men who've sailed along 'ere that there will be several more days ahead of us.'

'Well we've managed so far,' smiled Jason, 'in spite of a few diversions. I wonder what we'll have to face next.'

'Quite, sir, who can really know. Rumours abound – aye, that they do. Fantastical rumours some of 'em, spread by traders I'd say to keep away the competition.'

By late afternoon the channel had narrowed with land rising gently to either side. The breeze had abated and the crew rowed at a leisurely pace when Argos said: 'Ahead and over to our left, there looks to be a favourable landin' place. See what you think, young sir; your eyes are keener than mine. I make out a few 'ouses but not much else.'

Jason raised a hand to shield his eyes and peered in the direction indicated. 'Yes, there are – there are a few scattered dwellings but I can make out nothing further inland except for what could be a small village. I see no reason why we shouldn't sail in and shelter there for the night.'

'Aye, sir; we need little more by way of provisions though our wine is gettin' low since there was none to be 'ad from Amycus and the land of Bebrycia.'

'Low on wine,' Jason responded. 'Now that *is* serious. From the looks of it I doubt we'll get any from where we're presently heading. If we do have enough to spare I'd better make my usual offering to Poseidon and trust he and Athena will continue to look upon us with favour. Have we enough wine for this evening?'

'There's enough wine for tonight an' enough for a small libation, sir, yes, but later tomorrow we'll need to acquire more as well as fresh water; though from where I cannot say, nor do I know 'ow many of the people beyond this place will understand our dialect or even speak our language.'

They approached the land, seeing not far from the water a solitary stone house. Observed seated to one side of the door was an elderly, grey-bearded man in a loose-fitting peasant's gown. With their vessel brought close in and secured, Jason and his captain were first to clamber ashore.

112

'I doubt we'll need armed men hereabouts,' said Jason, 'but I'll take two with me all the same. Have the rest of our crew set up camp and I'll see what sense I can get out of that man over there although as yet he appears to be taking no notice of us.'

'There's two of our lads lookin' keen to step ashore,' said Argos, 'Calais an' Zetes. I'll 'ave 'em take up their arms an' join you.'

With his companions, each bearing sword, spear and small, circular shield, Jason walked up gently rising, grassy ground, but on approaching the old man closer they realized all was not well. He appeared pallid, drawn and hungry, perhaps aged beyond his years. Clutching his gnarled walking stick he turned to stare in the direction of the newcomers but seemed unable to look directly at them. When the man asked, 'Who is there?' it was obvious he was blind.

'We mean you no harm,' came the reply. 'I am Jason, son of Chiron who rules over Pelion in Thessaly and we are sailing to Colchis. My men are setting up camp by the inlet where our vessel is moored but we'll be gone in the morning. All we look for here is fresh -.'

'Jason of Pelion!' the old man cried, rising with the aid of the stick from the rough wooden bench. 'Jason of Pelion! Then – then by the gods my prayers are answered!'

'Your prayers are what - are you saying you know of me? By the - how could you possibly -?' His thoughts turned briefly to the old woman he had helped to cross the Anauros river. She, too, had recognized him – but then there was the ring on his finger and she had her sight.

'Know of you!' the man cut in. 'That I do!' He spoke as if fired with a new life by Jason's presence. 'I have waited many days and now at last you are here and we may speak.'

'Waited many-!' responded Jason, stepping closer. 'Then maybe I should know who *you* are!' Calais and Zetes glanced at one another and both shrugged.

Staring by Jason with pale blue, unfocussed eyes, the man replied, 'Let me tell you, sir, I am Phineus. I may be blind but I am favoured with sight beyond the world about me. I see as a prophet and because of this I was party to the thinking of the gods themselves. But years ago I transgressed, I unknowingly misused my powers when I divulged to others the thoughts of mighty Zeus himself. For that foolish act he rendered me sightless and brought a further curse down upon me. Yes, sir, I am doubly cursed.'

'Oh, really, a curse,' said Jason, peering by him to assess the house which appeared on the verge of dilapidation though it still supported a roof of terracotta tiles. 'You have me utterly puzzled. And apart from your loss of sight, what might that further curse be?'

'You doubt me, sir, I hear it in the tone of your voice. Ah, but now I think the day draws on. I feel this by the direction of warmth from the sun and the tang of afternoon air. I feel also those doubts will be driven from you and those who are with you by what is soon to occur. Then you will know why I'm obliged to live away from the village.'

'Do the village people deny you food?' Jason asked. 'You appear ill-nourished. Is it food you wish for now? If so then I'll grant you that but you'll tell me first how you know of me.'

'Food!' he exclaimed, raising his stick and turning his sightless eye to the sky. 'Food, you say. Tell me, sir, are there people coming out from the village? It is this time of the day when they do so yet I hear no voices.'

Much puzzled, Jason stepped to the end of the house, turned and called back, 'Yes, there are two men heading along the path towards us and each has with him a small basket!'

'Then you should stand well clear from me,' declared Phineus as Jason rejoined his companions, 'unless, as I hope, you are armed and prepared to use your weapons!'

The three stepped away to allow Phineus by as he hand-tapped his way along the wall to the corner of the house. They watched the two with the baskets approach, hurrying now and looking frequently upwards, one of them almost stumbling in his haste. They halted a few steps from the rear corner of the house, looked hard at Jason and his companions then dropped the baskets as one, called out, 'It's 'ere Phineus! Better be quick about it!' Both turned and scuttled away as though fearful of something as yet unseen.

Phineus tottered along the side of the house onto open ground, wagging his stick until it touched the nearest basket. He stooped, felt about until

115

grasping the handles of both baskets which he tugged and lifted awkwardly. Jason stepped forward intending to offer the old man help when without warning, shadows sped and circled over the ground all about them. A loud cackling was heard, a vortex of wind descended together with a whooshing, a whirring, more a metallic clatter that grew ever louder to shiver air that was suddenly charged with foul, swirling odours. Phineus, stick waving wildly above his head, stumbled back toward the house. Jason, Calais and Zetes looked up to see dark and sinister forms closing over them but in particular Phineus.

'By the gods what damnable creatures are these!' shouted Zetes as he and Calais backed away with their shields held high.

Phineus had almost reached the front of his house but these abominable beasts of the air, three in number, were swooping, flapping, landing and bounding about him as he attempted to gain the entrance. Sword drawn, shield held high, Jason stood his ground, transfixed by the sight of their faces – shrunken dark faces of ghastly but unmistakable female form. With baleful dark eyes glaring down at Phineus, their all but skeletal limbs bearing white-clawed hands and feet, their black, bat-like wings opened and closed as they lunged back and forth, demon-shrieking, attempting to seize the baskets from a crouching, beleaguered Phineus who was unable to take a single step forward. The food, bread and skewered meat, was spilling out, claw-seized by the fetid beasts as, prancing closer still they wrenched at the baskets.

'At 'em, lads!' Jason cried aloud. Striding forward, he Calais and Zetes dashed at the creatures with weapons raised, Jason driving his blade hard into the one closest to him while his companions thrust with their shields and struck with their spears to pierce the other two. The three men did not pause in their resolute assault but despite their screeching malevolent anger, the beasts were giving way, flapping, leaping from the ground as the three men continued their assault with grim determination. The foul creatures were rising into the air, cackling aloud but retreating ever higher. Soon they were circling way above the house, ever rising, soon becoming mere specks wheeling about against the blue vault of the sky until they altogether disappeared. Phineus, now on his knees, was attempting to rise from the ground, one hand reaching furtively about to recover fallen food. From the direction of the ship armed men were approaching, led by Argos, but Jason strode into full view and gestured to indicate there was no help needed.

Quite speechless, Calais and Zetes, were assisting Phineus to his feet when Jason stepped back to ask, 'What in the name of - what charming creatures were those? Where were they from and why did they attack you?'

Phineus leaned against the wall and clutching his stick and one of his baskets replied, 'They, sir, are the Harpies. Have you never heard of them?'

'Harpies?' queried Jason. 'No, my friend, I confess I have not.'

117

'Nor 'ave we,' agreed Calais with Zetes confirming he had not heard of them either.

'Well there's something else I've missed so far in life,' muttered Jason, glancing up at the sky then down at the blade of his sword. 'They appeared to be female and their blood is, er, green.'

'And stinks to high heaven,' said Zetes.

'I've some of their shit on my shield,' added Calais, holding the object in question away from himself.

'Are there many more of 'em in these parts?' Jason asked.

'There are not, sir,' replied Phineus. 'They are not of this or any other land, unless you call the kingdom of the gods a land, which it surely is not. They are the reason why I'm excluded from the village and obliged to live alone. Those vile things are the hunting hounds of mighty Zeus – forever ravenous. They defile with their excrement, their very presence. They steal the food of the accursed such as myself and often they will seize and carry off the souls of the dead. You, sir, have driven them away as others could not – no, would not dare to do. You have defeated them and now they will never again return to torment me.'

'Ah, what would life be if we couldn't help people out now and again,' responded Jason as he and his two companions wiped their blades and shields on the grass. 'But after our having driven off those damnable Harpies and so, as you say, lifted the curse, are you still able to prophesy?'

'I believe I still can, sir,' Phineus replied, nodding his head, 'but I fear if I say too much then

118

even greater ills may descend upon me. The gods listen in case I transgress. Always they listen.'

'All right but you must know more than just my name and where I came from. I'll not press you over that, but tell us where we might obtain fresh water and give us whatever advice you feel you can.'

'There is a fresh water spring close by the village,' he replied, 'and as you are sailing to Colchis you will have to pass through the Symplegades before you enter the Euxine Sea.'

'Pass through the what?' Jason asked, sheathing his sword.

'The Symplegades,' Phineus answered, 'the Clashing Rocks as many call them. Have all your men offer prayers to Athena before you attempt this passage and I know she will listen. More important still, you must sacrifice to Aphrodite when you approach Colchis.'

'Why Aphrodite?' Jason asked.

Phineus reached down to locate his second basket and replied, 'I – I must say no more but there is much ahead of you. My life, meanwhile, though in its autumn days, will be all the more pleasant for what you have done so I – so I must thank you.' He turned away and clutching his precious baskets, hobbled off to disappear inside his humble dwelling.

'You didn't get much out of 'im, sir, did you,' remarked Zetes. 'Not after what we just done.'

'Hmm, no, but maybe it'll be as well if we follow his advice since it won't cost us anything.'

That evening the fires burned and Jason sat by his captain. 'We thought at first they were great

119

birds,' said Argos, 'monstrous in size but birds all the same, maybe eagles, until we saw you fightin' 'em off. It was then I knew what they might be for I've 'eard mention of those 'Arpies on my travels.'

'Parts of them were human,' Jason explained in the glow of their fire, 'or at least their faces were - part women I mean, but blackened and – and shrunken the way real people look when they're starving to death. Except, of course, real people don't fly, do they. Er, please don't tell me some of them do – I've seen and heard enough for one day. I'm starting to think I'll believe almost anything – more so after listening to old Phineus. Maybe things will seem clearer in the morning. At least I hope they will.'

'There are many strange things in this world,' sighed Argos as they lay back to rest. 'Aye, young sir, there are, an' I doubt we've seen the last of 'em today.'

***

The light of dawn saw oars striking water as the Argonauts took their vessel out into the channel. Jason looked back across the inlet to see Phineus seated on his bench as if nothing had happened to disturb his peace that previous day.

The sun was at its highest, a fresh wind filling the sail and the oars drawn in when Jason and Argos sat in the stern of the vessel close to Tiphys the steersman. The channel was narrower, the boat pitching and rolling more than she had at any time since the voyage began. 'Before we enter the Euxine Sea,' informed Argos, 'we'll 'ave the Clashin' Rocks to contend with an' that's what we're about to do. We've sung the praises of Athena with Orpheus at 'is best and there's no more to be done.'

Jason, feeling a landsman's discomfort with the increased rolling of the ship and hearing the thunder of waves ahead, remarked, 'Yes, Orpheus was in fine voice when he led us all so let's hope the good lady enjoyed our collective effort.'

'Aye, young sir, let's 'ope, but as others often pass this way to trade for grain I dare say we'll suffer no 'arm.'

Their vessel heaved with the contrary currents, waves buffeting, water breaking over her to drench all aboard as *Argo* progressed through the channel. The cliffs and fallen boulders seemed to grow ever larger as if threatening to crush them. The waves pounded and roared in mockery of the Argonauts, their vessel's sail thudded in protest but still she sailed on and after a time the channel became wider and the waters calmer. Ahead of them, sparkling sunlight, lay an open and a more placid sea.

'Well it wasn't as bad as some like to make out was it,' grinned the captain.

'That is a matter of opinion,' said Jason, pushing wet hair away from his eyes.

'I've been through 'ere a good number of times,' informed Tiphys. 'Can be better, can be much worse.'

'Now 'e tells us,' said Argos, raising his hands.

'You never asked me, did you,' came Tiphys' response. 'I thought a man so well-travelled as you would know the route.'

121

'Well as I 'ardly do in this case, you'll know better than any which direction we 'ave to take.'

'There's only the one direction we *can* take for Colchis,' said Tiphys, 'an' that's easterly along the north coast of Bithynia until we reach where we want to reach. My travels 'ave always taken me north an' west but as I understand things, Colchis is maybe ten an' more days away so we'll 'ave a few ports of call.'

'I'm beginning to realise,' said Jason, gazing across the wide expanse of water, 'why that rogue Pelias had me make this journey. I suspect while I'm away he'll be plotting mischief and the Golden Fleece won't mean a thing.'

'But you'll not 'ave us turn back now, will you young sir – or will you?'

'No, I'll get my hands on that damned fleece and when we return I'll make him choke on it.'

***

It's time I had another say. Jason had met with two violent encounters hadn't he since leaving the sweet and oh, so accommodating ladies of Lemnos with despair at their departure evident on most of the Argonauts' faces. One of dear Jason's men had rid the land of that boorish oaf, Amycus, then they'd accounted for a good few of his followers and several of his boats. No great loss in my opinion and at least the waters around that part of the world as well as some of his neighbours on land would be all the safer for it even though still missing a few of their more valuable possessions.

As for the Harpies plaguing old Phineus, I think you'll agree Jason and a couple of his men sorted that one out rather well. Why Zeus, or any other of the gods, would want to create anything as hideous, as revolting to eyes, ears and nose as the Harpies is a mystery even to me. There are, after all, so many other ways of punishing people who upset you. Yes, there certainly are. And the Clashing Rocks – they didn't clash very much did they. That, if anything, is a case of rumour being inflated into fantasy as it gets passed from mouth to mouth among people who have no direct experience of these things whatsoever.

I, meanwhile, was getting on with what I'd been raised since childhood to do – follow in my mother's footsteps by developing a knowledge of what nature could provide in the way of herbs and potions to alleviate pain and suffering. Of course in finding out what is good and beneficial for people, you discover also what is best avoided. By now there were other things on my mind. That vessel from Thessaly was drawing closer with its image and that of the men aboard her becoming clearer.

***

Sailing fair along the north coast of Bithynia the wind had for much of the day been in their favour. The vessel rolled gently, her sail well filled and her oars shipped. Lines and nets were cast to ensure a good supply of fish and squid while Telamon was busied in relighting fresh kindle in a brazier, concentrating the rays of a mid-afternoon sun with his rock crystal. If ever a man possessed something of priceless value it was Telamon. Jason and his captain stood together in *Argo's* bow, both staring inland, hands raised to shelter their eyes from the sun.

'D'you see those horsemen,' asked Jason, peering to the high-risen land at their right. 'I suspect they've been following our progress ever since we turned east.'

'Aye, two of 'em I can just make out,' confirmed Argos. 'Your eyes are keener than mine – can you see anythin' more?'

'No, except that they don't appear to be armed. Could be they're just scouts. Tiphys says this land belongs to the Mariandyni who he thinks are peaceable but that's about all he knows of them.'

'Then why are they followin' us?'

'I dare say we'll find out when we go ashore later today but we'd better have our men on their guard. I've had more than my share of surprises since the day I set off to visit Iolcos.'

The sun was low to their stern when *Argo* was steered to moor in the deepwater shelter of a lightly wooded inlet. The men were disembarking with their arms and utensils when, through a gap in the trees, two horsemen were seen approaching.

'Are they the ones keeping an eye on us?' asked the captain.

'They may well be,' replied Jason. 'They appear well turned out, not brigands, and it really does look as if they're not armed.'

On reaching the edge of the trees and now in full view of all *Argo's* crew, the men approached Jason.

'I am Diores of the Mariandynians,' said the first man in a heavily accented but readily understandable Greek.

'Diores of the -?' queried Jason.

'Of the Mariandynians,' he repeated slowly. 'Do I now address the leader of your men?'

'You do, I am Jason - Jason of Pelion in Thessaly.'

'We bring you peaceful greetings!' declared the second man as both dismounted. 'We see from your vessel and her crew that your purpose here is other than brigandry.'

'That is so,' responded Jason. 'We stop only to rest for the night and will continue on our way to Colchis at first light tomorrow.'

'You are welcome to our land,' said Diores as they stood before Jason who was joined now by Argos. 'We are sent to give you thanks and to offer you gifts and all the provisions you need for the service you have rendered to our people. You have rid our lands of Amycus whose kingdom lies to the south of us. We heard much of what had happened from slaves who had fled his court after he died.'

'Who then is your king?' Jason asked.

'Our king? No, we have no king,' informed the second man. 'We have no great palace or walled city though we have our temples, our priests and our markets. We are a coalition of towns and villages ruled over by a council of elders and priests. Our lands are rich and our workshops the envy of many so we have no need nor have we the desire to steal from others as did Amycus.'

'And I trust there are no Harpies hereabouts,' smiled Jason.

'Oh, Harpies,' replied Diores, 'no, sir, we had instead Amycus and the Bebryces. Under *his* rule they helped themselves to our crops, our livestock and our goods whenever it pleased them. Because they lived only by plundering, almost all their men and many of their women were brigands. If ever we defied Amycus they would come at night to one of our farms, seize or murder its people then burn it to the ground. So as you see, we really are in your debt.'

'Yes,' said Jason, 'I saw some of what Amycus had stolen from other people. Now might be a good time for you to send a large and well-armed delegation to his palace and claim back whatever you can find of your property. Do it soon in case whoever takes over proves to be as bad as he was.'

'Aye, Lord Jason, we will,' said Diores. 'But was it you who killed the man?'

'Unfortunately not,' answered Jason, pointing toward his vessel, 'it was Polydeuces, the big fellow you see over there with that coil of rope over his shoulder.'

'Then let us thank him directly and ask for a lock of his hair. We will dedicate it in a shrine to him at our temple of Athena. You, your captain and the man Polydeuces must return with us for the evening and accept our gifts.'

'The best gifts you could give us,' said Jason, 'is bread, meat and a supply of good wine since we have little or none left on board. We'll ask nothing more of you.'

126

'Sir,' responded Diores, 'we produce the best wines in these lands so you'll have as much as you can carry on board that handsome vessel of yours. Wines are most essential here as many of the springs are tainted and their water unfit or even dangerous to drink, though there are enough safe wells further inland. And there will be food enough to satisfy all your men, and more.'

'Ah!' exclaimed Argos, 'I 'eard our steersman say findin' fresh water was exactly what 'e was goin' to do.' He looked toward the trees to see the man in question emerge carrying a clay jar and called out, 'Tiphys – don't drink that water, it'll do you no good! Throw it away! We'll soon 'ave safe water and good wine!'

Tiphys approached, clutching the jar and said, 'Don't drink it? Oh, but I - yes, fine, I'll get rid of it.' He emptied the contents of the jar into the grass then stepped over to the boat.

'Fine,' said Jason, 'we will return with you but we must leave here at dawn.'

***

As the sky began to lighten, straw padded jars of wine and baskets of food began to arrive, conveyed by ox and cart; welcome goods to be loaded carefully onto and under *Argo's* deck as well as space within the bow. With these provisions came Saron, a weather-beaten, short-bearded seafaring man used to bearing arms and having knowledge of the Bithynian coast as far as Colchis and the Phasis River. Jason readily accepted his offer as guide for the rest of their journey to Colchis.

Before mid-morning *Argo* sailed from the Mariandyni coast with Tiphys at the tiller. The wind was favourable but light so that the oarsmen were employed to assist the vessel on her course at an easy rate without the need of the captain's drum. It was one of the oarsmen at the very rear of the vessel who, shortly before midday, noted something was amiss with their tiller man. Tiphys was staring down with one hand on the tiller and the other clutching at his stomach. He appeared to be in pain. Others began to notice and before long, Tiphys groaned aloud, fell forward with one arm draped over the tiller and the other hanging loosely by his side. Argos was called for and made his way along the deck. There he placed a hand on Tiphys' shoulder and asked, 'What troubles you, my friend?'

Tiphys mumbled incoherently and would have slid forward onto the deck had not Argos held him. Jason stepped along to join him and helped lift Tiphys from his seat but the man grasped tighter on his stomach and was unable to stand.

'We'll carry him to the bow where he can lie in more comfort,' said Jason. 'Do we have another man to take over here?'

'Aye, sir, there's one at the oar, Ancaeus, 'appy to do that. I'll 'ave 'im replaced an' down 'ere on the tiller while we get this poor bugger up to the front.'

They laid Tiphys on a woollen blanket in the bow with his face shielded from the glare of a mid-morning sun. There he remained softly groaning, curled up and all but motionless.

'D'you know what might be ailing him?' Jason asked.

'I'm not at all sure, young master for 'e seems unable to speak, but I suspect 'e drank some of the water we was told not to drink an' now 'e suffers from it.' He peered along the rows of oarsmen then added, 'An' I regret to say we 'ave no one aboard to deal with the likes of this an' nothin' with which to comfort 'im.'

'Then,' said Jason, 'we must wait until we reach some place where he's able to rest and hope he soon recovers.'

The sun was past its highest when they discovered Tiphys was dead.

'We'll have to go ashore somewhere and find a place to bury or cremate him,' said Jason as he and Argos peered down at the still and pallid form.

'Aye, sir, an' we can 'ave one of the lads carve a marker to show where 'is ashes rests. In fact it's a task I can do myself if you'll allow.'

'Of course, and I see there's an island some way ahead to our left. There he could lie undisturbed if we can get ashore. Saron may know something about it – let's ask him.'

Saron joined them to assess the island and said, 'I never 'ad cause to set foot on there; it 'as no name I'm aware of. It's covered in trees an' I'm certain no one lives there as it's too small.'

The island was further from the coast than Argos had anticipated and the sun was low in the sky when they drew close.

'I see nowhere to land,' Jason said as the oarsmen took them slowly on. 'I see no signs of habitation so as our friend here said, it must be deserted.'

'Keep on sailin' around it,' advised Saron. As they reached the furthest side of the small island he pointed across, saying, 'Look, where that tree stands close to the water, you could 'itch your vessel to it; I don't recall seein' there's anywhere else.'

'Then we'll do that,' confirmed Argo. 'It looks not too steep a climb an' if there's level ground maybe we could camp ashore for the night. Poor Tiphys was always a bit of a loner so 'is spirit will not begrudge our choice for 'is final restin' place.'

'Is there anyone in Thessaly or elsewhere you know of awaiting his return?' Jason asked.

'None I'm aware of in Thessly, sir,' his captain replied, 'never 'eard the man speak of anyone there at all, not ever – spent most of 'is life at sea. Very sad to 'ave no one, I'd say, but there we are.'

Overhearing this, one of the crewmen said, 'Pardon me interruptin' but 'e did 'ave a woman on Lemnos he promised to return to. 'Er name I recall was Merope. She'll be expectin' 'im an' maybe expectin 'is child.'

'Then should we return to that island,' said Argos, 'you must take the sad news to her.'

With their boat secured, most of her crew clambered up the steep, rocky bank until reaching level ground overgrown mainly by laurel trees. Some of the crew carried wine jars in straw-lined baskets, Telamon swung on its chain a lighted ship's brazier from which they would obtain more fire but it was Argos alone who carried the cold body of Tiphys wrapped in sailcloth. Twilight was

130

close when they began to gather brushwood and timber for the funeral pyre and for their camp. Those looking up to yet higher ground before darkness fell might have noticed a small ruin close to the centre of the island and part hidden by tall trees.

In deepening night but with a full moon risen, Jason, his curiosity much aroused, made his way up to what appeared to be a modest stone temple. There he stood before the entrance where an ornately carved lintel was supported by much overgrown columns. Glancing behind he observed his men busily arranging wood for the pyre where Tiphys was to be laid and he listened a while as they called to one another. There was time to loiter so he moved forward, stooped slightly to pass beneath the lintel and, once inside, found himself enclosed by dark stone walls with only the sweep of stars above. The abandoned building offered no clues to its origin or dedication. Was the temple empty, he wondered, or did a carved image, perhaps in the form of some other worldly deity, lie waiting unseen a short way from where he stood? No light from the fires outside penetrated the interior but a profound silence closed about and possessed him as a spectral shroud. Lost in unfathomable stillness, Jason stood in a gently flowing contentment unlike any he had known. Time seemed no longer to matter and in that strange reverie he desired nothing more than to remain where he was. In that curious realm of contemplation he began to think upon the world he knew and of those worlds beyond he might never know. Then passed before his eyes a vague and shifting form – the face of that strange, that frail old woman who, months ago, he had carried over the Anauros River.

A call from some great distance beyond and his dreaming shimmered, then dissolved. 'Lord Jason, sir, the pyre is ready to be lit!' With aching reluctance he turned and stepped out into the open night where his men waited and Argos stood with burning torch held high. He returned to give his blessing and the pyre soon burned. Smoke arose above the trees, blazing wood cracked and flames threw glowing embers as memories into the night. Orpheus played and sang an elegy while the men listened in attentive silence.

Jason and his captain sat aside from the rest with Saron, each with goblet filled and fire reflected in their eyes. Jason, silent for a time, said, 'I wonder who it was built a temple here of all places.'

'It's said by some,' informed Saron, 'that the mainland and islands 'ereabouts were occupied once by the Amazons, women who devoted 'emselves to warfare and 'untin' and regarded men as chattels.'

'And are we to believe that?' Jason asked. 'Could those warlike women have built a temple here, one that seemed to me when I entered it a place of - of wondrous tranquility?

'Don't know if I believe it or if I don't,' replied Saron. 'I 'ear so many tales on my travels I'm not sure now and again what to think.'

'Well,' declared Jason, taking a gulp of honeyed wine, 'we encountered flying women the other day, if you can call those loathsome, foul smelling creatures women, though I did wonder when only half awake the next morning if it hadn't been a bad dream.'

'Oh, sounds like you mean the 'arpies,' responded Saron. 'Aye, I've 'eard of 'em – so they *are* real are they.'

'Unfortunately they are, or were, very real. But you, my friend, trade with Colchis so tell us something about King Aietes and his land as well as anything you've heard about this precious, this so-called Golden Fleece that's supposed to be guarded by a dragon or something else unpleasant.'

'An' whatever we can expect to meet on the way,' added the captain.

'On the way, and it's still a long way,' answered Saron, 'I doubt there'll be too many surprises. There's an odd rock formation further along, just off the coast that some talk about. When it blows 'ard it gives forth a sound like a man cryin' out in agony. The locals on the mainland, a pretty rustic lot, say it's the cries of Prometheus chained up there with 'is liver bein' pecked out by an eagle. I've sailed by it many times an' 'eard the noise but it really is a noise caused by the wind an' that's all it is – wind blowin' though gaps in the rocks if you see what I mean. An' I never saw no great bird 'angin' around there either.'

'Well that's a relief,' breathed Jason, refilling his goblet from the jar. 'And -?'

'Aye, as for the Colchians – they're a rough lot though their court is wealthy enough. But the 'omage they pay to that goddess of theirs – you'll see what I mean if you visit 'er temple an' see 'er statue; it's the ugliest looking thing I ever set eyes on.'

'You mean Hecate,' said Jason, 'yes, I've heard vaguely of her but there's not much else I know. This side of the world seems to be full of women no sane man would care to encounter.'

'Not so the young women of Aietes' court,' grinned Saron. 'They'll turn any man's 'ead an' more.'

'The Harpies turned my head,' commented Jason, 'and the smell of 'em nearly turned my stomach.'

'But as for this Golden Fleece,' continued Saron, 'I've never seen it meself an' don't know anyone that 'as. But there are tales of men who've tried to get their 'ands on it and 'ave come to grief. It's said this Aietes values it more than anythin' else in 'is kingom an' will order killed anyone 'e suspects might be wantin' to steal it. Last year I did witness a boat cast adrift downriver from Aia, Aietes' capital. No one could say exactly what 'appened to 'er crew since those few men left in 'er 'ad been dead many days before the birds started feedin' on 'em – some of 'em mutilated. But that boat wasn't one from these parts. As for Aietes 'imself, well -.'

'Well what?' Jason asked.

'Well 'e's a vain an' arrogant man but above all a man without mercy as you'll most likely see for y'self.'

***

Yes, very sad it might have been to lose Tiphys but more by far to Argos and no few of his men than I

134

suspect it was to Jason who hardly knew him. But now I was becoming more aware of them. In the loneliness of my chamber, in night-shrouded silence, I saw their vessel lying by that island on moonlight-glinting water. I saw the flaming pyre that consumed the one who earlier that day had departed this world. But it still wasn't clear to me what was the purpose of their voyage, other than that it was very important to Jason. As I was yet to discover, though I ought to have suspected it earlier and wonder now why I didn't, all he wanted was to reach Colchis as soon as possible, to negotiate for or steal, preferably steal the Golden Fleece, then sail off back to Thessaly. Once there he'd head straight to Iolcus, topple Pelias off his throne if the Fleece wasn't enough to have him give it up, kill him perhaps, and take over as the new king. But he was still a long way from Colchis and his men had so far gained, apart from the delights on offer at Lemnos, nothing other than hard work. They were expecting rather more than that before they landed back in Greece.

But as I've already made clear, Hera also wanted to see Pelias ousted or even dead, preferably dead, and as it became clearer to me later, it was her image he witnessed, if only for moments, in that long abandoned island temple. She was of course intent on seeing Jason's expedition through to ultimate success, as was Athena because of Argos and the well-conceived ship he'd dedicated to her. I knew that much because I was a priestess at Hecate's temple and she'd instill such information during my times of devotion. What she did not make clear, perhaps because it was not imparted to her, I would eventually discover much to my cost.

Chapter 6 - The Land of Colchis

More days passed, days uncounted, days of variable weather when men began to complain of heat or of rain when under other circumstances the latter might have been welcomed. Here it was not welcomed because it began for most to feel as if the journey might never end. They would go ashore wherever Saron considered supplies could be found and a decent camp safely established. After the wine of Mariandynia was gone, other wines were sometimes to be had though sometimes not. But no other wines could quite match those of the Mariandyni and often they were not worth drinking other than to slake the thirst of men labouring at the oars when the wind was not with them. The men rowed hard to the rhythm of Argo's drum but expressions of discontent evident on a number of their faces was not always the result of physical effort.

'There's unrest brewin' among a good few of 'em,' said Argos one morning when their vessel was under sail in a fresh wind beneath a cloudless sky.

'Be that as it may,' said Jason, 'they are all indebted to my father and have sworn to support me have they not.'

'Makin' promises is easy, young sir, is it not,' said Argos. 'Keepin' 'em not always so an' I doubt there'll be another Lemnos 'ereabouts to raise their spirits.'

It was a revelation from Saron that brought cause for optimism when he approached Jason and

137

his captain to inform them, 'We've turned north-east so that 'as us sailin' along the west coast of Colchis. That in turn means late tomorrow or the mornin' after will see us off the River Phasis. Further up the river lies Aietes' city of Aia.'

'So we sail upstream to Aia,' said Jason. 'You've not mentioned any harbour – I take it there must be one.'

'Aye, sir, there is 'arbour but I suggest you moor your vessel close to woodland further downstream from the city, set up camp out of sight there and take only those men you need.'

'So you consider mooring our vessel under the king's nose may be dangerous.'

Saron brushed a hand thoughtfully over his beard before responding. 'Well like I said, sir, this man Aietes, suspects every stranger enterin' the city of plottin' to oust 'im or steal 'is precious fleece. He might be a king but like I said, 'asn't the manners of any noble - no, far from it.'

'Hm, sounds as bad if not worse than the one that persuaded me to come out here. Echion can precede us and tell Aietes we're passing through his territory on our way north and looking only to buy supplies and wine for the journey. Sending a genuine herald ought to dampen his suspicions.'

'You could claim you're out 'ere to look for grain supplies,' suggested Saron. 'That might work since it's a common enough reason for trade around the Euxine Sea though not in Colchis.'

The water sparkled morning sun when they entered the Phasis estuary where fishermen and others in bobbing boats eyed their vessel with interest. The current was against them but the wind much in their favour so *Argo's* sail was filled, her rigging taut and the men rowed with ease.

'Not far now on our left there's a small, abandoned temple,' informed Saron, standing in the bow with Jason and his captain. 'There's a wooden jetty leads from it though very few use that any more since the 'arbour was built near the city a few years back. A boat like this can still be moored close in there an' it'll be part 'idden by the trees, but you'll need to take down the yard 'arm an' mast before enterin' or she'll snag on the branches. There's a track your men can follow; it'll be much overgrown since I last used it but should still be easy to see an' it more or less follows the river.'

'An' there'll be little chance of 'em blockin' our vessel in,' muttered Argos.

The sun was higher and *Argo* secured alongside the neglected jetty when Echion, herald's staff in hand, set off followed by two armed men. Telamon's fire-making pebble had done its work; braziers burned and the smoke from cooking fires drifted upstream.

The sun was close to its highest when the three returned to be met on the jetty by Jason and Argos. 'Were you well received?' asked Jason.

'King Aietes agreed to meet with you at his palace this afternoon, sir,' Echion replied, 'but no more than ten lightly armed men are to make up your party.'

'Which is pretty well what I'd planned,' said Jason. 'Go on.'

'Well, sir, he demanded to know more of your business so I told him where we were from and what you said about needing supplies for our journey north to trade for grain. He insisted upon knowing more but I told him it was my business only to arrange an interview and I was not permitted to discuss matters beyond that. He is an aggressive oaf of a man, sir, if I may say so, and a visit to his city may not, I think, be to your liking. You will witness what happens to those who give him offence.'

'Almost what I've come to expect,' said Jason. 'I'll gather a few of our men and we'll set off soon.' He turned to his captain, saying, 'Those items of value we have concealed in the bows of the ship – I'll collect some I consider worthy of a king if you'll nominate one of our crew to carry them; it will leave my sword hand free.'

'I'll 'ave Polydeuces do that,' Argos replied. 'No one will dare try to take 'em off 'im.'

With Jason at the head they set off along the path, much overgrown and enclosed by a forest of bushes. On this occasion he wore the fine cloak given him by Hypsipyle the day they had sailed from Lemnos. Beneath this, at his belted tunic, was concealed his trusted sword. Eventually the path opened out, they passed the harbour and its wharf where small boats swayed, and a short way beyond that arose the gaunt, cyclopean stone walls of Aia. About what appeared to be the main city gate waited some twelve fully armed men wearing bronze or scale-plated armour and ornate bronze helmets.

140

'How very considerate of their king,' said Jason, turning with a grin to face his men, 'it seems there's a guard of honour waiting to conduct us to the regal presence.'

Some of the men laughed but each rested a hand on his sword hilt as they moved forward. It could not escape the attention of anyone approaching from the river, nor was it intended to, that suspended by chains, high on the walls either side of the gate were displayed the corpses of numerous men in various stages of decay and decomposition. Drawing closer, Jason and his men observed how a few were already skeletal, others, still dripping gore. The air about the corpses was alive; a focus of attention for ravenous, frantically fluttering birds while other bodies hanging there were infested by black, scurrying, clustering flies and other unspeakable creatures that buzzed and busied themselves about eye socket, nose and mouth. Jason's men eyed the grim array but none spoke except Polydeuces who muttered, 'I've seen some pretty sights on the field of battle in my time but, by the gods, none to match a spectacle of death like this one.'

One of the guards, more elaborately appointed than the others, stepped forward to meet Jason's party and announced in an unfamiliar though comprehensible accent of Greek, 'You are to come before our king and you must say nothing until you are addressed by him.'

Jason did not reply but followed quietly as the guard led them beneath the massive stone lintel of the gateway with his men following uncomfortably

141

close behind, each with spear conspicuously raised. There were no others near the gate, no one passing through and no beggars to be seen.

'Looks like they've cleared everyone out of the way,' muttered one of Jason's men.

This appeared to be true for as they emerged from beneath the shadow of the gate people could be seen milling about and chattering some distance away at either side, citizens, young and old and tradesman with their stalls.

If anything other than dead bodies emphasised the nature of this strange land as they approached the palace, it was the architecture. Not to be seen were the stylized bull's horns running along the parapets of Aia's main buildings, nor were there the painted, downward tapering columns so familiar throughout most cities of Greece. Here were buildings of a more rugged, almost brutal aspect, some rising to three or more floors. Jason and his companions were conducted through the main portal then across a courtyard where fountains played and gowned courtiers passed back and forth chatting and laughing as if quite unaware of the gristly assemblage outside their main gate. The megaron of Aietes was more familiar for here were painted columns set about a great circular hearth, here were walls hung with the instruments of conflict, arms and armour interspaced with burning torches. The courtiers were colourfully but more heavily gowned than those of Jason's homeland, as though warmth was here of greater importance, the female courtiers being fully covered from the neck down. Opposite where Jason and his men had entered stood a richly adorned throne upon which sat the King of Colchis surrounded by his male attendants.

Jason and Polydeuces only were conducted by the leader of the guards to stand before Aietes whose broad face was framed in a heavy, curling and encroaching black growth from which peered small but harshly staring pale blue eyes. He wore no crown but a pectoral visible below his bushy beard and rings on his oddly delicate fingers bore glistening gemstones of numerous colours in gold and silver settings. He continued to stare unblinking at Jason but for a time said nothing. His face molded gradually into a smile but this was not a smile of welcome as he adjusted his stout figure in his throne and asked in rumbling tones, 'Tell me, what is the real purpose of y'visit then maybe we'll take wine.'

'I thought my herald had made that clear,' answered Jason. 'We require supplies to see us on our journey north but first I have gifts from my father's court at Pelion to offer you as one king to another.' He gestured for Polydeuces to step forward with the canvas bag which he placed at the foot of Aietes' throne. As the courtiers stood watching in silence Jason himself stooped to open the bag to reveal small ornaments and vessels in intricately designed bronze, gold and silver, a few embellished with precious inlay and gemstones.

'I thank you,' Aietes breathed, eyeing the gifts and leaning closer to Jason, 'but I'm *still* unclear as to the reason for y'journey. The coast from 'ere on turns north-west and the lands beyond are not so 'ospitable. Which town or city did you 'ave in mind? Say now if you will because I know of very few places worth the trouble.'

'It *is* trade for grain that interests us,' replied Jason. 'There is much demand in Greece for grain but its cultivation in our rugged lands is most difficult and this means there is seldom enough for the people of the cities. The Cretans have a virtual monopoly of trade with Egypt so we must find other sources.'

'Oh, it's still grain y'tellin' me,' growled Aietes, 'then I suggest you're 'eadin' in the wrong direction by comin' 'ere, then there is, of course, Troy. How d'you propose to avoid their interceptin' and taxin' y'vessels because that's what I 'ear they do?'

'Our own vessel is swift and we passed through the straits without incident. I expect we'll do so on our return.'

'Yer own vessel, really,' breathed the king. He stared upwards in exaggerated perplexity, then added, 'I'm told there's no vessel of yours to be seen in our 'arbour. How is this?'

'Because,' replied Jason, assertively, 'we had no wish to risk obstructing the passage of your own boats and we did not intend to remain here long.'

Aietes relaxed then said, 'I see - well, I suppose our traditions of 'ospitality are little different to those throughout Greece from what others tell me of 'em. So then – so I 'ave to offer you and your men food and wine while I think over your presence 'ere.'

144

Amidst the courtiers, who were now gathering around with interest, there was one who eyed Jason with feelings very different to those of her father the king. She gazed at him, transfixed, and Aietes, while occupied in issuing orders to his attendants was soon aware of it, though at the time he considered it of scant importance.

In an adjacent hall those crewmen of *Argo* who had accompanied Jason, including Polydeuces, were seated about a sturdy communal table where they were offered food and undiluted wine, the latter in liberal quantity. There they were entertained by musicians and women of the court who were soon to make it clear their sexual favours might be obtained in their chambers or in the privacy of gardens at the rear of the palace. Jason sat alone with Aietes, both having transferred to a private room off the main hall, lit mainly by wall-mounted firebrands. Outside, as Jason was well aware, there stood three armed guards. He and Aietes had taken their food and wine, a stronger wine than any he had encountered, with little conversation but now, with cups refilled to generous measure, it was Aietes who began, 'You find me suspicious of yer intentions do y'not?'

'That had crossed my mind,' replied Jason, calmly raising his goblet to drink, though taking care not to take the wine too quickly. Jason was here reminded of his interview at Iolcus with Pelias, a man who he already regarded as a less blighted individual by far than his present company.

'Then let me tell you,' continued Aietes, easing aside to pass wind loudly from his rear, 'there are

145

those who covet the throne of Aia, some of 'em my own family. They'd stop at nothin' to get it unless I acted first. Yes, unless *I* acted first! Four of my own grandsons, 'ardly more than kids, I 'eard were busy plottin' so one of 'em could take over. I listened an' I watched through the ears and eyes of others. I caught 'em out, though, and now they're locked away beneath the palace until I 'ave the bastards taken out in front of our citizens and blinded. Aye, they'll 'ave their eyes torn out as an example of what will 'appen to anyone with similar ideas. Then they'll spend the rest of their days in the vaults below 'ere grovelin' in their own shit.' He leaned forward and lowered his voice as if not wishing to be overheard. 'There were others encouragin' and connivin' with 'em, you see, aye, others, and I'm told there's people waitin' in villages outside the city ready to move against me at a day's notice. They may not realise it but it's reported to me by, shall I say, certain means who some of 'em are. So you see, I'll 'ave no one question my authority. No one at all. Trouble is, some of 'em in those outlayin' villages are related to my own guards so that needs tidyin' up before long.' He relaxed back then continued, 'And I'll tell you now, those men of yours in the dinin' 'all are well supplied with wine and women so let's 'ope when their tongues are loosened they don't say 'anythin to compromise 'emselves or you.'

'How very thoughtful of you,' remarked Jason, coolly, though the sarcasm of his remark appeared not to register with Aietes. 'But since we're not related to anyone hereabouts, perhaps I and my men, all fit and well-seasoned warriors, can help you to put down these enemies of yours.'

'Huh, fit and well-seasoned warriors are they,' muttered Aietes, gulping his wine, 'and not set out just to trade for grain like you said.'

'It is as I said but those men have to be armed because the Aegean Sea has more than its share of pirates and there was, as you say, a risk of encountering Trojan vessels when entering the narrows to the Hellespont. Now do you wish to consider my offer of help and what I would ask in return for its undertaking?'

'How many men d'you 'ave and what might you really be wantin' in return – gold, silver, exactly what?'

'What do I want,' smiled Jason, setting his unfinished wine aside while his other hand drifted discreetly beneath his cloak to pass fingers over the hilt of his sword. 'Let me see - gold, silver, yes that sounds like – no, wait - how about – yes, how about this Golden Fleece I hear people say you have? They talk of it but seem to know hardly anything. I understand you hold it in high regard but I'm sure you could get another one like it – oh, and I'd need a tablet baked hard with your seal to confirm its former ownership and prove to others where I and my men had been.' Even as he spoke, Jason regretted his words.

Aietes stared at him for tense moments, began to laugh loudly, then louder still, his mouth ajar, his eyes turned up to the beamed ceiling as he rocked back and forth in his seat. When he at last calmed and sat upright, Jason said, 'I'm glad you find my modest humour so entertaining. It's just a wager I had – nothing more.'

Huh, 'umour you 'ave and no mistake,' responded Aietes, leaning to peer closer at him, 'and very entertainin' it is. Almost pissed me'self laughin'! Aye, funniest thing I've 'eard in many a day. I like a man with a sense of 'umour, oh but I do.' He lifted aside passed wind again then added, 'One or two of 'em 'earabouts made me laugh so fuckin' much they're up there now decoratin' the city wall.' He raised the goblet, held it poised before his lips then said, 'I'll need time to think on y'reason for bein' in my city, so as you won't be leavin' today, I suggest you join those men you brought 'ere with you, 'ave a good time of it with our women.'

'I'd prefer to take a stroll around the town if you don't mind,' said Jason. 'I need to clear my head after that wine of yours.'

'If that's what y'want. Our main temple will be quiet this afternoon so y'might find that interestin' enough. One of my daughters, youngest of 'em as it 'appens, is priestess there as well - 'er name's Medea.'

'Maybe I'll do that,' Jason responded, lifting his goblet to down the remains of his wine, 'as long as I'm not followed around by your guards - I do find that unsettling.'

The king nodded his acquiescence and added, 'We'll continue our conversation later if you care to find y'way back 'ere around sunset – otherwise I leave y'to it.'

148

Jason arose, smiled and stepped across the room, followed by a shout from Aietes to his guards, instructing them to remain where they were.

With Jason gone, Aietes swiveled about and called, 'Damon, come over 'ere!' The captain of his guard emerged from columned shadows at one side of the room, a tall and burly, red-bearded man who removed his horned bronze helmet as, offering a small bow, he stood before Aietes to receive his instructions. 'You 'eard where 'e's probably goin'. Can't do no 'arm in the temple but two of your lads are to keep an eye on 'im when 'e's out an' about. Send one of y'men down river to the old jetty dressed as – as a nobody, a peasant sellin' whatever. There's a vessel moored there and I want to know 'ow many are on board or camped around 'er an' anythin' else 'e can see without raisin' suspicion - like what the buggers 'ave with 'em in the way of arms and armour.'

***

Now at last, in the darkness of my chamber, in the deepest recesses of the temple, closed off from all but myself and the priests, a place where the voices of the gods might be heard, I saw and I knew. What I knew surprised me greatly for it seemed to give answers to questions I had never thought to ask. It presented me with images I had not expected and aroused me with feelings entirely unexpected. I thought at first it was Hecate herself whose presence I felt and so I was unafraid, but there were others who moved unseen to possess my thoughts. I saw the vessel on our river, I watched them moor it amidst the trees, well away from the city. They had sent their herald and now he had returned they were on their way to the city to meet my father, the king. I knew no good would come of it because I knew my father well enough. I knew what had gone before and like everyone else I was aware of the appalling sight that greeted people at the main gate to our city. Then I saw the image of Jason for the first time; a fair and handsome youth, smiling and confident, determined in his course of life. I felt the arrow of Eros in my pounding heart and I heard myself whisper words that soared into the darkness about me, "You have travelled far on your journey. By the gods I know you. Oh, yes, yes, yes, I know who you are and why you have come to Colchis and I must be prepared."

I realized only later how I had been no more than a pawn in the plans of Aphrodite herself in order to satisfy the plans of Hera and Athena who were working in collusion. But at the time...

***

The afternoon air was heavy and humid as Jason, his head clearing, walked across the courtyard and out into the open square. He noted the area now appeared normal as might be expected in any such town, with men and women, traders, children, dogs and the odd official hurrying about his business. To his left arose the most notable edifice, one with colourfully decorated columns and banners flying from tall cedar poles either side of the heavily carved stone entrance where stout, copper-banded oak doors stood ajar. He approached the short flight of steps and glanced over his shoulder to ascertain whether or not any of Aietes' men were following.

There were two of them standing on the far side of the square. Were they watching him? At that distance it was difficult to say where their attention was directed but they appeared to be in conversation. 'Let 'em get on with it,' Jason muttered, then he stepped through the doorway into the cool interior.

It took a while for his eyes to adjust because there were no windows to allow in daylight, but it was obvious there were dogs present. They yapped, running here and there as Jason stood to look about, then they became quiet and slunk into the shadows. The smoke of incense hung heavily in the air to suppress any odours less pleasant. On the frescoed walls could be made out many strange, and to Jason, incomprehensible images, bizarre, unworldly beasts in some unfathomable ritual. On the walls, also, were mounted burning torches that helped illuminate the one major feature of the interior, a freestanding statue of the city goddess, Hecate. The darkly coloured statue, somewhat taller than she would be if a real life figure, represented a curious, a sinister cowled and robed woman whose large eyes stared out to infinity with vengeful intent. In each of her raised hands she held a burning torch which accentuated her grotesque image in shimmering light.

'Another outlandish woman,' Jason muttered. At the rear of the statue, to its left, a door indicated that the temple must extend further. As he stood bemused at the sight of Hecate, a voice touched his ear from behind. 'At last, Jason, you are here with me.'

'What!' Jason spun about with a hand falling instinctively to his sword. 'By the gods, who are you?' That she was young and beautiful drove all other thoughts from his mind. Her long hair, gleaming as polished obsidian, was held back at either side by golden clasps from where it tumbled loosely about her shoulders. A pale cotton robe graced her slim form, heavily embroidered at bodice, sleeve and hem with entwined geometrical forms and held in place by a red sash. Light from the burning torches fell on her prominent dark eyes and high cheek-boned face. The girl looked into his eyes and a smile livened her face.

'Who are you?' he asked again, this time in a whisper. 'And is there any point in my asking how you also know my name?'

'I am Medea,' she replied in a voice of compelling intimacy. She moved closer, her breath warm and sensual on his cheek as she added, 'I am a daughter of Aietes.'

'You,' he breathed, 'you, a daughter of -.'

'A daughter of Aietes,' she repeated, taking a small step back. 'But do not be afraid; I am not here by any design of my father's. I am priestess of Hecate; I serve here at this, her temple.'

'He did mention you,' smiled Jason while in his mind persisted an image of the statue that loomed directly behind him. 'And you knew my name. This is worrying since you're not the first complete stranger to tell me who I am though it is something I'm getting used to. Tell me how this is; I can't see how Aietes had time to explain anything.'

'I have my powers, Jason, which is why I serve here.'

'Yet you are as beautiful as that – that image whose temple you serve is disagreeable. No, it's damned ugly if you don't mind me saying so. But tell me more; tell me about this Hecate then more about yourself.'

'Hecate is a goddess of many aspects but mainly of the night, of witchcraft and sorcery. She possesses, too, a deep knowledge of herbs and of plants that may cure or may – or may do otherwise. Her true image is unknown and her statue was created uncounted years ago by unknown hands. As for me, I am the youngest of Aietes' daughters although my older sisters and brothers all have different mothers. I might be his daughter but I regret deeply that he is my father though I have always shown him my allegiance and my respect no matter how difficult at times that may have been, especially now.'

'Especially now?' queried Jason, reluctant to avert his gaze from her.

'Especially now,' she sighed, 'and better if we keep our voices down. I say what I say because my four half-brothers, all younger than you, he plans to have blinded and maimed outside the palace, yes, in front of the whole town, then thrown into some foul, vermin infested cellar for whatever is left of their lives. I - I cannot bear the thought of it.'

'Yes, he did speak of them, but give me your own reasons why he would do that.'

'Because he believes they were plotting to overthrow him even though it was no more than

153

hearsay. No one dares express sympathy for any of those accused or later executed. If someone is arrested or disappears, no one will dare ask why. Given the chance our people would rise against the oppressive tyrant my father has for so long been but are afraid to speak their mind in case they are denounced by someone close. He's demanded I help him expose his enemies but I tell him Hecate forbids it. I have risked pleading with him to be more lenient, to banish those four, to enslave them even, but he derives much pleasure from doing to people what he does. Those unfortunate men you will have seen hanging from the city wall; some he didn't have executed straight away but cut out their tongues and had them placed out there alive to prolong their suffering. Often, when any remained alive at sunset, he would set out with his bodyguard to stand with a goblet of wine and gaze up at them before returning to revel in the company of the palace women, usually our slaves. *That* is the sort of man you have taken wine with; a man who treats suffering and death as a kind of – of horrid entertainment.'

'Yes, how could anyone fail to notice those poor devils when near to the city wall – how could they not. And what crimes had most of those men actually committed?'

'They were accused of plotting or subordination,' she replied, 'but some, those reduced mainly to bone were men from the sea. They had – they had planned to do what you came here to do. The crew of their vessel he had tortured and executed then had their boat set adrift on the river where it would be carried out to sea.'

'What d'you mean when you say, what *I* came to do?'

'I mean they had planned to seize and to take away the Golden Fleece – to deprive my father of his power.'

'And how,' Jason asked, 'd'you know *that*? And only moments ago you spoke as if you expected me to come here. Was that knowledge also imparted to your father?'

'No it was not. I knew you were coming and I knew why because of – because of those powers handed on to me when my mother passed on. She was herself an acolyte of our goddess and many considered her divine. But this you must also understand – my father will suspect why you are here and will not allow you and your men to leave the land of Colchis alive.'

'Er, yes, he may already be convinced,' responded Jason, 'because over a goblet and more of his wine I played the fool and told him as if in jest I'd do a deal with him to get the Golden Fleece. I was curious to see what his reaction might be. I realise now how stupid that was but at the time those – those words just came out.'

Medea stared up at him in wide-eyed disbelief. 'Yes, that was - that was *not* a good idea. He doubtless gave you the strongest of our wines to loosen your tongue.'

'And he succeeded, didn't he. So when d'you think he'll make his move - d'you know that?'

'I believe he is presently undecided, in part because of those men you have encamped by the river so he wishes to entertain you further before he acts. He already has those of your men who came to the palace with you distracted by wine and the women of his court, as I'm sure you know. It is in his nature to torment, to lead people on with promises of great reward - of the Golden Fleece itself. In order to attain it they are offered ridiculous or demeaning challenges he knows perfectly well they can never overcome.'

'Then he'll doubtless be entertaining me in full this evening. Meanwhile I'll attend to my men as best I can and hope they're sober and willing enough to have their wits about them.' He looked up into the obscurity of the ceiling and muttered, 'Heracles, where are you now?'

'What was that you said?' asked Medea. Light from Hecate's torches danced brightly in her eyes.

'Oh, nothing. One question I will ask you; this so-called Golden Fleece; you must know more about it than anyone else. But covered in gold dust or not, it's only a damned sheepskin is it not, even if some people, like my own father, heard that it came from a golden ram. So why is it of such importance to Aietes and why have others risked so much trying to obtain the thing?'

'Yes,' she replied, 'it is as you say, just a sheepskin to those few who first set eyes upon it, but there is more you should know. My mother found it laying within an ancient altar beneath our temple but knew nothing of its origins. She took it to my father who saw it as a propitious sign for the beginning of his reign and had it announced to all by the priesthood that it arrived one night as a winged ram created by Hermes and had magical powers. He then had it dedicated to Zeus. Over the years the tale has spread wide and become ever more embellished. But one thing I do know because I saw it when I was a child; on the inside of the Fleece is written an incantation to some unknown god. My father will go to the shrine where the Fleece is kept and there he will speak this message. It is in a strange, an ancient language but he can recite much of it and claims he is able to ask who is speaking or plotting against him. He claims the voice of this god touches his thoughts and though it speaks to him only in riddles, he says he has learned to understand some of what is said. So you see, to my father, to the King of Colchis, the Golden Fleece helps to protect his wealth and his power. It has come to represent the soul and strength of the city and the whole of Colchis and that is why rumours of its worth have seeped out and spread so far afield.'

'And you believe his claims?'

'I – no, I think the voice he hears is in his mind only, but it serves to justify much of what he does. Some of those beyond our shores who have learned of its reputation through the words of travellers, like the man who sent you here, believe it is a direct link to the higher gods. Others believe the tales are fanciful nonsense but then, in the temples of other lands, there are objects of devotion that may have small material value but represent everything to those who possess them. At Troy they have the Palladium, just a carved wooden statue of a girl, yet

157

so highly do they value it that they claim the city will fall if ever it is taken from them. As for what the Golden Fleece really is, I have learned how the mountain people far from here obtain gold by staking out sheepskins in the gravel beds of their streams where grains of gold carried down by the water will stick to and build up on them. But that is of no importance to my father now that the one obtained by him bears its message and rests under guard in the holiest of places.'

'Then it might be worth my visiting these mountain people and grabbing one of their fleeces,' smiled Jason. 'Old Pelias back in Iolcos wouldn't know the difference as he's never been here, though I suspect he would still demand proof of its origin.' Jason hesitated, thought for some moments then added, 'But I doubt if my men would stand for an inland expedition when they still expect to make a profit out of this one. Look, when I've next spoken with Aietes are we to meet again?'

'Of course, we must, we have to meet again for your, for all our sakes. Return here after dark – I will be waiting, no matter how late. My father will be otherwise occupied with his female slaves. He prefers slaves because he can make them do what the nobler women of his court would rather not.'

Each gazed into the eyes of the other and Medea, pushing closer, whispered, 'Jason, dear, kiss me.'

Jason readily obliged as each slipped arms about the other. Medea's kisses were passionate and Jason returned them with equal ardour before whispering, 'Look, I have to go. Aietes mustn't suspect this is happening.'

'No he must not,' she sighed, releasing but slowly her hold on him.

159

Chapter 7 - The Golden Fleece

"Jason, dear!" Oh, yes, that's exactly what I said. I'd fallen for him there and then in full measure. Maybe you're thinking I above all should have studied him further, seen what might happen and let common sense gain more ground. But I was rather too impressionable to bother checking out the path of my own life just then, even had it been possible – not that, I suspect, it would have helped. No, there was too much opposition from on high. It was what they, the gods, intended.'

***

Jason returned to the palace, strolling casually as if at ease with a world that, in spite of sunlit skies, lay beneath a cloud of uncertainty and danger. He was watched closely by the guards but not challenged as he passed between them without a glance. Hesitating at the entrance to the megaron he saw Aietes throne was unoccupied and only a small number of courtiers and slaves were present.

Laughter and animated chatter drifted from the adjacent dining hall where, on reaching the doorway, he observed six of his men were still there, four amorously attended by women, two of them much under the influence of wine and seeming largely unaware of what was happening around them. The remaining four, he assumed, would have retired into intimate privacy with their women or returned to the ship. Only one in the room acknowledged his presence, Polydeuces, who though in the company of two of the palace girls,

160

appeared still to be in charge of his faculties. He realized Jason wished to speak with him so easing the girls aside he arose and made his way around the hall.

'Polydeuces,' said Jason, 'we need to talk somewhere away from here.'

'Aye, sir, I'm with you.'

They were soon in the courtyard where fountains played, also out of earshot and out of sight of the guards and Jason said, 'I'm sorry to curtail your pleasures my friend but you, me, all of us may be, no, probably are in considerable danger.'

Seeming relatively sober, Polydeuces grinned widely, saying, 'Oh, no, sir, I've already 'ad my pleasures so I'll 'ear all you 'ave to tell me.'

'You'll recall the measures we had to take to gather our men away from the charms of Lemnos; a task Heracles managed with considerable success.'

'Aye, sir, I recall it well – a paradise on Earth that was.'

'Well this town is no paradise at all unless you're cheered by the sight of those corpses hanging on display about the city gate. I must ask you to undertake the same task with our men here as did Heracles on Lemnos. They may not be sober but you'll have a far smaller number to deal with. While I'm back with Aietes, which will be later this afternoon, round them up and get those men of ours back to the ship, reluctant or not but as quietly and as quickly as you can while I keep Aietes occupied.'

'What if we're challenged?' asked Polydeuces.

'I don't know what instructions, if any, Aietes has given his men other than to keep an eye on me but – but if you *are* challenged away from the palace then ensure no message gets back to him – if you see what I mean.'

'You can depend on me, sir,' assured Polydeuces, raising his formidable right fist, 'an' I'll see to it all our lads see reason.'

'I'm sure you will, and once you're back at *Argo* have all her crew prepared for trouble.'

Now alone with time in hand, Jason strolled into the busy market square to peruse the stalls and traders; a square alive with chattering people, dashing children and yapping dogs. Listening to their conversation and seeing their attire, he concluded most of the traders were from lands quite unfamiliar to the people of Thessaly. Much of the food and the many spices and herbs on offer were also strange to him. He spotted leather sandals of a quality often seen at home and asked the owner of the stall. 'What will you accept in silver for those?'

The man's reply was coarse, guttural and barely understandable. 'I'll take them,' said Jason, offering the stallholder the small clipping of silver he knew would have been acceptable in the markets at Pelion. 'You never know,' he grinned, 'I might get back home without losing one of 'em.'

Deaf to his comment, the man accepted his silver eagerly and Jason wished he had offered less. He moved on to another trader, one whose speech sounded closer to his own. 'Do those corpses by the city gate affect your trade?' he asked.

'No, sir,' the man replied, 'people are used to all that, but we smell the poor buggers when the

162

wind blows this way. Hm, it's not at all pleasant, no it isn't.'

'I'm sure it isn't,' responded Jason, stepping back. Looking about the square he noted once more the two guards who had watched him earlier and had doubtless been there much of the time. The temple would probably be out of bounds to them when armed, as those temples in his own land were. Clutching his new sandals he strolled casually about the square until the sun had fallen well below the city wall and the traders were bundling away their goods. Eventually he re-entered the palace with the two guards closing behind and there made his way to the megaron where Aietes was seated on his throne in conversation with a group of courtiers. Aietes looked up, saw Jason and the guards approach, dismissed those in attendance, but not the two guards.

'So 'ere we are once again!' he declared, rising from his seat. Let's retire to my chamber an' discuss matters over a bit of food and wine.' With a slur in his voice, Aietes gave the impression of one already having indulged a quantity of alcohol. He summoned and instructed a male slave who hurried away, as Jason assumed, to the palace kitchens, then gestured for Jason to follow to the chamber where the initial face to face meeting with Aietes had taken place. There his guards were ordered to remain outside the door. Upon his small table stood an amphora of wine and a pair of ornate gold goblets. Jason placed his newly acquired sandals on the floor by his chair as both men sat to face one another each side of the table. Only moments after

163

Aietes had poured the wine with an unsteady hand, the door was opened and three plainly gowned young girls bearing dishes entered the room. The dishes, Jason suspected, must have been prepared in anticipation of his arrival. Among their cold contents familiar from his homeland were flatbreads, broad beans, olives, figs and sliced meat. He was provided also with a small knife.

'Well I'm honoured to be here dining with the mighty King of Colchis,' smiled Jason, taking his first, cautious sip of wine; a caution he intended to maintain until leaving Aietes' company.

'I don't get too many princes visitin' this town,' responded Aietes, gulping his own wine, 'especially ones lookin' to steal me property – though it 'as 'appened. But, yes, you are very definitely 'onoured because you 'ave 'ere before you beef rather than mule or 'orse. An' I'm told you prefer nice little puppy dogs f'dinner back 'ome. Aye, woof-woof-woof an' into the cookin' pot they go!'

Jason hesitated to stare amused at the man as he rocked back and forth in his chair, laughing raucously before he continued, 'An' you've met me daughter, aye, the one that spends most of 'er life in 'er temple. She's said to be good at seein' things other people can't but she doesn't see very much for me. Was she expectin' you, then? Was she accommodatin', if y'see what I mean?'

'She was amiable enough,' Jason replied as Aietes belched loudly.

'But let's get down to it 'ere an' now,' Aietes rumbled, leaning forward to glare hard at him. 'If you want the Golden Fleece, 'you 'ave to earn it so - so I've a proposition t'make.'

'Oh, really, a proposition!' exclaimed Jason, who saw no point now in maintaining the original excuse for his visit to Colchis. 'I was offered a proposition not so long ago by someone closer to home. That's why I'm here now. But do go on.'

'Well,' responded Aietes as his face broke into a leering grin, 'there's a field outside the city wall needs ploughin' an' I've a pair of excellent bulls ready to 'elp you do the job, both of 'em with breath that burns like fire - 'ot enough to fry yer arse. Then there's dragons' teeth kept in the main temple – these you cast about when the field is ready an' wait until they sprout armed men. Aye, an' once you've dealt with these the Golden Fleece will be yours to take all the way 'ome. All the way 'ome – if the dragon that guards it isn't lookin' when you go to fetch it.'

Jason continued to eat then said, calmly, 'You're too kind, really. I'll give this some thought then perhaps we can discuss it further in the morning.'

'Really?' mocked Aietes, 'I'm too, too fuckin' kind, y'say. But don't leave things too long, *I* say. Don't want to end up 'angin' about too long do we – might end up 'angin about longer than y'think, if y'see what I mean.'

He pushed aside his food, belched again, stared coldly at Jason but said nothing more. Draining his goblet which he thumped heavily down upon the table, he stood abruptly, gripped the edge of the table, clattered his chair noisily back then left the chamber with an unsteady gait, laughing to himself and muttering, 'Huh, end up 'angin' about – aye, 'angin' about the town wall.'

The door remained open and Jason, finishing his own food but leaving the remains of his wine, arose to find the guards, surprisingly, had also departed. There were people going about their business in the megaron where a fire in the great circular stone hearth at its centre blazed brightly. Aietes' throne was again unoccupied. Hand firmly on his sword hilt, Jason, glancing from side to side, left the palace, ignored by the guards at its main entrance who, to his surprise, sat resting against the wall either side of the door with their heads bowed. He crossed the courtyard, now in darkness, and stepped out into the market square where he hesitated to listen hard. There were subdued voices but one in particular, commanding in its tone, he recognized. Standing by a column, Jason watched the group of men heading toward the city gate though found it too dark to count their number. 'Polydeuces must have discovered another way out of the palace,' he muttered. 'Who needs Heracles.'

Under a moonlit sky he returned to the temple of Hecate eased open and stepped through the heavy doors to see again the torch-lit interior where the bizarre statue of the goddess loomed at the far end in the light of her own torches. This time there were no dogs present to signal his arrival so he closed the doors and stood to listen. Several heartbeats passed before he continued on to where he hesitated a few steps away from the statue. The silence was profound. Profound, so he imagined, as if he stood enclosed within a deep chasm. But still he waited.

Then Medea's voice as a gentle breeze in the night. 'Jason, I am here.'

Jason turned to look at her, saying, 'Ah, good, I wondered if you'd -.'

'Did you think I wouldn't be here waiting for you?' she asked.

'I'm not sure what I thought – this is all so strange.' He noted the linen bag she clutched under her left arm but thought it not important enough to question.

'You spoke with my father and I know what he's challenged you to do. He's done it before to others.'

'Yes, he intends to humiliate me,' said Jason. 'Is there any truth at all in anything he said – about these bulls, I mean, and dragons' teeth?'

'Yes, the bulls do exist. They are bred through a line of savage beasts and of those few men rash enough to accept the challenge, none survived the ordeal. Those who refused were – well, you have witnessed what he does to rid himself of people he considers undesirable. When there's no room close to the city gate he has them burned alive in the market square. So either way he intends you would lose. As for the so-called dragon's teeth; they have been contained here within an ancient oak casket for longer than anyone knows. It is believed they will do what my father told you they would, but the casket was opened only once and its contents never used because no one ever got that far.'

'I watched my men leave the city and make their way back to the river,' said Jason. 'I saw no one following them though Aietes had a couple of his men tailing me earlier. Strangely enough I didn't see any others around tonight except a pair of them lounging by the palace door as if they were asleep. Let's hope for their sake your father doesn't pass that way.'

'They really *were* asleep,' she said, 'and you would not see any others. I arranged the wine ration for all those on duty tonight. They will be soundly asleep until morning.'

'Are you – are you saying you have them drugged – all of them?'

'Yes, but if father finds out and sees your men are gone he'll call out the entire palace guard. He'll guess who was responsible and that could well be the end of me. I doubt he'd have any more regard for my life than he would for yours. You may think it improper of me to say this of my own father, but I believe the gods have deprived him of reason and as well as compassion. I believe he is possessed by demons.'

'Improper, no; he surely is as you say – possessed. He is also cunning and unpredictable; I'd say we're both clear on that. Tonight, though, he may be too drunk to care. And what's this about someone or something guarding his precious Fleece? A few moments ago you mentioned what others have said, including your father, that the Golden Fleece is guarded. He used the word, dragon. Is this some foolish tale to scare people

168

away for surely there must be armed guards posted there? If so, how many?'

'There are no men guarding it,' she breathed, 'because none are needed.'

'A dragon is more or less what he meant and yes, it truly exists; a dreadful creature created many years ago by the gods to guard the shrine. My dear father sacrificed much to obtain it, though mainly in secret. I have witnessed the thing awakened only in my visions but it is a truly fearsome sight. It bides its time but I have the power to know its mind in its lair and I tell you, it waits unseen for any who approach.'

'Sounds worse than the Harpies. Is it a creature of this or some other world? What I mean is, can it be killed?'

'It can be killed,' she replied, 'with the help of certain incantations I possess.'

'It seems you have many strange and wonderful powers. But these incantations – will you deliver them for me at the shrine? I must somehow get hold of that damned fleece and it's pretty obvious I have only tonight to do it.'

'Jason, dear,' sighed Medea, letting fall the bag then slipping her arms about him, 'I will help you but -.'

'But what?' he breathed, feeling the carnal heat of her breath. They kissed several times, each kiss more passionate than the one preceding, then she eased away to answer his question.

'But I must ask that you take me with you. My life will depend on this - and you must let me be your wife.'

169

'My wife! Look - I swear I'll get you away from here, but -.'

'Jason, this is escape to freedom for both of us but I will not be abandoned afterwards nor will I be dishonoured.'

Jason stepped back to reappraise her alluring form, her raven-black hair, her deep pool eyes, her full and inviting red lips. Even in the gloom of the temple her beauty shone as a flame.

'This will be your, our, one and only chance, Jason, darling,' Medea assured him. 'This town carries a stench of death. I have no wish to remain here as part of it.'

That she was a most desirable woman he had no doubt, and somewhat younger than himself, but her request was not at all what he might have expected. He stepped forward, placed arms about her waist as she did about his shoulders and though doubts stirred deep within he gave her the answer she so needed - the answer she demanded. 'When we're safely away from here, yes we will be married.'

He gazed captivated into eyes that reflected the light of the torches as she spoke again. 'And, Jason, I confided with Chalciope, mother of my four half-brothers who are held prisoner within the palace. She begs you to rescue her sons and to take them with us. I know where they are kept and the guards, as I told you, will not awaken.'

'What - rescue other people before I face this – this, whatever it is that guards the Fleece! Ah - yes, they are the ones he mentioned, as did you, and I recall what he intends to do with them, but -.'

'Please Jason, we can release them first and very soon and send them to your vessel. They of course know the path and when aboard they will serve as you wish.'

'Will they now. And this damned shrine – you say it's not far away.'

'No, not far at all. The Golden Fleece is held in a cavern on my father's sacred land a short way outside the city wall; I will take you there as soon as those boys are freed.'

'You also take a lot for granted,' declared Jason. 'You really did know we were heading this way didn't you and had all the time needed to lay your plans.'

Medea picked up her bag, smiled at him and whispered, 'Follow me now; I have prayed to Hecate to give you strength and to guide your sword, and in my dreams she has promised her help.'

'Well that's worth knowing,' he muttered. 'A sword is all I have with me – no spear, no shield and no armour.'

He eyed the bag that now had acquired some significance. Medea noted his interest and said, 'It's just a few of my personal things and – and some silver I have to take with me.'

'You're taking – damn! I paid silver for new sandals in your market place and left them in Aietes' chamber after out last meeting.'

'You cannot go back there now; you'd have to pass through the megaron.'

'You're right,' he breathed, 'it's too much of a risk and we've too little time.'

171

Cool night air bathed their faces as they hurried across the market square and into the palace courtyard. There were no guards other than those asleep at the palace entrance. Medea entered with Jason, sword part drawn, close behind. At one side of the short passage, illuminated by one of several burning torches, another two men sat with their backs against the wall, heads tilted forward, their helmets and spears resting close by. Before reaching the megaron, from where voices and music could be heard, they turned abruptly left to be confronted by a flight of stone steps that descended into utter blackness. Jason reached to lift one of the torches away from the wall and they proceeded cautiously down. On reaching the bottom they continued along a corridor that soon opened out into a torch-lit room where several men, some armed, lay or sat sprawled about the flagstones. Medea and Jason hesitated to look around and in those tense moments were aware of course breathing and spluttered snoring. From a wooden table where rested two wine jars and a number of earthenware goblets, Medea seized a metal-ringed cluster of keys.

'This way,' she whispered and they started down a second, narrower flight of steps with their own shadows swaying and dancing as black demons about the cold stone walls and low-arched ceiling. The air was chilling and damp when they reached the bottom and tainted by an odour of corruption. They entered a rough-stoned chamber where a number of heavy, bronze-reinforced doors were spaced apart in what would, were it not for the torch held by Jason, be utter, fetid blackness. Muffled voices and pitiful murmurings drifted from behind some of the doors but Medea stepped across to one and, trying three of the keys, found the fourth would release the lock. Jason, close by her side, reached to slide open two protesting bronze bolts. As the door grated inward she called in a harsh whisper, 'It's me – it's Medea. Come out of there. Hurry and we'll get you away from here.'

Four mop-haired figures, hardly more than boys, emerged cautious and confused from the cell, disheveled, begrimed and stubbled, their hands raised against the light from Jason's torch.

'You're free and there's a boat waiting,' said Jason. 'We don't have much time.'

None of the four spoke as, hands pressing against the side walls, they clambered up the lower stairs ahead of Jason and Medea. In the halfway room where the guards and others lay they hesitated and one of the young men turned to Medea and asked, 'Are these men properly out?'

'Of course they are,' hissed Medea, 'Come along now.'

'Wait,' said another and all four spread about the room to roughly haul about and divest four of the sleepers of their tunics, sandals, belts and swords while Jason took up a fallen spear, thinking briefly once again about the newly acquired sandals that had been laid aside in Aietes' chamber. With the youths clutching their newly gained attire and weapons they ascended the upper flight of steps, into the corridor, then out into the welcoming clean air of the courtyard. Jason, torch and spear in hand, expected they would head straight for the market

173

square then out of the town to the river, but here was to be yet another delay as the four escapees rushed to the nearest fountain. There they discarded their befouled clothes, drank and revelled in the cleansing embrace of fresh water.

'We don't have time for this,' Jason told her in impatient tone.

'We have to let them do it,' she replied. 'They've been confined in darkness and filth for many days.'

As she spoke, a figure approached from the darkness and Jason, grasping the burning torch high in his left hand, raised his spear ready to strike.

'It's Apsyrtus!' gasped Medea as she recognized the newcomer, a man of courtly bearing. 'He's one of Aietes sons.'

'Is he really,' breathed Jason. 'Then I'll ensure his silence once and for all.'

But the man, dark and bearded, barely older than Jason himself, halted some steps away and raised both hands in a gesture of defence. Jason, his spear levelled at the other's chest, looked questioningly at Medea who asked Apsyrtus, 'What are you doing here?'

'I couldn't sleep,' he replied. 'I came out to take the night air then I saw your torch and those men in the fountain. You have released them from beneath the palace have you not?'

Medea offered no reply then Jason said to her, 'Get over there and have them back with us before anyone else shows up.' She left his side and Jason, laying his spear on the ground with the free hand falling to his sword hilt, turned to Apsyrtus. 'Now

174

my friend, you have two options – you come with us or I cut you down.'

Apsyrtus stared wide-eyed at Jason, kept his hands palm up in full view and replied, 'Look, I take it you're from that vessel downriver and intending soon to leave. I'll go with you willingly, yes, willingly. I - I've no wish to stay here; my father and our entire house has many enemies inside and outside the city. It's only a matter of time before we're set upon in the market square or murdered in our beds so I'll gladly go – but where are you headed?'

'We return through the Euxine Sea on our way to Thessaly,' Jason informed him. The man showed no reaction.

Voices were heard as the four youths approached, busily tugging and adjusting newly acquired tunics over wet bodies then fixing on their swords. Medea stood some way back, wringing her hands with impatience over the delay and Jason's intentions toward the newcomer. The four, on recognizing Apsyrtus, appeared ready to tear him apart but Jason raised a hand, saying, 'One of you get another torch then all go to our vessel moored by the old jetty. You know where I mean do you not?'

'Yes we do,' replied one of the youths. He stared hard at Apsyrtus, laid a hand on his sword hilt, then asked, 'And what're you or what're we to do with him?'

'Remove his sword belt, take him with you and if he tries to escape, consign him to the river. Tell Argos, my captain what has happened and have him keep a close eye on our friend here. We'll be with you before sunrise or sooner.' Then he added under his breath, 'I hope.'

One of the four dashed back into the palace entrance to emerge moments later holding high a second firebrand. With Apsyrtus walking behind two of them and with two following him, the small group made their way in silence across the courtyard. Before they vanished from sight, Medea said to Jason, 'I don't trust that man and nor should you – no son of Aietes should *ever* be trusted.'

'Fine,' breathed Jason, sheathing his sword and picking up his spear, 'then if he makes it to the ship he'll be leaving with us. Come on - let's get this over with.'

'Apsyrtus is considered the king's favourite and next in line for the throne,' said Medea as they hurried on. 'No other of his sons would put himself forward for fear of his life. Those four young men you can trust because Aietes had them condemned to eventual death. One wrong move from Apsyrtus and they'll gladly kill him.'

***

In the cellars below Aietes palace there were voices. 'Some of 'em are snorin' so I say they're not dead but drugged an' some of 'em robbed,' declared one of the three newly arrived guards as they trod about, staring down at the sprawled-out figures. 'Who'll tell the king?'

'Not me,' declared the second, 'not at this time of the night either.'

'Not at any time of any night,' muttered the third, 'but someone 'as to.'

176

'Aye, we'll 'ave to tell someone as we're the relief for some of this lot,' said the first. 'We'll 'ave to let Damon know. He's 'ead of the palace guard so let 'im deal with it.' They agreed that was what they would do and set off to locate the man in question.

A short while later, with plumed helmet clasped under his left arm, the burly Damon approached Aietes' chamber with his three men where, at its closed entrance, two further guards and an aged male slave waited. 'Is the king awake?' Damon asked. 'I need to speak with 'im.' The two guards looked at one another then at the slave but neither spoke. 'You go in there,' Damon ordered the slave. 'Tell 'im there's important matter needs 'is attention and that I'm waitin' outside.' The slave hesitated. When one of the guards raised a hand to strike him the man backed wide eyed to the heavy oak door, turned and tapped three times. 'Harder!' snapped Damon, and the wretched man did so.

From within the chamber a voice barked. 'Who's that?'

'Get in there and tell 'im!' ordered Damon.

The slave, trembling visibly, opened the door and entered a room illuminated only by the swaying flame of a single small oil lamp. From a bed further inside, Aietes growled, 'This'd better be important.'

The slave spoke though his words were not intelligible from outside the chamber. Then Aietes' voice boomed, 'Then tell 'im to get in 'ere now and you fuck off out!'

Damon entered as the slave, head lowered, scampered by. With sufficient torchlight entering

177

the room, Damon was able to see Aietes sitting up in his heavily carved wooden bed. 'What's goin' on?' the king demanded. 'It's not even light outside.'

'My Lord,' replied Damon, 'the four sons of Chalciope have escaped and the guards as well as others in charge down there lie drugged and unconscious. Some of them are relieved of their clothes and weapons.'

'Drugged were they!' Aietes growled as he scrambled naked from his bed and reached for his robe. 'An' 'ow did they get fuckin' drugged – who did that and 'ow'd they fuckin' well manage it? Tell me that!'

'I know, sir, that your daughter, the Lady Medea, 'ad wine sent down to them but I thought little of it as she's done so before. It reached me earlier, also, that those men from the boat by the old jetty 'ave not been seen for some time.'

Pulling on the robe, Aietes stared hard at him, mouthing in ominous tones, 'Well *I* can guess what's 'appened all right – that, I can! 'Ave one of your men go find my daughter in 'Ecate's temple an' bring 'er straight to me – drag 'er 'ere if you 'ave to. Call out the city guard an' get our sturdier vessels manned double quick. We'll get after those bastards an' by Zeus I'll 'ave that bugger in charge of 'em an' a few of 'is pals decoratin' the city wall. Aye an' beggin' me for the quick death they'll not 'ave!' As Damon stepped away, Aietes called after him, 'An' get armed men with a couple of priests over to check all's well at the shrine!'

***

178

Two figures guided by one shimmering torch had set off some time earlier, hurrying across the market square and out through the main city gate beneath a starry sky. Jason had glanced up as they left the gate but the moon was in its first quarter and the corrupting corpses, so gruesomely evident in daylight, were hardly visible. With Medea stepping ahead they carried on, part skirting the city wall before they found themselves amid encroaching bushes on a barely discernable path. Jason said, 'I imagined the route to Aietes' famous shrine would be far clearer than this.'

'No, there are very few who care to venture close to the place other than priests who come to replenish the torches before nightfall. They return to make sacrificial offerings in the light of day and none of them care to remain a moment longer than is necessary. The creature sets out at night to claim its offerings and sometimes stalks the woods to seize and devour any living thing it comes upon - or any one.'

'And how often d'you make your way here?' he asked as they trudged on.

'I've been close enough only once to watch the priests at one of their brief ceremonies during the day when the creature is said to sleep, though it never truly does. I've never seen it awakened but I know of the thing by other means, as I already told you. It was never revealed to me from where it came. Why the gods gave it life or what my father sacrificed to obtain it was hidden even from Hecate but I believe it was one of his own children.'

As she spoke, lights appeared ahead and moments later their source was revealed. They emerged from the bushes into an ominously calm stillness, a stillness charged with impending menace. Directly before them across clear ground lay a cliff, dark against the night sky and rising to over three times the height of a man. At its base was a grotto, lit either side of its entrance by a burning brand placed on wall brackets less than an arm's length within. They approached to find close before the entrance a blood-drenched table, a wooden altar upon which rested an offering, the part-eaten remains of some large but unidentifiable animal. The carcass glistened, still wet in the light of the torches and they saw it was infested already by a myriad of small, writhing, wriggling creatures.

Jason sensed Medea's apprehension. 'So it needs to eat,' he said as they paused before the altar. 'If it needs to eat then it truly lives and can be killed.'

'It is as I told you,' replied Medea, closing her eyes as she clutched his arm, 'but of the few who avoided my father and got as far as this, none survived to speak of it.'

'This may not be the best time to ask,' muttered Jason, 'but what happened to them?'

'Two were seized and devoured by the creature and one escaped only to be caught later and executed with some of his men. Others from their vessel were condemned to the quarries where they were worked to death in chains.'

'I smell a foulness in the air,' said Jason. 'It was so with the Harpies but this - this is -.'

'It is the stench of pure evil,' she cut in. 'It is an evil beyond anything I ever knew.'

At the gloomy rear of the cavern Jason saw there had been placed upright a dead tree. From one of its branches hung the object of his quest. 'So that's Aietes' precious fleece,' he said, quietly. 'It's surely an ordinary sheepskin covered in gold dust yet men have given their lives trying obtain it.' As they moved closer he added, 'I don't see this so-called dragon yet.'

'No,' she whispered, 'you see nothing, but it sees us and it waits until we attempt to flee. I know Hera watches over you but I call as well upon Hecate because she is closer and knows the nature of beast.'

'Then here's to them both,' said Jason, handing her the torch while levelling the spear to test its balance, 'but I hope well-sharpened bronze might also come in useful.' He moved closer to peer inside the entrance but Medea lowered her linen bag to the ground and remained where she was with the torch held high and the fingers of her free hand raised to her mouth as she murmured, 'Jason, I regret more with each breath that we ever came here!'

The air was cold and small vortices touched him here and there as tiny insects scampering over his flesh. Until standing on the threshold of the cavern his attention had been only upon the fleece but now, able to see over the altar, his gaze fell to the floor he would have to cross. Between himself and that which he desired, the ground within the cavern arose in the manner of a hillock – but not one of earth or rock. Upon it Jason discerned a

181

pattern, a glistening pattern the nature of which became clearer as he looked on. The pattern resembled scales, not scales of bronze as worn by fighting men but scales that might be seen on a lizard, though very much larger.

He glanced back at Medea whose fingers now clutched hard at her cheek. 'Jason,' she called, 'forget the damned fleece! Please, I beg you! Let's run fast as we can to your ship!'

'I'll not run away now!' he cried. 'By all the gods of Olympus I will not!'

Switching his attention back to the grotto he laid a hand on the heavy altar intending to drag this and its gristly remains out of his way but within the cavern something stirred. A subterranean breathing, a coarse hissing arose to shiver the air as looking up at the sky Medea began to recite loudly her words. The scale covered mound heaved. It began to rise, extricating its half buried form from the earth. A white-clawed arm appeared, flexing, reaching upward. Now arose the dark reptilian head, large as that of a horse but flatter with dagger-like white teeth set within a gaping, drooling mouth from where flickered a glistening, tar-black tongue. Yellow speckled eyes, oddly human in form, fixed hard upon Jason as this insane nightmare continued to shed crumbling soil. Its other arm and rear limbs were visible then its entire body, larger than that of a bear as it writhed up from the hollow where it had lain. Transfixed by the sight of it, Jason, oblivious to Medea's desperate incantations, gripped the spear, thinking to hold back before casting as the creature appeared slow and cumbersome. With shocking suddenness it reared up and rending the air with a demented shriek it made to seize him in its claws. With one hand Jason grasped the table, its bloody contents skidding away as, crouching low, he raised it to use as a shield. The guardian of the shrine, eyes glaring, mouth wide, sprang forward but its head struck the table so hard as to split and hurl it from Jason's grasp. The creature reeled back with a howl of rage that might have reached the stars above as it poised for a final, murderous strike against this foolish intruder whose flesh it would tear, whose bones it would crunch in its jaws, whose warm blood it would gulp. Unyielding determination vied with fear as Jason leapt forward with his spear raised to strike. As he passed between the torches they flared out to illuminate the cavern as a blaze of raw sunlight that startled and dazzled the creature. Jason felt himself in possession of powers he had never known as with a cry he plunged his blade hard and deep between those murderous jaws. The beast raged and shook its head violently to dislodge the shaft but with sword flashing from his scabbard, Jason struck again, this time into the neck, feeling yet greater strength surge through his limbs as he thrust his blade again and again between yielding scales. Blood issued copiously and the creature, with head jerking back and forth, fell choking gore and sank back into the pit from which it had arisen. Jason heard its murmuring growl, watched it quiver, saw its eyes close, its clawed limbs settle and become still. He continued to stare, bloodied sword at the ready in case any sign of life should return.

Then a voice from behind, 'No longer can I feel its life force! Jason, the thing is dead!'

Jason glanced back at her. Medea stood by the shattered table, eyes wide, mouth ajar and with both hands clasping the torch. Lowering the sword but still cautious, Jason stepped by the guardian of the Golden Fleece, whose blood still issued freely. 'And now I have it!' he declared, reaching for the fleece with outspread fingers. It felt soft to his touch as, grasping one edge, he lifted it from the branch. The light within the cavern was returning to its former strength, the firebrand flames diminishing as he stepped back into the open to stand before Medea.

'Oh, Jason,' she breathed, reaching to touch the fleece, 'We – you have done what others suffered and died hoping to do.'

'I felt as – as though another was with me. And then the light brightened as I -.'

'The light - I don't understand. But let us go now! Please - now!'

He knelt to wipe his sword clean on the grass, saying, 'Yes, we have to get to the ship; I don't know how much longer this torch will last. We must get there and cast off before daylight or before Aietes discovers what's been happening.'

'My father will call out the city guard,' she said picking up her bag as he took the torch from her. 'Hundreds of armed men. We must hurry!'

'And this,' said Jason, holding the fleece tightly as they hurried back through the bushes, 'it may be covered in gold dust but it's a sheepskin like any other I've seen or held.'

184

They were soon approaching the city wall around part of which they would have to detour so as to gain the river path. They were passing a short way from the main gate and its macabre embellishments when Medea glanced aside to exclaim, 'Oh, I see lights showing through there and people moving about!'

Voices could be heard, there were shouts and the harsh, three times repeated notes of a ram's horn drifted from within the city.

'There are men carrying torches about the main square,' said Jason, following her gaze. 'Aietes must know what's been happening.'

'What if they see our torch?' asked Medea.

'It's a chance we'll have to take,' responded Jason as they hurried on. 'The sky's beginning to brighten but we'll still need some light on the river path and that's straight ahead. Come on, we're going to make it because we damned well have to.'

They reached the path and stumbled on, avoiding rocks and fallen branches that in the daytime would hardly have mattered, and now their firebrand was giving forth more smoke and less light then earlier.

'Does your father have many ships?' Jason asked at one point. The path seemed long – longer by far than he remembered.

'Yes, many,' she replied. 'He uses them to patrol the river and the coast for pirates as well as anyone he thinks might be a threat.'

'Really – then that must be just about everyone.'

On they hurried until at last there were fires visible ahead, a whiff of smoke drifted by and voices could be heard. 'We're almost there,' said Jason, as he hurled the faltering torch through the bushes and into the river.

It was Argos himself, standing on the jetty, who spotted two figures emerge from amidst the trees. He strode along, recognized Jason and called, 'Welcome back, young sir! Good to see you!' He eyed Medea and the fleece as Jason asked, 'How soon can we sail?'

'How soon – well certainly before sun-up - our vessel is all but ready, the wind'll be with us and the current is strong.'

'I assure you, my friend, it's vital we get away from here quickly as possible if not sooner.'

'Very good, young sir, and by the way, the white owl was perched above our bow last night when most of our men were ashore - Athena's owl that is. She's still with us, I know she is.'

'Nice to know we've got friends around here,' muttered Jason. Argos was back on board and shouting urgent orders as Jason assisted Medea from the jetty and onto the vessel. 'There's sheltered space in the bow for yourself and for this blasted sheepskin,' he informed her. 'Make your way down there and once we're under sail I'll be with you.'

The vessel was alive with movement and voices as Medea made her way awkwardly to the bow, catching the eye of each man she passed no matter how demanding his task. Men scrambled to the benches. Mooring ropes were freed. Oars were used to heave *Argo* clear of the jetty and overhanging trees then turn her to face downriver. As the oars were deployed for rowing, the mast was heaved into position, the yardarm hoisted up, the great sail hauled flapping and billowing and the rigging secured. Jason noted the four escapees seated close to the stern whereas Apsyrtus, the king's son, had located himself amidships by the mast where he stood gripping one of the stays. The River Phasis was taking them seaward but if any aboard had anticipated an easy escape, their confidence was soon to be challenged. Jason was in conversation with his captain and Ancaeus the steersman when the first arrow passed close over their heads to strike the sail then drop harmlessly onto the deck. They looked back to see Aietes' archers emerging from amid the trees and gathering on the jetty with bows raised. More arrows sped through the air toward them, most falling short, two striking crewmen but causing no more than flesh wounds, a small number clattering harmlessly about the deck where Apsyrtus now crouched low.

'We're almost out of range,' commented Argos, 'aye they'll give us no more trouble.'

'Maybe not those archers,' said Jason, gesturing upstream, 'but *they* might.'

Other members of the crew had already seen them and now so did Argos and Ancaeus.

'He's sendin' 'is ships after us!' exclaimed Argo.

'That he is,' responded Jason, 'and he'll not give up until he gets hold of his Golden Fleece. No, he'll not rest until he catches up with us.'

187

'Well, young sir,' declared the captain, 'no chance 'e'll catch up with my vessel an' our crew – no 'e won't! Are there many of 'em, can you tell from 'ere with your good vision?'

With a hand raised to shade his eyes from the newly rising sun, Jason said, 'I count five – no, there are six and – and some appear to be broader boats full of armed men.'

'Then they never will catch up with us, sir, no they won't.'

'No, I think they expected to reach the jetty before we cut loose and sailed off, but their leading vessel looks to be a trim craft not so different from our own and I suspect it carries Aietes himself with some of his palace guard and with armed men at the oars.'

'Aye,' said Argos, as their vessel ploughed ahead in lively waters, her sail well-filled and her oarsmen working steadily without their captain's drum, 'they'll follow us until we 'ave to go ashore, won't they; that's what I think.'

'And I say you're right,' Jason responded. 'Let's hope the white owl you spotted has noticed them as well. But what I'm wondering is how they managed to organize themselves so quickly. It's as if Aietes was warned of his prisoners' escape before we left the town.'

'Aye, young sir, an' by who, I might ask.'

'Yes, by who,' breathed Jason, turning to gaze along the ship 'I see one man taking at least as much interest in our pursuers as we do ourselves and he's been there in full view of 'em since we left the cove.'

188

'The son of King Aietes 'imself or so we're led to believe.'

'The very one,' answered Jason, 'and he really is a son of Aietes. He was keen enough to condemn his own father and having met the man it hardly surprised me at the time. I have to find the truth before long and I think there might be a way of doing that. Meanwhile, my friend, I trust you'll be able to coax our vessel and our worthy crew into putting more distance between ourselves and those Colchian vessels.'

'Aye, sir, I'll be on the drum again now.'

Jason made his way along the deck, passing Apsyrtus but saying nothing on his way to the bow of the ship where Medea waited.

The river had widened into an estuary and when open sea was in sight *Argo* was steered westward to follow the coast of Colchis in lively waters. Peering sternwards, Jason noted how first one, then another of Aietes' vessels fell back from the rest until there were three remaining. Before long, with a frequently obscured sun half way to its zenith, another was falling away. But as morning progressed, as the breeze increased and spray at times swept the deck, their pursuer, consisting now of only one vessel, appeared to be matching their speed and with well-filled sail, their oars flashed sufficient light for their progress to be measured. 'They'll not keep up that pace all day and nor will our own men!' called Argos from his seat.

'Quite so,' agreed Jason, 'but wherever we make shelter they'll follow and though we'll likely equal them in numbers I thought I spotted horsemen keeping up with us on land. If so then they're sure to be Aietes' men. They'll see where we moor our boat then they'll maybe call in local men as reinforcements. I doubt Apsyrtus will be aware of them as his attention's been elsewhere so for now I'll say nothing.'

Argo was making good headway, her captain continuing at his drum and her oarsmen maintaining a regular stroke in what had become a steadily increasing breeze. Apsyrtus had moved close to the bow and stood leaning aside to observe the pursuing vessel when Medea laid a hand on his shoulder. He twisted about, saying, 'Ah, Lady Medea, I knew you were sheltering but I had no wish to disturb you.'

Medea gazed furtively at the backs of the oarsman then below the sail to the stern where Jason and other members of the crew were preoccupied in watching Aietes' ship. 'We have to talk while they're otherwise occupied,' she hissed. 'Quickly, join me where we won't be noticed.'

Apsyrtus glanced about then followed her to the storage area beneath the bow, unnoticed so they thought, by the busy Argos. In semi-darkness they sat together amid folded leather tents, sparsely filled baskets for storable food, jars of wine, unstrung bows, arrows and chopped wood for Telamon's braziers. Pushed into a recess at the very front was the Golden Fleece. Apsyrtus stared hard and reached to touch it as Medea asked, 'What are you intending to do?'

'Now wait,' responded Apsyrtus, switching his attention to her, 'I was about to ask you the same question and I need your answer first.'

'Very well,' she replied, drawing closer to him, 'they – he, Jason, forced me to show him where the Golden Fleece was kept. I had to do as he said or he would have killed me – yes, he or one of those four half-brothers of ours he helped to escape would have done for me even there in front of you. I tried to get away from them but all the time they were watching me. Now Jason regards me as a hostage to trade for a safe passage if father catches up with him.'

'But the powers you command as a priestess of Hecate; your incantations, your insight into the minds of others; are they of no avail now?'

'I'm far away from Hecate's shrine and – and I feel there are powers greater than hers at work here,' A tear glistened on her cheek as she added, 'I - I don't know what to do.'

'Then listen to me - when I came out last night and heard voices in the palace courtyard I suspected there was something going on; a plot of some kind, maybe. I had no idea what but I found a slave and sent him to alert the guards on duty. He never returned to confirm what happened as I'd ordered so I came over to see for myself and like you I was obliged to go with them. That slave must have found someone eventually because father was alerted, albeit too late. Now he chases us and as he's not far behind I have to somehow disable this vessel. There are two ways I'm thinking of right now: I could wait and see if we get far enough ahead of him to find a safe mooring then at night, while they're ashore, I could cut through the rigging. They took my sword but I see it and other weapons stored in here. That would detain or slow them down until the old man catches up with us in the morning. Or if he's close enough during today I could put their steersman out of business with a knife across his throat. I could cut away the tiller, throw myself overboard, use it to keep myself afloat and wait to be picked up.'

'Yes,' she gasped, 'anything to save us; anything to get us back to Colchis. At last now there is hope.'

'Look,' he said, 'I need to be out on deck. The motion of this boat is making me feel sick.'

'I feel it, too, and you must be seen out there before Jason comes looking for you.'

Argos' drum meanwhile had ceased. The oarsmen could no longer row in rougher waters and had drawn in their oars.

Apsyrtus left her and Medea waited a while before emerging to face a clouded sky. And although the following breeze had increased to a brisk wind, it was not in their favour for it had assisted also those in pursuit. *Argo's* rigging shivered and she rolled in a buffeting sea. Apsyrtus crouched by the mast with a steadying arm about the rail. Medea, feeling spray on her face, grasped at rope stays and made her apprehensive way with much difficulty along the deck between chattering oarsmen, ignoring Apsyrtus as she stooped beneath the sail to push by him. Among the crew, separated now from one another, were her four half-brothers and each of these she acknowledged with a passing smile. As she neared the stern Jason turned, saw her, offered a steadying hand and said, 'If you wanted fresh air then today's the day.'

'Aye, fresh it is,' added the captain, 'an' I fear it may get fresher still but I doubt we'll be able to make land with those buggers following so close, that I do.'

'I hate the sea,' gasped Medea, clutching hard at a stay. 'I'm not used to this.' Then reaching to brush windblown hair from her eyes she asked, 'Jason, is Apsyrtus watching us?'

'No, he's hanging on by the mast and looks as if he'll soon be hanging over the side.'

'Jason,' she continued, glancing over her shoulder, 'I convinced him I was forced to come aboard and he confided in me. He *did* send to warn our father before he approached us near the palace. He wishes you and your men only harm and never would have left the city had you not forced him. He plans to cause damage to this ship so my father can catch up with us. He may attempt to cut the rigging while your men sleep, or worse, he could attack your steersman.'

'He doesn't look capable of attacking anything right now,' said Jason.

'Perhaps not now, but - but when we go ashore. It's what he said he would do and I know from his thoughts he means it.'

'Can he swim, do you know?' Jason asked.

'He – yes, he swims with others in the Phasis; I have seen him.'

193

'A pity perhaps - but by the time we go ashore I intend he'll no longer be with us.'

'Go ashore?' queried Argos. 'I can't see us doin' that as things are unless we take on those buggers be'ind us man to man.'

'I don't want to risk losing any more of our crew,' said Jason, scanning the landward hills, 'but maybe there's another way, It's heavily wooded country over there so if Aietes horsemen are still trying to follow, I doubt they'll be able to see us right now and not at all if we sail closer in and find a sheltered cove.' Jason turned his attention back to ashen faced Apsyrtus who was making his way unsteadily along the deck toward them. 'Good,' said Jason, 'this'll save me calling him over.' To Medea he added, 'And you'd better get back to where you were for a while and try to keep dry.

Apsyrtus pushed by Medea, reached the stern, glanced at the following vessel and asked, 'W-what's happening now? Where next are we headed?'

'You look rather pale, my friend,' said Jason. 'Does the motion of our boat trouble you?'

'Yes it does,' he replied, 'I've never been this far out to sea before and never for so long. I feel ill – yes, terrible. The sooner we go ashore the better.'

'Er, we won't be stopping tonight,' said Jason, nodding aside to Argos, 'but as your father isn't far behind and as you're next in line for the throne I think you should be with him.'

'Wh-what d'you mean!' gasped Apsyrtus. 'Ah-let go of me!' he yelled as Jason and Argos seized hold of his arms.

'I mean now's your chance to enjoy his company!' declared Jason. Ancaeus the tiller man watched in disbelief as they dragged the desperately kicking and struggling Apsyrtus to the edge of the vessel. 'Let's hope the mighty King of Colchis sees fit to welcome you aboard!'

'You - you bastards – no, I can't swim!' screamed Apsyrtus as they lifted and heaved him overboard.

'Well now's your chance to learn!' called Jason.

The crew, distracted by the shrill cry and sight of Apsyrtus plummeting into the water began to cheer loudly as the son of Aietes, arms thrashing, mouth ajar, drifted away. None cheered with more enthusiasm than the four newly rescued youths who then bawled obscenities at the diminishing figure.'

'If 'is old man slows enough to fish 'im out of the water.' Argos said, 'I'll get to the drum and 'ave our lads try to row 'ard for a while to give us better distance, bad sea or not.'

'Do that anyway,' ordered Jason.

Jason headed to the bow of the vessel, their captain urging his men to deploy their oars as he followed behind. At the bow they leaned aside to look back as Apsyrtus, frantically waving and yelling, appeared now a third of the way between themselves and the pursuing ship. 'Well he's still afloat,' Jason said. 'I doubt even the likes of Aietes would let his favourite son drown in front of his own men. Anyway, they'll want to find out from him what we plan to do.'

195

'The current's takin' 'im towards 'em,' Argos observed, preparing to raise his drumsticks. They continued to watch and Argos declared, 'Aye, young sir, they're lowerin' their sail so they are.' Then he called aloud to his oarsmen, 'Let's 'ave some speed, lads an' we'll be rid of those buggers!' The oarsmen responded eagerly. Their vessel surged ahead despite rough seas and her captain called to Jason, 'There's 'eadland before us an' once we've rounded that we'll be out of Aietes' sight! The wind's easin,' too, so our lads'll take advantage of that an' maybe we'll lose 'em altogether.'

Argos' drum continued, the wind was decreasing, the headland drawing closer and they observed Aietes vessel had fallen well astern with her sail still down. As *Argo* began to round the headland the pursuing boat was still in sight but considerably further away. 'We can ease back a bit, lads!' called the captain, setting aside his drum. 'Find your own pace but keep it steady!'

Jason peered landward and said, 'It seems now we have an advantage over Aietes and there's no sign of those horsemen. If we're out of his sight by sunset then I figure we can find somewhere to shelter for the night as must Aietes. And he might give up trying to catch us if he thinks we're to continue through darkness. The sky looks to be clearing so have Telamon use his fire pebble while the sun's out and have a few braziers going. Tell those men not rowing to cast their lines and pull in whatever they can. They'll need to cook our food before we land so we'll not risk giving ourselves away at night with campfires.'

'Aye, sir, I'll see that is done. Oh, an' despite this present lull, I feel the weather might worsen' again – soon before dark I'd say.'

Making her way along the deck past Argos, Medea rejoined Jason and, peering astern, said, 'I see my father's vessel is no longer keeping up.'

'He stopped to pick up Apsyrtus,' replied Jason, 'but he may try to catch up with us all the same.'

'I'm sure he will but Apsyrtus must still be alive or he wouldn't have taken him on board. He'll have done so to discover our intentions, otherwise he would have sailed on and later found another son to take his place.'

'I'm sure you're right,' agreed Jason. 'It's what you might call fatherly love.'

'Apsyrtus will have told him you actually do have the Fleece if he didn't know already,' assured Medea. 'He will never give up.'

Medea had returned to her refuge at the bow when they rounded the headland. But with the wind again blustering, the sail well filled, the sea buffeting and the vessel continuing to roll, Argos had his crew pull in their oars and rest after the sustained effort of that day. They had managed to light braziers and these were burning to accommodate a fresh catch of fish and squid. The headland was well behind but still there was no sign of Aietes' ship.

'D'you think 'e's given up?' asked the captain, rejoining Jason. 'Without 'elp from the land 'e might think 'is men would be no match for ours.'

197

'I doubt it. I have it from his daughter that he won't give up the chase and I believe her. At least this wind will prevent the smoke from our braziers giving us away.'

'Maybe so, young sir, but I don't like the way those braziers are swingin' about so the sooner they're extinguished the better I say. An' as daylight is fadin' an' rain clouds gatherin' we'll soon 'ave to decide where we make land for the night.'

Dusk was closing in and with the wind blowing hard, the vessel pitched and rolled with sea spray lashing her deck. Eventually, with a few oars deployed to assist steering, the sail furled and the yardarm lowered, they guided *Argo* with much difficulty into a narrow, tree-sheltered cove where she was secured at bow and stern. Rain was beginning to fall so the men carried their leather tents to higher ground and set them up beneath the trees where further strengthening winds banshee-moaned amidst the branches above.

'Aietes or no,' said Jason as he and Argos, in total darkness, adjusted their positions for greater comfort within the confines of a shivering tent, 'there'd for sure be no camp fires here tonight.'

'No, young sir, there would not. And if Aietes didn't find shelter in time then 'e'll be capsized or driven against the land where maybe sailin' men ought not to be driven. Whatever - Colchis is no seafarin' nation so I don't expect we'll 'ave sight of 'im again soon.'

'Maybe, maybe not,' breathed Jason, closing his eyes and saying with a yawn, 'I once severed a man's head, a leader of brigands intent on looting our town. I threw the head into his own boat. In Aietes' case I'd welcome a second chance. Sleep well, my friend.'

Chapter 8 - The Voyage Beyond

... So we'd escaped from Colchis and dear, brave Jason, with my invaluable help, had his Golden Fleece and me along with it. Like my half-brother, Apsyrtus, I'd spent precious little time at sea but unlike him *I* couldn't swim at all, though being on the boat had not affected me quite as badly. Mind you, I suspect his ailment, his affectation of nausea, was less to do with rocking around at sea than it was for fear of Jason suspecting his true intentions. As for myself, being a priestess of Hecate didn't get me into the water very often except for bathing each day in the perfumed privacy of my chamber with the pampering and *very* personal attention of my slaves. By now was I beginning to realise how much I missed all that and it was only the beginning.

The desires of the men, the crew of *Argo*, I could read easily in their eyes and sense in their thoughts when I was on deck, yes, more than I might have read in their casual glances. With the few items I had managed to bring with me I could at least continue in modest appearance. For those days at sea Jason had them make a kind of rope harness and in this I was lowered from the stern of the ship into the water each morning and afternoon in the flimsy gown of Egyptian cotton I'd stuffed into my linen bag. Once in the water I had a rudimentary wash and did also what nature demanded. And didn't those men love watching this damned humiliating ritual whenever they could! They thought it wonderful entertainment but I had no choice in the matter and I dreaded it. Apart from that I hate salt water and I feared what it was doing to my hair. The men of course had to take to the water also but all any of them needed to do was climb naked down a length of rope. They would wallow around a while then haul themselves back up again, often grinning at me in the process and hoping I'd pause to admire what they'd normally have concealed but was there in full view. Yes, I suffered the dipping penalty twice each day through the ill-disguised smirks of the crewmen, even on occasion Jason's captain who was at least twice my age. I ignored them all. I made it clear I wished to be entirely alone and spent more time at the bow. Yet I still craved the presence and the very touch of Jason and I kept telling myself it was only me he wanted.

Had Jason bothered to thank me for all I'd done? No, but then I told myself he had too much else on his mind. As I saw things, our relationship had to continue; apart from that, I could never return home for obvious reasons. Unless my father felt inclined to forgive me, which had never been his way, my life wouldn't be worth living even if it lasted long enough for him to make clear his displeasure. There'd be nothing public about my demise - no, I'd been too popular with the people of his own city for that to happen. I imagined my death might be an arranged suicide undertaken in a fit of remorse for the unforgivable offense I had committed in assisting his then worst enemy to steal his greatest treasure.

Yes, for now I remained smitten with Jason though we'd spent not much time together since leaving Colchis. My desire for him was visceral, it consumed me. I had persuaded him to marry me, yet deep down I knew this was wrong since he'd had little or no choice in the matter. Most nights he would be with me in our refuge at the front of the vessel where we took our pleasures together on a bed of folded tents but at daylight he would say little before rejoining Argos and the rest of his crew.

I mentioned clothing; it was during my time in the bow retreat, when Aietes still pursued us, that I discovered the cloak. It had been concealed behind those baskets containing wine jars. It was the cloak I recognized had been worn by Jason when first I saw him in audience with my father. It was the cloak of a nobleman. During that night of wet weather I'd remained alone on the vessel rather than going ashore with Jason and the rest but I had felt cold so I took the cloak and pulled it around myself to keep warm. There was a faint odour about it, a delicate perfume I could not imagine being worn by the likes of Jason. I was convinced it had been used by a woman not long ago. Pressing the cloak to my face I could almost resolve her image.

The well secured though still gently swaying vessel helped me sleep and in my dreaming I knew it was Hera who had sent the wind and rain. Jason hoped this would help shake my father off his tale. Perhaps for a time it might, but they didn't know him as I and a few others did.

Next morning the weather had cleared and we were once again at sea, now in calmer waters and under blue skies. I could do nothing other than watch the land and the islands drift by and though I derived much pleasure for the playing and singing of Orpheus, I needed more – much more.

***

The following days proved uneventful with the wind more often than not in the Argonauts' favour. There was no further sighting of Aietes' vessel. The men were now and again cheered by Orpheus and would sing aloud to his prompting, which was preferable by far to the insistent beat of Argos' drum. Most remained captivated, too, by the sight of ever pensive Medea when she sat close by the stern to listen.

Yet their mood was changing. When they were free to talk, conversation among the crew was at times guarded and often would cease altogether when Jason or his captain passed close. Their vessel was steered south from the Euxine Sea but only after they had navigated the restricted channel where lay the so-called Clashing Rocks. There sea spray would have doused Telamon's braziers had he not left them unlit and sheltered beneath the lower benches. It was after they had sailed by the land of the Bebryces and entered the Propontis that trouble begin to stir.

They had passed the point opposite to where, on the outward journey, Jason and his two companions had gone ashore to encounter Phineus the blind prophet and to drive away the foul Harpies that afflicted him. The wind and sea had been lively and the oars were needed only to manoeuvre *Argo* into a more open yet secluded cove as daylight waned. Brushwood had been collected and fires were beginning to liven the night when Polydeuces approached Jason and his captain as they grilled their fish. Even before Polydeuces sat close by to speak, conversation among the men had all but ceased.

'Lord Jason,' Polydeuces began, 'we've followed you faithfully on the long voyage to Colchis and you've gained the prize you sought. All we've gained, 'owever, is nothin' other than 'ard work when most of the crew expected to leave Colchis with enough plunder to keep 'em 'appy for a good while. The men feel they've fulfilled their obligation to your father but are not willin' to disembark at Thessaly and return to their own lands empty 'anded. Some, over 'alf or more, talk of leavin' the ship at Lemnos an' rejoinin' those women if there's nothin' else on offer an' I can't say I blame 'em. Should they do that, you'd not 'ave enough crew to man the vessel.'

'And the rest?' Jason asked.

'The rest,' continued Polydeuces, 'they want to see a bit of action. We've soon to pass Troy and as Troy takes readily from others who owe 'em nothin' to begin with, our lads see no reason not to take a measure of it back – and that includes some of their wine since ours is runnin' low again.'

The captain rubbed a hand thoughtfully over his mouth then said, 'Maybe so but I know Troy better than anyone 'ere. Troy is a mighty, well-fortified city, stronger by far than Aietes' capital an' well used to conflict on land and sea. They'd 'ave us surrounded with no chance of escape an' let me tell

204

you, they don't look too kindly on brigands for that's what we'd be.'

'We'd better forget about that,' said Jason, 'and hope we get by in one piece. We have gifts left over here on our vessel but not nearly enough to spread fairly among our crew.' Jason looked across at the groups of men seated about their fires. 'Hmm, a tricky situation. It seems I have a duty to lead them further and not yet return to Thessaly as I know I should. My father will be anxious and the King of Iolcus more than likely convinced of my death.' He thought hard for some moments then said, 'Well, my friend, it seems I have no alternative but to comply with the wishes of our crew. As you know that part of the world better than any man, what other opportunities might we have if we're to avoid Minos' ships?'

'Aye, young sir, there may be possibilities if we sail south down the Aegean Sea then west, keepin' close to the mainland and continue so we pass well north of Crete. Then we could sail to the island of Trinacria that lies south of Italy. It's a big island, aye, very big, with many different peoples an' many towns. Some, as I recall, are of considerable wealth an' most of 'em 'ostile to Greeks, includin' the Cretans, so we'd be quite justified in payin' 'em a visit – if you see what I mean. Then there's Italy itself though all that I speak of is at least as far away as was Colchis. But once clear of the Peloponnese, where Pylos would 'ave to be our last call, there's open water with no sight of land for three an' more days an' nights dependin' on the winds which are usually from the south. It may be no easy journey so we'll need to fill our jars with spring water as well as good wine an' 'ope the stars are out to guide us through the dark.'

By now the men were silent and most turning heads toward Jason, Polydeuces and Argos. Jason arose, stepped over to the group of campfires and announced, 'I understand your concerns, I share your feelings and you have honoured the promise you made to my father! Our good captain tells me there could be much to be gained by our passing north of Crete, entering the great sea then sailing west to Trinacria, a place with which some of you may already be familiar. We'll take our vessel there if all of you agree.'

There was further silence then one of the men announced, 'Yes, I'll agree; I know some of the island and there should be rich pickings.' Then others followed with, 'Aye, count me in,' 'Yes, and me.' Within moments all had given their agreement.

'Then we have a new goal,' declared Jason, 'so let us make it profitable for all!'

A tide of chatter ensued and as it waned, one man called, 'An' after that I'm off back to Lemnos!' Others laughed aloud, many declared the same intention, perhaps facetiously, perhaps not.

Orpheus, lifting his lyre, announced, 'Well here's a song - I mean yet another song I've composed about the women of Lemnos.'

***

They had passed by Troy under sail and oar without incident then entered the Aegean Sea, cruising east of Lemnos as they turned due south. Being in sight for a time, the island was subject of much comment

206

by the men as their oars were drawn aboard. *Argo* continued briskly under sail in a favourable wind with her crew observing a number of other vessels. At one point, the distance to Pelion being not so great, Jason was tempted to make for his home port but knew his men would find this delay unacceptable. There were many opportunities amidst the islands to set up camp ashore and for obtaining supplies until having passed north of Crete where they continued westward into more open seas. They now were seeing fewer vessels than earlier but on the afternoon of that day they observed in the distance three large ships of sinister aspect proceeding south-eastward. Each on its broad sail bore the image of a double-headed axe. Argos, standing with Jason close by Ancaeus at the steering oar, said, 'I recall such vessels from my earlier days; they patrol these waters and others close to Crete and her allies by order of Minos.'

'I hope the great King Minos' men don't regard us as brigands, remarked Jason, eyeing the ships.'

'No, young sir, I doubt they'll do that an' even if they did this 'ere boat of ours would not be easy for 'em catch, swift as they are.'

'Most reassuring but I tell you, my friend, I don't look forward to spending too many nights in the middle of nowhere aboard this or any other vessel and I feel truly sorry for Medea.'

'I fear for now we've little option,' said Argos, 'but with clear skies an' steady breezes I'll ensure we're in sight of Trinacria on our fourth day.'

A new day had dawned and warmer winds flowed now from a southerly direction. All sight of land as well as of all but a few larger vessels was gone. Orpheus played and on occasion sang. Those of the crew at their benches rowed at a leisurely pace when needed; otherwise there was hardly anything else to do during the day other than cast for fish, chatter or gamble with board games. Medea, usually close to the bow, occasionally the stern, her long hair swaying in the breeze, kept whenever possible to herself.

***

Keeping to myself was just about all I could do during those long days in open water and from the start I'd dreaded the very thought of it. I wasn't going to walk along the deck to be leered at by those stupid men unless I absolutely had to. Heroes they might have been, or so dear Jason had assured me on more than one occasion, but that was of little concern to me by then even though one or other of them cooked and served me my food – mainly the fish and squid which I had to eat since there was nothing else available. One member of the crew whose attention I did find comforting was Orpheus. He would speak to me, assure me all would be well, and on occasion bring me food and wine.

Jason spent most of the day with his men while I was left to my own devices, wishing yet again for the luxuries of home and my hot bath. All of these seemed now, with the almost unbearable discomforts of the ship, a vision of paradise lost, particularly when I was subjected to that demeaning twice each day ritual of being lowered into the water.

In the bow at night, when Jason slept, I prayed silently to Hecate and though distant she assured me things soon would change. I took her words to mean change for the better was on its way and realized only later why she may not have been more explicit. I trust you can imagine my feeling of relief when one day, from inside my shelter, I heard someone call out that land was seen ahead.

Chapter 9 - The Perils of Trinacria

'Aye, there she is,' announced the captain as the coastline of Trinacria loomed out of a hazed dawn. 'A welcome sight for us all.'

'A welcome sight as you say,' agreed Jason as they stood together at the bow. 'Tell me more of this island.' All eyes were turned to study the grey landmass ahead but all noted the arrival of Medea as she emerged from below to join Jason and Argos on deck and there witness the land of Trinacria for herself.

'We approach the south-east of the island,' informed the captain. 'There's not much there as I recall other than small fishin' villages where we can find shelter for the night. For larger towns we'll 'ave to follow the south coast much of tomorrow an' more, then turn north before we reach anythin' bigger. Somewhere on the island is reputed to be where mighty Helios pastures 'is sacred cattle if that's to be believed and many seafarin' men do.'

'And you say it's an island of considerable size,' said Jason.

'Aye, sir, it is, an' it's along those western parts in the old days we met trouble an' were obliged to quit their shores or be set upon. But then we were lookin' for 'onest trade whereas now we 'ave a boat full of seasoned warriors who'd stand no nonsense from anyone.'

'Does Minos' navy not deal with the problems?' Jason asked.

'Aye, young sir, that 'e does if 'e catches 'em at sea but Trinacria bein' the size it is, no one could ever track the buggers down.'

'Are we soon to go ashore?' asked Medea.

'That we are,' replied Argos, 'as soon as we spot a village with olive groves an' vineyards.'

'And plenty of fresh water, I hope,' said Medea.

'That is so, lady,' grinned the captain. 'Many rivers enter the sea along the south coast.'

'I wasn't thinking of rivers,' she muttered.

***

No, I wasn't thinking of rivers. What I had in mind was a bath full of hot water, preferably with an ample showering of flower petals and some personal attention. But still it seemed I wasn't going to get anything of the sort for the time being.

Over the next two days we sailed along the south coast as intended and, just to be off that damned boat and on dry land for a while, I went ashore with Jason when he and his men traded with the local villagers. Then we were at sea once more. There was no trouble until we turned north where the towns, as expected, were hostile. The unexpected arrival of Jason with sixty and more well-armed men, most battle-hardened, resulted in enough plunder to encourage further effort and none of his men were lost. Their incursions, their quick visits as I saw it, I did not of course attend. Some time later, listening to their conversations, I knew there was substance to old Argos' misgivings.

***

'Now then, young sir,' said Argos as they negotiated the headland and turned eastward, 'this way takes us all along the north coast to the straits between Trinacria and the mainland. Most sailin' men will not attempt to go that far an' claim what lies thereabouts is evil an' that many 'ave died because of it. I've travelled this direction but once and on that day we sailed further to the north because the men insisted upon it. As for the narrow seaway where we turn south, the waters then were calm, the currents slow an' the wind with us though I felt there was somethin' very wrong about the place. Many others 'ave since assured me me 'ow lucky I was to 'ave survived such a journey so there must be a risk of sorts even though much is 'earsay. D'you wish to continue?'

'We have to continue do we not' replied Jason, 'unless we go back the way we came. If we sailed westward it seems we'd carry on to the end of the world.'

'Aye, sir, then we sail on eastwards. If we find safe anchorage tonight then we'll reach the straits on the mornin' after tomorrow.'

They followed the coast under sail and oar, mooring in a broad bay where Argos remembered there were thermal springs and their vessel could be safely beached. The hot springs were welcomed by Jason and his men and proved a consolation also for Medea who found an opportunity to bathe alone unobserved. On this occasion she chose not to remain on their boat but to sit by Jason at the camp fire.

'The hot springs have revived my spirits,' Medea informed him as Orpheus played, 'but throughout the day I am alone among many with whom I do not speak and you are otherwise occupied.'

He slipped an arm about her shoulder, seeing firelight dance in her eyes as he spoke. 'It's unfortunate, yes, but I must be with Argos and my men most of the time. They expect me to be there while they're at their oars and wish to discuss matters with me when they're not.'

'There is misfortune ahead – I know it,' she whispered. 'And not just because of what Argos has said, or has not said.'

'What d'you mean?' he asked.

'The feelings I have,' she replied, squeezing his hand, 'they are confused; I sense danger awaiting us but all is confused. A portal of promise opens but here are cries of anger, torment and death. Without the peace and solitude I need there is little more I can tell you.'

'Perhaps you're troubled by no more than dreams brought about by the discomfort of the boat and long days, as you say, without the company you once had. I'm with you at night, I know, but perhaps if we take our food together more often.'

***

Perhaps, or so he said, but the demands for his attention continued much the same as we sailed on. And though I had sensed danger ahead of us, the second day proved one of good fortune for *Argo's* crew.

213

Passing close in to the shore, a beached vessel was observed, about which some twelve or more men busied themselves. Jason had us sail in closer still to see what the men were about because his captain was certain they were pirates and not traders. The men by the beached vessel were hurriedly arming themselves so that created an incentive for Jason to investigate further. Clever old Argos located a deeper channel nearby so our vessel could get in closer without grounding. Jason was able to wade ashore with half our ship's complement, all fully armed, to be met as expected by flying spears which his men managed to avoid. He looked brave and determined with the plume of his bronze helmet swaying as he strode at the head of the rest. I stood watching from the bow as the other vessel's crew, with much shouting, were driven away with three of their number struck down by spears. They stopped but kept their distance with no choice but to gather beyond spear shot from where they yelled pointless abuse. On examining the ship Jason discovered her hull had been damaged when she ran ashore but she was loaded, overloaded as he later told me for a ship of her modest size, with goods of much value stolen by her crew.

I learned one of the stricken men lay wounded but far from dead. What Jason or one of his men did to make him talk and cooperate I care not to think, but it transpired those brigands hoarded more of their ill-gotten gains inland. Jason called over for ten more of our own men to join him and to bring bows and arrows. Once ashore they loosed their arrows at the remaining pirates, bringing four more down and causing those few left to scurry well beyond range. I watched some twenty of our men proceed from the beach up a gully, taking the injured pirate with them, while the remainder clambered aboard the abandoned ship. I watched them return, some carrying armfuls of precious plunder which they stowed away beneath the deck with smallest items placed in the bow where Jason and I spent our nights. There were objects of gold and silver, some I imagined were temple offerings. There were many more items of personal adornment, trinkets arrayed with gemstones and pearls, all taken by force or stealth from others.

Meanwhile, the party having gone inland were guided to an inconspicuous cave, little more than a cleft in the rock face hidden by bushes. On squeezing inside they discovered the passage opened out and there they found more loot. Lots of it – mainly small items but all of high value. The men made their way back to the shore, each carrying whatever he could, then returned to our vessel. Welcome, also, were the jars of good wine that had contributed also to the pirate vessel's weight. All of this added to the weight of our own vessel but Argos maintained that she would still handle well.

Their last act before leaving, Jason's men set fire to the crippled boat – made possible by Telamon with some gathered kindling, his fire pebble and a strong sun. Heading out to sea once more we watched her blaze and billow black smoke to our crew's wild cheering.

They set up camp on a rocky shore that evening and all was well. The men's morale had much improved after their windfall and after some consideration and liberal quantities of wine they agreed that what had been recovered from the pirates would serve every man's expectations and returning to Thessaly would be our next priority.

Later that night I spent alone because dearest Jason, thinking always of me, as you know, celebrated the day with his men and fell asleep by his fire after a surfeit of wine. As I slept, Hecate spoke to me and opened the door to dreaming. In those dreams I heard sweet music, sweet and compelling, but I felt it meant only death to those enticed by it. There were cries, then screams of insane laughter that went on and on and on. There were creatures at once beautiful, at once hideous and utterly evil. I saw them, I saw what they were, but I did not fully understand until later.

When I awoke I knew we were nearing danger and that it was not far away. Should I have made my dreaming known to Jason? I worried now, after their good fortune, that he and the rest would have considered me foolish. No matter how seriously they accept at times other people's prophesies, mine would not have suited their intentions and most probably would have been ignored. I allowed myself that essential dip into the sea, thinking afterwards I might change my mind, but still I said nothing.

***

216

'The air is oddly tainted,' said Jason as sometime after passing another wide bay they approached a solitary island.

'It's sulphur, young sir. It's sulphur you smell and it's to be found in places where the earth breathes fire and sometimes around 'ot springs. I've 'eard there are many such features in parts of Trinacria an' at sea to the north of the island, an' I've 'eard also of other, stranger things that seem to me a result of delirium brought about by certain plants that cause the mind to go astray. Aye, that cause a man to witness things that aren't there or ought never to be there.'

'Well, my friend, I hope whatever is floating around in the air right now doesn't have that effect.'

'Oh no, sir, this I've encountered often enough. What's in the air now seems to come from that island we're soon to pass by. It's unpleasant, as you say, but 'armless unless you get too much of it – then you choke to death.'

'You're very reassuring at times,' smiled Jason. 'So I take it you are familiar with this island.'

'Not this particular one, no. Last time I sailed this way we went further north an' closer to the mainland. The crew I 'ad at the time demanded as much with some very strange tales.'

There was not enough breeze to swell the vessel's sail but the oarsmen worked at an easy pace without need of the drum while Orpheus gave rhythm with his songs, singing loudly and much to their pleasure. Medea emerged from her shelter at the bow to join Jason, Argos and Orpheus and once there glanced ahead to the island. Noting her expression Jason asked, 'You look troubled – are you feeling unwell?'

She drew breath looked up at Jason, at his captain then once more at the small, treeless island basking in crinkled silver water beneath a hot sun. It now was looming close. 'Steer away from - from *that*!' she gasped. 'Steer well away, I beg you!'

Jason peered ahead then turned to her. 'We're not sailing too close in but all I see there are blackened rocks with smoke rising above. Is that what bothers you?'

'It'll not cause you any problems, My Lady' Argos assured her, 'but we'll not sail too close in.'

Medea closed her eyes, nodded and raised hands to her face. 'No, you don't understand – the place is evil–evil-evil and I beg you now to take us well clear of it. Take us further than a voice might carry. Please do that for me! Do it for *all* of us!'

Jason turned to the captain. 'Look, you said your previous crew wanted to avoid it so do as she asks. It might make little difference but it could be the smoke that's upsetting her.'

Medea pressed hands tighter to her face and Argos said, 'Aye-aye, sir. I'll 'ave Ancaeus steer us further out.' But by the time he had made his way along the deck they were close enough for figures to be seen by those men not at the oars; pale figures moving amid the boulders of a bleak and barren landscape. Orpheus himself, noting the distractions, ceased singing. A number of the oarsmen, too, were glancing aside to see what was of interest. Medea turned away, supporting herself against the railing with her head bowed. Argos was now with his steersman but both realized, as did Jason, that they would still be within hailing distance of the island. Jason, a hand raised above his eyes, stared hard to observe five female figures peering toward their vessel from behind a disordered array of black rocks. Closer now and those men intent upon watching the figures perceived them as young women - women of most beautiful aspect but visible only above the waist. Honey-blond hair cascaded about their full and naked breasts and as they swayed from side to side in seductive unison their voices could be heard. They raised their hands, pushing aside their hair, smiling and running fingers slowly, invitingly over their breasts. And although the boat was skirting wider than at first intended, their voices drifted clearly across the water - voices that sang in wondrous harmony, voices that arose as a blessing to sea and sky. They sang in a manner so compelling, so utterly enchanting, that the oarsmen slowed and others stared transfixed as did Argos on his way back to rejoin Jason. The voices were an invitation, a call of sensual promise that soon, it seemed, might not be denied.

'Jason!' Medea's cry shattered his reverie, rang through his mind as a clash of sword against shield. Her eyes were wide and within them glinted dark fear as she grasped his arm. 'Jason – have Orpheus sing aloud to overwhelm their voices! Have your men work their oars as if their lives depended upon it for I swear to you they surely will!'

Gazing into her eyes, Jason believed her and was seized with a chilling fear. As his captain at last joined them he ordered, 'Get to that drum! Beat it

219

loudly! Have our men row hard as they ever did and harder 'till we're well away from that island! And you, Orpheus, sing loud – loud enough to drown those voices! Do it!'

Argos scrambled to his drum and the men at their benches, though confused, responded to his beat and heaved on their oars. The vessel surged forward. Jason tuned to gaze at the island and saw they were now at their closest. Medea tightened her grip on his arm and cried, 'Jason – don't listen to them! Listen only to Orpheus. Don't move from my side!'

But one man, a tall and powerful man but not one of those straining at an oarsman's bench, had stared across, had listened for too many heartbeats, had looked and listened until the voices had overwhelmed and confounded him. Despite the drumming, despite the splash of oars, the creaking of *Argo's* timbers and the soaring voice of Orpheus, he heard only the Sirens call. He saw only what they wished him to see and through his mind swept an all compelling tide of words, "Oh, such charm, such grace, such beauty and you call me – you call me!" He stepped close to the stern and grasping the rail, heaved himself overboard and into the water.

'By the gods - Butes!' cried Jason. He would have to rushed forward, but Medea held him tighter still as the man swam strongly, thrashing water in blind determination to reach the island. With their vessel passing the rocks, both could see the spot to which Butes was headed and would soon reach. Laying about the rubble beach were the scattered timbers of vessels and the skeletal remains of their crews, most bleached white but some with flesh not yet rotted away. The figures emerged from behind the rocks and onto that beach of horrors as though to welcome Butes who, now drawing close, seemed unaware of what was about to greet him. Below the waist they possessed the legs and clawed feet of great birds and above the waist where beauty had once declared itself, their flesh was pallid, their eyes large and glowing baleful bright. And though the wondrous, soaring voice of Orpheus continued to defeat that of the Sirens it was clear to those who watched that the creatures were laughing, shrieking evil malice and scampering toward Butes as he struggled out of the water. He arose and staggered forward. He saw them approach and perceiving what they really were he turned in horror back to the water, gazing in disbelief at the ship from which he had so recklessly departed. His arms flailing wildly, his desperate calls for help ignorrd, Butes had reached the water when they seized hold and dragged him back. His screams now were loud enough to be heard over the thrash of oars and the voice of Orpheus and Argos cried out, 'By Zeus they're tearin' 'im apart - they're eatin' the poor bastard alive!'

Butes' cries, like those of a screeching sea bird, swept across the water then ceased abruptly.

'Don't look!' exclaimed Medea. 'Look ahead at the sea and the sky then into my eyes.' Jason did as she demanded but the scene on the beach would only be erased for a short while. 'They would have dragged your very soul to hell,' Medea breathed as her cheek touched his.

221

Argo was passing clear and though the oarsmen, facing astern, were able now to see the island, its foreshore and beach were shrouded by swirling, sulphurous vapours that drifted from the inland crater. The voice of Orpheus calmed then ceased as he also peered back at the island.

That night by an onshore campfire, an afternoon's sailing away from that accursed place, Jason said to Argos, 'I don't know, unless it was the will of the gods, why I so suddenly believed her.'

'Just as well you did, young sir. Aye, just as well for us all except poor Butes.'

'No man should die like that,' breathed Jason, downing in one gulp half a goblet of red wine.

'Women again wasn't it,' muttered Argos, raising his own cup. 'Why do so many of these evils manifest 'emselves as women? But then it was one that 'elped save us was it not.'

'Yes, the one I committed myself to marrying back in Colchis.'

'Do I sense, Master Jason, that you're troubled now with second thoughts?'

'I – no, a promise is a promise and I – we, owe her much.'

'Well tomorrow,' said Argos, stirring the fire to greater brightness, we turn south through the straits and that'll 'ave us on our way 'ome.'

***

Once our vessel was secured in a sheltered bay I expected I would spend another night alone in the bow as Jason was drawn into conversation with the crew over that recent and terrible event. He did, however, eventually appear. After taking wine, and other pleasures with him I fell asleep. It was a deep and longer-lasting sleep by far than I might have wished for. Perhaps I needed to exclude from my thoughts the horrors we had witnessed that day but later, in that strange, elusive land of half wakefulness I heard a distant booming. It sounded like thunder but it continued without any breaks. The time of dreams was passing, when I realized the boat was already at sea, rolling but not as gently as it usually did, and still there was a sound of distant thunder. I had no recollection of Jason leaving my side but slivers of daylight showed about the edges of the small doors that closed off the bow space. I sat up and reached for my gown but the sound was ever there and growing louder. No longer could it be thunder and deep in my mind the nature of what we were to encounter was becoming clearer. I pushed ajar one of the doors, felt sea spray on my face so had no intention of going out onto the deck. Yes, as the waters were rough and the vessel becoming ever more unsteady, I decided to remain where I was, confined within the bow rather than risk getting soaked. Before long I was to sense acutely the fear of the captain and his men. Jason, too, because it was a fear of something he could not fight or kill.

***

'The currents are stronger,' said the captain, standing with Jason close to the bow as they proceeded due south. 'Aye, much stronger by far than they were when I passed through 'ere all those years back. An' just you ear' that noise – it's gettin'

223

louder as we approach an' the water's becomin' livelier.'

The strait was getting narrower, the land either side rising, soon becoming almost vertical to their left. Argos gestured leftward, saying, 'Those rocks, they 'ave a terrible reputation. Sailin' past them is said to be invitin' death. It's said the creature they call Scylla lives among those rocks, a dark an' monstrous thing that 'as a cravin' for 'uman flesh. They say that it seizes an' feeds upon the men of passin' ships.'

'Is it female by any chance?' asked Jason.

'Aye, sir, they say it is.'

'May the gods preserve us,' muttered Jason 'I thought we'd had enough of evil women. But I take it you yourself have never witnessed this Scylla creature or whatever it is.'

'No, sir, I've not an' I've no wish to take a chance on doin' so - not today, not never. An' that's why we're steerin' far away as possible an' I 'ope it's far enough.'

Jason peered at the dark, cavern-pitted cliffs rising above but *Argo* was already passing by on the swift current. Though aware of what was by then an ominously loud rumble he continued nevertheless to look upward, thinking that from one of the caverns he could see emerging a large black, snake-like object that squirmed about the ledges and rocks. He stared a while longer, wondering if what he saw was an illusion fuelled by Argos' comments but other matters had become more pressing. Their vessel heaved and rolled and as he turned his attention to the scene ahead the captain called to him, 'What lies

224

before us I've 'eard called Charybdis. It's not at all as I remember 'ere, no it isn't more's the pity. Right now it looks unlike anythin' I ever came upon an' we some'ow 'ave to get around it or we're done for.'

Jason gazed by Argos but it took him some moments to realise how the sea before them was rotating in a great circle with a depression at its centre. As they drew closer it became in appearance a vast, foaming bowl, stirred as if by some monstrous unseen hand, slow at its outer edges but swirling rapidly about its centre. *Argo's* sail billowed, her stays shook and groaned in protest, her hull quivered like a living entity as they drew closer to the gyrating torrent.

'It's good the wind and current are with us,' called Jason, drenched as were they all by intensifying sea spray, 'but our men will have to row very hard!

'That they will - 'arder even than yesterday if that's possible an' my bangin' that drum will be of no 'elp! They'll all' 'ave to watch each other!' With that the captain yelled at the top of his voice to the oarsmen, 'Row 'arder lads - 'ard as y'damned well can then 'arder still!'

Argo ploughed toward the seething monster, the green hell maw of the maelstrom, and in moments they were teetering on the edge of a thundering turmoil that threatened to consume their fragile vessel in one all-devouring gulp. But as the spray-lashed men strained to their utmost, driven by a primordial desire to survive, the wind further strengthened in their favour and though pitching and

225

rolling wildly, *Argo* maintained her precarious course ahead. They were contesting what many of the crew regarded as certain death but were gradually defying such fate to make their way clear. Their vessel surged on but steadier now. At last the passage grew wider and the roar of the whirlpool diminished as they entered calmer waters. Gasping hard, the oarsmen relaxed their strokes and slumped forward, few as yet able to observe the welcoming seas that lay ahead.

Jason stood with eyes closed, breathing a deep sigh of relief as his captain spoke. 'I believe it all, now – everythin' I was told. They said she could drag down far larger vessels than ours then disgorge the wreckage and the bodies of their crews in calmer waters to feed the creatures of the deep. Aye, I believe it all an' should 'ave taken more notice.'

'But what,' Jason asked, 'would your alternative have been?'

'Alterative? Why, sir, my alternative would 'ave been never to sail around Trinacria at all an' never again will I.'

'And you referred to that thing, once more as "She."'

'Aye, sir; the one that drives it is said to be a daughter of Poseidon if you please.'

Chapter 10 - The Marriage

… Well we got through that, our latest trial I'm glad to say, though I emerged from within the bow feeling ill as never before and needing to hang over the side of the ship and grasping my hair to keep it out of the way. And while this journey had for me long since become an ordeal, at last we were sailing in the right direction - back to Thessaly, however many days that might take. Now in calmer seas and returned to my hideaway, I gave thanks to Hecate and in my sleep later on she acknowledged this. At the same time I knew one above her was party to our exchange, one who I knew strove to guide our fate, or should I say, that of Jason. It was Hera who deserved our thanks because it was she who strengthened the arms of the oarsmen and power of the winds when it mattered most. My thoughts turned to Jason. Perhaps, if or when our dangers were ended, he would give some thought to the promises he'd made to me in Colchis.

We sailed more or less southward for two days and nights with Trinacria to our right, then back into open waters of the great sea with land no longer visible. The skies were often clouded and at night it must have been the gods who determined our course because without sight of the moon and stars our captain could only estimate through observing wind and current. Dear Jason, worried as much as anything over where we might next make landfall, spent more time with me than he would otherwise have. The men, temporarily bereft of anything else to do, occupied themselves mainly in gaming, arguing about one thing or another, fishing and cooking. It was fortunate that Telamon, when on occasion the sun managed to shine through, had been able to start an initial fire after our leaving the straits, and drying out the wood stowed under the deck.

It was on the morning of the third day, with the sky clearing, that we saw land ahead and a few small and larger vessels going about their business. No one was sure just where this might be so heading there was regarded as vital in order to discover exactly where we were. And while this time I sensed no great danger awaiting us, I felt some concern over our as yet uncertain destination.

***

'Ah, we're a bit further north than I'd 'oped to be,' announced the captain, 'but I do recall this land – that I do.'

'Then hopefully,' responded Jason, 'we'll find wherever we are more welcoming than we've experienced of late.'

'Aye, sir, we'll soon be approachin' the island of Scheria in the land of the Phaeacians, a seafarin' people. I sailed around 'ere years ago lookin' for trade. We should carry on down the coast because it's there the town an' 'arbour lies.'

Argo continued under sail in a lively and sunlit sea, and soon after midday a sizeable town was visible situated above a sheltered bay accessed by a south facing inlet that soon widened out. With the crew once again at their oars *Argo* was steered into the extensive bay where were gathered many other vessels with some passing to and fro under sail and oar. Observing from the bow a town whose buildings appeared not dissimilar in style to others he had visited, Jason peered at the harbour as his captain remarked, 'There, young sir, I'd say it looks peaceable enough, don't you think?'

'Yes, as we draw closer I see people going about their business. It appears a wealthy enough town.'

'Provided we don't go marchin' in like brigands,' said Argos, 'I believe we'll be greeted with civility unless things 'ave changed. After my time 'ere I learned Scheria was ruled over by King Alcinous - a good man as I recall other travellers sayin'.'

'Then once we're docked I'll send Echion ahead to announce our purpose and I'll choose gifts for Alcinous or whoever now rules the place.' Only when they were closer to the quay and the crew shipping most of their oars did Jason point across to exclaim, 'Don't I recognize those pennants!'

'By the gods that you do,' responded his captain. 'I can 'ardly believe my eyes! I recall their like flyin' from Aietes boat when they pursued us. What are men from Colchis doin' this far from 'ome!'

'Yes, that *is* one of my father's ships!' Medea declared as she approached from behind. 'He is still pursuing me – pursuing us! Why else would his men have sailed all the way here when they never did before!'

'That we'll soon find out,' said Jason as their vessel swung about to moor beside a jetty and men scrambled over to secure the ropes, 'but they cannot possibly have known we'd show up here today. We may need to look to our arms but I'll have Echion find out what their purpose is before I make that decision.'

Their arrival at the town drew scant attention from its people and Argos said, 'Ships from all lands come an' go from this port so we're not quite the novelty we'd be elsewhere – maybe not even those Colchians are.'

They watched Echion stride along the jetty in flowing white gown with staff held before him. He attracted moderate attention from passersby as he proceeded toward what Argos had confirmed was the royal palace, a building no more pretentious than that of his father at Pelion. The sun had traversed some way across a cloudless sky and the crew were occupied with their various tasks and diversions when Echion was observed making his way back across the bustling area between town and harbour.

'Our worthy herald appears quite at ease,' commented Jason as Echion stepped onto the jetty. 'I expect that's a good sign.'

'Most encouraging,' agreed his captain. Medea remained silent but watched intently as Echion boarded the vessel to stand before them.

'Well, my friend, were you received in courtly manner?' Jason asked.

'I was indeed received in courtly manner, sir,' replied the herald. 'Most odd, though; it was before the king's wife, Arete, and two of her palace guards that I was first summoned. She is their queen, very young and beautiful but it seemed to me with all the confidence and astuteness her situation must demand. I explained briefly how we had been driven off course and were now making our way back to Thessaly. She accepted my account then explained how her husband, King Alcinous, does not readily interview casual or unexpected strangers. That is because his town is usually full of them and he finds their presence at times overpowering. I was shown into the megaron because of my status and there I stood before him to be questioned further.'

'Did he tell you what the Colchians are doing in this part of the world?' asked Jason. 'And is Aietes with them?'

'I queried their presence, sir. He told me Queen Arete and her attendants had spoken with them whereas he himself had declined. Of Aietes they had heard nothing. Alcinous tells me the Colchians have been moored in the harbour for almost a month, trading or paying for their needs but for much of the time, as far as he knew, most of them had remained on board or close to their vessel as if they were ready to sail at short notice. It seems the King's wife was not favourably impressed by them, which is why they never reached Alcinous himself. Should you care to return with me then Alcinous is willing to see you this afternoon as you offered the courtesy of myself as herald when the Colchians could offer none.'

'I'll certainly do that,' responded Jason. He turned to Argos, saying, 'And you, my friend must accompany me and I'll have you carry gifts for

Alcinous. We've enough plunder as well as our own remaining valuables to choose from.'

'I will also go with you,' put in Medea. 'I am after all a daughter of the Colchian king and can tell Alcinous whatever he might care to know about them.'

'Or might not care to know,' added Jason. 'But yes, you should be with us. Your presence will be reassuring though our own men must remain on their guard while we're away.'

In the heat of the afternoon the three followed Echion along the jetty and to the busy open area where people traded noisily from stalls or rumbled to and from the numerous ships with ass or ox-drawn cart. It was Jason who, scrutinizing the Colchian vessel as they went, noted the attention her crew were paying to his own ship as well as to himself and his small company. 'They've obviously recognized our pennants,' commented Jason. 'I wonder who their captain is.'

'Of course they've recognized us,' said Medea under her breath. 'It's us they've been waiting for.'

At the palace entrance they were greeted amiably by a robed and bearded attendant of modest build, accompanied by two armed but bare-headed guards of considerably greater stature. As they followed through a dancing-fountain courtyard with great storage jars arrayed along one side, it struck Jason how much in common so many cities of Greece had in spite of their frequent conflicts.

Within the megaron smoke and flames swirled upward from the great circular hearth. Torches set about the walls combined with light from small windows high above to illuminate frescoes that depicted sea vessels engaged not in combat but in peaceful trade. About the familiar pastel coloured, downward tapering columns, courtiers stood about or sat in easy conversation, children played tag and slaves awaited their summons to duty. The white-haired bard played his lyre as bards in many other great halls did, but as the visiting party was conducted past the hearth a polite silence fell throughout the hall. On his scallop backed, richly cushioned alabaster throne sat Alcinous, beardless King of the Phaeacians. Long, dark hair, held in place by a white, gem-studded band, fell about the shoulders of an unpretentiously patterned linen tunic. Seated by his side on a richly draped wooden throne, long fair hair cascaded about the shoulders of her gold-threaded gown of Egyptian cotton, his slim young, wide-eyed queen smiled at the newcomers, first at Jason then harder and for longer at Medea, where her attention remained. Jason himself, in admiring the face and form of Arete, was at once aware of her interest. Alcinous laid aside his gold goblet and peered at Jason, who stepped ahead of Argos and Medea. Alcinous addressed him in a gentle but commanding voice, 'I'm told you are Jason, a son of Chiron, King of Pelion close to the Aegean Sea.'

'I am,' replied Jason. He gestured to those in his company, adding, 'This is Argos, my captain and as worthy a seaman as you'll ever meet, and Lady Medea who is a daughter of Aietes, King of Colchis and high priestess of the temple where Hecate is worshipped. She has endured the journey

233

with us since leaving Colchis. Our vessel is the *Argo* and so we call ourselves the Argonauts. We have sailed far west of Crete. We have faced great danger in passing around Trinacria and have been driven far from our intended course. We are here to trade for food and wine, and perhaps a day or two of rest from the sea.'

'Oh, Argonauts are you,' he smiled. 'Well I know something of Pelion and her famous horses though traders from that area seldom reach us here by sea. Of Colchis I know nothing at all other than that the vessel from that distant place, in coming here, has sailed where their men have never before ventured. They have occupied a mooring at our harbour for some considerable time awaiting – awaiting possibly yourselves. Am I right?'

'It would seem so,' answered Jason, taking the canvas bag from Argos. 'But, please, I hope you will accept these gifts I offer on our king's behalf as custom requires.'

'Gladly, then I, too, will offer gifts and our hospitality so that after you bathe and take refreshment you may tell me in full about your long voyage and something of the Colchians.'

'I'll do so and gladly.' Jason replied.

'But Lady Medea,' said Arete, smiling as she rose from her seat, 'you don't want to wait around with these boring men to hear them discuss what I presume you must already know. Come and share wine with me in private. You must be careworn after your time at sea and needing to relax.' She summoned a waiting attendant, leaned close and exchanged discrete words. With a nod of acknowledgement from Alcinous, Arete stepped gracefully away from her seat and gestured for Medea to follow.

***

She was quite right of course. I did *not* wish to sit and listen to what I already knew. I sensed her concern for me was genuine and I needed the company of another woman after my time with all those leering men on the ship. I followed her around the great hearth and across the megaron, passing finely attired courtiers while much aware of my own less than courtly appearance and unkempt hair. We left through a side door, passed along a short corridor and stepped out into a small, partly sunlit courtyard replete with potted plants that presented a riot of colours and delightful perfume in the still, afternoon air. From there we ascended steps to the floor above to enter a modest, softly furnished room whose brightly frescoed walls were alive with scenes of nature depicting what I took to be the Phaeacian countryside. I knew she must have arranged in the megaron what followed. Firstly, her slave, a young, willowy boy, appeared from the direction we had entered grasping an amphora and two embossed gold goblets which he positioned on a small tripod table close by before leaving us. We sat in that quiet, most pleasant of rooms, her private retreat I concluded, for it overlooked a small but beautiful sunlit, walled garden with the hills rising beyond. Just then it seemed my time on the vessel was a distant dream, except that I must have appeared more like a peasant than a temple priestess let alone a king's daughter. With jewel-ringed hand she dispensed red wine and said, "I find it odd that you, one of your status and one so young, should be so far from home and travelling abroad with a boat full of men. I'm sure it all must be very interesting, perhaps rather trying."

I admitted to her, also, how very glad I was to have left the vessel and her crew behind for a time.

"Would you care to talk further about your experiences after bathing?"

"I'd be happy to do so," I informed her on tasting what struck me as a most agreeable honeyed wine. As she did not attempt to question me at that point we drank in an expectant silence with myself glancing out often to her private garden. From behind a leather-curtained doorway opposite to the one we had entered I could make out muffled voices and the sound of running water. There was a growing hint of perfume in the air, though not like that of any garden and my thoughts turned again to the comforts I once enjoyed at my now forsaken home. I was shaken from my reminiscing when Arete at last said. "When our wine is finished I will leave you to bathe and afterwards you'll be offered new clothes." She glanced aside at the curtained doorway, adding, "We enjoy here many of the luxuries of Knossos though on a more modest scale of course."

"I've heard often of Knossos," I told her. "Even in Colchis, Knossos is spoken of, though much as people speak of legends as no one from my country seemed ever to have been there. They speak of it almost as a dwelling of the gods."

236

"Knossos is no legend," she smiled, "though it is a place of wonders as I myself have witnessed. As with Mycenae, however, its ruling family is beset by problems we fortunately do not have here."

"They can't be any worse than the house of Colchis," I assured her.

I was finishing my wine when the curtain from behind which I had noticed those sounds was pushed open and a breeze of warm, richly perfumed air flowed from within. At the doorway stood two smiling, bright-eyed girls, hardly older than myself, one with copper-sheened hair, the other fair. The long hair of both was held back by ornate, gilded clasps and belted floral gowns hugged their slim figures.

"My personal attendants, Hesperia and Maia will see to all your needs," said Arete. "After that I will return and we will take more wine together."

Her timely, her oh, so gladly anticipated offer tempts me now to reminisce. It promised a wholly welcome change from being lowered over the side of that ship in a rope harness that chafed my skin, into water that chilled me to the bone, had my hair end up feeling like stranded seaweed and my lips like parchment. Her two girls, smiling widely, moved apart to confirm my presence was awaited. I stood to thank Arete who simply nodded in the direction of the waiting girls as she, too, rose from her chair. I stepped across to enter a modest sized chamber where I beheld a vision of paradise lit by afternoon sunlight from a window that also overlooked the garden. Across the stone floor were scattered colourful woollen rugs and the pale walls were painted with sea creatures in all their vibrant colours. Blue dolphins, exquisitely rendered, leapt about amidst smaller fish while above and below the main scene were depicted stylized plant forms. But the main features that greeted me within the room were a brightly painted earthenware bathtub from which wisps of steam arose. A pair of two-handled copper urns placed close to the door must have been employed to convey hot water to the bath by slaves. A smaller bowl for basic necessities stood beside the bath and a low but wide, blanket-covered bench rested by the wall opposite the window. In a large, polished bronze mirror standing on a table set before the window I studied my reflection with misgiving and desired nothing more than to immerse myself in the waiting bath. Hesperia and Maia pulled away the pale, much sullied cotton robe I had worn when first I encountered Jason in Hecate's temple. They guided me to the bath and assisted me over the edge so I might lower myself gently and most gratefully into the warm, perfumed and petal-strewn water. Wondering briefly how cold water could first have been introduced into the bath, I noted a dripping ceramic pipe and a swivel copper lever of sorts protruding from the wall slightly above. I settled with indescribable bliss, immersing myself from head to toe. The two girls, now divested of their own gowns, introduced a further dash of perfumed salts which they stirred into my glorious, wonderful bath.

They left me alone for a while but when they returned with a large cotton towel I gathered I had revelled there for long enough and stood while they dried my upper body. Another, larger towel was laid on the floor and onto this I stepped as they held my arms to steady me back over the edge of the bath. Ever smiling, humming softly, Hesperia and Maia continued to dry me. It seemed that royal courts throughout much of Greece and some beyond, strove to emulate the luxuries of Knossos. The closer they were to Crete, the more in evidence this was, though hearsay travelled much further. Cretan court women were said to abhor body hair, as these girls so obviously did, and because of this I was most self-conscious, having neglected my appearance through conditions imposed upon me. I stood in silence until Maia said, "Lift your arms please and we'll make your body all smooth again."

I was momentarily reluctant then amused, after all they were only about to do what they must do for their royal mistress and what I and members of the court had been used to having done even in the less refined surroundings of Colchis, so I smilingly complied. With bronze strigil and pumice stone they removed with infinite care that which I had acquired on the journey. As they worked I sensed within Hesperia and Maia a smouldering sensuality and I could not deny my own arousal though they offered only small talk. When they had finished I stepped away from the towel which they gathered up, removed and replaced with a new one. Hesperia produced a ceramic flask, patterned with tiny sea creatures and said, "Let us treat you with perfumed oil before you dress then you will leave us as one of Lady Arete's court."

I stepped onto the new towel and as each poured oil into the palm of her hand I lifted my arms and closed my eyes. They plied warm, delicate oil about me from neck to toe, Hesperia at my front, Maia behind, their hands, their fingers caressing, fluttering fire moths, and I felt the heat of carnal pleasure rising within. No part of my body was denied their touch and soon the flames of passion were consuming me. I was catching my breath, I was murmuring, "Oh, such pleasure you give me," when they placed the flask aside. They slipped their arms about me, plied tingling kisses and Maia whispered close to my ear, "Let us lie together a while."

I gazed in turn into their eyes - eyes of wanton desire, but could say nothing, nor did I wish to as they guided me to the bench. There we lay, kissing and caressing, intimate and uninhibited, locked together, as glistening serpents in mortal combat, each crying out in turn as that ultimate of pleasures overwhelmed.

When it was over, when we arose from the bench, I could for a time say nothing. I stood to watch as from an oak chest Maia lifted clothes and soft boots, including a gown fit for a lady of the court though not as pretentious and not as revealing above the waist as at most courts. When we all were dressed, Hesperia let down my hair and as I sat before the mirror she ran an ivory comb through with sensuous care, teasing and pinning it back until both confirmed their satisfaction. I arose, reborn a new woman and as I parted the curtain to leave we kissed and I sighed, "Thank you, sisters of

Aphrodite." I backed away and the curtain closed. I hoped Arete would not be there. I hoped she would not have heard what transpired but I turned to find the room was empty. I suspected Hesperia or Maia had signalled to her from their window because little time had passed before Arete reappeared, followed by her slave who replenished our goblets before retiring.

As we sat I noted the sun was low enough to cast long shadows over her garden and Arete said, "Now you are refreshed and relaxed you must tell me whatever you wish about Colchis, your long journey and about Jason and his Argonauts, and I will listen."

I began my tale with Jason and his men arriving at Aea from where my father ruled over the land of Colchis. I described my father in no uncertain terms; his merciless intentions toward my young half-brothers and his treatment of those he suspected of opposing him. I explained how I had helped Jason to defeat that dreadful creature appointed to guard my father's precious Golden Fleece in return for his promise to take me as his wife. Arete had me repeat in part the account of our taking the Fleece and our escape from the River Phasis with my father's vessels in pursuit. I explained how later, Jason's disgruntled men had obliged him to undertake a long and hazardous sea voyage so as to acquire the plunder they had until then been denied. I told of how we had sailed around the great island of Trinacria, how we had witnessed the murderous Sirens and survived perilous waters in passing between Scylla and Charybdis before reaching Scheria.

"But now," said Arete, "your father's men have caught up with you. They must have inquired from others over the direction of your journey and hoped you might find your way here. They'll demand back this Golden Fleece and you with it will they not."

"No doubt they will, but Jason won't let it happen – I know he won't."

"You have much faith in the man, I can understand that, yet still he has not fulfilled his promise to marry you when the captain of his ship might have been prevailed upon to do so."

Arete was right but all I could say was, "Yes but other matters overwhelmed him – overwhelmed us all." I hoped that remark sounded more convincing to her than it did to me deep within. When the sun declined and the sky began to darken, Arete's slave reappeared with a glowing torch to conduct us to the floor below. There, together with Jason and his captain, we were to dine at the table with Alcinous. By then he would know far more than I had imparted to Arete as Jason's account would have begun with his leaving Pelion.

***

Burning torchlight threw shadows about the modest but colourfully frescoed private dining hall. At the head of the ornately carved wooden table sat Alcinous with close by his side, Arete. Opposite sat Jason with, at either side, facing one another, Medea and Argos. When their meal was finished, attendants cleared away dishes and knives but the wine remained. Small talk prevailed until Alcinous, addressing Medea, said, 'Those men from Colchis presently moored in our harbour have requested an interview with me before midday. I think you know what they will want.'

'I know perfectly well what they'll want,' she responded. 'They'll demand return of the Golden Fleece, such is its value to my father – and they will demand to take me with it.'

'Their business may be of no concern to me,' remarked Alcinous, 'but you are my guests and therefore under my protection. That may not be the custom in Colchis but it is so on the island of Scheria and throughout all of Phaeacia.'

'You were to be married were you not,' said Arete, glancing from Medea to Jason. 'Surely, if you are married to the prince of another kingdom your father Aietes can no longer claim jurisdiction over you – or does that not apply in Colchis?'

About to drink, Jason poised his goblet and Medea replied, 'I believe it does apply, yes.'

Jason remained silent and Alcinous said, 'Then we must arrange for your marriage at our temple of Poseidon where it will be announced to the gods and recorded upon tablets. Both of you, Jason and Medea, are born of a king and have the power to make your own decisions without reference to the formalities of others, especially here where I am king. The ceremony we can arrange for sunrise tomorrow should you both agree.'

Medea, Alcinous, Arete and Argos all looked hard at Jason, who lowered his goblet to the table. He paused for several heartbeats then replied, 'Well, yes, we should do that – first thing tomorrow.'

'And this Golden Fleece,' said Arete, 'I trust you intend to keep it?'

'I most certainly do,' he answered.'

'I will send for their leader tomorrow,' declared Alcinous, 'and I'll demand they sail from here before midday.'

'They may not agree to that,' Medea said. 'My father, being what he is, will not accept failure. Those men of his will be desperate to obey him. Yes, their very lives may depend upon it.'

'I will have armed men of our own standing by in case they offer violence,' said Alcinous.

'And I'll be there at your service,' declared Jason. The first of those Colchians to come ashore armed I will cut down.

'Aye,' agreed Argos, 'and me an' our crew will be ready to join you.'

'Tonight,' said Jason, 'I'll remain with your palace guard in case they try anything sooner and I'll have some of our men keep an eye on that Colchian vessel.'

'Then you,' said Arete, placing a hand on Medea's shoulder, 'must stay in one of our private rooms with two of our guards outside.'

***

Nothing untoward happened that night and I slept without dreaming. As arranged at sunrise the following day, Arete, with her guards, escorted me to the temple of Poseidon where with due, albeit unpretentious ceremony and with several more armed guards posted outside for assurance, Jason and I were married; this recorded by the temple scribes. Arete had loaned me the dress she had worn at her own wedding and Jason wore the gown he had acquired at Lemnos, the one I had discovered in the bow of the ship. On the way to the temple and on the way back we looked across at the Colchian vessel but there was minimal sign of activity on board her or on board *Argo*. After our hurried wedding we did manage to celebrate in a modest way, at least modest for people of royal lineage, with Orpheus playing and singing for us. Alcinous ensured all the men of our crew were supplied with good food and enough wine to accompany it but not so much as to have them forget about the Colchians moored close by. It should have been a momentous occasion but for me it did not feel at all like that. I have not troubled to describe the temple ceremony in detail as it would pain me to do so. Of my reasons for that you will understand later.

***

Jason, Medea and others of the king's family and companions were later being entertained in the megaron by Orpheus once again, as well as other musicians and dancers of the court, when Alcinous was approached by one of his staff. He listened to the man's words then summoned Jason to his side.

'The Colchian captain and two of his men are outside and ask to speak with you,' said Alcinous. 'Shall I have them returned to their ship under guard and ordered to quit our harbour or d'you wish to hear what they have to say?'

'I'll speak with them. They need to understand the situation then maybe they'll give us no trouble.'

'Then,' said Alcinous, 'I will take to my throne and you, with your new wife, must be at my side.

The Colchians will stand before us as supplicants. Your actions and your words I will support by my authority and if necessary with the palace guard.'

He ordered the musicians and the dancers to stop and to move in silence with most others to the far side of the hall. Jason and Medea followed him and there stood as requested with three armed guards a short distance away. A court official appeared, followed by three leather-kilted, bearded and burly men, evidently disarmed. They approached around the great hearth until commanded to halt before Alcinous.

'What is it you wish to say?' asked the king.

The three eyed Medea, then glanced at Jason, who had allowed his gown to fall open enough for his sword to be in plain view at the side of his tunic.

'Your Lordship,' answered their captain, 'we are commanded by King Aietes to find those who took away the Golden Fleece that is most sacred to him; to reclaim this and to return to Colchis with it and with our king's daughter, who we see here before us.'

'By custom throughout these and other lands,' Alcinous responded, 'the Lady Medea can no longer be obliged to return with you since she is married to this man, a prince of the House of Chiron, King of Pelion in Thessaly.' He looked aside at Jason, adding, 'As for this Golden Fleece, the decision must be in his hands and his alone.'

The eyes of the Colchian captain were hard on him as Jason said, 'The Golden Fleece I will not let you have but you can go inland from Colchis to the mountains where you may find yourselves another

246

like it. That shouldn't be too difficult from what I've heard and Aietes must himself be aware of it.'

'But – but from what we are told,' insisted the captain, 'the one you took has properties possessed by no other – and therefore is mightily desired by our king.'

'Oh, you mean the inscription it carries,' said Jason. 'Then we'll have it copied onto a clay tablet and baked hard so you can give that to Aietes. Problem solved, I think.'

The three shuffled uneasily, murmuring, staring from one to the other then the captain asked, 'Lord Alcinous, may we talk among ourselves for some moments then return here to you?'

'You may do so, yes,' replied Alcinous, gesturing to his right. 'Take yourselves over to those columns, decide what else you have to say but do not test my patience.'

'Nor mine,' added Jason under his breath.

The three stepped across the megaron, halted where indicated and with hands in animated gesturing they conversed in harsh whispers. They became silent, looked across then returned to stand before Alcinous. The one who had spoken first began, 'My Lord, I as captain of the vessel that brought us here and these, two of my most trusted men, ask humbly that you – that you allow us to remain and take us into your service.'

'By Zeus!' exclaimed Alcinous. 'Are you not in the service of a king who has trusted you?'

'If we return without the Golden Fleece and Aietes knows we encountered you here, as he must if one of the crew speak of it, and that surely will

247

happen, his anger will be turned upon us and our lives may be forfeit.'

'He speaks the truth,' said Medea. 'I know my father well enough. He will punish their failure just as he would have rewarded their success.'

'They might end up decorating his city wall,' added Jason. 'I've seen what Aietes does.'

The fire at the centre of the megaron flared, spat and settled as Alcinous considered his response. 'And if I were to look favourably upon your request, what about your crew; how many are there?'

'Some thirty of us,' answered one of the captain's men.

'Aye, that's so,' confirmed the captain, 'and once they know we three are not returning and why, they'll not care to do so either. My Lord, if you'll grant us our wishes we'll hand over our vessel, all those things of value for trade it contains and all our arms. And – and the vessel herself; she has been long in your harbour and may in any case be in need of repair.'

'And what of those families I'm sure you have in Colchis?' Medea asked.

'What can we do?' responded the captain. 'They'd suffer rebuke or worse if we returned but if nothing more was heard of us then silence could not harm them. King Aietes will most likely think we were lost at sea.'

'Aye,' added the third man, 'we've been gone from Colchis long enough to 'ave disappeared many times over.'

'Return to your vessel and stay where you are,' said Alcinous. 'I will give you my answer in the morning.' As the three Colchians departed he turned to Jason and Medea to ask, 'As you know these people better than I, what would be your decision?'

'I think their not returning would be better for everyone concerned,' answered Jason. 'Aietes won't know whether they or we have been here and will have no idea whether or not we returned to Thessaly.'

'I agree,' said Medea. 'If my father knows nothing of their fate he is more likely to beg at our temples for help than he is to send more men this far out.'

Alcinous appeared satisfied with their replies and the activities of his court returned to normal.

***

Well there you have it, I was married to Jason, and the problem with the Colchians was settled. As I said our somewhat hurried wedding ceremony was no great royal affair with courtiers swarming in from all sides with gifts and unwanted advice. As for relatives, I certainly would have wanted none of mine.

Arete, bless her, had given Jason and I one of her private rooms with ornate oil lamps, luxurious bed, more romantic you see, and amenities similar to those I had previously enjoyed but without, of course, the assistance of her two girls. After dining with Alcinous, Arete and his closest courtiers, Jason left me alone and went to visit the ship while I, having retired, made good use of the facilities granted to us and awaited his return. Wearing only my Egyptian cotton gown, I was gazing out over the moonlit garden when he reappeared, grinning like a mischievous child. In his arms he carried the Golden Fleece.

"Why have you brought *that* here?" I asked.

"I'm going to lay it over our bed," he informed me. "A special occasion like ours deserves something as special as this. I'd also like to think what Aietes would say if he knew we were using his most valued possession to celebrate our marriage."

"Well, Jason, dear," I responded, "he isn't going to know whether we fuck on that or as we've been doing all along in the bow of your ship – but all right, we'll do it on there tonight if it pleases you."

You'll have gathered, I wasn't overjoyed with the idea but I wanted Jason just then in the same way he wanted me so the Fleece was put to a somewhat different use than previously intended with both of us rolling about on it. Afterwards, when the one meagre lamp we'd left burning was extinguished and darkness possessed us, I lay thinking of my father in distant Colchis. Had he been able to see us that night he might have had a seizure. Oh, and how some of his people would have rejoiced.

Chapter 11 - Conflict at The River

The sun was yet to rise when, under a peerless blue sky, *Argo*, well provisioned by order of Alcinous, set sail on her home journey. By midday, riding lively waters in a fair breeze that spared the efforts of the oarsmen, the island of Scheria was becoming hardly more than a pleasant memory for the men, though a fateful one for Medea.

'I know these coasts well enough now,' said the captain, 'an' if the nights are clear then, wind an' weather permittin', we'll be back 'ome, in five days.'

They proceeded south and continued on without incident, keeping close to land where nighttime camping proved safe and convenient, sailing between the islands of Ithaca and Kephallenia before reaching the coast of the Peloponnese. Further south yet and they passed close by the great city of Pylos set in her fertile plains. There some of the crew wished to go ashore but Jason insisted they continue on, uppermost in his mind being the possible situation at Pelion. Turning east they passed between the cape of Maleia and the island of Kythera before steering north-east into the Aegean Sea, passing Attica on their left then turning north-west to follow the coast of Euboia. Argo's estimate for their arrival proved true, for early on the fifth day they steered into the bay where the harbour of Pelion came into view.

With sail furled, most of the oars shipped and Ancaeus at his tiller, they approached the quay

251

where people of the town, having already spotted *Argo's* pennants and sail some way out, were gathered in growing numbers to cheer and wave.

'Well, young sir,' beamed the captain, 'doesn't seem like there's been any trouble 'ere.'

'No,' said Jason, shielding his eyes from the afternoon sun with raised hand, 'and I see my father coming down to greet us. I'm sure he'll have much to tell me and I'll have a great deal to tell him.'

Medea stood close by in a courtly gown given her by Arete, her long hair clipped back so as to appear less unkempt than this last stage of the voyage had once again rendered it. Arms folded, she studied the people on the quay but said nothing.

***

Argo was safely moored with her crew ashore and returning to reclaim their camp. All but pressed in by an eager throng, Jason and Medea proceeded with Chiron to the palace where, once clear of their citizen followers, they made their way through the great hall to his private chamber. On their crossing the megaron there was one who, clouded by remorse, watched from amidst the milling courtiers. Clymene was no longer a slave. Clymene no longer would be required to serve her former master and lover. She gazed at Medea and knew her own image had passed from Jason's thoughts as a flame extinguished in a breeze. It seemed for Jason another flame was lit but Clymene wished only for a return to her previous status when she would be called once more to attend him.

'Your vessel was reported approaching from some way out,' said Chiron as they sat before the circular wooden table in a small chamber overlooking the harbour, 'so I have already arranged a feast and entertainment later today for your captain and your men.'

'That they will much appreciate,' said Jason.

Two male slaves entered bearing an amphora and three gold goblets that they placed reverently upon the table. With the wine poured, Chiron dismissed the two and glancing at the still silent Medea who, cup in hand, sat looking pensively toward the window, said, 'This lady you have brought to my presence has yet to be introduced. Will you do so now?'

'We are man and wife,' replied Jason, sensing her mood of detachment. He was about to say more when lowering her goblet she announced, 'I am Medea, priestess of Hecate and a daughter of Aietes, King of Colchis. Jason and I were married six days ago at the temple of Poseidon on the island of Scheria.'

'Oh, married were you,' smiled Chiron, 'then I must congratulate you both. But finish your wine, retire for a while to bathe and prepare yourselves to rejoin me where we can talk at greater length. I'm sure it will be a most pleasurable evening. You, Jason, have been away from Pelion far longer than I expected and doubtless will have much to tell me.'

When Jason and Medea arose, Chiron remained at the table. He watched them leave, the image of Medea hovered, but his smile was gone.

In those rooms of the palace assigned to Jason, Medea found herself able to bathe in warm water and pampered by two girls in a manner she considered deserving of her royal status, though not to quite the degree of sophistication or intimacy that she had experienced in Arete's private chamber. Nevertheless, the oils and perfumes, the attention to her hair before a polished bronze mirror and the use of those adornments she had taken with her on the long journey prompted a return of confidence. Suitably attired in courtly robes she joined Jason who, in plain, belted tunic, assessed her carefully and remarked, 'Well now you do look the part and I'm sure my father will be impressed.'

'He may appear to be impressed,' said Medea, adjusting her brightly pattered, ankle-length flounced dress, 'but I know he will not truly be so.'

'How can you say that? You've hardly met him and he surely said nothing that could have caused you offence.'

'No he did not,' she said, quietly, 'but still I know it.'

'I think you misread my father, powers of perception or no,' responded Jason. 'I'll send to say we'll soon join him then we'll make our way down there.'

As Jason gave his instructions to the man waiting outside, Medea breathed, 'I did not misread him. I do not misread people, no, except perhaps for you, Jason, dear.'

They found Chiron waiting outside the megaron where he said with a smile, 'Let's go together into the garden where we can sit in peace and you can relate what has happened to you, to Argos and to those men of your crew over these past months. There is food and wine waiting for us and the evening is most pleasant.'

They sat beneath the light of a three quarter moon and abundant display of stars while close by played the delicate tune not of a lyre but of a fountain. Jason raised his goblet to drink then began to recount the events of their long voyage. He told how they had abandoned the ever boastful Heracles, how they had driven away the bizarre and ravenous Harpies who had victimized blind Phineus. Chiron was amused to hear of the boxing match that saw the defeat and death of Amycus, pirate king of the Bebryces at the fists of Polydeuces and their welcoming reception by the Mariandyni for his having done this. When the meal was finished, more wine was brought and Jason spoke next of their arrival at Aietes' forbidding town and the grim spectacle it presented at the main city gate. He spoke of his encounter with Aietes, his meeting Medea in the temple of Hecate. Chiron raised his hands with enthusiasm as Jason related in greater detail his seizure of the Golden Fleece, the slaughter of its guardian and their escape from Colchis with her king in pursuit. Medea's attention was by now occupied wholly by the fountain.

'Wonderful!' declared Chiron, swirling wine about his goblet. 'What a tale you have to tell! But for all the time that has passed since you left Pelion there must be far more to relate.'

'Perhaps so but what happened after Colchis was a result of our men's dissatisfaction. They had gained little from our journey other than hard work so on returning to the Aegean Sea we continued on westwards.' Jason related all that had followed until their reaching the Phaeacians and the unexpected presence in their harbour of a Colchian vessel.

Until now, Medea had remained silent. 'And don't forget to tell your father more of our royal wedding will you, dear,' she said at last, adding under her breath, 'after all those endless days at sea on that damned ship.'

'How could I forget such an occasion,' grinned Jason.'

'And talking of ships,' said Medea, 'the four young men, my half-brothers we rescued from Colchis – they served with Argos' crew throughout our journey but now they're here and have nowhere else to go.'

'True enough,' Jason responded, turning to Chiron. 'They know well the use of weapons and are familiar with court life even if it was only that of Colchis. I will vouch for them.'

'I'll think on it and speak with them tomorrow,' said Chiron. 'I'm sure we can take them within our fold and make Pelion their new home.'

Jason took another mouthful of wine then said, 'But since we sat, this has all been my – our tale and I know nothing of what's happened here at home.'

'We have remained at peace,' Chiron responded, 'but trouble simmers in Iolcos. I'm informed that Pelias is now convinced you are gone forever and is laying his plans against us. I have two men of our own over there, one as a visiting priest of Poseidon and the other as a trader in ingots of tin, a valuable enough commodity to take him closer to their king and others who may have loose tongues.

Your returning here at this time must be the work of the gods as one or both those men of mine are expected back with us any day now and will report all they have learned.'

'Then let's hope none of Pelias' own men have spotted our vessel,' said Jason.

***

Two sunlit days passed during which time the plunder gained at Trinacria, with silver to even out each man's allotted share, was divided among *Argo's* crew at their camp and Medea enjoyed what she regarded as a well-earned rest amid the comparative luxuries of Chiron's palace. Several times did she pass close by Clymene. The girl appeared always preoccupied and said nothing, but Medea knew her thoughts and could feel strongly her resentment.

Around midafternoon on the third day a bearded rider in rough tunic rode through the city gate with a second ass on tow behind, this burdened by satchels of tin ingots hanging either side of the wearily plodding animal. He reached the steps to the palace entrance, dismounted, ascended to where the guards stood waiting and, obviously known to them, passed inside without hindrance.

'Ah, Polydamos,' said Chiron, 'you were seen approaching. What news have you from Iolcos?'

Polydamos halted before the throne where Chiron sat with Jason standing by his side. He eyed Jason with surprise, not having known of his return, then replied, 'My Lords, these last nights I have spent time in a tavern close by their palace – a tavern frequented by members of the palace guard.

257

The wine had loosened their tongues and revealed their enthusiasm so I learned this: the fighting men of Iolcus are being readied by order of Pelias as I speak with you and it would seem they are promised full freedom to seize everything of value here, including our young women and your horses, and to burn all of this town.'

'And do you know when Pelias intends to make his move?' Jason asked.

'I believe from what I heard,' replied Polydamos, 'that it will be in three days' time. It is planned their spearmen and archers will leave Iolcus before dawn when the moon is full and cross the River Anauros at daybreak. They will arrive here as our people are about their morning business or insufficiently prepared even if warned of their approach. The afternoon before, Pelias will have men disguised as traders come here to ascertain for certain that his forces are not expected. I thought it better to leave before my appointed meeting with his dealers this morning to acquire silver in exchange for tin, as matters seemed most urgent, and so I still retain those ingots I was about to sell. I heard also that Andron, my colleague who presented himself as a visiting priest was denounced as an imposter by one of those serving at the temple of Poseidon. If that is so he could be subjected to torture and might reveal my own presence and purpose there.'

'But at this time of the year,' said Chiron, 'the Anauros is in full flood and can be treacherous. How does Pelias plan to have his men cross it in safety when burdened by their arms and armour?'

'There was talk, My Lord, of pulling carts full of men by oxen where the river is at its widest and therefore slowest – just above the rocks where today I myself managed to cross though with some difficulty. Two of those carts I saw being prepared outside the city wall as I left.'

'I know the place on the river you speak of,' said Jason. 'I lost a sandal there when I – well never mind that; I know it and we must plan our own moves. The men you say he'll be sending in advance – d'you know who they are?'

'I regret, Sir, I do not.'

Jason and his father considered Polydamos' words then Jason said, 'You may leave us now but I'm sure my father will reward you for the risks you've taken.'

'That I will,' agreed Chiron, 'but we must think hard over what you have told us.'

Having offered a short bow Polydamos stepped away. With father and son now alone, Jason said, 'If Pelias is sending men to check on us it means he probably knows nothing of my return or of those men we still have camped outside our main gate. They'll have to relocate elsewhere and soon.'

'Whether he knows of your return or not,' said Chiron, 'we must be prepared to do battle and I say we meet our enemy at the river.'

'Perhaps, but many of our own men will die even if we defeat Pelias. I say we use to our advantage his ignorance of my being back here. When his spies visit us, they must see nothing untoward – no tents, nothing at all and that includes

259

Argo. Our vessel must be taken out today and moored along the coast where she'll not be seen.'

'That is so,' agreed Chiron, 'and I'll deal with these matters shortly.'

'Good, they must see our people and our traders doing what they always do as if we suspected nothing. His men will return and report to Pelias and he'll think we're to be overwhelmed by a surprise attack and our town picked clean.'

'So,' breathed Chiron, 'it sounds as if you've already worked out what has to be done. Would you care to enlighten me?'

'Just upriver of the crossing place is heavily wooded on both sides. Tomorrow we gather a group of men skilled in felling trees and cutting timber, then -. Look, shall I call for wine and then I'll go into more detail.'

'Yes, call for wine,' answered Chiron, 'I may well need it.'

***

The stars were gone from the sky, the moon a pale ghost of its once shining glory. The sun was yet to rise but the birds were singing as always they did at this time of a brightening day. Anyone nearing the Anauros in the cool, calm air of that morning would have seen or heard nothing to break the peace other than the gushing waters of the river. A few people were gathered by the riverside. Fishing lines were cast into turbulent waters, children called out as they dashed to and fro, dogs yapped and scurried and women watched in case their children ventured too close to the water. On the same side but further downstream a lone figure stood unnoticed; a fragile, stooping figure dressed in black gown and hood with her face part concealed.

There were sounds that did not belong; indistinct at first against the rush of water but still they did not belong. There was distant shouting. Heads were raised. Where the river bank opposite rose gradually away there was movement and as people looked on, menacing forms arose against a lightening sky. Soon it was obvious; there were men approaching in force. There were horsemen, there were pairs of oxen pulling carts and in each of those carts there were tightly packed many more men with light glinting ominously on a bristling of bronze spearheads. Men by the river abandoned their fishing, women called shrilly for their children and, with dogs circling, began to usher them toward the path leading back to the town.

A short way upriver where the trees began stood a figure in rustic gown. He had observed the solitary dark figure waiting further down and knew her, but now was not the time to reflect on that. He gazed across at the burgeoning hoard as it descended the gentle slope to the Anauros. The snort of oxen and creak of carts reached his ears. And though there was no opposition to confront them on the other side of the river a drum began to beat from the leading cart and men started to chant aloud. While the majority of the men, spearmen and archers, occupied the six ox-drawn wagons their leader was obvious enough as he pulled ahead to the water's edge in a four wheeled wicker and hide chariot drawn by a pair of gaudily plumed black horses. Unlike most of his men whose armour was

261

varied, whose helmets were of bronze or of interlocking boar's tusks, his ornately crafted bronze corselet gleamed bright, as did his banded helmet topped by many quivering plumes. He paused and waited as his host reached churning water that would deter any man attempting to cross on foot encumbered with arms and armour. As the big carts prepared to cross, as their leader gestured for them to continue on, those few men on foot clung to the sides and rear of the carts wherever they were able.

A ram's horn blared out, raised by the man standing upriver by the trees. Those beginning to cross the Anauros paid no heed to it; those who did notice took it as a signal from one of their own. Two carts had entered the water side by side and, splashing, jolting over riverbed rocks, would soon be half way across with two more close behind. With the cacophony of the river and their own chanting, they could never have heard the thunder of hoof-beats as over sixty armed riders appeared from the direction of the town. But these new arrivals they saw easily enough as did their leader who himself, almost part way over, called his men on in confidence of knowing he outnumbered very greatly the men of Pelion who were dismounting to so foolishly oppose him. His men were shouting insults and some, fuelled by enthusiasm cast their spears, though only one man on the river bank was struck because the lumbering wagons spoiled their aim. The leading pairs of oxen were about to struggle up the embankment when the first log stuck. None of the men from Iolcus had seen that log and others approach, heaving and rolling, from upriver. It slammed into one of the second pair of carts, splintering the side, rearing, driving into the men it contained, heaving the cart aside to collide with its companion that swayed precariously then heeled over to discharge its human cargo into churning water. Several horsemen, too, were struck down as others attempted to back away and turn. Jason's men were cheering wildly when moments later another log collided with the leading pair and added to the blind chaos that had erupted close behind them. Screams of the wounded and dying joined cries of panic, bellowing oxen and snorting horses as further logs ploughed into the wagons already stricken and into those pulling the third pair which veered aside then shuddered to a standstill. Men were floundering in the water, some, where close enough, scrambled to regain the river bank, others were seized and hurled away by a current that dashed many against the rocks further downstream. Witnessing this catastrophic turmoil their leader had managed to pull his horses about and was struggling to reach dry ground with a man clinging in desperation to a side of his cart that was beginning to break away in his grasp. Pelias drew his sword and hacked through the man's arm so that, with screams consumed by the uproar, he joined his companions to perish in that blood tainted tide of death. Pelias looked over his shoulder at the carnage then he saw, and he knew, who was responsible for the defeat of his enterprise. Jason, his peasant's smock cast aside, had rejoined his men.

263

The horsemen of Pelion had dismounted and spread along the river bank with swords drawn to cut down or take prisoner any man who attempted to escape on their side of the wreckage-sweeping Anauros. More men were approaching from the town with Chiron himself at their head, mainly archers with their bows at the ready. Those of the enemy, thinking themselves safe through having gained dry land opposite, now began to fall as a deadly, bronze-tipped flock hissed over the river.

'There goes the man who planned to destroy us,' said Jason as he and Polydeuces watched Pelias, who fleeing beyond range of the flesh-seeking arrows, disappeared over the rise.

'Why did you order the archers not to aim at the bastard?' asked Polydeuces.

'Because,' replied Jason, 'I swore an oath before the priests of his own temple - one that I'd be unable to keep should he die first.'

***

I had followed them although Jason didn't know it. I'd had a slave prepare a small chariot and take me following behind his horsemen but ahead of the archers. I remained out of sight somewhat further back on higher ground from where I witnessed the whole scene. I watched the enemy wagons shattered by those logs, their men crushed and drowned or their lives brutally ended by sword or knife while trying to drag themselves from the river. Their cries, their screams, arose to the heavens – to the very gods themselves. I watched the man I knew was Pelias, King of Iolcus, flee with those of his men

264

who survived scurrying to follow him as best they could.

Killing other men was what Jason did well. I was proud of him then; proud of his skills and his leadership at such a time of adversity. And although I sensed on occasion, usually in the depths of night, a demon of doubt stirring deep within me, always it curled up and refused to arise.

But I saw more when at the Anauros. I saw the one standing downstream, the one Jason had told me about, the frail old woman swathed in black. Frail and old as she wished others to see her but I knew who she was and she knew I was there also. I knew she was laughing and the bloodied waters of the river were laughing with her.

***

'A splendid idea and how well it worked,' said Chiron as they sat that afternoon in the palace courtyard with an ample quantity of honeyed wine.

'I thought a novel approach might do it,' smiled Jason. 'I had our men collect whatever there was to be recovered of their arms and armour on our side of the river.'

'How many men d'you think they lost?' asked Chiron.

'I can make only a rough guess but it must exceed two hundred of his best – maybe far more.'

'And now?'

'Tomorrow,' replied Jason, 'I pay our friend Pelias a visit. I owe him the Golden Fleece do I not and he owes us his throne.'

'He owes *you* his throne, don't you mean? It is rightfully yours and yours alone.'

265

'Yes I – I thought of it that way until I set out on my journey. Now I see Iolcus as joined to our own kingdom under one ruling house - yours. I have no wish to spend my days in Iolcus.'

'You're still restless, my boy; more restless than ever you were in spite of your long journey.'

'That I am,' Jason agreed, 'more than ever I was, as you say. But first things first – how many horses can we spare? I'd like to take with me thirty well-armed men including a few of those who sailed with me to Colchis. That should be enough; I doubt there'll be much fight left in Pelias.'

'No problem. Thirty good mounts you shall have and I'll make sure they're ready before sunrise tomorrow. Meanwhile I'll have Argos and his men set off to bring our vessel back to the harbour.'

'Then for now,' said Jason, 'I think it as well if I join my newly acquired wife. I've not seen much of her these last few days.'

'Is she to join you tomorrow?' Chiron asked. 'After all, Medea is your only sound evidence that you went to Colchis at all and as for your procuring the fleece she is your only witness.'

Jason thought for some moments then replied, 'Yes, she *is* my only witness. I'll take her with me.'

***

The slowly lightening sky was part clouded, the breeze fresh when they set off to pass through the city gate, Jason at their head with the Golden Fleece draped across the neck of his horse, a prize white mount from his father's stable. Each man wore crested bronze helmet, a bronze or boiled hide cuirass over his woollen tunic and wool-padded

266

greaves at his lower legs. And while each wore a sword at his side, some also carried a short spear and small round shield. In their midst, pulled by two horses, a four-wheeled, wooden framed, oxhide chariot carrying a battle-hardened warrior, Polydeuces himself, as its driver and Medea in the plain dark dress of a priestess as its passenger. Descending to the plane they passed traders on their way to Pelion, these obliged to stand aside and look on as the armed party passed them by. Others were already about their business in orchard, vineyard and field.

The clouds were dispersing when they approached the Anauros to observe it as lively as it had been that previous, memorable day. A short way upriver of the rocky crossing, water cascaded over smashed wagons, fallen oxen and horses. Ominous dark birds swooped, hovered, pranced and pecked about the wreckage amid which lay dead men heaped in grotesque disorder. Other bodies could be seen sprawled about on the far bank likewise attended by those creatures, including flesh-tearing jackals, who saw about them a feast unlike any other.

'No one's yet been to claim their dead,' observed one of Jason's men as they drew to a halt. 'And many of those on the far side appear still to possess their arms and armour.'

'I imagine,' said Jason, 'those at Iolcus are not yet recovered from the shock of what has happened.' They remained a short time to survey the scene of victory then Jason called to his men,

'We'll ride close by to the right of them! The water there is less turbulent!'

The water was deep but not so lively that they were unable to cross without incident or regard at closer distance the splintered and bloodied wreckage. The chariot carrying Medea crossed with some difficulty. On the far side they passed close to the bodies of those felled by the archer's shot, scattering to the air many of the attendant birds but not the busy flies.

'You can draw lots for their arms and armour on our way back,' declared Jason. 'And when we reach Iolcus we let no one stand in our way!'

The sun was past its zenith when Jason and his men approached the city gate of Iolcus. About the vineyards and orchards life appeared much as it might at Pelion though men and women looked on anxiously as the party rode by. They passed beneath the main gate where sheltered the pitiful destitute then into the market square which they found almost deserted and oddly quiet, as was the sacrificial area before the temple of Poseidon where Jason's oath had been so foolishly sworn. Crossing the square they dismounted at the steps leading up to the palace entrance. There the two guards moved aside, offering no challenge, as Jason, with the fleece hanging over his left arm, Polydeuces and one other of his men entered the building with Medea following close behind. Others of his men gathered about the entrance ready to act if called upon. Jason well remembered the way into the great hall where, on that fateful day, he had been persuaded to undertake a journey the likes of which he could never have imagined. In silence they passed through deserted annex and corridor until pausing before the entrance to the megaron. There were voices as they entered.

The atmosphere within the great hall was more that of a deserted temple. The central hearth contained only smouldering ashes, no torches burned about the walls, daylight was not sufficient to dispel the gloom and the air was altogether free of cooking odours. Pelias was seated at his great wooden table in conversation with Lycon, his aide. Two armed guards stood close by. There was cold food and a wine goblet set before Pelias but no chatter, no music, no sight of the bare-breasted female courtiers who once fluttered before his regal presence. On seeing the newcomers the guards appeared confused, one of them dropping a hand to his sword hilt. Pelias raised a staying hand, glanced at Jason then dismissed his own men. He did not attempt to raise his pot-bellied bulk from the high-backed, ornately carved and gilded chair. Pushing aside his embossed gold cup he gazed hard at the Golden Fleece, by now not quite as golden as it had been when first removed from its shrine. He growled at Jason, 'I was informed of your approach an' after yesterday I knew you'd get around 'ere sooner or later.' His manner of speech suggested a considerable quantity of wine had passed his lips.

'And now I have,' said Jason, holding out his arm to display in full the object of their wager, 'and as you see, I have kept my side of the bargain. And if your priests are able to read the holy text displayed on it I believe they will confirm your

269

Golden Fleece to be genuine.' Pelias, rocking gently in his chair, continued to stare at the fleece as Jason added, softly, 'How unfortunate it is you decided to attack my father's kingdom; so many mothers now have lost a son, so many wives a husband.'

Medea, standing close to Jason, muttered, 'Beware of him. His thoughts are ruled only by vengeful anger.'

Pelias, with thundercloud expression, grasped the edge of his table, part rose from his seat, pushed back the jewelled leather band that circled his broad head and declared, 'All was in the 'ands of the gods! Aye, it always was, but that soothsayer of mine, Elymos, assured me you'd never be seen 'ere again an' all would go as we wished. We made the necessary sacrifices an' 'e told me, aye, 'e told me all the omens were good. Well 'e won't be makin' any more predictions unless 'is 'ead's able to do the talkin' without the rest of 'is fuckin' body!'

'Unlucky for him as well,' muttered Jason as Pelias struggled unsteadily from his chair. 'But now I confirm my right to this kingdom and all its lands. You, my friend, must gather your possessions and go, unless you wish to join your soothsayer in Hades. And *this* can go with you.' So saying, he cast the Golden Fleece onto the table in front of Pelias, adding, 'I and my men will take up residence here tonight and ensure your departure by sunrise tomorrow, together with those who remain loyal and wish to quit Iolcos with you.'

Pelias glared at the fleece and exclaimed, 'Inscription or no, where's the proof? That's what *I* want to see. Where's the tablets from their priests an' royal seal of 'oever was their king?'

'I am proof!' declared Medea. 'I am daughter of King Aietes of Colchis and priestess of the temple of Hecate. I was with Jason when he took the fleece from its shrine and when we fled the city.'

'You?' Pelias growled. 'He could 'ave picked *you* up anywhere. I don't believe a fuckin' word!'

'Believe whatever you like,' Jason responded. 'The matter is ended.'

The four would have left without another word but they had taken only a few steps when Medea cried, 'Jason!'

The swish of a blade caused them to spring apart and turn to face Pelias who, seized with drunken rage, his sword raised high, lunged at Jason with a cry of, 'This is all you'll 'ave!'

But Pelias was not a man built for physical action and Jason dodged the swinging blow as his own weapon flashed from its scabbard. He seized Pelias' sword arm, struck him hard and deep through the middle then stepped back to wrench the blade free. Pelias froze, stared at Jason in wide-eyed, mouth-gaping disbelief, let fall his sword then like a stricken ox, crashed to the floor with a rattling gasp, arms akimbo. The three watched the final quivering moments of his departing life then Jason bent to wipe the blood from his sword with the dead man's robe. He sheathed the blade, dragged the Golden Fleece from the table, drew it over the one time king's body then stood back to gaze down in

271

satisfaction. 'Like I said,' he breathed, 'The matter is ended.'

'Hera in those last moments turned his mind,' breathed Medea. 'She intended always that he should die at your hand.'

Further along the corridor leading from the megaron they encountered Lycon and the two guards dismissed by Pelias. 'Better go to your master,' said Jason, 'he seems to be indisposed – and, Lycon, I'll speak with you at sundown in Pelias' private chambers. Be there.'

The two sat facing one another in the small, frescoed, chamber, opulently appointed and having a view of the sea. And although the dying sun still touched nearby hills with soft light, wall-mounted torches were already lit. The pair of plainly dressed female slaves who had placed food and wine between them now stood beyond the door to await further summons.

'Lycon,' he began, 'I trust funeral arrangements are in hand for your now departed king.'

'They are, My Lord, and our priests will conclude ceremonies tomorrow at his tomb outside the city wall.'

'Good, then I, as you must know, am his rightful successor. Yesterday at the Anauros Iolcos lost a good many of its best warriors and many lie there still. Most of our men wait at Pelion and will march here fully armed at once if necessary but this is not what I or my father wish to see happen. Pelion and Iolcus should join together in friendship, each in support of the other. That way both will be stronger. Do you consider I speak the truth?'

Lycon peered down in thought then replied, 'It would be in the interests of both our kingdoms for there must be greater strength in unity, but why do you share your thoughts with me?'

'Because it's you I wish to retain in a position of trust. You were a close confidant of Pelias. You know well the workings of his court and those who were closest to him.'

Jason picked up his goblet and waited, visibly relaxed, but Lycon once again appeared lost for words. Eventually he said, 'My Lord, I served the king well enough in spite of occasional difficulties and it - it would please me to continue in your service provided it was also in the interests of my own people. I take it you yourself would wish to reside here.'

'I think possibly not and if that were so you would be answerable directly to my father, Chiron, who is King of Pelion. You, a number of your elders and members of your priesthood must therefore return with me and swear allegiance to him as ruler of our joint kingdoms.'

'I will do so willingly, Lord Jason. I know much about your father and from all accounts I believe he is one who will ensure justice and good governance prevail over Iolcus also.'

'Good, then we'll drink to that and before you and I leave tomorrow we will call together an assembly of elders, priests and the palace guard to announce our intentions. The men who came here with me will remain at the palace. I'm sure you understand.'

'Yes, Lord Jason, that will serve us both well. But perhaps you will permit some of our people to recover the bodies of those who fell by the Anauros.'

'Yes, they can follow us unarmed as far as the river and do just that, but as victors my men claim the arms and armour of those fallen.'

274

Chapter 12 - Betrayal

Three days had passed when, with Lycon and his entourage departed for their return to Iolcus, Jason sat with his father in a quiet chamber away from the chatter of the great hall.

'We have made sacrifice in thanks to the gods for what you have done,' Chiron said. 'The remaining men who heard my summons and who served you so well are departing their camp outside the city wall and through your actions the kingdoms of Pelion and Iolcos are joined as one.'

'I would suggest,' said Jason, 'that a good number of our fighting men remain in Iolcus and a number of theirs serve here at Pelion.'

'I think so. Trust can depart like chaff in the wind but your presence would have ensured its continuation. Are you quite sure you wish to leave Pelion for other lands?'

'Father, I – I have seen more of the world than I ever could have imagined and I'm not yet ready to take my place in Iolcos. There can only be one king and that is you. I need to see and know more of this world before I settle down. I believe Lycon will keep to his word, especially with our own men there to support him. Apart from that, you have many years ahead of you with a sound kingdom and I'm sure this will be much as it is when I return.'

'And your new wife, will she be contented to follow you – is she as restless as you are?'

'Oh, Medea, yes – I've seen little of her these past three days and our time together has not been

275

as any woman should expect, but then I'm not sure she would be happy to stay here. She feels you have not taken full liking to her.'

'No, I think there's a part of her that remains hidden - hidden perhaps even from you, though you have told me of her powers. But then the fault may lie within myself as I hardly know her. During the day she's kept largely to the company of other women and when we have spoken she's always had other things on her mind, as if other matters pressed for her attention.'

'Our marriage was one side of the bargain,' said Jason. 'Without her I never would have taken the Golden Fleece and might never have escaped Colchis.'

'Yes, I - I do understand,' said Chiron, gazing down at his wine cup. 'So what d'you have in mind?'

'I feel we should go first to Corinth and spend some time there. I have inquired much over these last few days and among the men who were our crew, some spoke of Corinth, saying this is a great city, larger than that of Aietes in Colchis, much larger than Iolcus and -.'

'And therefore much larger than Pelion,' put in Chiron.

'Well - yes, but I know we have good trading relations with them.'

'That we do and I myself was in Corinth some years ago. It is a fine and busy town, far enough away but only a fraction of the distance you have travelled. Her king, Creon, will be pleased to welcome a son of mine as he not so many years ago welcomed me.'

'Yes, and it's not so far away that I couldn't return here within days if necessary. I have it in mind to take *Argo*. She is in much need of repair after our long voyage so I will take her to the isthmus of Corinth which I'm told is sacred to Poseidon. There I will dedicate her to the god himself who I'm told also by our own priests has a shrine there.'

'Yes, that is true and I have seen it,' assured Chiron. 'But what about your crew? Most of those who manned your vessel have now left us.'

'I'll have our good Argos recruit enough men to take us there but they'll need to find their own way back. The one man I must take is Echion who served us well as herald. I'll have our arrival announced in advance.'

'That you must, my boy, and you have of course to take gifts for Creon – something to please him highly. I hear he's had many troubles within his own house since I was last there. And while you are gone I will take myself over to Iolcus to see our men and reassure Lycon of our commitment.'

***

Such glory has dear Jason enjoyed, but I return from now on with much more to tell – more than ever I thought I might. After Jason had settled his account with the King of Iolcus and we arrived back in Pelion, I found time to re-strengthen my relationship with Hecate. There was no shrine dedicated to her at Pelion, she was not recognised there and never would be. But when alone in my

277

chamber with only the wavering flame of a small oil lamp for company, as the scented plumes of incense arose and spread, I called her name and she answered. Her spirit came to me out of the night, which is her domain, and she reconfirmed my powers.

When Jason informed me that we were to go to Corinth I agreed, for I still nurtured a passion for him that defied my own reasoning. And where else would I care to go since I never thought I could find contentment at Pelion. There were Chiron's less than amiable feelings toward me – and there were all those snorting, clattering horses! The sound and smell of them I found most disagreeable. No, this town was not for me. Then there was that little slut Clymene, an ex-slave. She wanted to charm herself back into Jason's bed and have me out of it. Yes, her thoughts shone through even when she didn't look at me. I knew she'd been praying at the temple of Aphrodite and I knew she'd been making frequent offerings in the hope of rekindling his affections.

After all his wanderings and his victories it was clear to me how Jason wanted more of the good life. He regarded Corinth as an open door but gave no thought as to what might lie beyond it. He didn't ask me if I wanted to go there but simply assumed I would follow him. I'd learned less about the place than he had but I had no choice. Jason had accomplished the task Hera had contrived for him but what of the good fortune bestowed upon him to satisfy her vengeful scheming? Now her hand in his affairs was gone, what might be the fate of this all too mortal man - and was I destined to share it?

The night before we left, Chiron had organised a feast with musicians, acrobats, a fire eater and a sword swallower, the last two I wish had misjudged and accidentally killed themselves. I was in no mood for such petty entertainments. There was no ceremony arranged for our departure because Chiron wanted people to think Jason did not intend to be away for long but was rather undertaking a journey of diplomacy. And the reason for this pretence? Chiron considered there may have been those in Iolcus unhappy over the new arrangements with Pelion and keen to regain independence.

I'd had no desire to venture out to sea again but Jason assured me it would be quicker and safer than going overland, though I sensed he had other reasons for so doing. We departed the harbour early next morning with his captain in charge of the vessel but with dear Jason looking somewhat dazed after a surfeit of wine that previous evening and needing the hand of Argos to help him clamber into the ship. As most of those who'd manned the boat to Colchis and taken us around Trinacria had departed, our vessel had a different crew for the journey to Corinth. The hired crew, some of them appearing hardly more than ruffians were all armed in one way or another. Had they known how much of value we carried it might not have been safe at all. I wore only the plainest of clothes, kept as far away from them as possible and conversed only with Jason and Echion. Argos had assumed the role of steersman and delivered his orders to the crew from the stern. He seldom needed his drum.

The journey was not as tiresome as I had feared though our boat had begun to leak and two men were kept busy from time to time baling out water with copper buckets. We had two days of easy sailing with clear skies, the wind in our favour and always close to land where, mercifully, I could go ashore when the crew set up camp to eat and sleep, and I could carry out those other necessities of life away from prying eyes. At around mid-morning on a clear, breezy day we reached the wooded Isthmus of Corinth where, overlooking the unobstructed beach, stood a somewhat grand but presently deserted temple dedicated to Poseidon. Argos had the crewmen take to their oars and row hard until our vessel was grounded. Once everyone was ashore Jason had them haul *Argo* further up the gently sloping beach, toward the temple, until she was high and dry. Our possessions were still on board, stored out of sight in small boxes and satchels in the enclosed bow area I knew so well.

"*Argo* is now an offering to Poseidon," he informed me, "She has fulfilled all that was asked of her but is no longer as seaworthy as she was. Also I have no wish to have this vessel used by others after all we've been through with her. She will keep our memories and ours alone."

Such sentiment, I thought, ill-suited him. But in spite of my aversion to sea voyages I also felt a degree of remorse over what had been a much loved vessel now being abandoned. I stared long, seeing in her qualities I'd not appreciated before. Athena I knew had been her protectress but no longer did I feel the goddess was present. Other people, a few fishermen and children stood looking on out of curiosity but did not approach closely.

"Argos and the crewmen," Jason explained, "will make their way over to Corinth. He'll hire wagons there and return them overland where my farther will pay them for their work."

Before leaving, Jason and Argos stood apart from the crew in conversation, each man grasping the forearm of the other as if to express a final, sad, farewell. Once the men had departed, Jason and Echion unloaded our possessions from the boat, including those items a woman needs to keep herself presentable. Echion, before fulfilling his duty as herald to Creon, would go inland to procure a horse and cart to take ourselves and our belongings to the city.

The sun had passed its highest when Echion returned with horse and cart and an extra horse in tow.

"It's no great distance to the city," he informed us. "The path is well paved because they sometimes drag vessels on wooden rollers from here to the city. This they do to avoid their needing to sail all around the Peloponnese. I will ride ahead to inform their king of your approach. If you proceed after me you should reach the city while the sun is still high and I will be waiting at the main or at the southernmost gate." Echion mounted the spare horse and Jason handed up to him the herald's staff. We watched him leave then Jason turned to ask me, "Have you ever driven a horse and cart?"

'No I have not,' I replied. And I had no intention of so doing.

"Neither have I," he grinned. "Horses, yes, but never with a cart - so let's get our things in there and we'll see how quickly I learn."

We took our belongings from *Argo* and placed them into the cart where I sat. The demands upon Jason were not great since the horse, on climbing the modest rise to the road, knew exactly where it was supposed to be going and took us along at its own easy pace. We spoke very little on the way but it was not long before the busy harbour and the city wall of Corinth came into view with her buildings rising above. But above all else, beyond the city, there arose an imposing flat-topped mountain. The harbour was packed with vessels of all sizes with many coming and going. A sign of prosperity if ever I witnessed one. We continued on through olive groves, vineyards and orchards until nearing a great stone gateway. Standing before it with his staff raised high was Echion and two robed men who proved to be royal attendants. I saw about the walls the stylised bulls' horns hewn out of stone that were said to reflect those seen at the great palace on Crete. The closer any city was to Knossos, the more her influence was evident and the more talked about was her might and the power of her navy.

When at the city gate we climbed from the cart, Echion informed us the two officials were to take our belongings to chambers in the palace already being prepared for us while he himself would carry those items we intended to present to the king. Jason and I followed them through the gate and I was aware of there being no beggars or destitutes present. As we crossed the busy market square on our way to the palace and temples, it struck me how well ordered, how harmonious the city appeared to be under a warm sun. The sea, too, can be like that. It can sparkle calm in sunlight until aroused by the winds. Until it rises in anger to destroy the unwary.

We approached the palace, this building, too, replete with stone horns, painted white and set about its upper walls, its galleries supported by downward tapering columns in russet, ochre and white. We passed inside then entered the megaron where was revealed the now familiar, though here colourfully tiled circular hearth with just beyond it the king's throne. Familiar, too, were the richly frescoed walls spaced about with arms, armour and fire brands. Except that here, all was on a far grander scale than at Pelion. The courtiers, dressed as brazenly and as colourfully as any I had seen, ceased chattering and stepped aside to allow us through. The richly robed King of Corinth appeared fit and strong but was older by some years than Jason's father, his moderately long hair and beard the colour of straw, his weathered, blue-eyed face that of one who had travelled much. Standing by his throne was an attractive young girl of no more than twelve years old, her long blond hair pinned at the sides by ornamental, gilded clasps and falling over the shoulders of her white gown. Close at hand were three female crinkle-haired, rouge-cheeked attendants in the long flounced dresses that left their breasts exposed. I need not tell you where Jason's attention next fell.

"My Lord," announced Echion, "may I present Lord Jason and Lady Medea."

Creon rose from his marble throne and stepped down from its low plinth to greet us.

"I trust you remember my father, Lord Creon," said Jason, stepping forward to offer a brief bow.

"Of course I remember your father," smiled Creon, "I remember him well indeed. It's not so long since he came here to discuss trading with us. I therefore welcome yourself and your wife to Corinth as our royal guests and to my palace where you must remain for as long as you wish." He turned to the girl, who stood grinning with hands pressed flat together at her covered bosom, and said, "This house has seen many troubles of late; I lost my wife ten years ago and never cared to remarry but this is my dear daughter, Creusa."

I smiled and dipped my head in momentary gesture, a gesture I at once regretted as one of my status, or Jason's, ought not to have considered it necessary. I didn't feel like speaking, either, and didn't think I needed to. I looked from Creon to the girl and sensed at once how deeply impressed she was by the manly appearance of dear Jason. This I ascribed to her adolescent immaturity. Echion, having set out the gifts we had brought, bowed himself from the king's presence and left the hall. He would return to Pelion with Argos. Court activity was resuming its normal level and Jason seemed to be getting on very well indeed with the King of Corinth who expressed much interest in all we had seen and done.

We were conducted by Creon and two of his male attendants, those who had waited with Echion at the city gate, to apartments reached by torch-lit corridor some way from the great hall. You may remember what I said about the palace of Alcinous on the island of Scheria in the land of the Phaeacians, of the luxuries that were accorded us by Arete, his queen. Here even those comforts were exceeded. Here were gorgeous furnishings and exotic fabrics. Here the brightly frescoed walls with scenes of nature to beguile the eye. Here a room set aside for bathing, its walls alive with leaping dolphins and numerous other sea creatures. It occurred to me then how the same artists, or at least their students, must travel and offer their services throughout all of Greece. In the room intended for bathing, a pool was set into the floor with, at one end, a means of draining the water and there was a bronze valve in the wall above from which cold water would be allowed to issue. Suspended by a chain close to one end of the bath hung a large bronze vessel full of steaming water, presently attended by two slave boys. Below this burned a sunken fire intended to keep its contents always hot. From the vessel extended a lever which would serve to tilt it and empty hot water into the bath. There also was a bowl designed to accept and flush away that which I need not mention. On the shelves I noted the small jars of unguents, perfumes, combs, razors and, praise the gods, close by a beautifully polished bronze mirror, all of which instilled me with pleasurable anticipation. Small pottery oil lamps were placed all about, one left burning so that from it others could be lit.

"The luxuries we enjoy at Corinth," declared, one of Creon's men, "are second only to those of Knossos."

"Yes," agreed the other, "and perhaps not so second. And our city is well supplied with good water from the hills."

"You treat us well," commented Jason.

The bedroom we entered was most welcoming with its luxuries and looked out onto a modest though colourful garden where a multitude of small fountains sparkle-danced in the afternoon son.

"I trust you will find all here to your liking," said Creon. "We will leave you now but I will have the two slaves standing by to await your summons. After sunset you both must join myself and others in our dining hall where food and wine will await."

We were alone and familiarising ourselves further with our surroundings, in particular the bedroom, when Jason said, "Pity we still don't have the Golden Fleece to lie on."

"As far as I'm concerned," I responded angrily, "I never want to see the damned thing again, nor do I even wish to speak of it!"

I gazed across the garden. The sun was very low and we would soon be expected to join Creon and his company. I turned my attention to the clothes laid out mainly for me. Jason would no doubt wear the robe given him on Lemnos but I decided, after bathing, I would comply with courtly fashion and display my breasts as did the other women of this and other royal houses where Cretan manners were followed. I was determined my looks and my physical appearance would not be bettered by any of the women of Creon's opulent court. My hair, not yet arranged in the crinkled style of the courts, I would simply pin back and leave to flow freely about my shoulders. The jewelled band, one of my treasured possessions, would not be amiss. Jason assessed me in my new finery, smiled and offered favourable comment as we stepped out into the corridor. There were the slaves waiting to escort us to the megaron and dining room; this time two willowy females of dusky appearance, both too old to attract Jason's eye.

We entered the dining hall where torches burned bright about the walls and an odour of cooking greeted us. Creon and a small number of his closest companions, male and female, were already seated or about to be so at a circular table replete with food, wine jars and goblets waiting to be filled by gowned attendants who evidently were not slaves. The music of strings and pipes sweetened the air and amid that smiling company I was soon to feel entirely at ease.

**

I had no idea how long we might stay at Corinth and Jason was reluctant to discuss the subject. He and Creon appeared to bond well. Too well as things transpired. They drank together and soon would be seen riding out beyond the city wall with a few armed men to go hunting deer or, on occasion, lions. One day they returned with one of their men so badly mauled that he soon died. It was a risk they seemed willing to take.

287

The days had become months and when it became clear that Jason had no intention of our departing Corinth and that Creon had found an ideal companion, I, taking advantage of my position and daytime freedom, set up a modest shrine of my own devoted to Hecate in a small, disused building close to the market square. I established myself there as a healer and a diviner. Many people in Corinth had heard of Hecate but their priests were not favourably disposed and regarded her as alien. I discovered that the high priest himself, Norax, was a younger brother of Creon; the king having placed him there to keep him away from the court. The gods had not impressed upon Norax the benefits of brotherly love.

It was not long after we had established ourselves in Corinth that I found I was with child. Jason ought to have been more interested than he appeared to be, especially when I gave birth to a healthy boy. His father, Chiron, might have shown a greater degree of enthusiasm had he known, because the boy would have been eligible for the combined thrones of Pelion and Iolcus. Some nights, as well as days, I saw little of Jason but I felt disinclined to question his absences directly or otherwise. Knowing the ways of men I preferred not to be confronted by unpleasant truths as I was still devoted to him.

I became ever more preoccupied in my new role. I gained a reputation with the city people for my healing powers and my ability to see beyond their thoughts though with the women of the court I sensed a growing undercurrent of envy.

I was with child once more – the first now being a year old. Life had become settled with oh-so dearest Jason losing himself to the pleasures of the hunt and to court life. He and Creon might have been blood brothers. It seemed, too, that Jason, though often attending to my needs at night, was not really with me at all. Nevertheless he and I drew admiring crowds whenever we went about in ceremony together, as happened on festive occasions. Creon was becoming a figurehead, almost a demigod, and continued to preside over or attend only the most sacred events.

Yes, a tide of popularity had swept over Jason and myself. They saw us, perhaps, as future rulers of Corinth. But of course tides wax and tides wane.

***

Five years passed with Corinth remaining prosperous and at peace, though accounts of trouble in other lands as well as at the royal house of Mycenae to our south, were ever present. Creon had armed patrols ride out each day to ensure no groups with hostile intent would approach Corinth unseen. During that time I gave birth once more; another boy.

Within the town I still had a devoted following, much to the ever increasing displeasure of Poseidon's priesthood which was obvious enough to all. Oh, how they disapproved of Hecate. They disapproved also of the offerings I received at her shrine which, modest by comparison, they considered ought to have been theirs. They scorned what I was doing and had begun to foster rumours about my dabbling in the evil arts. Should any one of those attending my shrine die without obvious cause, the holy men put it about that they could have been poisoned or cursed by me. I carried on and kept myself occupied even though demands of those who visited my shrine were lessening.

The king's daughter, Creusa, had already come of age and had taken her place in her father's courtly gatherings but without the decorum of a ruler's daughter. Her lips were scarlet, her naked breasts rouged as a blatant offering, though for one of her status a personal choice of partner might not be permitted. But she had from the beginning nurtured an interest in Jason and now he paid her a degree of attention that gave rise to whispered comment. Creon was aware of what was happening but chose to ignore what had become a delicate situation. I had no doubts over Jason or any man finding Creusa most desirable and I well perceived that little bitch was a tinder waiting to ignite, to blaze as a flame of sensuality and that it was Jason who she intended would feel her heat. I told myself again it was the way he and all men were until I saw them alone together one evening in the courtyard. The words of intimacy that passed between them were not intended for other ears, especially mine, yet it was upon my ears they alighted. It was there and then the veil placed over my eyes by Aphrodite, in collusion with Hera, fell suddenly away. The sun burst through as a cold and bitter light to starkly illuminate hidden truths – truths that those on high had concealed from me but now were revealed as opportunism and deceit. Yes, Jason had wanted me at first as I had wanted him, but after Colchis and

290

over the following months, I had become an increasing burden, though it had taken him some time to admit this fully to himself. His desires now were centered upon dear little Creusa and her alone. What games were the gods now playing? Such sadness, such bitterness afflicted me. Then anger. I needed to think hard but I intended not to reveal my feelings. At least I did until one day in our own chambers Jason summoned wine, sat down opposite me, filled our cups and said quite calmly, "I wish for our marriage to end. Yes, it shall be ended."

Though I had sensed what he was likely to say, I acted as if his words were unexpected and replied, "Oh, but why, Jason? Tell me why you wish to renounce the promise you made to me those few years ago at Colchis. Tell me why you now refute the ceremony where we were joined together at the temple of Poseidon in the kingdom of Phaeacia?"

He set aside his wine, stood up, stared at me a while, then said, "Medea, it was circumstances guided and compelled me. I had to take the Golden Fleece and, yes, I wanted you but – but I had not enough time to consider the future after Colchis. I kept my word though, did I not."

"Yes, because you felt shamed into doing so by Arete. It wasn't clear to me at the time but it is now. Do go on, Jason, please do."

"Creon has no son," he continued, "only a brother, a high priest of Poseidon who he holds in low regard."

"Oh, yes, I know all about him; he preaches against me in the temple. He lies to the townspeople about Hecate and therefore defiles my own image.

He is turning the people against me day by day. Jason, I beg you not to dishonour me."

"I've heard much of that damned priest," he said, "and I do regret it happening. But Creon now favours my marrying his daughter. He favours my becoming as one with the house of Corinth and *that* I feel strongly inclined to do. My father still has many good years ahead of him so an alliance between Corinth and Pelion would be of advantage to both."

Well I couldn't see how an alliance between the two kingdoms would benefit either since there were a number of large cities and some rather mountainous country in between, not to mention the sea journey. I don't think Jason had really considered it, either. No, what he saw before him was an easy way to the throne of Corinth when Creon stepped aside; a far greater kingdom than Pelion and Iolcus combined would be his. And in the short term he'd have that little slut Creusa in his bed, officially that is. He was obsessed by her and much else hung upon that. She averted her eyes when passing by me in the megaron and I knew Jason often shared her bed when not with me at night. But I decided there and then to let him go on for there was not much else I could do.

"I promise you and your – our children will lack for nothing," he assured me one day, "nothing at all. I will elevate the status of Hecate and therefore that of yourself as priestess. What I'm proposing will be of benefit to us both."

Easy words, honey sweetened words I thought, but if I still had any trust in him it vanished as chaff in a breeze. I stood to face him, saying, "The fact is, Jason, I am betrayed, dishonoured and now maligned before all the people of Corinth and so it seems are you! Most of them respected me – they came to me with their ailments and their pains, imagined or not. But rumours abound in the city about us both, fuelled by Creon's priestly brother. He preaches and I hear his words; he tells them you have gained their king's trust these past years but plan to subvert his rule once married to his sweet little daughter. He tells them I am a witch and a sorceress and a considerable number are now thinking his words are truth, though a few still do not believe him."

"A witch - a sorceress," he grinned, "I thought you were."

At this puerile remark, anger flared within me. I seized my almost full goblet from the table and dashed the contents into his face. He raised a hand to strike me but at once let it drop. As he stood there the grin, now mocking, took hold once more across his dripping face, then he laughed aloud, turned and strode from the room. As I stood there another yet deeper anger possessed me, an anger cold and dark that arose to spread its roots into my very soul and would not be shaken free until…

Chapter 13 - And Revenge

Jason and I seldom conversed after that, and then only infrequently in the megaron because I had forbidden him to visit me again in private day or night, especially at night. Another month passed but word had spread throughout Corinth that Jason had denounced our marriage and was to wed Creusa. A growing number of people regarded him now as a man not be trusted, a man not worthy of the close association he enjoyed with their king. Through those years at Corinth I had never been entirely at one with the women of Creon's court but their attitude towards me now was becoming less amiable. I was beginning there to feel alienated but as well as Hecate's shrine I found I could devote some of my time to the three boys.

Then another blow. It was made clear to me by Creon's attendants, no doubt with Jason's urging, that I was no longer welcome in the megaron and most of the palace though I might retain the chambers I still occupied, the nursemaid who looked after my children when I was absent and my two slaves. My two slaves were of course girls and as satisfying as their personal attentions might be when I needed them, there were times when I wanted a man. One of the palace guards had on occasion eyed me with a look I well understood. Passing by me one evening in the corridor leading to my chambers he had hesitated, ostensibly out of sympathy for my situation, to say, "I hear much of your sad circumstances, Lady Medea, so perhaps when not on duty I might be of service?"

He was, as are all palace guards, a tall and soundly proportioned man much in the image of Jason. A handsome man with the uncompromising name of Gyas.

"You may bring me wine," I replied after a suitably contrived hesitation. "If you're available this evening, that is. If so then I'll have a slave by the palace steps ready to show you the way."

He was, of course, available that evening. Yes, he was available for a good number of evenings thereafter as on other occasions were two of his companions. They provided the diversions I needed and at first it appeared they were discreet. Then again I also needed to spend time alone. Time to think. I could go outside plainly dressed and as I was by now no longer idolised people tended to ignore me.

One day, when the sun was low in the sky, I was seated by a fountain in the town square when his shadow fell across me. I looked aside to see a well-built, fair-haired man in pale tunic. That he was a man of some quality was obvious and he wore a royal seal on a finger of his left hand. Close behind him waited another with whom I was familiar, a plainly gowned man with few teeth and puckered mouth, a priest of Poseidon who stood leaning on his gnarled stick.

"Lady Medea," smiled the distinguished man, 'forgive my intrusion but I saw you sitting here alone. I am Aegeus of Athens. Are you waiting for someone?"

I'd heard much about Athens and Aegeus, heard how he occasionally passed through Corinth on his way to and from the temples of Delphi and I assumed the priest had identified me to him. I stared up at the man and said, "Ah, *the* Aegeus," then added, "You are Aegeus the King."

"The same," he responded. "May I speak with you a while?"

Hardly likely to refuse, and bathed in sudden and exquisite relief by his presence, I eyed him intently and replied as if another had put the words in my mouth, "My pleasure, I heard you left Athens some time ago to visit Delphi."

"Did you now," he responded, sitting down next to me. "And there was I thinking such information had never been put about for reasons of security – my security, that is."

Being as close as he was to me I hoped my perfume was sufficient to hold at bay the odours of the square as I remarked, "We all need security."

"That's so," he continued, "but I believe mine may be less pressing than yours in the short term." *That* information had, I knew, been imparted to him by the priest who now stepped away. "In my case," Aegeus continued, "it is concern over the succession in Athens. It's a matter of great importance to myself and my people. It will, I hope, be resolved in time, though the priestess herself at Delphi was not at all clear in her message."

Hearing the way he addressed and confided in me, I was sure now of Hecate's presence. "It will be resolved in time," I assured him. "The fates will have it so."

"Really," he smiled, "I wish I had your confidence yet I wonder how it will be resolved."

My confidence; well I'd had little enough of that of late but now – here was a man of great importance paying attention to me.

"But," he continued, "I understand you yourself are in a difficult situation." He looked about the square and at its complement of haggling tradesman, hurrying slaves and yapping dogs, then added. "Sitting here by the fountain is pleasant enough but it will soon be dark. Will you not join me for a cup of wine? My men and I must leave for Troizen by first light tomorrow."

Troizen, a town some way south of Athens, I'd heard of, but knew nothing more.

"Wine?" I queried. "You'll not get wine fit for a king hereabouts except in Creon's palace and since I am forbidden to enter I regret I'm unable to accept your offer."

"Oh, so it's true what I heard," he said, "but the palace is where I shortly have to go."

Fearing now the possibility that he might be about to leave me once more alone I leant closer and gazed into his eyes. I gazed and as I did so I felt my feminine powers returning. This stranger, this man, this King of Athens returned my gaze and for some moments time seemed to stop. When an ox-drawn cart rattled by to break his attention he said, "Now, look, perhaps I may be of help here. Tell me why you find yourself in this situation. Are the rumours of a conspiracy true?"

"Conspiracy?" I answered. "I'll tell you what is true if you care to hear it."

He reached out a hand to rest on mine, saying, "Yes, tell me as much as you wish."

"Very well, I take it you know something of Jason."

"That I do," said Aegeus. "Several men of his crew came from or passed through Athens and were quite free with their accounts of the voyage you took to obtain the Golden Fleece. They spoke of the many dangers that were encountered by your Argonauts."

"Then you should know, I was married to the great Jason. I was hardly more than a child when he landed in Colchis but I was besotted from the very beginning. I travelled with him and his Argonaut friends when he set out, defying my father to steal the Golden Fleece. I used all the secret arts of our land, all those forbidden spells handed down through our family to help him gain it. I used my powers to help him even when I should have known better. King Aegeus – if you care to dig for further rumours, you will doubtless hear of the so-called evil deeds ascribed to me when with Jason, but I'd rather you did not."

"If true," asked Aegeus, "are they deeds you regret?"

"Lies and truth entwine like serpents but whatever I did I thought necessary at the time. It is too late for regret. In due course we ended up here in Corinth where Jason met that little tart, Creusa - Creon's blue-eyed daughter. They lodge here at the palace. He dares not face my father and imagines Creon will protect him from the many enemies he's made, including me. He no longer cares a damn

298

about me or our three children but I'll have my revenge when the time is right. Believe me, I will." My remark about Jason not daring to face my father was, of course, there for effect. Jason never would, regardless of all else, wish to see Colchis again.

"But you yourself may suffer harm,' responded Aegeus. 'Return with me to Athens. There I'll give you sanctuary. That I promise."

"No, not yet. There's much I have to do here in Corinth." I placed a hand on his cheek and this simple act seemed to fire him within as I spoke again. "But there are two things I will say. Firstly I will come to you in Athens when I'm done here in Corinth. Secondly, I foretell you will have the son and heir you so desire."

"But lady," he breathed, rising to his feet, "How can you be certain of that?"

I stood to face him, saying, "King Aegeus, of that I am certain." I arose, turned and hurried across the darkening square to my chambers.

***

One night, in the incense laden darkness of her shrine, Hecate spoke and told me what I might do and so my plan was formed. Over the days, with affable manner, I let it be known to those few who visited me that I had forgiven Jason and now wished him and his forthcoming bride well. There was one who still came often to see me, one for whose afflictions I had offered herbal cures that had given her ease and comfort. Her skills lay in making fine clothes. She had a workroom within the palace and there, on occasion, she and her helpers made clothes for the king and some members of his court. I approached her saying that I knew the kind of wedding gown Jason would find pleasing for his new wife to be and that if she or the woman doing this for me would make the dress at her own home, with my guidance, I would pay her and present the completed garment myself. She, of course, understood the importance of secrecy except that Jason would be told by her not to concern himself over it because the gown was in hand.

The gown I had made for Creusa, with Hecate's blessing and guidance, was of finest Egyptian cotton, long and elegant, intricately laced and patterned with coloured fabrics. It cost me much in silver but that hardly mattered. Many days had passed when, after dusk, she delivered the finished gown to me in linen wraps. I had already dismissed my two slaves when she arrived so I thanked and paid her the remaining amount owed then took the dress into Hecate's shrine. There as the goddess instructed, I laid it upon her altar and extinguished the small lamps standing either side. I returned to my chambers where I sat alone to take food and wine, then afterwards I summoned my slave girls. They bathed me in perfumed water, we took our pleasures as women know so well how to do, then having dismissed them, I retired contented to my bed. In darkness I lay, hearing a distant yelp of dogs and play of water in the garden outside my window. I thought of the wedding gown and I knew already it was charged with bad spirits.

Two days later, on the morning of the wedding, I had one of my slaves deliver the gown to Creusa with a discreet message - that message being, "Here is the gown desired for you by Jason." It was a propitious day for such events and the priests had announced the omens as favourable,

As was appropriate, the wedding took place early that afternoon at Aphrodite's temple. Dressed in a plain dark gown that covered me entirely I attended but remained at a distance. Jason was bedecked in his Lemnian robe as well as other finery and Creusa in the gown that I'd had sent to her. All through the ceremony I was tense for though I knew something was to happen I didn't know what because I had not myself determined it. Eyes of courtier and citizen from time to time were turned upon me – most with a look of distaste, a few with sadness.

During the wedding ritual nothing unusual occurred so after this I followed the royal party and attendants back to Creon's palace where a sumptuous feast, with musicians and entertainers had been prepared in the dining hall. The odours of cooking food lay heavy in air that was livened by chatter and laughter. Fires danced and glowed beneath bronze tripods upon which rested vessels of food or meat on turning spits. Jason had walked ahead of Creon with his darling Creusa and two of her giggling female attendants following a few steps behind her father. The musicians were already playing and I, feeling chilled in that otherwise warm evening, had begun to think Hecate had abandoned me.

Then it happened! A muffled crack reached my ears and as I stood watching a scream cut through the air. A pottery vessel had split asunder on its tripod as the bride passed by. It plunged down into the flames, causing bright embers to cascade directly over Creusa. Her dress was suddenly ablaze, entirely consumed by wild flames as if the breath of the forges was all about her. She shrieked aloud. Her father sprang to help, beating frantically with his arms to no avail and with his kingly robes starting to burn he fell to the floor. In the ensuing chaos and shouting, Jason had pulled off his own gown and with the help of two slaves would have attempted to stifle the fearsome blaze but could not get close enough. The flames brightened further then subdued as quickly as they had arisen, as though smothered by an unseen hand. But as the smoke cleared, as others gathered around in confusion and disbelief, it was obvious from her blistered, her flesh-charred form and the smouldering remnants of her hair that Creusa was far beyond mortal help. I was appalled at the sight of her when I ought not to have been. I ought not to have been because I had witnessed what my father had done to people, but still I was appalled. This, after all, was my doing. Creon himself, though not appearing badly burned, lay close by, but when his attendants tried to raise him, they announced that he, too, no longer lived. In those terrible moments I concluded that his heart must have ceased beating through the shock of what had happened.

Only the sound of spitting flames from below the tripods broke the silence as I backed away from those gathered speechless about the bodies. What could I say? Where was I to go? Why did the King of Corinth also have to die? Surely this was not intended. Surely this was not the work of Hecate. I hurried from the hall and out from the palace into warm evening air. There I paused to ease my breathing and to attain calm by looking up at the sky. A pale half-moon hung above the silent square and the stars were beginning to shine. All was so peaceful. All so shockingly innocent.

I gathered my wits and walked across the deserted square to Hecate's shrine, past the small table where I often sat to discuss matters with those who wished to consult me. I stepped into the utter blackness where her altar stood and gazed into what at that moment I imagined was infinity. "Why Creon?" I asked under my breath. "Why him?"

Her voice came from all about, from near and from afar, approaching, receding. "I had no hand in his death. I gave no thought to what he might do. No thought to his heart. No thought at all."

I fled anguished back to my chambers and there I took to my bed, hoping the darkness would spirit me away to some faraway land.

Over the following days all the city lay enveloped within a cloud of murmured gossip. I soon learned that Norax, Creon's unloved brother, had moved to take the throne and had the palace guard under his command. Rumours spread about the taverns and squares spawned in particular by the temple of Poseidon's priests. People were saying the gods had punished Jason and Creusa because of Jason's undue influence over Creon but in part because of the way I had been betrayed. These latter sentiments were based upon tradition rather than any true sympathy for me. Norax preached that

303

Jason had planned to usurp Creon, who the people loved, and what had happened at the wedding was willed by the gods. Jason's bride was dead, he would suffer for the rest of his life and in their fickle manner they began to scorn this man who was earlier a hero. When Jason stepped out from the palace some turned their faces away but others dared to pass insulting comments. His royal attendants withdrew their services on the orders of Norax and only slaves stooped to his command. He approached me on three occasions when in the market square but I turned away each time and mingled with the crowds to discourage his following me. On the third and last occasion the expression on his face spoke of a man afflicted by doubt and remorse.

With the antagonism of Norax and ever increasing disdain of the people, there was no point in Jason remaining in Corinth. He could have returned to Pelion or have himself hired in the service of any royal house, so I thought, but just then I cared hardly anything for whatever plans he might have. And so, one morning, Jason departed Corinth alone in a horse-drawn chariot.

Adverse as he had always been to displaying evidence of wealth on his person, he would have concealed about him and in the satchel at his side, silver and items considerable value. His skill with the fine sword he carried at his side would ensure few men would be foolish enough to risk acquiring anything from him by force.

Only much later did I discover, through Hecate, what became of Jason.

I saw no choice other than to carry on as best I could until matters became clearer. And yes, for a short while those people who had remained sympathetic still came to see me – as did Gyas on certain evenings. But only for a short while. Norax and his acolytes turned their vile attentions now upon me. They began to preach in temple and in public places that it was I, also, through my bringing Hecate, an alien deity, into Corinth, who had displeased Hera and Poseidon and fuelled cause for such terrible retribution against their king and his daughter. Word got out that I was responsible for Creusa's dress and had laid a curse upon it. Perhaps they had spoken to the woman who had made it for me - that I never ascertained, but how quickly their antagonism burgeoned. The priests condemned my potions as poisons, my pronouncements as false and as the days wore on *all* the people of Corinth began to accept their words. Much ill feeling, much resentment was turned upon me. I noticed it in their accusing glances and in their furtive conversations when I passed by. Some still visited my shrine but their numbers by now were so few that on an increasing number of days I saw no one at all.

Worse was soon to come. A minor earthquake struck, wells and streams dried up for a time. Before long a sickness spread throughout the city and rats were common in the streets. Many older people and young children died. This was no plague and such maladies are not so uncommon after a quake or when temperatures are at their highest, as at that time they were. The sickness was soon to pass yet the priests laid its blame entirely at the feet of Hecate and therefore me. The mood of the city changed, the townspeople people were becoming ever more aggressive. I was openly insulted, sometimes spat upon and not only myself but my three children, young as they were, threatened with violence. I entered my shrine early one morning to find vessels smashed and Hecate's altar fouled with excrement. I rushed back to the safety of my chambers. I took my children from their nursemaid, she being one of very few who had kept faith with me. I hurried them to the temple of Hera, hoping they would be safe there because, in spite of the priests, her temple was regarded as a refuge and a sanctuary in times of trouble. When I left, the taverns were rowdier than usual and there were groups of men roaming about, singing, shouting and brawling.

I overheard late that afternoon from the gossip of others that during celebrations for the lifting of the sickness the temple itself had been forcibly entered by a drunken mob. I set out back to the temple and demanded from the priests to know where my three boys were for they were not to be seen. No one claimed to know or would say what had happened to them. I could do no more just then because darkness was falling and I felt that being seen alone and recognized, I might be assaulted. On reaching the palace I headed straight to the megaron to demand from Norax the whereabouts of my children because I was convinced he must be responsible for what had happened. Outside the entrance to the great hall stood two armed guards. I demanded they let me through for I could see across the circular hearth where a fire blazed, Norax perched in arrogance upon Creon's throne. No longer the image of a holy man, he was in full regal attire and surrounded by a group of men, some of them priests, others scribes busy recording his words. I shouted but they ignored me. The guards would not allow me by and one, raising his fist, threatened to strike me down if I refused to leave. I returned to my chambers where waited my two girls. Seeing my distress they thought to console me but I was in no mood even to talk. I dismissed them, drank much wine then took to my bed where in utter darkness I called for Hecate. Whether I was wholly consumed by sleep or part awake I cannot say, but I recall a distant voice saying, "Your fate is to hand." The message was repeated as the voice faded.

Before sunrise next day, bathed and dressed, I determined I would try yet again to confront Norax in the great hall below but I never got that far. There were raised voices outside my door and I emerged to find standing there the shaven-headed, beardless, round-faced Norax. Once more wearing holy robes he was in the process of dismissing my two girls. Behind him stood the two guards.

"Why are you doing this?" I demanded. "Why – and where are my children?"

"They are no longer yours," he answered, "and I can tell you nothing more."

I did not believe him. I continued my demands but these he ignored, telling me only that, "You and that abomination you choose to worship have brought much trouble to our city and so you must leave. We have prayed to Hera and to almighty Zeus himself to drive the evil one away from Corinth and our request has been granted. Take whatever you can from here and be gone by midday. These men will see to it that you do." With that he turned and left. Standing dismayed, I could say or do nothing more. Before they also left, one of the guards told me that which threw me into yet greater depths of despair. "Your three kids," he said. "The mob dragged 'em away. I'd say they're no longer in this world. I'd 'eard they were stoned to death but I witnessed none of it."

He said it not with malice but with a touch of pity. He was one of the men with whom I had enjoyed an intimate relationship. I should never have trusted those children to the temple when knowing the influence Norax had there. Whatever had happened to them was my fault and I was utterly grief-stricken. Bewildered, not knowing where I was to go, I gathered together all the valuables I could wear on my person or contain in a linen bag small enough to conceal within my gown. It was a decorated crimson gown of the court, held in place by a black sash, for I had decided I ought still to maintain an appearance of nobility for I had always belonged to a royal house no matter what its reputation. Hidden beneath, I also carried a curved bronze dagger. If anyone tried to accost me I swore to myself I would use it whatever the consequences. On stepping outside I made my way to the market square because I could think of nowhere else to go. There was the occasional passing insult but most people simply ignored me. To them I was no longer a person of importance in spite of my appearance, no longer even to be rebuked, though several looked at those items of value I was unable to conceal until I feared someone might attempt to take them from me. I kept my hand close to the dagger.

Near to the centre of the market square where I had encountered Aegeus the fountain played. At least the busy water was life of a kind and carried with it no hate. So by that same fountain I chose to sit and rest a while, aware of odours of ox and ass, of cooking and other sources less pleasant, odours I once cared to endure for only as long as it took to cross the square. Bereft of all hope I closed my eyes and I prayed in silence to Hecate. I asked why she had abandoned me and if she had not altogether done so then to give me courage and direction. But what Norax had told me must have been true – the higher gods had driven her away from Corinth. I gazed into the water as it swirled about the base of the fountain. I had to do something, to go somewhere but could find no answer as the day passed and the sun began its inexorable descent. If I made my way to the port to take passage on a vessel, where was I to go? There was Pelion or even Iolcos, of course, but then Jason might also return there and life would be impossible. But if he did not return why should Chiron accept someone with whom he was not at all pleased in the first place, especially when his own son had deserted her. There was Thebes or Athens, much spoken of by others, though neither had I ever seen. Yes, Athens! Of course, Athens, because that is where Aegeus their king had said I might go. But walking to the port, attired as I was, could present grave perils so for the moment I was afraid to consider it. There were taverns in Corinth but as in other towns, these were not places for a woman alone, especially one possessed of valuables. Such was the situation that I worried that I might be lucky to see another sunrise. Some of those who had seen me by the fountain earlier and now passed by again to find me still there would pause to stare and make comments I cared not to hear. I worried that if I stayed much longer I might be set upon and robbed of all I had. What was I to do?

I returned my gaze to the water. It swished, it hissed, it whispered. Not words, just sounds; but sounds that seemed to have meaning. I arose from the fountain side, passed by a small group of ogling men and sneering women. The market was not so busy this late in the day and the traders were soon to begin packing away their wares. I stopped where garments hung on display at the rear of a merchant's stall and there I saw what I needed. It was a plain, dark cloak with a belt and a hood, all of coarsely woven linen, fine for an outdoor worker on cooler days. Seeing who I was, the stallholder wanted more than its worth and I gave him a ready to hand piece of silver without comment then pulled on cloak and hood. He stared, half amused, half puzzled as I walked away with my arms tucked inside. I made my way back across the square and passed beneath the city gate, grateful in finding I was no longer an object of unwelcome attention. The harbour had to be my destination whatever the risks and it was to Athens and to King Aegeus I was determined to make my way. On reaching the harbour I saw only two boats moored nearby with men aboard, wide-bellied vessels being loaded at the quayside, I guessed, for the following day so the first of these I approached to query the destination of their cargos from one of the men working on board.

"Both goin' across the straits to Boeotia," he replied, "then on by cart to Thebes."

"Does no one sail for Athens?" I asked, and although I should have known what his answer would be I regretted hearing it.

"Athens? No, you'll need to cross the isthmus to the lower 'arbour. No one sails to Athens from this side."

No, of course they wouldn't because it would involve a voyage of some days around the Peloponnese in open water. What choice now did I have? Twilight was looming. My setting out to cross the isthmus would have me walking alone in darkness. Wild dogs might be a danger, and did lions roam the area at night? And if I arrived safely – if – there might be no one there to offer me help. There was *Argo*, resting on dry land but what if she was now taken over by vagrants or those seeking parts of her for some use of their own? In desperation I asked if I might go aboard the ship. The men were busy loading cargo and seemed not to care whether I did so or not, so I clambered down into the nearest boat where crates and straw-padded amphorae were already loaded. There I found myself a bundle of sacking on which to curl up unnoticed for the night and part cover myself,

311

though the sacking smelt decidedly unpleasant. It occurred to me that others must from time to time do what I was doing which was why I had attracted so little attention. I prayed to Hecate, hoping she might offer me comfort, but her whispered message contained only the words, "Go where you must go for now but keep faith in me."

"For now," she'd said, but what else was I supposed to do?

The night was clear, the air calm, yet sleep eluded me. When the sky began to lighten I kept low but could hear them preparing the vessel to depart. The yardarm was being raised, the sail unfurled and the oarsmen heaving the boat away from the quay. I remained where I was but propped against the planking with my eyes open in case they might think I had died in the night and reach to touch me. The breeze was light, the boat rose, fell and swayed gently, and though thirsty and hungry I was heartened when sunlight spilled across to bathe me in warmth. At one point a wiry, sea-weathered man stepped close to offer a cup of water and a pastry for which I mouthed my thanks. The rings from my fingers I had concealed in the linen bag but he stared at my hands as I took the food and drink and must have realized I was not at all used to menial work.

The sun was high above when, with the captain calling out his orders, we reached the Boeotian port and the vessel was manoeuvred alongside the jetty. Hardly had the boat made jolting contact with the timbers when I clambered over the side. There were goods waiting for the vessel to collect but first what it carried had to be unloaded and for these goods awaited a number of wagons drawn by oxen. There were children scrambling on and off the carts so seeing how far away the city was, I intended to take advantage and avoid needing to walk the considerable distance once the cargoes were exchanged. There were vendors with small carts selling food and drink to the sailors but with what could I pay? The bag I kept hidden contained, among other things, my coiled length of silver and a pair of bronze clippers. I moved away from the jetty and discreetly cut off a few small pieces of silver, having no idea of their worth when exchanging one each for a cup of rough wine and mutton pastry. The expression on both the vendors' faces left me thinking they'd had by far the best of the deal.

The sun was past its zenith when I joined two of the children in easing myself onto one of the wagons. We jolted through orchards and olive groves until passing beneath the massive city gate then on to the market square. In appearance the city was larger and her walls higher and stronger even than those of Corinth but I did not feel as disorientated as I had expected. I left the wagon and asked where was the main temple of the city. I was informed it stood on a rise outside one of the other the city gates so I made my way there to find this was no temple dedicated to Poseidon or Athena but to Apollo, a son of Zeus himself. Even so, having removed the cloak I was able to introduce myself - my true self that is as a king's daughter, to the chief priest, hardly more than a boy bearing a wreath about his head. I explained how I was also a

313

priestess of one who had fallen out of favour in Corinth and should there be no shrine to Hecate in Thebes then might I offer my services at the temple of Apollo. I asked also if I could bathe and refresh myself. He agreed at once to this second request but to the first replied that he knew of Hecate and would consider the first before we met again next morning. He meanwhile offered me food, wine, the services of a slave and a room to rest for the evening and for this I made a grateful donation to his shrine. I afterwards spent the rest of the day wandering about the town disguised in my linen cloak and cowl, returning to the temple after sunset. That night I prayed once more to Hecate but yet again the message she whispered at my ear was, "Go where you must for now but keep faith in me." I was hardly any wiser than before but I somehow knew I was not destined to remain in Thebes.

Morning came and with it yet another misfortune. I was to be taken later in the day before Thersander, their king, where I should have expected further welcome. In the company of two priests of Apollo I entered the city and there was conducted to the palace. It was upon passing by the guards and entering the otherwise deserted megaron that I saw them and halted by the great hearth. Standing by the throne of Thebes' long-bearded, hoary old king were three officials of the Corinthian court and two priests of Poseidon, all of whose faces I recognized. What their business was in Thebes I had no idea but they had obviously been informed of my arrival. They and Thersander stared at me coldly with one of the priests shaking a finger in my direction as he uttered words unintelligible to me at that distance. I resumed walking with hesitant steps but again stopped several paces from the throne. The king arose slowly, saying, "We hear you represent a deity alien to our city – a deity of darkness we cannot accept."

"The woman is a witch and a conspirer!" exclaimed one of the priests. His voice echoed ominously about the great hall. "The death of Creon, our king, was in part her doing!"

I was tempted to respond but realized there was nothing I could say as their verbal poison had already done its work and the gods of Thebes were frowning upon Hecate. Thersander raised his right hand and declared, "You are not welcome at our court and must depart Thebes. Leave us now."

I was consumed with anger as I and the two priests of Apollo turned and left the hall in a menacing silence that pursued me as a dark shadow. The expressions on the guards' faces confirmed his orders would be enforced as they trod close behind us to the palace entrance. Hurrying ahead of my two priests I returned to the temple and without a word to anyone, collected my belongings and pulled on my cloak. I departed Thebes by the gate I had entered then stopped to watch in hopeless resignation as ox-drawn carts and asses loaded with merchandise passed in and out of the city. I had become a homeless wanderer but in despair I again thought of Athens. Where else was left for me yet how was I to get there safely from Thebes? I bought wine from one then food from a second vendor where I asked that very question.

"There's two ways," the man replied. "Sometimes but not off'n, parties with lots of wagons goes overland but it's rough country. Aye, they needs armed guards an' it takes all the daylight hours. Otherwise, get a boat to Corinth an' join a party crossin' the isthmus. It may take longer that way from 'ere but it's safer by boat from the south 'arbour."

Return to Corinth? I remained some time barely able to think. The sun by now was low in the sky and I considered somehow getting back to the harbour. But even if I could, there would possibly be no one sailing at night and it would be too dangerous to loiter. It occurred to me that I might have to join those wretched souls who huddled beneath the city gates. There would be company of sorts until the next morning and at least I had my dagger. No, I could never do that. Never! Then I saw what charged me with hope. Several armed guards on horseback emerged from the city gate with behind them four heavily loaded, ox-drawn wagons, these in turn followed by more armed guards. Tightening hard my cloak and belt, I stepped across to ask one of the guards at the rear, "Where are you going?"

"To Corinth," he replied.

I pushed stooping in front of his horse, tottered along by his side, eased down my hood, shook loose my hair, smiled up at him and said, "Good - then I'll find a place for myself on one of your wagons."

He nodded and grinned widely so I rushed to scramble onto the back of the wagon directly in front of him, found a place to lodge myself amidst bales of wool and pulled the hood back over my head. The goods in these wagons had to be important to be taken at night under armed guard but I would be there early in the morning. After nightfall, despite the rocking, jolting and timber-sighing of the wagon, I slept well.

My luck, if such it may be called, was to hold the next day. Before the wagon I occupied entered Corinth that morning I climbed out to watch what was happening and to consider how I might get across the isthmus. One of the wagons did not enter the city but remained by the gate while some goods were removed and others loaded under the eyes of officials and scribes. This wagon I learned, by listening to the conversation of others, would continue across the isthmus to the lower harbour where it would exchange cargoes with a vessel destined for Athens. Wonderful news! But a number of goods would not be ready to load until after darkness had fallen so I would have to wait throughout the rest of the day. I bought food and wine from sellers attending to the wagon party. There were woodlands not so far away, woodlands and a stream I knew well, so I decided it was to there I would retreat and bide my time. The day was becoming hot. I hoped to find peace and somewhere to rest until the wagon was due to leave. Pulling my hood closer to avoid recognition, I passed by those gathered about the wagon, made my way up a gentle rise and trod some way in among the trees.

Here was quietness. Here was solitude. The trees arose as sentinels of peace, their spreading canopy pierced by shafts of sunlight. All I desired

317

was somewhere to rest with my thoughts until the sun was low in the sky then I would return to the wagon. There were no paths to be seen but the undergrowth was not so thick as to prevent my going further inside. Here too, on the woodland floor, were some of the plants whose berries, leaves and roots I had not so long ago gathered and used for my brews and potions in Corinth. There were ruins somewhere deeper within. I had once glimpsed them and taken little interest, but now I sought them out. Soon I came upon the overgrown remains of what must once have been an important shrine though some of its stone blocks were now fallen. There was an elaborately carved altar, its long neglected form picked out just then by a shaft of light from above. I sensed echoes of a spirit here. One of the fallen blocks close by looked fit to serve as a seat if I laid my cloak over it. There I decided to check over those items of value I carried with me and ensure I had sufficient pieces of silver ready in my bag to pay for anything I was likely to need.

As I sat deep in thought there was whispering, but not from the trees. I thrust the bag into its place of concealment inside my gown and slipped fingers over the hilt of my dagger. Then a voice.

"Medea, I am returned to you."

"Lady Hecate," I breathed, "why now and why here?"

"Here where you find yourself was long ago a shrine dedicated to me. It was a focus of my presence until the greater gods of Olympus determined otherwise and it is no longer remembered. Now you should know, their interest in Jason, particularly that of Hera, began to wane after the defeat of Pelias. They have dismissed him from their thoughts."

"So is that what helped the people of Corinth turn so easily against him and then against me in spite of all I had done for them."

"Perhaps," she whispered. "People are as fickle as the gods themselves but do not fear; the powers I instilled within you will have returned when you reach Athens for Athena herself never regarded me with disfavour."

"And will King Aegeus remember me?" I asked. There was no reply but the leaves about me rustled gently and I knew she was gone. I was heartened by her words – yes, after the desecration of Hecate's shrine in Corinth and murder of my children, after the abuse the insults and discomforts I had suffered there, and the time so wasted in journeying to Thebes and back, I was much encouraged. I was impatient and pulling on my cloak and hood I took to walking here and there, all the time willing the day to pass by more quickly.

At last, as the sun was setting, I made my way down from the woods to where the wagon waited. I remained until, in near darkness, another wagon appeared from the direction of the city, led by four men carrying spears and burning brands. There was an additional horse drawn cart trailing close behind them and this contained four busily chattering young women. The men transferred goods to the waiting wagon and when they were done three of them joined the women in the cart. I did what I was now used to doing and hid myself on board the

319

wagon just before the ox, driven by the fourth man, was prompted to haul its charge on the way to the lower harbour with the cart following behind. The journey would not be long but with the comfort of my cloak I managed to sleep for a while.

We were stopped when I awoke and darkness embraced the land. There were sounds of laughter, an occasional cry and I peered out far enough to see a fire burning on the beach. That and a half moon were enough for me to observe what was going on. All were naked with four women and a man seated by the camp fire and three men returning with raised voices from the sea to join their companions. Their more intimate activities I had evidently missed and as I continued to watch it appeared they soon would settle down together in contented slumber. That of course meant much of the night was yet to pass and therefore I would try to do likewise.

Hearing voices I arose some time before dawn and clambered from the wagon to see the women walking back to their cart where they waited for the men to rejoin them. Knowing the four men would soon afterwards return to the wagon I retreated to bushes above the path from where I watched them take the wagon all the way down to the beach. A band of light smeared the eastern horizon and soon the sky would lighten so, feeling chilled in a freshening breeze, I stepped out to see what was happening. There were two vessels in the bay, one moored at the jetty. Crewmen were exchanging cargoes between this and the wagon. The sky was now bright but the sun still to appear when the exchange of goods was completed and the four were returning with their wagon. As it rejoined the cart carrying the women and all prepared to leave, I hurried down to the beach. There I stopped, lost in thought, to gaze across at *Argo*, still resting where she had been drawn high above the water those five or six years ago. The ship looked sad and forlorn with much taken from her, her mast gone and her planking in places sprung and rotting. Yet in her dissolution she somehow remained proud and aloof. As I looked on, all those reluctant days I had spent aboard her passed fleetingly though my mind – reluctant days, yes, but even so I was much saddened at the sorry sight of a once proud vessel that for a time had been my only home.

I continued down to the water and suddenly felt unclean, almost wishing I could dip into the sea as I approached the jetty. At the trading boat moored there I encountered her captain who, for a modest amount of silver, agreed to take me with them as long as I kept to myself and offered no distraction to his crew. With that I was in full agreement and despite my aversion to sea travel I climbed aboard in gratitude, having first been informed by him that the journey eastward would take most of that morning before his vessel sailed into the Athenian port of Phaleron. The captain assured me also that King Aegeus still ruled there. I kept my head covered and stayed in the bow of the ship as her men hauled up the sail and deployed their oars. When we departed the isthmus to enter open water the sea was turbulent, there was little shelter from the wind but I didn't care because I was at last on my way to Athens.

321

The morning sun was high when we moored at Phaleron and I left the vessel. From where I stood at the harbour, Athens was clearly visible with the great rock they call the acropolis rising high above the city. There were several carts being loaded for delivery there so I simply sat in the rear of one of these together with two other women and no one seemed to care. After an uncomfortable ride we passed through the main gate of the imposing city wall to where the carts would be unloaded. I stepped into the bustling market square to be assailed by the cries of traders and there I paused a while to look about. Here was a city at least as wealthy as Corinth and more impressive than any city I'd seen. Many of the buildings displayed those downward tapering columns in harmonious colours with which I was rather familiar. I walked on to ask a passer by the way to the temple of Aphrodite and to the palace of Aegeus. The temple was but a short stroll away but not the king's palace – this was situated high above on the acropolis with the temple of Athena nearby.

On finding myself a few steps from Aphrodite's temple I slipped off the cloak and handed it to a disbelieving peasant woman who, from her appearance needed it more than I now did. I entered the temple to find torches illuminating her inner shrine and numerous female acolytes in attendance. When the priestess in charge came to ask my business, I lied - or it was at least a part lie. With my cloak now gone she was able to assess my noble though somewhat care-worn attire though I kept hidden some of the valuables I still possessed. I explained how I had travelled from Corinth on an important mission from the palace to speak with King Aegeus but had been much delayed by circumstances on my way. I declared I would make an offering at Aphrodite's shrine and asked that they help in letting me tend to my needs, to refresh myself as well as to prepare me in appearance for my interview. On seeing the precious, gem studded ring I removed from my finger for presentation to their shrine they agreed to do all I asked of them. I was taken aside by two of her girls to private chambers, offered all I required, allowed to cater for every necessity then to bathe to cleanse and attend, with their assistance, to the most intimate pampering of my body. This was after all the temple of Aphrodite.

I asked many questions and the girls who attended me revealed much about Athens and her king. I learned how Aegeus was estranged from his brother, Pallas then conflict and famine were spoken of. They appointed a slave of the temple, an older woman, to fashion my hair in the manner of high ranking female member of the court and I sat in perfumed contentment for a while before the bronze mirror as her nimble fingers did their work with ivory combs. The jewelled headband I had managed to keep with me would now find a use. The girls obtained a dress appropriate for my destination, a dress for one of Athens' royal court, similar in style to those I had worn in the palace of Corinth. It was tiered, flounced and colourfully embroidered, reaching down to my ankles where it part concealed the short leather boots they had also provided. The dress held in my waist but the short-sleeved bodice left my firm and full breasts exposed. Oh, how proud I was of my body, how wonderful it was to wear that dress, and what man, I thought, could resist the sight of me. Not even, as I hoped, the King of Athens. They rouged my cheeks then reddened my lips and that I liked a lot. My sullied but still regal gown I left to their care.

I was going to stand before Aegeus, not as a refugee begging favour but as Medea, member of a royal house, daughter of a king, though fortunately one whose reputation must be as little known in Athens as it had been in Corinth and elsewhere. I did not wish to delay longer. I was eager to continue on. I stood transformed but could not cross the temple or step outside until given a belted gown, long and plain, to cover myself completely. It would be quite inappropriate, as I knew, to be seen as I was in a public place.

A warm, clear afternoon greeted me when I left the temple but the sun was well down as I approached the base of the Acropolis. Finding the stairway that I had to ascend in order to reach my goal was easy enough - climbing it considerably less so. At the top I stepped through the gate of a surrounding wall of imposing masonry. The gate was lightly guarded and in the open area before me were a number of people, mainly of official aspect, going about their business or conversing in small groups. Ahead lay the palace, a linear building of mainly two floors, its upper level partly open with rows of russet painted columns. On I went toward what had to be the main entrance but now I hesitated and was assailed by doubt. I assumed Aegeus might as yet be unaware of Creon's death but what if he'd forgotten all about me and about the promise he'd made by the fountain in Corinth? He might refuse to see me and order me dismissed as I had been at Thebes. But I had to go on and so I quickened my pace. At the entrance I was challenged by one of several guards and again I insisted I had urgent business with the king. The guards were convinced by my manner and my appearance, at least from the neck up, that I was no ordinary supplicant and so they allowed me in to what I saw to be an open courtyard where, to my left, stood a wide, columned entrance to the main building. There we stopped until one of the guards had summoned a court attendant. I was by then gripped with apprehension. The attendant, a man in courtly attire, stepped out, assessed me closely, asked who I was and what was the purpose of my visit. I repeated my tale about important business but declined to give my name and insisted Lord Aegeus would know me at once. He nodded to the guards, conducted me further inside to an anteroom then had me wait while he pushed aside a heavy curtain to enter the megaron from which I could hear sounds of conversation and the gentle strumming of a lyre. My confidence returned so there and then I slipped off the gown and laid it aside. The lyre ceased playing, I held my breath, the curtain reopened and the attendant, visibly taken aback by my newly revealed presence, gestured for me to follow him through.

The layout of the great hall was not unfamiliar. Daylight slanted low through upper windows to illuminate the frescoed walls, the displays of arms and amour and the circular hearth beyond which sat enthroned Aegeus. As I was conducted across to stand before him conversation lowered and people turned to look at me. At least my dress attire was not out of place for other women of the court were likewise attired. I halted before the throne and the attendant stood aside as I announced, "Lord Aegeus, I come here to claim the sanctuary you so generously offered me when we met in the town square of Corinth some time ago."

He stared at me a while, visibly surprised at my ready for the court appearance, then rose from his throne, saying, "Lady Medea, I do indeed recall our meeting but your name just now was not announced."

Others continued to stare as I explained how I came in disguise to Athens by wagon and how the women of Aphrodite's temple had offered me many comforts and suitable attire for my appearance before him.

"But why travel in disguise?" he asked me. "And why do you now ask me for sanctuary? Athens has suffered much these past years. More than I care to speak about."

"Much of Greece has suffered has it not," I responded.

Raising a hand, Aegeus announced that he wished us to be left alone. The courtiers and the old man with the lyre filed in obedient silence from the hall. On their departure he gestured for me to sit

326

close by him and I said, "Lord Aegeus, you will recall what I told you. You will recall how I, one of royal status, had been abandoned by Jason for Creon's daughter, that same Jason to whom I had been married."

"Yes I remember much of what you told me," he said. "You were treated dishonourably I thought."

He continued to regard me with intensifying interest. How could he not. I sensed how he was impressed by the sensual perfume I wore and how the sight of my naked breasts had him thinking of more than just my tale of misfortune. On my arrival Aegeus had appeared careworn and glum. But now it was clear his fascination for me was renewed and the flame I had ignited within him at our meeting in Corinth was lit once more. He nodded for me to carry on speaking for he desired to keep his eyes always upon me as I revealed my experiences with a degree of harmless embellishment. I considered that to mention Hecate might not be in my interest just then.

"I begged him not to marry that girl," I declared, "I demeaned myself before him but all he would offer in return was cold silver with – with no more sentiment than some farmer tendering payment for a farm beast! No one cared about that since in Corinth he was their shining hero." I lowered my head for some moments then continued, "In the night, in my dreaming, the spirits of my ancestors came to me. I called to them for vengeance the way my ancestors did and they told me what to do. In the light of day I had a gown made for Creusa as a wedding gift and sent anonymously. Think what you will of this but the day she wore it the gown caught fire and she was burned to death where she stood."

Aegeus turned away from me with a frown and breathed, "Burned to death. By the gods, burned to death. And you would have me believe that was your doing?"

"As I said, Lord Aegeus, think what you will. The Corinthians certainly did. Some of them set out as a drunken mob to find me and my children. I had sent the children to the temple of Hera for sanctuary but they were dragged away from the altar and murdered, yes, stoned to death. When I heard what had happened I took up my possessions and escaped to Thebes. The Corinthians had earlier turned upon Jason and he was gone from their city before me. My reputation for casting spells had followed me to Thebes and though I had done nothing to offend them, nothing at all, I again had to flee. Now I am here to claim the pledge you made to me. I can offer you much, Lord Aegeus. I can offer you a son – and I know a son is what you desire above all."

His gaze was again upon me and without thinking I reached to touch him.

"And what might the people of Athens make of your reputation?" he asked, placing a hand on mine. "It seems to spread with the winds."

"Athens is over the worst of her troubles," I replied, basing my words upon what I had recently been told, "and none of what has happened can be ascribed to me. Whatever I do here will be for the good of yourself and the city."

"No," he replied, raising a hand, "Athens is far from over the worst of times but that greatest of tragedies I will not discuss though all the city and beyond knows about it, as will you if you don't already. All mention of it is forbidden in Athens but whispers are whispers and, like smoke they will seep through the strongest walls."

"Yes," I assured him, "I am aware of what has happened, but they are events spread too wide afield and involve the gods themselves. There is nothing within my power to alter such affairs."

What he referred to was, I sensed, a tragedy that all but overwhelmed him. But its causes and its details were yet to be revealed. I sensed he found me alluring. Yes, irresistible. We arose, we stood to face one another and Aegeus took me in his arms. We retired to his private chamber and there he called for wine and refreshment. We talked alone for long. The flames of oil lamps cast our shadows swaying on the walls while Haemon, his bard and musician, played his lyre in a room close by. Aegeus had me describe in detail all I had witnessed, all I had been through and he listened eagerly to my every word. As my account drew to a close I well knew there were other things on Aegeus' mind. He leaned forward, caressed and kissed my lips, then my breasts.

Shortly after, we retired to his bed.

Chapter 14 - The Curse Upon Athens

We were married with great ceremony at the temple of Aphrodite. The priestesses blessed us. The scribes recorded all on their tablets. There were pipes, drums, singers and acrobats and I made out as if enjoying them all though I hardly did. Most of Athens seemed devoted to celebrations on that day. Crowds packed the square outside the temple and the street traders did brisk business. At last Aegeus had his queen and a true queen is what I intended to be. I'd fled my own temple at Colchis, spent endless gruelling, sometimes perilous days at sea and been cast aside by the man to whom I had been devoted. I'd had my children murdered in Corinth then been driven from the city to wander aimlessly for days with fear of being set upon and robbed, or worse. I had much to make up for.

A second throne was set up next to that of Aegeus in the megaron and there I sat by his side in my regal finery to assist in interviewing supplicants, visitors and dignitaries from within Athens and from other towns and lands. I loved the renewed power it gave me, the power I had experienced with Jason at Corinth. Within the palace I also enjoyed once more the services and pampering of my own attendants and slaves as well as private rooms where I might retreat and be alone – if alone I wished to be.

But the tragedy I mentioned weighed always on Aegeus' mind even in our most private, our most intimate moments. I sensed it strongly day and night yet, having told me I would in time know the truth, it was still a matter he, like others, seemed determined not to talk about.

I'd heard mention of bad relations with the house of Minos at Knossos on Crete. I heard it said there might even be Cretan agents here at Aegeus' court, perhaps among those close to him. I thought at first to consult Hecate or to sense the thoughts of others, but no, there appeared otherwise to be day to day harmony at our court and I had no wish to delve, to discover and pass information on to Aegeus that might result in discord. Should the rumours be true, should agents of Minos be exposed, this might have the Cretans take more direct action against Athens' trade at sea. King Minos, as all were aware, possessed a navy fit to overwhelm that of anyone else. But I *was* Queen and should therefore be told and know whatever I wished to know by Aegeus or someone close to him. There were his, *our* courtiers, of course, but regardless of all else there was one man I was aware everyone could trust - aged, white-bearded Haemon who played his lyre for the king's pleasure and related in song the great deeds of old. One morning when Aegeus was out hunting with his companions I had Haemon summoned to my private chambers. He arrived, followed by a slave carrying his precious lyre, and with a gentle smile asked, "Do you wish me to play for you, My Lady?"

"Not now," I replied, "I wish for us to talk together." I had Haemon sit in cushioned comfort to ease his old bones and ordered the slave to bring us honeyed wine. Once we both were relaxed I said to him, "There is a matter of deep concern to my husband, the king. I sense others are aware of it but are forbidden to speak. Please tell me what this is - I will sooner or later have to know."

Haemon gazed at me a while in silence then lowered his eyes.

"Yes," he said at last in solemn tones, "it is forbidden to discuss the matter openly but I'm surprised Lord Aegeus has not told you, though the event of this year occurred only days before you arrived in our city. It is a sad affair and much to the shame of Athens but - but yes, you must know of it for all too soon it will be upon us once more."

We drank a little wine then Haemon continued, "It is a complicated affair but for now, if I may, I will offer you the main tale. Some years ago when the annual Athenian Games were due to be celebrated, King Minos sent over a team of men to participate. One of these was a son of his, Androgeus, who remained incognito so as to deceive us all into assuming he was an ordinary citizen of Knossos. After the games had ended he returned not to Crete but rode to the south of Attica to join a number of armed warriors who'd arrived by sea from Crete. Knowing we would soon hear of it, his envoy informed our king these men had been sent by Minos to help rid people in the Plain of Marathon of the great bull abandoned there by Heracles after his taking it from Crete. Our king did not believe this and sent spies to see what the Cretans really intended. It transpired that Androgeus had continued on alone to Thorikos to confer with our king's rogue brother, Pallas. This man claimed the throne of Athens as his own by birthright and had sworn to assert that claim by any means. It was reported to our king that Androgeus had promised to aid Pallas in seizing the throne of Athens if he would ensure Athens and her allies would keep their vessels away from Minos' most important markets. Pallas was not well liked by the people of Thorikos and there were those at his court most willing to disclose this information to agents of his brother, our king.

When Androgeus rejoined his men in the Plain of Marathon, our king sent his captain, Metion, out with a party of soldiers to ambush them. Androgeus was killed but one of his men, though wounded, made it back to Crete via Thorikos and informed Minos of his son's fate."

By now I was convinced listening to Haemon was far better than my consulting Hecate who, having had no involvement, of that I was sure, might not have been so direct so I encouraged him to go on.

"Minos gathered his ships and landed forces on the mainland west of Attica. He sacked the town of our ally, Megara then arrived before the walls of Athens. But our king was forewarned, our livestock and much food brought within the city wall and our gates secured. Our city wall is strong and the Cretans, used to fighting mainly from ships at sea, could not maintain a long siege and soon had to withdraw with considerable loss of men and arms. Unknown to us, Minos then called upon every shrine on Crete and throughout his empire to have mighty Zeus avenge his son's death and that was when our troubles really began. A powerful earthquake struck the region, water supplies dried up for a time and this was followed by plague. Our trade suffered and was made worse when our vessels were harassed at sea and in foreign ports by Cretan ships full of armed men. Pallas took no advantage of our situation in case it carried the plague to Thorikos but he hoped it would leave Athens weak enough for invasion later.

Our priests went to Delphi where they begged at the shrine of Apollo for guidance. They were told they must send a delegation to Knossos and negotiate for peace terms but Minos sent them back with demands that would damage the reputation of Athens throughout all of Greece. Aye, he demanded a tribute each year of seven young men and seven young girls. Our king was furious but our elders and priests as well as some of our citizens believed this must be done to alleviate our suffering. Things were getting worse so we had to agree and all concerned met at Delphi where they swore their oaths at Apollo's shrine before Cretan emissaries who had scribes record all of it on their tablets. Not long after the first group of young people were sent to Crete the streams began to flow again and the plague was lifted. Our king said this must be coincidence. He wanted to denounce those oaths but copies were lodged at Delphi as well as at Knossos and this would have brought great dishonour upon Athens and the House of Aegeus. Alas, the sacrifice we make each year remains a terrible burden upon us for all time. The Cretans support Pallas rather than attempting further invasion to remind our king of Athens' obligations."

I part raised my goblet, saying, "Then I understand fully why he remains so troubled. But what happens to those men and girls who are sent to Crete? Have any returned?"

Haemon lapsed once more into silence, hands clutching his goblet, his head lowered. When he looked up to speak his voice was raised hardly above a whisper. "None have returned. None at all. There is a rumour, a rumour carried by some who trade with Knossos, that our young people are sacrificed to some dreadful creature that dwells in darkness beneath the palace. Let us pray to the gods that it is nothing other than a rumour."

Even before Haemon left, I was determined to find out more but would say nothing of it to Aegeus. After dark that same day I sat in silence with only a single flame to illuminate coiling incense. I whispered her name and eventually Hecate replied, "I am with you," her voice at first drifting from far away beyond the gloom of my chamber.

"Tell me," I began, "the young people who are taken from Athens each year to Knossos on Crete – what is their fate?"

There followed only silence and in those infinite moments I wondered if the goddess was still with me. At last her voice, still at a distance. "Those you speak of go to their deaths." I held my breath until she continued, "There is evil at Knossos. Deep

335

beneath that great and glorious palace, beneath the wonders people see there, beneath the light, the life and laughter that flows all about, there prowls a creature of darkness, a beast that craves human flesh. It is an abomination feared even by those who rule there though one among them helped to create it. Yes, they themselves dread the shadow of the beast in case one day that shadow falls upon them."

"So those taken from Athens are given as sacrifice to this – to this -."

"Yes, but to those outside of Knossos all of what you have learned from me is no more than rumour."

"Even to Aegeus?" I asked.

"Even to Aegeus," she whispered, then I felt her presence receding.

I arose, took up my small lamp and left the incense to burn itself out. I felt that in her sensing that evil its breath had touched me also. I swore to myself I would never speak of it to anyone, including Aegeus.

***

In the spring of that following year, when the citrus groves and orchards were alive with colour and the fields sown, I bore my royal husband a son. Sacrifices were offered in thanks at Athena's temple and three days of celebrations and feasting were ordered throughout the city. Aegeus appeared pleased enough to those about him but to me that smiling face was but a mask that concealed unease. When poised upon the verge of sleep I saw misted images – images of a woman and child, images of something buried beneath dark earth. I heard distant voices passing back and forth – echoes all but lost in a vastness. These I tried to dismiss as those spirits of the night that sometimes descend upon us with no reason at all and for a time I succeeded.

Numerous of our over-attentive, ever fussing courtiers debated at length upon a name for the child I had brought into the world. I cared for none of their suggestions and insisted he should be called Medeus so that in the end was what the scribes recorded on their tablets. The child's nursemaid and attendants were appointed but Aegeus, although continuing to express his satisfaction over there now being a male heir to the throne of Athens, still had buried deep inside those thoughts he could not reveal.

I determined to set up a shrine to Hecate in Athens, one with a modest altar for offerings. The shrine would not exist to tender advice and offer potions to other people as that would hardly be appropriate to one of my newfound status. No, it was to thank and to return my attentions in full to the deity I once served fully in Colchis and for a time in Corinth. This shrine would be in a private chapel set aside from the palace, but those close to me, those I trusted, would know about it and would have full access to my skills and my arts.

I'd heard it rumoured at court that Medeus had been born earlier than expected for Aegeus to have fathered him. That was so, a little early perhaps, but few would have maintained that it was *too* early. Shortly after I had established the shrine another rumour began. It started first in the palace but soon was prowling in murmurs about the city. Medeus

337

was some months old but his features did not reflect in an obvious way those of Aegeus. I strove to ignore this idle gossip but I sensed Aegeus did not, though he hinted nothing of it to me. But rumours have a life of their own; like birds that flutter here and there to settle wherever they will to deliver their message. Idle courtiers, then others, spoke of my deceiving Aegeus and so the townsfolk of Athens offered a less than enthusiastic welcome to the child when they saw him brought down from the palace to be taken about the city. To me they rendered the greatest respect but more through formal obligation than true feelings. It was also put about for a time that my shrine to Hecate, not being accessible to the ordinary citizen, as were other temples, was a focus of necromancy. It had me thinking how foolish are people who make far more of what they don't know than what they do. Nevertheless theirs was far from the animosity I had experienced in Corinth so I hardly cared. My life now was raised above the banal and tedious existence of most others as it ought all along to have been.

It was not long before I witnessed that which Haemon had described as the shame of Athens. By then, having told me nothing, I knew Aegeus already assumed I had discovered all by the whispering of others. I knew there was something of importance due to happen when our courtiers were busily preoccupied in what struck me as a most sullen, unsmiling manner. Members of the palace guard, too, were more in evidence than was usual and much of the market square was being cleared of traders. I was tempted to ask Aegeus what was happening but he, with grim expression, knew what was on my mind just as I knew it was something he wished still not to discuss. He behaved now not as a king but more as a man crushed in spirit.

I heard talk of a vessel coming into the harbour, a vessel that was not welcome. All others about me were so preoccupied that I felt like a stranger within my own court. I had stepped outside the palace when Aegeus hurried by in plain, unadorned tunic of dark linen, hair tumbled about his shoulders, his gaze fixed resolutely ahead. I returned to our chambers, pulled on a plain woollen gown, left the palace and made my way in bright morning sunlight to the low wall that circled the Acropolis. From there I was able to see across the market square and out to the harbour. A vessel was being manoeuvred toward the quay – a large vessel with a sail that bore prominently the image of a double-headed axe. This I knew was the emblem of Knossos. Men scrambled about the mast and rigging as the sail was lowered and I continued to watch as oars were shipped, the boat secured and her crew began to disembark. I could make out men carrying something but they were soon hidden by the city wall and all sight of them denied by the buildings.

Eventually the party reappeared at the entrance to the market square. I wanted to be closer, to see more of what was happening, so I headed for the stairway leading down from the Acropolis. Standing ahead of me and close to the bottom was Aegeus accompanied by Metion, three armed guards and two city elders. I carried on further down but stopped just over half way as it seemed my presence

339

would be inappropriate below. There were many people gathered at the one side of the square, citizens and trades people, all staring in silence. I felt their anger as the newcomers entered from the further side. There were men carrying two gilded chairs, each bearing a Cretan noble. Part way across the party halted and the nobles stepped down from their chairs.

Closer to my vantage point, behind a palisade of spears held by grim-faced guards of the palace, were assembled many of the healthiest young people of the city – all between the ages of fifteen and twenty years. All were attired in a simple manner, the males in plain white, short-sleeved belted tunics of linen, the females in long dresses of sparingly patterned fine wool that covered them from neck to ankle. Aegeus' attendants were moving among them, ushering boys to their right, girls to their left. The young people appeared agitated as they watched the Cretan nobles approach, each with his long, richly pattered robe lifted clear of the ground by a slave boy. Both envoys carried upright a gilded staff topped by a small, double-headed axe that glinted gold, again the emblem of Knossos and symbol of Cretan power. Seeming indifferent to the gravity of the situation all around them, the two nobles chatted together while, naked to the waist, strode the longhaired, clean-shaven ceremonial Cretan guards, six in front with six following. Each bore a stout spear with gleaming blade, each displayed a short sword at his side. The citizens of Athens maintained a tense silence though agitated dogs barked and circled about. Passing across the market place, the Cretan entourage halted at mid-point where both envoys turned to look up at Aegeus. They bowed slightly and Aegeus acknowledged them with no more than a slowly, part-raised hand. I listened transfixed as one of the pair called to him in Cretan accent. "Lord Aegeus, we are come to carry out the task allotted to us by Lord Minos, ruler of Knossos, of Crete and of the wide seas, whose eminence is decreed by mighty Zeus. I request we be allowed to proceed without hindrance - at your royal pleasure, that is."

I noted the barely suppressed sarcasm in the man's request as Aegeus nodded his assent with a hardly audible, "Yes, you may proceed."

Murmuring broke out here and there. It spread through the crowd like the droning of bees and I wondered if it might soon break out into torrents of abuse. "Shame," someone called out as the two envoys strode toward members of the city guard behind who were gathered the youngsters. Aegeus must have felt the resentment of his people for he appeared bowed. The city guard parted ranks, allowing the envoys to pass through. There the two Cretan nobles moved apart, one stepping over to the young men, the other to the girls. Angry faces looked on as they appraised each male, each female, touching the left shoulder of first one and then another, then gesturing for the chosen among them to walk over to where the armed Cretans waited. Once more, murmurs of, "Shame," arose from the crowd to spread as a breeze through swaying wheat. The envoys ignored it and themselves proceeded

341

back across the square. Again the word, 'Shame.'
This time it spread like a flock of dark birds about
to rise in anger. In an atmosphere charged with
resentment, the Cretan party, with their chosen
fourteen, and the nobles returned to their chairs,
walked in solemn procession back toward the city
gate. I did not stay long enough to watch the Cretan
vessel depart but returned for comfort to the shrine
of Hecate.

I later joined Aegeus in our chambers. I sensed
his feelings – feelings that overflowed from a
chalice of despair, but I had to wait until he spoke.
"I am their king," he breathed, "but I ask myself
how much longer will the people of Athens tolerate
what has been happening. How long before their
anger rises up to destroy me."

For many days after he remained sullen and
subdued, seeing no one unless pressing affairs
intervened. But certain other matters would become
clearer as time went by.

I was as close to Hecate as I had been in
Colchis and had been for those years in Corinth,
until my troubles there began. Thoughts of Jason
entered my mind from time to time and when they
did it was the goddess I served who kept me
informed. Jason had wandered from place to place,
never returning home to Pelion, often given to self-
indulgence until much of the silver and many other
things of value he carried about his person were
gone. He had offered his services to towns and
cities about the Peloponnese, about Thessaly and
further north, but the gods had imbued him with a
greater than ever urge to wander. He never

remained anywhere for long nor did he find lasting attachment to another woman. Medeus was entering his third year and twice more I had witnessed the spectacle of those young Athenians taken away to Crete where a dreadful fate awaited them. One evening as I sat in the near darkness of Hecate's sacred chamber with incense rising, I asked, "What news is there now of Jason?"

The flames of my two small lamps wavered and her voice was close. "Jason is dead."

"Oh - dead!" was my response. "Dead, and why and – and how, and what happened to him?" My curiosity I could not contain as images of Jason flashed through my mind; images of the brave Jason I once loved, the man who altered the course of my life then almost destroyed it.

"He sought a new dawn in his affairs," she answered, "a return of the fame and the fortune he once possessed but the gods would not grant it. He returned south and went to Delphi where he consulted the oracle but her message only confused him as it so often has confused others until someone else ventures to shine light upon it. In despair he returned to the land of Corinth, not to the city where he would not have been welcomed, but across the isthmus to the lower harbour which at the time was deserted. There, as the sun vanished below the horizon, he stood to gaze upon the decaying vessel that once he had so proudly commanded. Much of her stern was broken away, but there still remained the railed platform over her bow with, curving high above this, a slim and delicate device in the shape of a horn. With those few possessions he still had and with the precious sword at his side, he remained there even as darkness fell."

I held my breath a while. I imagined him standing alone, deep in thought beneath a glowing sweep of stars and hearing the gentle lap of waves from the shoreline. Did he relive those memories I also shared? Yes, how could he not recall our meeting in Colchis? How could he have forgotten the appalling sights created by my own father close by the city gate and the hideous creature he slew in order to gain the Golden Fleece? How could the pursuit and journey across wide waters to Trinacria, the pirates, the Sirens where the voice of Orpheus saved us from death, the passage through Scylla and Charybdis, and our marriage, how could all of these not have returned to possess his thoughts?

"And how did Jason die?" I asked once more.

"A white owl alighted upon the bow; the owl of Athena. Seeing this he walked over to *Argo* and hauled himself up onto her deck even though her timbers were unsound. He made his way to the bow where he thought to rest inside for he was much wearied by his wanderings. As he approached, the owl raised her wings and flew into the night. Jason saw her leave but did not care. He was too tired to care. He had returned to his ship and there would lie down to sleep and to dream of once more roaming the seas. But the much weakened timbers could not for long support his weight. As he slept the bow itself gave way and all its weight fell upon him. He lies there now in final sleep."

"So the vessel claimed him," I breathed, "and the world knows nothing of it."

344

"Yes, the vessel claimed and now possesses him."

***

Two years and more passed during which my son Medeus reached his fifth year. Aegeus was as satisfied as might be to have an heir but never showed the boy that degree of fatherly love I had hoped for. He was, however, even at that early age, allowed to accompany Aegeus and his men on the hunt. My life at court remained amiable enough and though I tried to improve my status in the eyes of the people by the promotion of festivals and sporting contests, talk of Medeus' legitimacy still from time to time arose. Then there were those at court and temple who claimed my influence over Aegeus was too great. Tales of conflict reached us, carried by traders from other parts of Greece but Athens, under the watchful eye of her king, was for now secure and increasingly prosperous in part through the exploitation of her nearby silver mines. There were also persistent rumours concerning Aegeus' conniving brother, Pallas. And although supplied with arms by the mighty King Minos, Pallas' plans were thwarted by continuing unrest in his home town of Thoricos to our south, encouraged partly by agents from Athens.

The images that from time to time invaded my sleep, those I earlier had mentioned, were growing ever stronger. I felt danger of a sort was nearing so decided I must press Hecate over the matter as she had previously revealed nothing about these. So concerned had I become that one night, while Aegeus slept, I pulled on a warm gown and left our

345

bedchamber carrying a small pottery lamp. Cold beneath my bare feet, the stairs and corridor leading to Hecate's shrine were illuminated by burning torches but her sanctuary, until I entered, was steeped in profound darkness. From my lamp I lit sticks of incense to enrich the air. I sat before her altar and as the vapours began to coil I whispered her name. I waited in silence until delicate wings of sound fluttered here and there about the gloom, then her voice, "Medea, I am with you."

"Lady Hecate - the images that so trouble my sleep - you know of these but you have told me nothing. I beg you to explain their cause.'

"I have said nothing because there was no certainty of their outcome and because I wished not to cause you distress. The matter that troubles you is not yet resolved but when it is, if it is, I then will have more to say."

"But - but tell me what it is you know this far for I must know it also."

When she next spoke, her voice was no more than a whisper close to my ear. "Aegeus has an older son."

I caught my breath. I felt suddenly cold. Very cold. "Tell me all," I breathed. The vapours of incense swirled lazily and my heart beat many times before she spoke again.

"He is a young man of some twenty years and his name is Theseus. His true mother is called Aethra, she is daughter of a king and their home is the town of Troizen in the Peloponnese. He was left there as a child with a peasant family for his own protection, not knowing his birthright. At the time it seemed that Athens and her closest ally, Troizen, was threatened with invasion by Pallas, aided by Cretan forces. Pallas had used Cretan gold, so it was feared, to buy the loyalty of some at Aegeus' own court – even members of his palace guard. Had Athens fallen then one of Pallas' many sons would have been nominated heir to her throne and Theseus, had they known of him, would have been in mortal danger."

"And - and right now -?"

"From childhood he was educated in courtly manners and trained in arms but hardly understood why. He was sent to Delphi to present a lock of his hair to the priestess and there he would receive her blessing but he has this very day returned to Troizen. His mother will reveal the truth to him but I do not know if he will accept it."

"And this truth you speak of," I asked, "when is this Theseus to know it?"

"Two days, perhaps. Until then there is no more I can tell you."

Then silence, and I knew she was gone. I returned to our bed where Aegeus slept soundly but I remained awake to see the sky grow lighter and hear dogs yapping from somewhere close to the palace as they had for much of the night. I arose after Aegeus, bathed and had my girls prepare me straight afterwards for the megaron. I entered to find Aegeus seated and in conversation with a small group of city elders. The ill-fitting smile that moulded my face as I stepped across to sit beside him did not come from within. It was a courtly smile and as they acknowledged me I felt suddenly

347

vulnerable and wished my breasts were not bared, court custom or no. With the elders departed, we moved to the adjacent private chamber where Aegeus had a slave bring us wine and small dishes of food. We talked a while about city affairs but all the time my thoughts dwelt upon Hecate's words. The wine and food done with, Aegeus pushed his goblet aside and said, "You seem preoccupied - is there something that bothers you?"

I looked at him with a frozen smile I hoped he found reassuring and replied, "No, nothing to speak of other than a little tiredness. Last night was hot and the sound of dogs kept me awake for much of the time."

"Hot?" he smiled. "I thought the night rather cool when we retired. But today I planned to gather a group of men for the hunt. You might wish to join us as you have before though on this occasion I would not advise it. Lions are reported to have taken two of our men working in the fields and this has to be dealt with or others will be afraid to tend their crops."

"Of course," I said, 'you must do whatever is necessary as long as you take good care but I have no wish to accompany your hunt today. Should any matter arise that needs court attention then you know I will be here to deal with it,"

"Yes, and what man could have at his side a more dedicated woman than you. But should anything untoward, should any danger arise then as always you have Metion to call upon."

Hah, Metion. Metion, in charge of the palace guard, and what a fine figure of a man he was. I'd

348

caught his eye a number of times but I felt it too much of a risk to allow even a merest suggestion of intimacy. Now I was alone, preoccupied by my thoughts and not wishing to take my place in the great hall. No, I would have the elders stay there in attendance and have the court go about its affairs with both thrones unoccupied until later in the day.

***

I stayed clear of Hecate's shrine for two days. In trying to bar her last words and their possible implications from my mind, I steeped myself in court conversations and entertainments. I sat by Aegeus to hear elders, priests and supplicants and in between I listened to the sweet notes of Haemon's lyre. At night with Aegeus I behaved as I ought and as he would expect me to. But when the lamps were extinguished, when the stars were visible beyond our window, that which I had held at bay flooded in as a chilling tide to dominate much of my restless nights.

At sunrise on the third day, with Aegeus already risen and gone to ride out with his companions for another hunt, I hurried down from our chambers and along the corridor to the shrine. Having forgotten in my haste to take a lamp I found myself in utter darkness once beyond the heavy curtain but that hardly mattered, except I was not able to offer incense. I spoke her name softly, I clasped my hands together, held my breath and waited. For a time I thought nothing was to happen, I thought perhaps my ill prepared visit might not have been to her liking. But when I felt the air stir all about I knew she was with me.

"Medea, I am here," she whispered from within the blackness.

"What news have you of this Theseus?" I asked.

"I watched and I listened. His mother took him before sunrise to an ancient stone pillar by the road outside Troizen where she explained all. Close to this lay a heavy stone slab which she had him raise. Beneath this, concealed twenty years before by Aegeus, was a precious sword, one fit for a noble warrior, and a pair of sandals left there as a symbol that he was to travel. These were intended as proof of what she had told him – that he was rightful claimant the throne of Athens."

"And he believed her?"

"Yes," Hecate replied, "and tomorrow he will set out from Troizen on his journey to Athens."

I sat in numbed silence as the true import of her words uncoiled as a dark serpent, then I said, "But that will mean -. No, it is *my* son, Medeus who must inherit the throne of Athens and not some outcast who never trod the meanest back streets of this city! It must be the son who was born and raised here at the court of Aegeus!"

"Medea, this you must know; Aegeus will see Theseus as having the greater claim. He is older of the two and his parentage is certain. Doubts have often passed through Aegeus' mind, and that of others who have his ear, that he may not be the true father of your own son and I tell you he is not."

I was again silent, my mind a whirl of confusion, then I asked, "And - and how long before this Theseus arrives in Athens? Tell me that."

"I cannot say. I cannot predict what lies before him or even if he will reach Athens alive, for should he walk, as he intends to do, his journey will be one of many dangers. But your own powers are enough for you to discover if and when he draws close. They are yours to use as you wish are they not."

She was gone. I remained for some time seated in darkness then said aloud, "No, this cannot be! No one must take away what is rightfully mine and that of my son. I will wait and I will watch, and when the time approaches I will know what to do."

Chapter 15 - Theseus

Each day I hurried to the shrine of Hecate and, as smouldering incense gave forth wraiths of spectral smoke, the vague images that began at Troizen became each day clearer until, "Ah, I see you. You have travelled far on your journey. I know you. Oh, yes, yes, yes; I know who you are and why you have come to Athens and I will be prepared."

Seated in the darkness of Hecate's shrine I became aware when, late on the twelfth day, he entered Athens. His presence was strong but I sensed also his weariness and I watched as he sought rest for the night at the Inn of Poseidon. There he was subjected to scorn and insult by a number of those unsavoury peasants who frequent these taverns. I wondered if now, almost at the end of his journey, this might also be the end of his life for killings in such places were not uncommon after dark, but he struck down the one who arose to challenge him, a big and brutal man. He drove out the rest of them at sword point and thereafter spent his night in peace.

Hate smouldered within me, hate not so much for this Theseus but for what he, however unknowingly, was about to accomplish. It was only through taking one of my own herbal preparations that I managed any sleep at all that night.

I harboured no ill feelings toward my husband but I had to plan carefully how best to deal with what was to confront me the following day. When offering Aegeus wine I would include a potion that, otherwise harmless, would have him needing to concentrate harder upon matters being dealt with, and so be far less aware of whatever else was taking place about him.

***

Aegeus was occupied in conversation with a noble of the court when, on the morning of that thirteenth day, the one I awaited entered the great hall. He was fair-haired and clean-shaven, a band of blue linen about his head, a leather bag slung over his shoulder, a fancy sword buckled about the waist of a plain scallop-edged tunic. Followed by two armed guards he stepped around the great hearth to approach our twin thrones. Aegeus, still deep in conversation remained, as I intended, quite unaware of his approach through the bustle of the court but I watched him intently and as he looked directly at me I smiled and acknowledged his presence with a gently raised hand, though my heart was pounding. I gestured discreetly to my left where a slave boy waited close by with an ornate gold goblet resting upon a bronze tray. This I indicated should be offered to the newcomer who stood now only four paces from Aegeus and myself. Theseus had heard of me, oh, yes, he knew who I was so as it was offered to him, he lifted the goblet from the tray expecting now I would alert my distracted husband to his presence. I of course made no attempt to do so but at that point Haemon stopped playing, coughed and bent aside put down his lyre. This, to my dismay, caused Aegeus to turn and seeing Theseus he asked, "Who stands there looking at us? How did this man gain entry, unannounced?"

The eyes of those close by were also turned to the newcomer. Voices were lowered while the two guards, part drawing their swords, readied themselves to act if called upon. I leant close to Aegeus. I whispered in his ear, "He is an intruder sent by your brother Pallas to harm us both. In the night I foresaw his coming. He managed to slip past the guards but they're waiting to cut him down. We want no blood on the floor but once he drinks from the cup he will no longer be a danger to us. Let him drink." In my thoughts blazed the words, "Drink it now! Drink! Drink! Drink!"

"Then why did you not warn -?" began Aegeus, then his attention fell to the sword at the intruder's side. "Wait!" he called aloud, glancing at me. "What are you offering him?" He looked hard at the young man then rose promptly from his throne to demand, "Name yourself!"

With goblet raised the newcomer declared boldly, "Lord Aegeus, I am Theseus. I have journeyed from Troizen to find you, as my mother Aethra said I must. I drink the wine the Lady Medea has offered me in greeting!"

"Don't drink that!" cried Aegeus, striding forward, arm outstretched to dash the goblet spinning from Theseus' hand. The goblet rang on the flagstones to roll aside in a pool of spreading liquid while Theseus stood in mute confusion. Aegeus stared down at the sword hilt, reached to run fingers over it, glanced at the countryman's sandals on Theseus' feet then, very slowly, he placed his hands on the young man's shoulders. In the charged moments that followed a dark anger arose within me and close behind it swept a tide of fear.

"At last it is you," breathed Aegeus, gazing hard at him. "At last, my son. You have Aethra's eyes and her hair. There is no mistaking it, no, not even after all these years." He turned to the bewildered courtiers and cried aloud, "My son is arrived! Theseus – the son I have waited for is with us! I thank almighty Zeus, I thank all the gods!"

The courtiers glanced at one another then at Theseus. They began to chatter, all the time pressing closer to see for themselves the handsome, youthful figure who stared about bemused.

Aegeus turned to glare at me as, hands clutched to lift my skirts, I was in the act of leaving. "Stay where you are!" he ordered, then with a gesture to the guards who had followed Theseus he called, "Seize her! Get that damned woman out of my sight! Lock her away - and her son with her!" As the guards moved toward me Aegeus returned his attention to Theseus. Tears welling in his eyes as he spoke. 'Long ago I dismissed all hope of seeing you because I so feared disappointment. Yet deep down a flame of hope still burned. Now you are here, that flame is arisen to fill my house, my world, with light!'

I cried out in anger as the two men seized and dragged me from the megaron while others stood staring. "Where are you taking me?" I demanded.

"Where we takin' 'er?" one guard asked his companion.

"The king didn't say, did 'e." replied the other as they propelled me along the gloomy corridor.

"Yeah, I know where I'd like to take 'er," leered the first as we slowed and they eased their hold on me.

"An' me," agreed the second as we stopped with both ogling my breasts. With my arms freed I was able to reach into a fold of my skirts to where my dagger nestled. Ready to draw it out I felt suddenly calmer, eased my grip on the hilt and informed them, "If my husband the king knows you've harmed me he will have you both executed – you know that, don't you. Don't you!" The two looked at one another, each at a loss for what next to do, so I added, "Why not return me to my private chamber? Find my son and bring him there also then stand guard on us both. The king will see no wrong in that."

"Sounds good enough to me," agreed the first. "Where's the boy?"

We resumed walking and I answered, "He'll be playing with others in our private garden." It was an easy way out for them as well as for me and so that's what was done. Later that morning, with Medeus returned, we were confined together in comfort until such time Aegeus would appear to announce our fate. And what might that be? I called upon Hecate but she was not to reply just then. What could she have said or done? She was after all no Zeus, no Hera. I looked at Medeus, playing with his toy chariot – whooping to himself as he pretended to charge at an unseen enemy. I had plotted to kill Theseus so that same fate could now fall upon me, but surely not on my five year old son for no crime had he committed. He understood nothing of what had passed. But as we waited my anger returned in full measure and I considered the three men I had best known in my life. My father who was a mindless brute, Jason, who in the end wanted only glory and the good life, and now Aegeus who, long unknown to me, had years before my coming to Athens already fathered a son. And was he the father of *my* son? Perhaps, perhaps not. There had been other men on hand for those pleasures Aphrodite had bestowed upon us but none of them mattered in the end and if you were to ask me their number it might take me some time in reckoning before I could reply.

I now hated men. All men. I closed my eyes. I breathed the words, "Pity I could not join the Sirens on their bleak rock. Oh, yes, to be one of them. To sing ever so sweetly. To entice men ashore then tear them limb from limb."

There were voices from the corridor outside – one I easily recognised. Aegeus entered, followed by the two guards. He looked hard at me and said, "Had I not recognised the sword he carried you would have murdered my one true son before my eyes. Yes, eyes that now are fully opened to who and what you are."

Medeus pushed aside his model chariot and remained on the floor staring up at him as Aegeus continued, "Death is what you deserve but I cannot bring myself to countenance it. No, I cannot. I understand your motives and the desperation that must have afflicted you. Instead you will suffer banishment, not just from Athens and my kingdom but from all of Greece. Rumours of what you intended here will spread through this and other lands; I will make sure of that. There is a trading vessel from Italy berthed at Phaleron. It leaves at dawn and returns with our goods to its homeport on the east coast. Directly before it sails I'll have you escorted out of the city by armed men and placed on board with those of your possessions the vessel's captain will allow."

I remained silent but when I glanced aside at Medeus, Aegeus said, "Should your son go with you he will grow to manhood and through your influence will doubtless seek vengeance, perhaps even joining with our enemies. He is, of course, innocent of any crime and so need not suffer."

I tried to form my words. I wanted to ask him what he intended for my Medeus but it proved unnecessary as Aegeus glanced aside at him and spoke again. "Your son, in many respects my own, will remain at court as such and will be younger brother by a woman of our court and companion to Theseus."

"What - !" I began, but Aegeus raised a silence gesturing hand.

"I'll hear no argument from you," he declared. "You spared him scant attention. His comforts and his company have been largely those of attendants and slaves so he'll accept your absence soon enough."

Aegeus stooped, picked up the toy chariot, took the hand of Medeus, raised the boy to his feet then turned once more to me, saying, "You will see neither of us again nor these men will ensure you are on board the boat at first light tomorrow."

358

I could say nothing. Open–mouthed, I watched them leave, followed by the guards. I stood numbed, in crushing silence. Was it Hecate who softened Aegeus' decision? After some time in thought, I told myself, there had to be a last time for everything did there not. The last time I had seen my father, despicable as he was. The last time I had kissed – the last time I had spoken to Jason. And now, the last time I would enjoy the luxuries and the comforts of this court. This and perhaps any other. And when would I last have sight of a setting sun? Yes, there had to be a last time for everything. For all of us wretched mortals.

***

I'd not had my slaves nor had I anyone to help me prepare for that final morning when the guards arrived. The court dress I had laid most carefully over the bed. Why so carefully, I don't know. I wore my old regal dress and over this a plain linen gown with a cowl for my head. The leather ankle boots were reassuringly comfortable. Apart from those things of value I had concealed about me, including the knife, a number of less valuable items I had in two small canvas bags. They were all I could carry.

The sun was yet to rise but a swathe of light defined the horizon as I was conducted in cool but breezy air aboard the vessel, taken ahead of the mast, and confronted by her beady-eyed, bushy-bearded captain with a crushed parchment face. I had no time to ask the questions I wanted to ask as he announced, gruffly, "Make yer way to the bow, madam, an' keep yerself t'yerself.'

The bows of vessels I was well accustomed to but here I had no other choice as the ship was filled with cargo, either side of which were only those few rowing benches needed for negotiating within a harbour. This vessel's journey would be mainly under sail. As the ropes securing his vessel were being loosed from the quay the captain made his way along and sat close by me.

"We're takin' you to Italy," he confirmed. "Aye, east coast of Italy to the first town where Greek is spoke. You don't look the sort to be keen on salin' but 'ere's wine to 'elp you face up to it."

"How right you are," I replied, accepting the flask he offered me, "I'm not keen on sailing and the sooner we reach land the better."

"Well we're leavin' now an' since I've no intentions of sailin' at night it'll be end of today when we goes ashore an' makes camp."

He left me alone but I was dazed, almost unable to think beyond my present situation. The boat was being heaved away from the quayside and her sail prepared for raising as I crouched with my possessions in what limited space there was. I had sworn never to suffer another sea voyage and now I was taken with dread at the thought of this one and determined to leave the vessel as soon as an opportunity arose, no matter where. Italy was a long way from Attica and I wondered what other instructions had the captain been given about me. I had to concentrate on the day ahead.

We were clear of Phaleron and turning south in a brisk northerly wind. I recalled how we would soon steer more to the west, passing between the

Peloponnese and the many islands close by. The voyage proceeded with a handing out of dried mutton, bread and diluted wine, the only event to punctuate my day. But the wind was becoming variable and the sea lively under grey skies. I feared getting sea spray over me, pulled tight the gown and hood and crouched lower.

With much chatter the few oarsmen this vessel had were working to make headway with none of the crew attempting to cast a line for fish. And had they the means of making fire, it would have been to no avail. I heard from comments that we were further away from the mainland than was intended because of the adverse wind and as the barely visible sun was by now low in the sky a refuge ashore was to be sought as soon as possible. Ahead to our left lay a small island, lone amid the wide sea and toward this the vessel was steered. The captain approached and said, "My men are to camp on that island for the night. There's food but it'll be cold unless we get a fire goin', but at least you'll eat."

"What's the island called," I asked, "and what people live there?"

"It 'as no name I know of," he answered, "an' nobody lives there – not even goats."

"No one at all?" I queried.

"No one at all, no, an' never 'as been or wants to. The island is said to be 'aunted an' we're only goin' there because we 'ave to, otherwise I'd not go near the place, ever. But you'll stay on the boat, madam, 'as that's what I'm told you 'ave to do - 'till we reaches Italy, that is."

"But, please, I have to go ashore. I'll need to - if you see what I mean."

He peered down at me for some moments then grinned, "Oh, aye – I see what you mean."

The sea had calmed with the wind eased to a modest breeze as we entered a small inlet. What few clouds remained in the sky were flaming veils now the sun had fallen below the horizon. The men were clambering over the side of the ship, some peering at me out of curiosity though only my face was visible and I remained huddled where I was. Once the crew were ashore I quickly finished what little wine and food I had left, took up my possessions and eased myself over the side of the boat onto a rocky beach, glad of the boots protecting my feet. Night was closing in and I saw the men had somehow contrived to get a small fire burning. Despite the bushes and uneven ground, I managed to skirt about their small camp unseen, pressing upward through bushes and trees, leaving behind their laughter and chatter until reaching smoother ground. There was no path, nothing to indicate anyone had ever been there, but I felt compelled to go on. With the sky clear and a three-quarter moon shining above I made my way higher still. Soon I entered a more open area with the sweep of stars, gleaming jewels against a black vault. From there I was able to see the other side of the island, no further than I had already walked, with moonlight glinting on the water beyond.

But why had I abandoned the vessel and her crew to reach the centre of this small, deserted island where other people had no wish to be? There would be no food, perhaps no water and perhaps no more ships for months. I no longer cared. I no longer cared about anything. I was contented. The air was most pleasantly warm and there was utter calm here. I was alone with the stars for company and this island was the most important place in the whole world. Mine and mine alone. I closed my eyes.

Then came her voice, "Medea, I am with you."

"Of course," I sighed. "Of course, and is it not why I'm here?"

"Yes, I guided you. It is why you are here. There is nowhere else in the world for you."

"No, there is nowhere else. And now?"

"You have served me well. I with the moon my companion, with earth and underworld as my domains may also bring good fortune to those in need, and this I offer to you. Leave this world and its foolish people behind. Join with me beneath the stars. Join with me now."

When darkness lifted, the men from the ship would find me gone. They would call for me. They might for a while search, but they would find nothing. Nothing at all.

Other novels by this author

SHADOW OF THE BEAST
THE MAN WHO SOUGHT ETERNITY
RETURN OF THE HERO
THE DEVIL IN EDEN
THE SINGING STONES
HIDDEN WORLDS Volumes 1 and 2
Further works by Jeff Clarke may be found on
www.jeffreypeterclarke.co.uk

And on his author page at:
https://fiction4all.com/ebooks/a1549.htm

www.ingramcontent.com/pod-product-compliance
Lightning Source LLC
Chambersburg PA
CBHW011402010726
47495CB00009B/2746